King Kelson's Bride

King Kelson's Bride

KATHERINE KURTZ

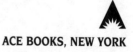
ACE BOOKS, NEW YORK

KING KELSON'S BRIDE

An Ace Book
Published by The Berkley Publishing Group,
a division of Penguin Putnam Inc.,
375 Hudson Street, New York, New York 10014.
The Penguin Putnam Inc. World Wide Web site address is
http://www.penguinputnam.com

Copyright © 2000 by Katherine Kurtz
Cover art by Jon Sullivan

First edition: June 2000

Library of Congress Cataloging-in-Publication Data

Kurtz, Katherine.
    King Kelson's bride / by Katherine Kurtz.
        p.   cm.
    Includes indexes.
    ISBN 0-441-00732-5
    I. Title.
    PS3561.U69 K49 2000
    813'.54—dc21   99–048047

Printed in the United States of America

10   9   8   7   6   5   4   3   2

For Robert Reginald,
who is also Brother Theophilus:

faithful fellow venturer
into the exotic lands East of Gwynedd,
where many things are very different, indeed. . . .

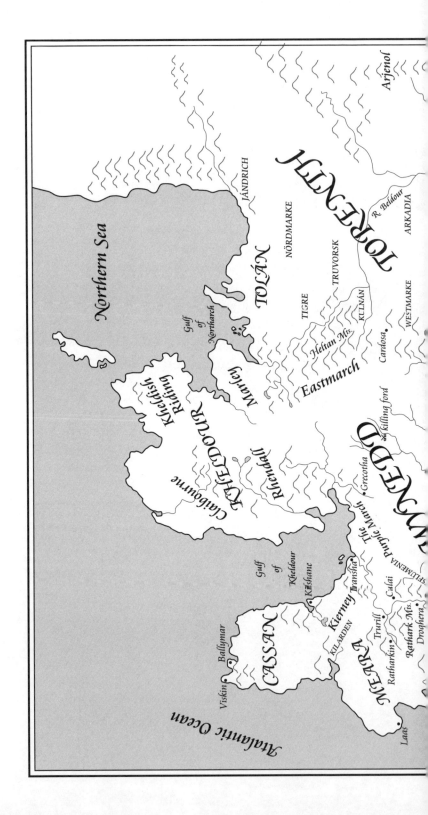

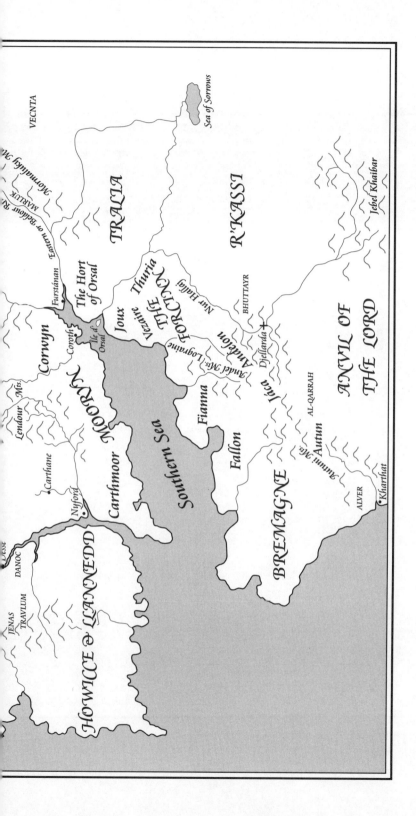

PROLOGUE

He that is greedy of gain troubleth his own house.

Proverbs 15:27

"*M*ark me well, my brother, for I tell you truly that Kelson of Gwynedd means to wed. He must, now that he has agreed to allow the return of Liam-Lajos to Torenth. The way of kings is that of expediency. And it is expedient for the King of Gwynedd to provide his kingdom with an heir before his rival can do the same."

The speaker was Count Teymuraz, acting regent of Arjenol and a younger brother of its duke, Mahael, who was seated across from him. The latter was one of the regents of Torenth, and both men were kin by marriage to the woman who had summoned them to this meeting at domed Torenthály, country seat of Torenth's kings.

The Princess Morag Furstána, widowed sister of the late King Wencit of Torenth, was standing in the opening of a long, brass-trellised window that looked westward across rolling fields, lush and verdant in the brightness of a sultry June afternoon. Co-regent with Mahael, she was also the mother of the previous king, of the said Liam-Lajos, who was the present king, and of Prince Ronal Rurik, the ten-year-old heir presumptive.

"If you are telling me that Liam-Lajos soon must wed, I think it premature," she said quietly, hooking the be-ringed fingers of one hand through the brass grillwork.

"Premature?" said Teymuraz. "He is fourteen, two months into his majority.

And the precarious nature of his situation does put a certain urgency on the matter."

She turned to look at him. The dappled sunlight filtering through the pierced brass set aglow the gauzy folds of veil and trailing sleeve and touched with fire the bands of gold embellishing the royal purple, shimmering around her like the magical Deryni auras all of them could conjure forth at will.

"Do you think I am not aware of that?" she asked. "Yes, he is fourteen. And we have no idea what manner of man he has become, in these four years held hostage at the court of Gwynedd. Best determine first whether he is fit to be king, before we speak of the getting of heirs."

"Harsh words, from the one who bore him," Mahael replied. A faint smile curled within the close-clipped black beard. "And yet, for the sake of the kingdom, we must all of us acknowledge that it could prove necessary to pass over Liam-Lajos in favor of one better suited to rule."

As she glanced at him sharply, Teymuraz gave an amused snort.

"Since my brother has been responsible for the training of the young king's brother, who is the present heir, I can only think he alludes to four more years of his own regency, if it were necessary for Liam-Lajos to give way to Ronal Rurik. We are all of us aware that Mahael harbors no ambition of his own regarding the throne."

Mahael feigned languid interest in a massive seal ring that he wore on his left forefinger, dark eyes heavy-lidded as his thumb absently caressed the design cut into the murky bloodstone.

"I would not see either of my nephews come to harm," he said neutrally, "but if any had a right to wield the might of Furstán after them, it would be myself."

"No one disputes either part of that statement," Morag said briskly, coming to sit between them. "It is an unnatural mother who does not wish success for her sons; but not having seen my elder one for several years, I cannot, as regent, speak for his readiness to rule this kingdom. We do not know how he may have been tainted by contact with the court of Gwynedd. He has had his training from Duke Nigel Haldane, who has ever been a fierce and loyal advocate for Gwynedd's interests—which rarely coincide with Torenth's interests. And I like it not that, as a condition of his return, we must endure the presence of a Gwyneddan 'advisor' always among us, until my son attains the age of eighteen."

"We need not 'endure,' if the situation becomes too inconvenient," Mahael remarked. "Human advisors can be gotten around, and I doubt that young Haldane will long risk leaving one of his few Deryni intimates among us."

"You're aware that if interference is detected, you risk war," Teymuraz said, his voice trailing off in question.

"My dear Teymuraz, let us not speak of such unpleasantness," Mahael said silkily. "But even if the Haldane should leave one of his Deryni among us . . . accidents do happen."

"Aye, even to princes," Teymuraz murmured, not looking at either of them, for the previous king, Morag's eldest son, had died under circumstances many might term "convenient," shortly after attaining his legal majority. Suspicions of Haldane conspiracies had emerged very quickly from the backlash of shocked grief and outrage—though without a shred of evidence—but it could not be denied that two of those present had greatly benefited by the boy's death, simply resuming their regency of the previous four years. That one of those regents was the boy's mother had not stopped speculation in some quarters.

The Princess Morag ignored the comment, tossing her head with a musical chiming of tiny golden bells at ears and throat, and retrieved the wine she had abandoned earlier. The stemmed goblet was of delicate green Vezairi glass, almost invisible against the rich moss-green of the brocade table covering. The wine was the color of blood.

"Teymuraz, you spoke of the Haldane's intention to wed," she said, holding the glass to the light after she had sipped from it. "Have you heard aught regarding whom he might choose?"

Inclining his head, Teymuraz said, "I have cause to wonder whether he might yet persuade the Nabila Rothana to marry him. She and her young son are reported to be visiting Rhemuth; no one knows why."

Mahael flicked his long braid back over his shoulder with a dismissive gesture and leaned forward to pour himself another glass of wine.

"The boy's paternal grandparents live in Rhemuth," he said. "There is no mystery to that. Furthermore, Rothana has stated publicly that she will never marry again—and you know the stubbornness of the House of ar-Rafiq. No, I think it far more likely that the King of Gwynedd seeks a queen among the daughters of the Hort of Orsal's court. His mother passed the winter there; did you know?"

Morag looked startled, and Teymuraz sat back in his chair with an appraising glance at his brother.

"Why was I not told?"

"It was not a state visit," Mahael answered. "The ostensible purpose was to assist in preparations for the coming nuptials of one of the Orsal's nieces, who is also a grandniece to Queen Jehana by marriage."

"That would be one of the Princess Sivorn's daughters," Morag observed, arching a dark eyebrow at Mahael's complacent nod. "Interesting. They *are* of marriageable age, aren't they? And Haldanes, too."

"Surely not of a sort we need worry about overmuch," Teymuraz said, with a disparaging wave of his hand.

"And why not?" Morag asked.

Teymuraz shrugged. "Their father was Duke Richard Haldane, uncle to Queen Jehana's late husband—hardly a contender so far as Haldane powers are concerned. Besides, the elder girl is soon to make a Mearan match, arranged by Kelson himself—and 'tis said that the younger is all but betrothed to Prince Cuan of Howicce."

"Then, it seems the Haldane demoiselles are safely out of the equation," Morag said. "That takes us back to the Orsal's daughters—but surely they're too young."

"The eldest isn't," Mahael remarked. "She's called Rezza Elisabet." On his lips, the name carried a sibilant frisson that caused both his companions to glance at him sharply, though for different reasons. Teymuraz quickly schooled himself to a more neutral deference before his elder brother.

"I thought," said Morag, "that we were talking about a bride for Kelson."

"Oh, we are," Mahael agreed. "But the King of Gwynedd is not alone in his quest for a rich and nubile bride." He shrugged in amusement at her expression of distaste. "You *have* continued to spurn my offers of matrimony, dear Morag."

"Darling Mahael, I adore you," she replied, with a faintly poisonous smile, "but we should kill one another within a week."

"But, oh, what a week of passion it should be!" He chuckled as she rolled her eyes heavenward. "Perhaps not. Failing your capitulation, however, I must confess that the prospect of a suitable consort has been on my mind of late. In fact, my brother will be greatly relieved to learn that it isn't the Orsal's daughter who has caught my fancy, but his niece, the fair Araxie. That flower would be wasted in Howicce, dear Teymuraz."

"True enough," Teymuraz said, much relieved. "But what about Prince Cuan?"

"He is a boy," Mahael replied. "And he is not Deryni."

Morag smiled mirthlessly and shook her head, pushing back a fold of her purple veil. "The poor girl hasn't a chance—or the boy. However, this still leaves us with the question of why Jehana has spent the winter at the Orsal's court. Do you suppose she *is* seeking a bride for her son among the Orsal's daughters?"

Mahael shrugged. "Alas for my brother, I think it possible. And from a Torenthi perspective, it is a far less dangerous match than many being proposed—though marrying into the von Horthy line almost guarantees an heir within a year, if the Haldane does his duty; they are notoriously good breeders. His council would approve of that. Nor would they object to the fact that she is also wealthy and not overly clever."

"I object to neither, in the bedchamber," said Teymuraz. He sighed resignedly. "Ah, sweet Elisabet, thou luscious and succulent peach, ripe for plucking. Fortunate the man who claims thy maidenhead!"

"We *must* find wives for *both* of you!" Morag muttered. "Either that, or a better quality of serving maids. Now, may we please return to the reason I summoned you here?"

Mahael cast an admonitory but indulgent glance at his younger brother, then returned his attention to Morag.

"Despite my brother's obvious disappointment, I reiterate my recommendation regarding the Orsal's daughter. Such a match would have no immediate ramifications for any of the other lands surrounding Gwynedd. More to the point, I see little likelihood that it would change any of the favorable trade arrangements we have in place at present with the girl's father."

"A telling point," Morag agreed. "Nothing can be allowed to compromise our southern ports."

"Our southern ports would be served just as well if *I* married the girl," Teymuraz said a little petulantly. "On the other hand—" An odd look came upon his handsome face. "Dear me, I've just conceived a far better reason to see her married to the Haldane."

"Which is—?"

"Just this: Mahael, you said that Queen Jehana had gone to the Orsal's court to assist in the nuptial preparations for her kinswoman. Have you considered the very unpleasant possibility that she might be arranging for *two* Haldane weddings in Meara?"

Mahael gazed at Teymuraz appraisingly, slowly nodding as he leaned back in his chair. "A possibility I had not, indeed, considered, my brother—and unpleasant, to be sure."

"What possibility?" Morag demanded.

Mahael returned his attention to their sister-in-law.

"We have alluded to the upcoming nuptials of Araxie Haldane's sister, the Princess Richelle, but without taking adequate note of her bridegroom's identity. His name is Brecon Ramsay, and he has a sister also ripe for marriage. Perhaps you will now understand why I regard this possibility as unpleasant."

"Ramsay," Morag repeated, going very still. "Reacquaint me with the particulars. I seem to recall a Ramsay marrying into the old Mearan line. . . ."

"Indeed," Mahael said with a grim smile. "About a century ago, one Edward Ramsay, a younger son of the Earl of Cloome, took to wife the fair Magrette, youngest daughter of the last Prince of Meara, who had died without surviving male issue. It seemed a safe enough match at the time, since the eldest daughter had married King Malcolm Haldane—an act intended to settle the Mearan succession on the children of that union.

"But the Dowager Princess of Meara had refused to accept the Haldane marriage settlement, and began promoting the cause of her middle daughter, twin to Malcolm's queen. Successive Haldane kings down to Kelson himself dealt with that rival line and eventually eradicated it, including—to Kelson's sorrow—the ill-fated Princess Sidana. Even I would not have guessed that her own brother would slay her at the altar rather than see her wed to a Haldane.

"That leaves Mearan pretensions now resting with the descendants of the third demoiselle, who married a Ramsay, of which line one Jolyon Ramsay is now the senior representor—and Brecon is his eldest son and heir."

"Interesting," Morag said. "However, I have never heard that the Ramsays entertained any designs on the throne."

"They don't," Teymuraz chimed in. "And the reason they've survived is probably because they've remained outside subsequent dynastic wranglings of the Mearan royal house."

"And with the more senior lines extinguished," Mahael went on conspiratorially, "those who continue fighting for Mearan independence may not long allow this last branch of the Mearan line to remain quietly on the sidelines. It is bad enough that Brecon, the heir to their last hope of a prince of their own, is set to marry Richelle Haldane, Malcolm Haldane's granddaughter. A marriage between Kelson and Brecon's sister would strike a double blow at any further thought of Mearan independence."

"I see," Morag said, thoughtful as she turned her wineglass in her fingers. "Are there any other siblings?"

"One more brother, conveniently in holy orders," Mahael replied. "With stability in Meara at last, Kelson could turn his full energies toward Torenth—and toward any thought you might entertain of recovering the Festillic legacy for yourself and your sons—both of whom are still quite young. Now, do you understand my concern?"

"I do, indeed. How is the girl called?"

"Noelie."

"I see," Morag said. "And perhaps intended for Kelson of Gwynedd. A shrewd alliance, if true. It would achieve exactly what Kelson tried to do with his ill-fated marriage to Sidana of Meara. But this time, his queen's brother would be safely married to another Haldane."

"*T*here is still that rather inconvenient second brother," said the frail and elderly woman sitting as one of the coadjutors of the Camberian Council, that august and secret body of Deryni mages self-constituted to oversee the affairs of Deryni in the Eleven Kingdoms. They were convened beneath the great purple dome of their hidden mountain eyrie, discussing the same potential match being examined with such wariness in Torenth—though as friends of Kelson Haldane, not his mortal enemies.

"He has entered holy orders since we last discussed this match," said Laran ap Pardyce, the physician among them, consulting a list. "He is now *Brother Christophle*—affirmation of a vocation recognized in childhood. They say he studies for the priesthood."

A heavy sigh drew all eyes in the direction of Bishop Denis Arilan, a man well-qualified to speak regarding priesthood, for he had been the first of their race in nearly two hundred years to be successfully ordained a priest—and had seen others fail and die for their presumption. With an easing of the political climate in Gwynedd, and having risen to the episcopate, he secretly had begun ordaining other Deryni priests—and there was a second bishop come to his priestly status without Arilan's help—but Denis Arilan was still the only cleric to sit on the Council since the time of Camber himself.

"Need I point out that the priesthood has been no bar to Mearan pretensions in the past?" he asked. "Witness the Prince-Bishop Judhael, whom Kelson finally had to execute. Furthermore, I think the king would be very wary of another potential Sidana. The parallels between Noelie, Brecon, and Christophle Ramsay are altogether too close to Sidana, Ithel, and Llewell."

"True enough," Laran agreed. "On the other hand, it would be a great personal triumph for Oksana Ramsay."

Mild amusement rippled among five of the six present. Sir Sion Benét, seated farther around the great octagonal table, cleared his throat and shifted in his chair, looking like a perplexed lion with his yellow eyes and beard and mane of tawny curls. At forty-two, he was the Council's youngest member and, in the absence of its most recent appointment, the most junior—though by only a few months. The Council had filled its last vacant seat only at the end of the previous new year, bringing its full complement to seven. (The eighth chair, in the North, remained always vacant and was known as Saint Camber's Siege.)

"I . . . gather," Sion said, "that the lady harbors some motivation beyond mere motherly ambition, to see her daughter make this particular match."

"Ah, that girl!" Vivienne exclaimed, throwing up her hands. "Willful, even as a child!"

Dark-eyed Sofiana, sovereign princess in her own land of Andelon, cast a faintly amused glance at the dismayed Sion.

"You must forgive Vivienne," she said, not unkindly. "It was something of a scandal at the time. I well remember the gossip in my father's hall. Oksana Ramsay is distant kin to Vivienne's late husband, and also to the Hort of Orsal's line. That descent, while noble, was unlikely to attract a royal match, but nonetheless she set her sights on first Brion and then Nigel Haldane. Unfortunately, both princes chose others. She has never forgotten the slight."

Sion nodded. Himself an under-chancellor to the royal House of Llannedd, he was currently dealing with another headstrong young woman at home: the Princess Gwenlian, half-sister to the King of Llannedd, unmarried and high-spirited, who had already been discussed and not yet discarded as a potential bride for Kelson.

"I quite understand, now that you've explained," he said. "But she did marry well enough."

"Not well enough to suit *her*," Arilan said drily. "Jolyon Ramsay may bear the name of the last effective Prince of Meara, and even a trace of the blood, through the youngest daughter of that prince, but he is still a simple knight, descended in the male line from a cadet branch of a rather minor earldom at the back of beyond."

"Mearan separatists regard that lineage with rather more respect," Laran pointed out. "A difference of opinion over which your king has already fought one war, and been left a widower before he was truly a husband. Still, marrying the Mearan problem may still be the best way to resolve it, in the end. Tell me, has he shown any interest in the Mearan girl?"

Arilan shook his head. "No—though they were thrown together often enough last summer, when the marriage contract was being arranged between her brother and Kelson's cousin. It was certainly not for the mother's want of trying."

"Let's move on," said blind Barrett de Laney, the Council's second coadjutor. "We've discussed this match before. Laran, who is our next candidate?"

Laran ap Pardyce, serving as recorder for the proceeding, consulted the parchment sheet before him, ticking off another name. "Kelson's other cousin, Araxie Haldane," he announced.

Sion looked up sharply, lips pursing in a silent whistle, but before he could speak, Vivienne shook her grey head.

"I've said it before: a dangerous match," she declared. "Double-Haldane blood. Impossible to predict what the children would be like."

Sion cleared his throat, shrugging slightly as all eyes turned toward him.

"Court gossip in Llannedd has it that, any day now, an official announcement will be made of a betrothal between the Princess Araxie and Prince Cuan of Howicce."

"An interesting notion," Barrett said, as several of the others murmured among themselves. "Harmless enough, politically. Rather a waste of Haldane blood, however—especially if, as we now suspect, the Haldane gifts may be some form of Deryni inheritance. Who knows what else might surface in the children of such a union?"

"Yes, who knows?" Vivienne retorted. "One shudders to contemplate! What the Haldanes need is a good infusion of Deryni blood to stabilize things—and there's Deryni blood in the Orsal's line. Marry him to the Orsal's eldest. Good bones and teeth, sturdy heirs, and no surprises!"

Sofiana smiled as she leaned her head languidly against the high back of her chair. "I still like the idea of a double-Haldane cross."

"One would think we were talking about breeding horses!" Arilan grumbled. "I, for one, should be glad if Kelson could summon up some enthusiasm for just about *any* prospective bride besides Rothana!"

"Be careful what you wish for . . ." Laran murmured.

"You know what I mean. Could we just get on with it? I need to get back."

"Yes, we all have other duties," Barrett said. "Laran, how many more are on the list?"

"Five," Laran said. "But I suppose we can eliminate the Princess Janniver."

"Hmmm, yes," Vivienne agreed. "A pity about that, but nothing to be done. Let's return to the Princess Gwenlian."

CHAPTER ONE

Whoso findeth a wife findeth a good thing, and obtaineth favor of the Lord.

Proverbs 18:22

*M*arriage was very much on the mind of Kelson of Gwynedd as, later that evening, he paused before the door to the chapel royal at Rhemuth Castle, royally arrayed—though the marriage about to take place within was not any of those the Camberian Council had in mind. At twenty-one, he had been resisting the Council's "guidance" for a full third of his life, and would not have been surprised at the antipathy they held for the woman he shortly would lead before the altar.

Growing impatient, he glanced back at the squire waiting behind him and brushed distractedly at a bothersome wisp of black hair escaping from the queue at his nape, braided and doubled back on itself with a wrapping of gold. He had cause to regret the latter gesture at once, for the glint of gold on his left hand drew his attention to the narrow band gracing the little finger, next to a signet of his Haldane arms as king—a ring he had given to other brides in other times, one slain and another forever beyond his reach. But he must not let himself think of that; not now.

He straightened and drew a fortifying breath, determined not to let his disquiet show when the bride appeared. Mindful of his rank—and hers—he had arrayed himself in Haldane crimson for the small, almost clandestine ceremony shortly to begin. Though only a plain gold circlet adorned his brow, not the crown of state, the border of his crimson mantle was embellished with the emblems of his House: a favorite pattern of lean, stylized running lions, their legs and tails interlaced in an ancient design, echoing the larger lion *rampant guardant* worked in gold bullion on the breast of his tunic.

He smoothed the lion absently and drew another deep breath. Waiting beyond the door were a carefully chosen handful of his closest intimates, whose lives had long been intertwined with his: his uncle, his cousins, even the young hostage king, Liam-Lajos, who had endeared himself to the royal family during his four years of squireship under Nigel.

The Deryni Bishop Duncan McLain was also among them, though not as celebrant of the nuptial Mass about to begin—for this marriage would provoke controversy. Presiding instead would be Kelson's personal chaplain of the past year, a young Deryni priest called John Nivard.

Also within was Duncan's son Dhugal, Kelson's blood-brother and perhaps his closest companion. And standing across from Dhugal, her mere presence enough to tear out Kelson's heart, would be the woman who should have been his bride but had sworn never again to wed: Rothana of Nur Hallaj, here to witness for the golden-haired young woman who now shyly set her hand on Kelson's arm.

"Sire?" she whispered.

Nervous as any bridegroom, the king turned to smile down at her as he covered her hand with his, thinking that he had never seen her look so lovely.

"Courage," he murmured. "You are a bride to make any man proud."

She flushed prettily, the high color in her cheeks rivaling the pale pinks and creams of her bridal bouquet and the rose wreath crowning the mane of golden curls. Her gown was of silver samite, befitting a royal princess.

"Sire, you do me far more honor than I deserve," she said. "Not many men would—"

"Not another word," he said, with a shake of his head to silence her protestations. "The altar is prepared, and we have business there, I think. Shall we go in?"

Her color faded, but she nodded, briefly biting at her lower lip before turning her face toward the older woman waiting to open the door before them. The Duchess Meraude, Kelson's aunt, had dressed the bride and brought her to the chapel door, and leaned closer to gently kiss her cheek before opening the door and herself slipping inside to join her husband.

Kelson's appearance in the doorway with the Princess Janniver on his arm elicited a soft murmur of anticipation, quickly stilled, rather than the trumpet fanfare that should have greeted a royal bride. She had opted not even to have the choir Kelson could have summoned with a word, to sing the responses of the entrance antiphon. He could feel her trembling against his arm as Father Nivard began merely reading out the antiphon as the two of them walked down the short aisle.

"*Adjutorium nostrum in nomine Domini.*"

"*Qui fecit caelum et terram,*" the witnesses responded.

"*Domine, exaudi orationem meam.*"

"*Et clamor meus ad te veniat.*"

Our help is in the name of the Lord . . . Who made heaven and earth . . . O Lord, hear my prayer . . . and let my cry come unto thee. . . .

Kelson kept his gaze averted as they walked, not for the first time regretting the circumstances that required this marriage to be solemnized in private. But it was better than might have befallen the unfortunate Janniver, who had never asked for the fate that befell her en route to another set of nuptials some four years before. Though then betrothed to the King of Llannedd, both he and her own father had utterly rejected her following her violation at the hands of a now-dead Mearan prince.

It was Kelson who had avenged her, and who had found her a sympathetic refuge in the household of his aunt; but it was one of his former squires who had lost his heart to the shy and gentle Janniver, and who now stepped forward almost reverently to take her hand from Kelson's, adoration mingling with awed incredulity at his remarkable good fortune. Not often might a mere knight aspire to the hand of a royal princess.

With a nod and a smile at Sir Jatham Kilshane, Kelson set his hand briefly over their joined ones, then bent to lightly kiss Janniver's cheek before stepping back beside Dhugal. Father Nivard also smiled as he moved forward to greet the couple, inviting them to pray.

"*Dominus vobiscum.*"

"*Et cum spiritu tuo.*"

"*Oremus.*"

Only when the prayer was done and Nivard began to speak briefly about the institution of marriage did Kelson dare to lift his gaze to the other woman standing near the altar, now holding Janniver's bridal bouquet—the woman for whom he gladly would have sacrificed almost anything within his power, if only she might consent to the vows Janniver and Jatham shortly would exchange.

Rothana of Nur Hallaj: a princess of ancient royal blood, full Deryni, and his match- and soul-mate on every level. Standing there on Janniver's other side, with dark eyes demurely downcast over the bouquet that should have been her own, she was gowned in the simple grey habit worn by the Servants of Saint Camber, whose patronage she had taken up following the birth of her son. Though the Servants were not a true religious order, she had covered the blue-black splendor of her hair beneath a nun-like fall of snowy wimple and veil, perhaps intending to remind him that she considered herself no more obtainable now than she had been when first they met—a vowed novice in the abbey where Janniver had broken her journey to another bridegroom never meant to be.

It so nearly had been otherwise. Herself as drawn to Kelson as he was to her, Rothana had tested the strength of her religious vows and eventually set them aside, intending to marry him, persuaded that her higher vocation lay in becoming his queen—and a queen for the Deryni.

But when faced with Kelson's supposed death, as all the court believed, she had allowed his cousin Conall to persuade her that she now should be *his* queen, and still a queen for the Deryni, and had married him, borne his son. It mattered not that their brief marriage, of less than a month, had been based on deceptions that had ended with Conall's execution as a traitor, leaving her free to marry again; Rothana had lost faith, and regarded herself now unworthy to be Kelson's queen.

Father Nivard's prenuptial exhortations concluded, and Kelson returned his attention briefly to the rapt bridal couple as Nivard now addressed first the groom, in the formal reiteration of betrothal that preceded the marriage vows.

"*Jathamus,*" he asked, "*vis accipere Jannivera hic praesentem in tuam legitimam uxorem juxta ritum sanctae Matris Ecclesiae?*"

"*Volo,*" Jatham breathed, his word of assent hardly audible for the joy welling in his eyes.

"*Et Jannivera, vis accipere Jathamus hic praesentem in tuam legitimam maritum juxta ritum sanctae Matris Ecclesiae?*"

"*Volo,*" she replied, her eyes never leaving Jatham's.

They exchanged vows then, but Kelson hardly heard them. Even with Dhugal at his side, he had never felt so alone, never been more aware that, unless fate took a drastic turn, it was likely that he himself would never experience even a small part of the joy so obviously surrounding the couple before him. But he did his best to mask his own sorrow as the ring was blessed, the nuptial Mass celebrated, the bridal bouquet laid as an offering before the statue of the Queen of Heaven, over at the side of the chapel royal.

Afterward, when Kelson had led the bridal party to his own quarters for an intimate wedding supper, he set himself to play the gracious host as they dined on venison and roast fowl and poached salmon and savory pies. Three of his aunt's ladies-in-waiting had undertaken to provide musical accompaniment for the meal, and their sweet voices mingled with the gentle strains of lute and dulcimer that drifted through the open door to Kelson's bedchamber while the guests washed down their fare with ample portions of fine Vezairi wines brought up from the royal cellars. By the time the debris of the main courses was cleared away and the squires began laying out little cakes and honeyed dates and other dainties, he had let the wine blunt a little of his personal hopelessness.

He was seated directly across from Jatham and Janniver, on one side of a long trestle table laid out in the center of the withdrawing chamber adjacent to his private quarters. Meraude and Nigel flanked the happy couple, with Rory and Payne Haldane and young Liam ranged around the end of the table on Nigel's side, the young Torenthi king looking almost like another Haldane, save for the bronze glints in his clubbed hair. Under the indulgent eye of Rory, recently knighted, both younger boys had been partaking freely of the wine brought up from the royal cellars, and had elicited more than one raised eyebrow from Nigel.

A smothered snicker from Payne earned the pair a raised eyebrow from Kelson as well, but he made himself smile as he pushed back his chair and got to his feet, taking up his goblet. At least this part of his hosting duty would be a pleasure. Dhugal sat at his left hand, across from Duchess Meraude, with Duncan beyond him—and then Rothana, safely between him and Father Nivard. It was Meraude who had persuaded Rothana not to forego the wedding supper, since she was as close to family as the Princess Janniver could claim, on what should have been an occasion for family rejoicing on both sides.

Kelson cast a furtive glance in her direction as conversation gradually died away and all eyes turned in his direction, his thumb unconsciously worrying at the ring on his little finger—the ring she had cast into the moat before her marriage to another, believing him dead—recovered that next summer, through no little exertion of the powers of several of his Deryni associates. He knew she would not long linger, once the formalities of the meal had been concluded. Knowing his own sorrow, he knew hers hardly could be less.

"My friends," he said, putting aside the sorrow as he scanned the smiling faces upturned toward him, "it is now my happy privilege to offer a toast to Sir Jatham's fair bride. But before I do that," he went on, turning his focus on the pair, "I have something to say to the two of you." He set down his goblet and cast an inquiring glance at Nigel, who nodded minutely.

"My lady Janniver, I should first like to point out that I have given you to a husband I took great pains to bring up properly—which is no mean feat for a king who is hardly a year older than his squire." The droll observation elicited smiles and a few chuckles as Kelson continued. "I can assure you, however, that I regard Sir Jatham Kilshane as a credit to my court and to whatever bride he might have chosen. Little did I realize that he would choose a royal princess—though every bride is a princess on her wedding day."

Janniver blushed, Jatham ducked his head sheepishly, and gentle laughter rippled among the wedding guests.

"This leaves us, however, with an interesting point of protocol," Kelson went on. "It is long-established custom that a bride takes the rank of her new husband on her wedding day, no matter how exalted her birth—which means that you, my dear princess, rank now as the wife of a simple knight."

Before she could make indignant protest, a smiling Kelson held up a hand and shook his head. "Now, I know you'll say it doesn't matter, and I have the distinct impression that the two of you would be quite content to live together in a humble cottage somewhere in the woods," he continued, "but even for a simple knight and his lady, that's hardly suitable. Furthermore, it would require your departure from court, which is not a prospect I relish. Not only would I miss Jatham's useful counsel, but I would lose one of Rhemuth's loveliest adornments. I have, therefore, decided to remedy the situation in my own way."

He glanced again at Nigel, who had reached behind him to retrieve a rolled scroll adorned with pendant seals along its edge, which item he passed across to the king. Kelson did not unroll it; merely held it out to Jatham, who rose uncertainly to receive it.

"You don't need to read it now," he said, at Jatham's look of bewilderment. "I'm sure you see enough royal writs in my chancery that you don't need to read one on your wedding night." He favored Janniver with a fond smile before continuing.

"Suffice it to say that, with the consent and enthusiastic approval of the Duke of Cassan"—he gestured toward Dhugal, who bowed in his chair—"I have this day revived the ancient barony of Kilshane, in the earldom of Kierney, and have created you Baron of Kilshane." He ignored Jatham's look of astonishment and Janniver's little gasp of surprise. "This comes with a grant of the castle of Kilshane and all the rents and incomes thereunto appertaining. After all, you now have a baroness to support—though I'll still expect the pair of you to spend a reasonable amount of time at court each year. I would have made you an earl, Jatham—and I do hope to revive the old Kilshane earldom, which has long been extinct—but Nigel pointed out that it might be more appropriate to let you prove yourself as baron first."

Delighted laughter greeted this remark, along with a general pounding of hands on table in approval. A teary-eyed Janniver had risen to clasp her new husband's arm in adoring affirmation, and Jatham turned the scroll in his hands as if unable to believe what had just happened.

"Sire, I—"

"No, not another word. The title is yours—my wedding gift to the pair of you. We'll confirm it in open court in the morning—or maybe in the afternoon, depending on what time you two decide to emerge from the bridal chamber," he added with a wink. "You needn't worry about the details. Your new overlord will organize what needs to be done."

"I will, indeed," Dhugal agreed, clearly delighted to be sharing in the king's largesse.

"I—Sire, we thank you most humbly," was all Jatham could manage to murmur, as the two of them sat down, exchanging still-disbelieving glances.

"You're both very welcome," Kelson said, feeling pleased with himself as he took up his goblet again. "Given what's just been done, then, I ask everyone to be upstanding for a toast to the bride's health." He paused as all of them rose in a scraping of chairs on stone, except for Janniver, who was dabbing at her eyes with the edge of a sleeve.

"I give you the bride: the new Baroness of Kilshane. May her life with her bold new baron be long and happy and fruitful." He lifted his cup. "To the bride!"

"The bride!" the others chorused, also raising their cups in salute before draining them.

When the toast had been drunk—and another to the king, offered by the now-recovering Baron Jatham—the guests settled back to nibble on the sweetmeats and candied fruits, while the bride fed the groom bits of honeyed cake and the wine continued to flow. Almost immediately, Kelson withdrew to his private chamber, dismissing the musicians with his thanks and a purse of silver and sending a page to request Rothana's attendance before she could depart. She came; but she clearly was uneasy to have been summoned away from the others.

"Thank you for coming," he said, when she had given him a formal curtsy and the page had left them—and before she could speak. "I wished to advise you, before I left for Torenth, that construction is nearly completed on the chapel to be reinstated for Saint Camber. I believe Duncan has been in communication with you, regarding its consecration. I look forward to the presence of the Servants of Saint Camber on that historic day."

She averted her eyes and sighed. "My lord, I have told you that I would be there on that day. But you must not continue contriving these meetings in private, which but cause us both pain. I have told you I will not marry again."

"And I must believe you," he said quietly. "I suppose that, in time, I must accept it, too." He sighed and dropped his gaze, unable to bear the sight of her with the candlelight gilding her cheek. "I cannot promise that my heart will ever accept it, though. How can you ask me to break the bond we have shared?"

"It *must* be broken, Sire," she whispered. "And you must forge a like bond with another, for the sake of your kingdom. The faith of your queen must never waver."

"The queen I would wed *never* broke faith with my kingdom, even when she thought its king had perished!" Kelson replied, looking up at her. "Can you not see that?"

She paled in the candlelight, her dark eyes like twin caverns burned in the pale mask of her face. "I see only that the one you would have made your queen lost faith in you," she said miserably. "You deserve better! *Gwynedd* deserves better!"

He closed his eyes and turned his face away, head drooping onto his chest as the breath caught in his throat. Only after a long moment did he find his voice.

"We must agree to disagree on this point," he finally said, bracing his shoulders again.

"Yes," she managed to answer. "We agree on that."

"Thank you." He swallowed painfully. "There is—another matter I would discuss with you. In this, perhaps you will permit your heart to soften. It concerns your son—who might have been *our* son."

She stiffened. "Sire, my heart is resolved in that regard as well. Albin is promised to the Church."

"Rothana, he is a Haldane prince. If that is *his* choice, if it is *God's* choice, then so be it—Haldanes have served thus before. But do not presume to make that choice *for* him!"

"It is the best choice," she said, "and better *that*, than that he should someday challenge your own line. And do not remind me that holy orders give no guarantee against the lure of secular pretensions—well do I remember the fate of the Mearan prince-bishop!"

So did Kelson. It was he who had been obliged to order Judhael's execution.

"Rothana," he said, "until I wed and sire heirs of my own body, Prince Albin Haldane is still my next kin after Nigel, no matter what you do. No cloister wall can alter that."

"And if you were to have no sons," she said, "I should be well enough content that he succeed you and Nigel. But *you* must have sons. And what I fear is that my Albin should someday be turned against those sons—sons by a proper queen. . . ."

She turned her head away on a sob, and Kelson bowed his head again.

A proper queen . . . She was his proper queen! He could not tell her how he had watched her that afternoon from a window that overlooked the castle gardens, as she and Janniver gathered flowers for the bridal bouquet, the two-year-old Albin trundling happily behind them with a wicker basket to carry the blooms—the very model of a Haldane prince, with his fair skin and pale eyes and shock of night-black hair. Whenever he saw the boy, Kelson found it all too easy to wish and even to pretend that Albin surely must be his own son, not the traitorous Conall's.

But by now he had heard the same arguments often enough from Rothana to know she was firm in her plans both for herself and for Albin; and with a sickly, sinking feeling, he feared he was starting to accept them.

"It—seems, then," he heard himself saying, as if from very far away, "that I must start thinking seriously about a—proper queen."

Her strangled little gasp told of the pain that statement cost her, as well as himself.

"I am—pleased to hear you say that, my lord," she said, her voice steadying after the first few words. "To say that I do not love you would be a lie—and you would know it—but we must, both of us, get on with our lives. I have made arrangements for my future, and for Albin's, and I—have made certain inquiries concerning your own. If—If you will hear me, I—believe I may have found you the queen you require."

"*You* have found—"

Shocked and stunned, he turned away from her, unseeing, not in rejection of her offer—for it bespoke a love beyond mere human yearning—but in dull recognition that what remained of their relationship was about to move beyond any hope of reconciliation. And there was nothing he could do to prevent it.

"Can there be no hope at all for us?" he whispered.

"None." Her voice was stark, strained. "But there must be hope for Gwynedd—and for that, you must have sons. If—If you will give her even half a chance, I think that the bride I would propose will please you."

"I am all too well aware of my duty to provide Gwynedd with sons," he said. "As for pleasure—"

He shook his head dismally, unable to go on, and flinched as she laid her hand gently on his forearm.

"My dearest lord, you have so much love to give," she murmured. "Whatever queen you take, you must share at least a portion of that love with her—for your own dear sake, as well as that of Gwynedd, and the princes you will sire, and the woman who will bear them. To do less would be to vow falsely before God's altar—and the King of Gwynedd that I know would never break his holy oath. Besides"—she released him and turned nervously aside—"the bride I have in mind is already known to you. You got on very well when you were children."

He blinked at her in mute astonishment. Then:

"You're speaking of someone I already know?"

"Well, of course. I would not see you wed a total stranger." She eyed him cautiously. "Kelson, I have not been idle while you have been pining, these past three years. After Albin was born, I took him to Nur Hallaj, so that my parents might meet their new grandson—for he is that, whatever else he may become. I returned by way of the Ile d'Orsal, for the Orsal's line are distant kin to my family. It was that summer that Gwynedd's envoys first approached your great-aunt Sivorn regarding marriage between your cousin Richelle and Brecon Ramsay."

"If you're thinking of Brecon's sister, Noelie, I only met her last summer, when she came to Rhemuth for her brother's betrothal—though my council would certainly approve of the match—as would her mother!"

"And being vexed with the pressures being brought to bear by both the mother and your council," Rothana said with faint amusement, "no doubt you failed to mark the Lady Noelie's interest in a different Haldane prince besides yourself."

"What?"

"Kelson, Kelson, it is Rory she should wed, not you," she replied. "They were most discreet, but their mutual attraction did not go unnoticed by my uncle Azim, who has served as my good agent in searching out a bride for you. Oh, both will marry where required, for they are bred to duty, as we all have been—but think on it: a marriage between Rory and Noelie would further bind Mearan loyalty to Gwynedd, just as your council desires, with Haldane heirs to succeed them. And in the meantime, you could have an ongoing Haldane presence in Meara, for Rory might live there, where you could not."

"Rory and Noelie," Kelson repeated dazedly. "But it . . . does make sense—especially if, as you say, there's an affinity already. . . ."

She glanced at her hands, twining her fingers to stop their fidgeting. "It is a great blessing when needs of the state can be made to match desires of the heart," she murmured.

Her declaration immediately brought Kelson back to the original direction of their conversation, reluctant though he was to take it up again.

"You—said that I already know the woman you have in mind for me," he said quietly. He could not bear to ask the question that naturally followed on that statement, but at his hesitation, she smiled and sadly shook her head.

"My dearest prince, we *must* go on," she whispered. "Tell me truly, did you pay no mind at all to Richelle's sister?"

"Araxie? You mean my cousin? But she's all but betrothed to Cuan of . . . Howicce . . ." His voice trailed off as Rothana slowly shook her head. "She isn't?"

"A smoke screen, my lord. Oh, marriage certainly has been discussed at length—but not between the two of them. They regard one another as brother and sister."

"But—that isn't possible. All the court gossip—"

"—is precisely that, with as little substance as usually pertains to gossip. In fact, Cuan wishes to wed his cousin Gwenlian."

"*Gwenlian?!* But her brother *hates* Cuan! He'd never allow it."

"Indeed," Rothana replied. "Hence, the need for misdirection, in which Araxie has been only too happy to conspire."

Through his own stunned consternation—for his own cousin had never even crossed his mind as a possible royal bride—Kelson felt an accompanying tug of sympathy for Gwenlian, whose brother was the very same King Colman who once had been affianced to the Princess Janniver. But he was only vaguely listening as Rothana launched upon a clipped précis of the convoluted succession laws operant in the United Kingdoms of Howicce and Llannedd, whereby the present heirs of Colman—still unmarried, after his broken betrothal to Janniver—were his sister Gwenlian in Llannedd, but their cousin Cuan in Howicce, since women could not reign in that land.

Araxie. His cousin Araxie. The notion was so unexpected that he could not, for the life of him, conjure up more than a vague recollection of what she even looked like, grown to womanhood, though he knew he must have seen her with Richelle the previous summer. Presentable enough, he supposed, for he would have noticed if she were not, but quiet and unpresuming in the shadow of her vivacious elder sister, who favored her Haldane blood and, as the prospective bride of Meara, had been the focus of the family's visit.

More vivid were childhood memories of a laughing, snub-nosed little girl with knobby knees and freckles and flaxen braids, who had romped with him and her sister and Conall in the royal gardens, and fled squealing and giggling with Richelle when he and Conall decided it would be good sport to tease and chase the girls.

"The thought that Cuan should inherit even Howicce is abhorrent to Colman," Rothana went on, "but the only way he can prevent that is by producing a male heir of his own, who would then take precedence over even Gwenlian and inherit both crowns. Of course, he must make a suitable marriage first—which is proving difficult, since no decent house will entertain his suit after his shabby treatment of Janniver."

This last declaration was delivered with some satisfaction, for Rothana was a staunch partisan of the wronged Janniver, even though the marriage just celebrated was a happy resolution to the princess's ill fortune.

"Meanwhile, did he know of it, Colman would do his utmost to prevent a marriage that would eventually allow Cuan to sit on both thrones," she concluded. "Did he even suspect, he would lock up Gwenlian, or worse. Hence, the illusion that an understanding exists between Cuan and Araxie."

"Then, she is *not* contemplating marriage with Cuan," Kelson said, after a beat.

"No, she is not. Nor with any of the other suitors who have, from time to time, sought her hand. Think of it, my lord: She is a Haldane, your distant cousin, so no one could take political exception to such a marriage—and there is Deryni blood through her mother's line. It may even be that she carries some form of the Haldane potential you possess."

Kelson thrust his hands through his belt and began pacing restlessly before the fireplace, hardly daring to look at her. In truth, not even his council had ever suggested his younger Haldane cousin as a potential bride, believing her already matched with Cuan. Nor had he paid her much note on that visit last summer, being focused on the Mearan match. Now he was beginning to recall brief glimpses of a tallish, fair, vaguely attractive girl who looked a lot like his Aunt Sivorn.

"My cousin Araxie," he finally murmured, feeling disloyal already. "I . . . suppose she *is* grown by now," he ended lamely.

Rothana cast her glance heavenward with an exasperated sigh. "Men pay so little attention. Sometimes I truly do despair. Of course she's grown. She's nearly nineteen."

Kelson cleared his throat, trying unsuccessfully to merge the blond imp of childhood memory with an imagined Araxie now become a woman, wearing the crown of Gwynedd's queen consort.

"Rothana, I can't do this," he said. "I confess that you've presented very sound arguments, but I—I really do hardly know her."

"You knew her as a child," Rothana replied. "You know her better than any of the other candidates your council has been pushing in your direction for the past five years. And you certainly know her better than you knew Sidana, before you married *her*."

Kelson flinched at this reminder of his slain bride, his hand closing unconsciously on the ring he had given to her *and* Rothana.

"It would still be a marriage of state," he said woodenly. "Besides, what makes you think Araxie would have me?"

"Because I have asked her," Rothana replied, only blinking at his look of startled panic. "Be assured, it was not a sudden whim—either the asking or her acceptance. But she has indicated her willingness, if you consent."

He was staring at her speechlessly, stupidly, unable to believe she had taken this upon herself.

"She *is* fond of you, Kelson—or at least of the boy you were," Rothana said softly. "I cannot think she will be any less fond of Kelson the man. You both could do far worse. She is intelligent, well-read, attractive—and a Haldane with Deryni blood, though not so much as yourself. But she has some ability emerging—and shields. My uncle Azim has been giving her instruction for some time."

Kelson hung his head, fighting the lump in his throat.

"You seem to have my future all planned out," he said bitterly.

"It *is* a future, for you and for Gwynedd," she ventured.

"For Gwynedd, at least."

"For Gwynedd and for Araxie *and* for you, if you will have it so," she amended. "And for children of your union. Without them, I cannot speak for the future of Gwynedd."

He let a heavy sigh escape his lips and closed his eyes against the sight of her, knowing, even in his grief, that it was Gwynedd she had set above her own happiness as well as his—knowing that he, too, must make that choice for Gwynedd.

As the silence between them deepened, she dared to touch a hesitant hand to his sleeve, recoiling when he drew back as if stung, looking up, all his thwarted longing writ across his face for her to see.

"Please, my lord, do not make this more difficult than it must be," she pleaded, her voice barely a whisper. "Will you consider it?"

His heart shrank from it, every fiber of his being begged him to gainsay her; but a cool thread of logic and duty tugged at his will, bending him to hers.

"If—that is what you wish," he said dully, after a moment.

"I do wish it," she said very softly, blinking back tears as she drew herself up bravely, head high. "I am—told that you will be calling in at the Ile d'Orsal, en route to Beldour with Liam of Torenth," she went on. "She is there at the Orsal's court now, helping her sister prepare for the Mearan marriage. Azim is there as well, for he is to represent my father at the investiture in Torenth. You have to but request it of him, and Azim will arrange a private meeting with your cousin."

"Is it your intention that I should propose marriage at that time?" Kelson said, turning his face away from her.

"The opportunity is timely," she replied, "and you cannot afford any long delay. The ministers of Liam-Lajos will not delay to see him wed, as soon as he is back among his own people. The getting of heirs will be a high priority for him, and so it also must become a high priority for you."

"Rothana, please don't make me do this—"

But she only shook her head, closing her eyes to his entreaties. "You *must* wed, my love, and I cannot marry you," she whispered. "At least marry the woman I have chosen for you. She will make you and Gwynedd a wise and worthy queen."

CHAPTER TWO

Look at the generations of old, and see.

Ecclesiasticus 2:10

*T*he wedding guests affected not to take particular notice when Rothana and then the king rejoined them, for all were aware of the convoluted history that lay between the pair. Rothana appeared reasonably composed—if one ignored the new hint of sorrow in her dark eyes—and Kelson managed to convey a credible impression of equanimity; but both seemed palpably relieved when, after only a few minutes, Meraude rose and, with a nod and a smile, indicated to Rothana that it was time to convey the bride to her marriage bed.

The women departed. In the next quarter-hour before the men followed, Kelson continued to play the consummate host, joining in the gentle teasing of the occasionally blushing bridegroom, calling for a last flagon of wine, dutifully lifting his cup to drink with the rest as Rory offered a traditional toast to the groom's joy of his bride.

Later, Dhugal would say that it was the wine that caused a momentary crack in the king's façade—and it was only he who caught it, and only for an instant. As they rose to conduct Jatham to the bridal chamber, several of the other men taking up torches to light their way, the king misstepped while entering the stairwell, apparently intent on Jatham, who was disappearing upward.

Dhugal saved him from a spill; but raw emotion came blasting through the link that was always present between them on at least some level, and especially with physical contact. And Kelson's whispered plaint, heard by no one else, wrenched at Dhugal's heart as the king shook off his touch and murmured, on a sob, "Happy Jatham! Can he comprehend his great good fortune, to have wed where he loves?"

He only shook his head at Dhugal's look of sympathetic question—shields slamming down, jaw tight-set, quickly putting back a mask of geniality fitting for a wedding celebration as he fell in with the others at the tail of the procession, Jatham gone subdued in their midst. Dhugal followed but said nothing, for as their torchlight ascended the turnpike stair, Rory and then Nigel began softly to sing a traditional Transhan wedding air. When Payne and even Liam joined in, Nivard started to weave in harmonies, which were soon picked up by Duncan and Dhugal; but Kelson did not sing. By the time their party emerged before the bridal chamber, whose lintel bore a swag of roses and true-lover's knots, the men had turned the song's refrain into a haunting three-part canon that they repeated twice more before falling silent.

From inside, women's voices took up an even older canting song between the bride and her beloved, answered by the men—Meraude and the ladies who, earlier, had played and sung at supper; but as they emerged to fetch the groom, Rothana was not among them. Kelson craned his neck to peer after them as, still singing, they led Jatham behind a screen beside the curtained bed; but Rothana seemed nowhere in evidence.

When the groom, now adorned in a fine robe of scarlet silk, had been conducted to his bride, Duncan came into the room to bless the couple in their marriage bed, then withdrew with the ladies for the final song, sung outside the door, which was also a bridal blessing. Kelson fled before this last song ended, and Dhugal hurried after, only catching up with him two flights down.

"Kelson, wait," he called softly. "Kelson!"

The king faltered and then stopped, head bowed, but he did not turn. By the time Dhugal reached him, his face was a taut mask, his eyes blank, unreadable. He winced as Dhugal grabbed him by the bicep and turned him toward the nearest torch.

"What's wrong with you? You look like death!" Dhugal said. "Did you and Rothana quarrel?"

Kelson closed his eyes and shook his head, lips pressed tightly together, but he would not open his shields to Dhugal's anxious query.

"I'd rather not talk about it yet," he said quietly. "I have something I need to do. You're free to come along if you wish."

"You'd have a hard time stopping me," Dhugal muttered, though he doubted the king had heard him, for he was already heading down the next flight of stairs.

The pace Kelson set was brisk, and he said not another word as he led the way, not back to his own quarters but down to the library on a lower floor. After trying the latch, he shook his head and muttered something vexedly under his breath, then crouched to set both hands over the lock. Dhugal guessed what he was doing, though not why, so was not surprised when light flared briefly from under Kelson's hands and the door moved slightly inward.

"Wouldn't it have been easier to use the key?" Dhugal asked, attempting to lighten the mood as Kelson pushed open the door and entered.

"No, because Father Nivard keeps the key nowadays, and then I would have had to explain to him." Handfire flared crimson-gold in the king's hand as he headed purposefully toward the dark bulk of a reading desk that backed up between a pair of dark-draped window embrasures. "Close the door, would you?"

Dhugal said nothing, only pulling the door closed and shooting the inner bolt as Kelson began sorting through several piles of books stacked on the desk. The light of the handfire cast blurred shadows amid the crowded shelves that lined most of the walls, doing little to dispel the mood Dhugal sensed was brewing.

"I'm sure you're wondering why I brought you here," Kelson said, bending to read the gold-stamped title on one large, leather-bound volume. "I need to check some family history."

"Family history?"

"Hmmm." The muffled sound conveyed neither agreement nor denial as Kelson opened the book and scanned down an index. "You asked if Rothana and I had quarrelled," he said distractedly. "Far from it. It seems she's arranged a match for me. With a cousin. *My* cousin. I thought I ought to check the exact relationship."

"*Rothana* has arranged a match?" Dhugal repeated, stunned, as Kelson abruptly closed the book and tucked it under one arm, heading off toward the shadows to their right. "Kelson, are you serious?"

"Unfortunately, *she* was."

This dispassionate statement was accompanied by a harsh clatter of metal curtain rings as Kelson reached up to yank aside a dark curtain screening what Dhugal immediately presumed to be a garderobe niche—except that he did not remember this room having a garderobe. It appeared to be a very ordinary garderobe, with access opened into the thickness of the common wall between this room and the next, and the latrine shaft itself let into the outer wall of the building; but Dhugal had never heard of one being added to an existing building so seamlessly.

He was staring at it stupidly, trying to decide how it might have been done without bringing down this entire wall of the building, when he realized that the cut-stone directly before them, the back wall of the newly created access to the garderobe, seemed to ripple on its surface with a darkling glimmer of vaguely dancing motes that were not quite light, on which his eyes somehow could not quite seem to focus.

"What *is* this?" he whispered, abandoning, for the moment, all further thought of Rothana. "I don't remember a garderobe in this room."

"There wasn't one, until fairly recently," Kelson said neutrally, looping back the folds of curtain behind a black iron finial. "And it isn't just a garderobe— though that's all that most people see."

"It doesn't seem to be a Portal," Dhugal ventured, leaning past Kelson to look around, then reaching out to touch the strange wall, which simply felt like rough-cut stone.

"If you'll step on in, I'll take you through," Kelson said a trifle impatiently. "Unless, of course, you aren't coming."

"You'll not be rid of me *that* easily," Dhugal murmured, moving into the niche with the king, expecting to be taken through a Portal despite his inability to detect one.

He flinched and closed his eyes as Kelson's hand clasped the back of his neck and drew him slightly closer, aware of the wall very close to their noses. He braced himself for a stormy onslaught as he started rolling back his shields, for the king's preoccupation and inner turmoil were apparent.

To his surprise, the other's touch of mind to mind was deft and gentle, all but impersonal, though it bespoke tight-shackled emotion just beyond reach. Settling into the familiar link, Dhugal sensed a reaching, a stretching—and then a Word of power bloomed like a starburst behind his eyes, leaving only tranquillity as the star-burst ebbed and he was left to surface at his own speed.

"Step forward now," he heard Kelson say, as if from far away, as pressure at his neck also urged him forward.

He stepped, sensing the faintest of resistance, as if moving against an upright screen of loosely stretched silk. Then the resistance gave way in a briefly felt surge of cold as they penetrated the Veil.

"We're through," Kelson said, releasing him and pushing aside another physical curtain on the other side. "I've been meaning to show you this, anyway."

Though he faltered in midstep, Dhugal stabilized immediately, opening his eyes to the sound of Kelson's fingers snapping and another flare of crimson-gold handfire blossoming above the king's opening hand. That light revealed a room perhaps a third the size of the one they had just left, with another reading desk set hard against the opposite wall, at right angles to a smaller window embrasure. More bookshelves lined the wall to the right. Well attuned now to the probability that the room shared in the magic by which they had entered, Dhugal caught the faint but decisive ripple of psychic energy that declared the presence of a live Transfer Portal somewhere in the chamber.

"I see you've felt it," Kelson said, as Dhugal moved cautiously forward, feeling out the reverberations. "That's why the door was punched through, and why I've taken such extraordinary measures to guard it. Nigel and I discovered it last winter, while you were off in Transha. We were looking for a way to expand the library. This room had been disused and locked up for years—and when we finally got it opened, we found out why. The Portal is centered there on the square flagstone. It's probably how Charissa got into the castle the night before my coronation."

Dhugal crouched down and laid both hands flat on the stone, a thrill shivering up his spine as he locked the Portal's unique coordinates into memory.

"No wonder she seemed able to come and go at will," he murmured, glancing up at Kelson. "This is an old one—and it's still in use, isn't it?"

"Not by me," Kelson said sourly. "I only know a few Portal locations—the other two here in Rhemuth and the one in Valoret—and Arilan's one in Dhassa, but he's forbidden to show me any others." He shook his head. "The Camberian Council had the audacity to demand access to the library—which I gave, at least to this new section, which houses all the references I've gathered on the Deryni. But in return, I got Arilan to help me set up *that*"—he gestured toward the Veiled doorway—"to keep them from wandering around the rest of the castle at will." He looked vaguely pleased with himself.

"The only ones who can pass in either direction are those of my blood and those I've authorized, like Morgan, and Father Nivard, and Arilan himself, and now you. It's also occurred to me that this Portal might be useful as a bolthole, if we have to get out of Beldour quickly—provided, of course, that we could access a Portal there."

Dhugal nodded as he rose, absently dusting his hands against his thighs, well aware of the ongoing tension between Kelson and the Deryni bishop, and between both of them and the Camberian Council, if for different reasons. Common to all of them, however, was concern for the potential dangers awaiting Kelson in Torenth—and this newly rediscovered Portal might well provide an avenue of escape, if things went sour. But as Dhugal's gaze lit on the great book still clasped under Kelson's arm, he remembered why they had come here, and realized that, at least tonight, Torenth and its dangers were far from Kelson's most urgent concern.

"This match Rothana's proposing—you just found out about it tonight, didn't you?" he said, cutting right to the heart of the matter. "I can't say her timing was the best, following right on the heels of Jatham and Janniver's wedding."

Kelson shrugged and moved to the edge of the window embrasure, there to sink listlessly to a seat on the edge of the single step up.

"I did provide the perfect opening, by insisting on a private meeting. And from her perspective, the timing couldn't be better. She was here, I was here, and I'll be seeing the lady in question on our way to Torenth." He opened the book flat on his lap. "So, let's see what the old stud book says about her."

Dhugal grimaced at the term, for he was beginning to experience subtle pressure from his own vassals to marry and begin producing heirs. But as he sat down beside the king, beckoning the handfire closer, he knew his own pressure could be nothing beside what Kelson was feeling—and Rothana's proposition must have devastated him. It suddenly occurred to him that he didn't even know which of Kelson's cousins Rothana had put forward.

"In a way, Rothana's right, you know—about my marrying a cousin," the king said. His light tone was at odds with the taut muscles around his mouth as he began paging through the book. "If I can't have the woman I really want, a bride of my own blood makes perfect sense. She's been raised as a royal princess, so she'll understand what's expected. And she's a Haldane—which means she might even have potentials similar to my own. Apparently Azim has been working with her, and he and Rothana both have spoken with her, and she's willing to take me on."

"Kelson, you're talking like it's all been decided already," Dhugal said, when Kelson finally paused for breath. "And it would be useful to know which cousin you're talking about."

"Didn't I tell you? It's Araxie Haldane."

"Araxie? You mean, Richelle's sister?"

"Yes."

"But—"

"I know: Everyone thinks she's going to marry Cuan of Howicce. Apparently, she isn't." Kelson turned another page and bent closer. "Ah, here we are: little cousin Araxie, second daughter of Duke Richard Haldane. We called him Uncle Richard, but he was actually my . . . grandfather's half-brother." He gave a taut nod. "Well, at least that's far enough removed that a dispensation won't be difficult."

Dhugal leaned down to follow Kelson's finger sideways along a bristling genealogical chart.

"It's a good line on her mother's side, too," the king went on, scanning up and down. "Hortic blood. After Uncle Richard died, his widow married a Tralian baron, but she was born the Princess Sivorn von Horthy, sister of the present Hort of Orsal. That makes Araxie doubly royal."

"But not Deryni," Dhugal said.

"Well, no, but there's Deryni blood in the Orsal's line—unknown just how much, because they pretty much take such things for granted—shields and such—but it's there. And being a Haldane should count for something."

"I—suppose so," Dhugal conceded, as Kelson carefully closed the book. "Ah—what's she like?"

Kelson sighed. "I have no idea."

"But—surely you saw her when her family came to Rhemuth for Richelle's betrothal."

"I did have a few other things on my mind!" Kelson retorted, slamming the book down on the ledge beside him and springing to his feet. "Not only was the prospective groom's mother trying to match me with her daughter, but the negotiations proved far more delicate than anyone expected, for Richelle and Brecon." He shook his head in a snort of near amusement. "I suppose it's some consolation that the two of them at least seem to *like* one another!

"As for Araxie—do you know that I can't even remember what she *looks* like, for certain? I've been trying for the last hour, but I just keep jumbling blurred impressions of a younger, blonder Aunt Sivorn, with childhood memories of a funny little girl tagging after her older sister, with big eyes and straggly blond hair done in plaits!"

The mental picture brought a faint smile to Dhugal's lips, despite the desperation now unfolding, but Kelson rattled on unchecked.

"Believe me," he said, "I was in no mood to think about a bride for myself! Not that this stopped all and sundry from thrusting marriageable heiresses in my direction, as *always* happens when there's a formal court function. Having gathered for a betrothal, everyone was also eager to see *my* betrothal! Araxie didn't even figure in the equation." He laughed mirthlessly, verging on a sob.

"Do you know what I remember most about that week? Brecon's mother, trying to make his marriage with Richelle contingent on a match between me and Noelie—who, I've just found out, has apparently developed an attachment for Rory, of all people, and he for her."

"*Rory* and Noelie?" Dhugal breathed, sitting up straighter in surprise. "But, that's a brilliant match!"

Kelson stopped pacing, looking slightly dazed. "It is, I know," he whispered. "I suppose I should have thought of it myself. And it's doubly brilliant, if they care for one another. Rothana's promoting *that* match as well. She's—"

He choked back a sob as he buried his face in both hands, finally succumbing to the full hopelessness of his plight.

"Kelson—I am so sorry," Dhugal whispered.

Shaking his head, Kelson stumbled back to the other's side, sinking beside him on the step in a huddled, miserable heap.

"Dhugal, what am I going to do?" he managed to croak out, half-blind with tears, fighting for control. "She won't have me. She's even chosen someone else for me. I hoped, I prayed, that eventually she might change her mind, but I—think I may have to accept that this is the way it is; she *isn't* going to change.

"And tonight—" He paused to swallow noisily. "Tonight she played that final piece, called Duty, that I can't ignore, no matter what my heart may say." He opened his eyes to gaze blurrily at the handfire hovering above their heads. "She reminded me that when I return young Liam to his people, *he'll* be under the same pressure I've been—to marry and produce an heir as quickly as possible. That means that for the sake of Gwynedd, I must do the same."

"But, could you actually do it?" Dhugal whispered. "Could you actually marry Araxie, knowing how you feel about Rothana?"

Kelson lowered his gaze to his hands, and the rings upon them—at the lion signet of Gwynedd, to which he was wed by oaths far more binding than any marriage vows, beside the lesser ring he once had given to Sidana.

"I have married before, out of duty," he murmured. "At least this queen would not be an enemy, with a brother waiting to slay her for daring to marry me."

"Kelson, don't do this to yourself," Dhugal breathed.

"Have I any choice?" the king whispered.

CHAPTER THREE

Hast thou a wife after thy mind?

Ecclesiasticus 7:26

*D*ull heartache and a numb, stolid hopelessness accompanied the king as he and Dhugal made their way back to the royal apartments. While they finished what was left of the wine—far more of it than Dhugal really deemed wise—what words passed between them grew ever more maudlin, marked by longer and more painful silences. When he at last let Dhugal help him stumble off to bed, it was to sink at once into heavy, dreamless sleep.

He woke to a queasy, pounding headache, fully-clothed, with Dhugal dozing in a chair beside him, feet propped up on the edge of the bed. Across the room, a sliver of sunlight was streaming through a crack between the drapes drawn over the balcony doors, dust motes dancing in its beam. Its angle suggested a far later hour than Kelson had intended.

"Dhugal!" he cried, levering himself up on his elbows and at the same time kicking at the other's feet. The abrupt movement woke Dhugal with a start.

"What?"

"Wake up. What time is it?"

"How should I know?"

"Damn you, she'll have gone by now!" Kelson said, rolling from the bed and nearly falling as he staggered toward the drapes. "I might have changed her mind."

Dhugal sighed and got to his feet, coming after Kelson to help pull back the drapes, wincing at the burst of sunlight.

"Kelson, you wouldn't have changed her mind. You just would have muddled yours. She's made up her mind. You know that; I know that. Meanwhile, we only have a day before we leave for Torenth. And you've a last council meeting, and the Torenthi envoys arriving later today—"

"Maybe she hasn't left yet!" Kelson murmured. "Where's a squire? Ivo! Davoran!"

His bellow brought the sound of running feet, followed by an anxious-looking clutch of squires and pages. Davoran's furtive glance at Dhugal made it clear that Dhugal himself had given the orders allowing them to sleep so late, but Kelson ignored them both as he beckoned one of the pages closer, crouching down to the boy's level.

"Niall, I want you to run down to the stables as fast as you can, and find out whether the Lady Rothana and her son have left yet. If they haven't, they're not to leave. If they have, I want to know when. Have you got that?"

The boy nodded, dark eyes wide and somber with the obvious import of his mission, and took off at a run. Immediately Kelson began stripping off the finery of the night before, flinging items left and right, calling for his riding leathers while Davoran directed the other squires and pages in a hurried version of the king's morning toilette. Dhugal settled for a quick wash and a change of shirt, watching the king with a critical eye, wondering whether the previous night had pushed him completely beyond rational behavior.

Kelson was pulling on a boot, Davoran trying to finish with his hair, when Niall came bursting into the room, followed less precipitously by a concerned-looking Rory.

"Sire, the lady has already gone," young Niall blurted. "They left last night."

"Last night?"

"Kelson, she's been gone for hours," Rory said, catching Kelson's arm when he would have dashed past the boy, and then supporting him as he deflated, biting back a sob. "Kelson, what is it?"

With a warning look at Rory, Dhugal shook his head and shooed the squires and pages out of the room. By the time they were gone, Kelson had somewhat recovered himself, standing before the window with his back to both younger men, gazing out sightlessly.

"When, last night, did she leave?" he asked.

"Probably not long after we lit Jatham to the bridal chamber," Rory said. "I don't remember seeing her when we all dispersed. She may not even have gone there." He paused. "Kelson, she'll have had at least an eight- or ten-hour head start. What did she say to you last night?"

Kelson only shook his head, not looking at Rory—though it occurred to him, through the dull finality of the other's words, that he had within his power the means to salvage at least something from the devastation of the night before.

"Actually," he said at last, "your name was mentioned."

"My name?" Obviously surprised, Rory glanced in question at Dhugal, who gave him a noncommittal shrug.

"Yes." Kelson turned to look at his cousin, smiling faintly. "Tell me, what do you think of Lady Noelie Ramsay?"

Rory stiffened minutely, his handsome face reflecting a bewildered mix of caution and wistful longing, but he met Kelson's gaze squarely.

"If you ask me that as king," he said carefully, "I am well aware that both her mother and the council would see you marry her. If that comes to pass, she would be my cousin's wife—and my queen—and I should owe her all duty and honor—"

"Rory, I'm not asking you as king," Kelson broke in, his smile broadening. "I'm asking you as a man, and I want you to answer me as a man. If I assured you that I had no intention of making Noelie Ramsay my queen, would it please you to take her for your wife?"

Rory cast an incredulous look at Dhugal, who was doing his best not to grin, then back at Kelson.

"You're serious, aren't you?" he whispered.

"I am." Coming closer, Kelson set his hands on the other's shoulders, looking him straight in the eyes. "Rory, listen to me. A second Haldane match with Meara would be extremely useful, but it doesn't have to be with me. I feel no attraction to Noelie—but I'm informed that you do. If I can arrange it—and don't remind me of all the obstacles to be overcome—would it be your pleasure to marry her? Answer from your heart."

"I—I would gladly marry her!" Rory said. "Kelson, I never dreamed—"

"*Someone* should be allowed to dream," Kelson said, briefly ducking his forehead against Rory's, then pulling him closer in a quick, fierce hug.

"Go ahead now," he went on, releasing him. "Say nothing to anyone until I return from Torenth. I don't want any word of this getting out until I've had a chance to think it through. Nothing can be allowed to jeopardize that first Mearan marriage."

"I understand, of course," Rory agreed, wide-eyed. "I take it that means I mayn't write to Noelie."

"And possibly have to contend with her mother, on your own, while I'm gone, if she found out?" Kelson replied. "I think not! No reflection on you, cousin, but she's hoping for a king for her daughter's hand—not a prince. I shall be hard-pressed enough to persuade her that love more than compensates for the lesser rank."

Rory shrugged sheepishly. "I don't envy you *that* task. But this may be the most difficult secret I've ever had to keep. I can't thank you enough. If you knew what this means—"

"Oh, I have rather a good idea," Kelson replied, though he managed to smile as he said it. "Go ahead now, and try to look merely hung-over from last night; I know *I* am. We'll join you later."

When Rory had gone, Kelson exhaled a deep sigh and turned to cast a sidelong glance at Dhugal again. Dhugal now was grinning unabashedly.

"You've made Rory a very happy man this morning," he said. "Do you have something definite in mind, to actually make it happen?"

Wincing, Kelson rubbed at his aching forehead, allowing himself an ironic smile. "Not yet. But *I'm* not going to marry Noelie Ramsay, so there's no reason why *he* shouldn't, if he's so inclined."

"Then, are you going to marry Araxie?" Dhugal said quietly.

Kelson glanced at the floor, trying to push that possibility to the back of his mind.

"Dhugal, I honestly don't know. I can't deal with that yet. But maybe I *can* at least set things in motion for Rory, before we leave for Torenth. Nigel needs to be aware of this, in any case. The match will be even more critical, if I shouldn't come back."

"Don't even *think* about not coming back!" Dhugal muttered.

"I *have* to think about it; I'm the king," Kelson said. "And Nigel will be the next king, if I *don't* come back. That is always a possibility, especially when dealing with Torenth.

"In which case," he added, managing a bleak smile as he thrust a sheathed dagger through the back of his belt, "it becomes *Nigel's* problem—so let's go find him. He'll be at Mass with the squires and pages. We'll catch him there. If I don't attend, he usually briefs me right after, before we proceed with the business of the day."

"Are you sure this is a good time?"

"No, but there may not be a better one, before we leave. Once the Torenthi envoys arrive, I'll need to focus all my energies on Liam and the hand-over."

They slipped into the back of the chapel royal during the Offertory. Young Payne was serving the Mass, looking somewhat bleary-eyed and underslept in his lace-trimmed cotta and his cassock of Haldane crimson. Father Nivard was presenting the elements soon to be consecrated: a slender, rapt figure in green vestments lifting the chalice filled with water and wine which, by a mystery more potent than any magic of the Deryni, would soon be transformed into the holy Blood.

"*Offerimus tibi, Domine, calicem salutaris . . . ,*" Nivard was saying. We offer Thee, Lord, the chalice of salvation. . . .

Signing himself with holy water, Kelson eased into an inconspicuous corner niche at the back, Dhugal at his side. In contrast to the previous night, the little chapel was filled nearly to capacity, for many of Gwynedd's nobles not customarily resident at court had been arriving during the past week or two, some to accompany Kelson on his mission to Torenth and some to remain at the capital during his absence. A knot of Kheldouri knights in the service of Ewan Duke of Claibourne were standing just ahead of him and Dhugal.

Even Queen Jehana had returned to court a few days before, to take up duties as part of the regency council, which would govern Gwynedd in her son's absence—and also to lend her weight to the increasing pressure on him to marry. Kelson could see her kneeling at her own prie-dieu, very near the altar: a wraith-like shadow in the white coif and nun-like white robes she had affected since her widowhood. Standing nearby were her chaplain, a handsome young priest called Father Ambros, and Sister Cecile, a somewhat older woman who had been her companion of several years.

Putting her mission from his mind, Kelson let his gaze continue roving over the congregation, looking for Nigel—and spotted him at last, farther to the right than was his usual wont, standing amid a number of his squires and pages. Some of the squires were as tall as he, and almost shielded him from view.

The golden chiming of the Sanctus bell recalled Kelson to the Mass, and he sank to his knees as Father Nivard intoned the venerable hymn of praise:

"*Sanctus, Sanctus, Sanctus Dominus Deus Sabaoth. Pleni sunt caeli et terra gloria tua. . . .*"

But Kelson's mind was only partially on the Mass. Using the drone of the familiar prayers to help him focus, he buried his face in one hand and turned his thoughts to what he must say to Nigel—to the practicalities that must be considered regarding a match between Rory and Noelie—for love alone, or even fondness, was not sufficient motive when disposing of the marriage of princes.

Most fortuitously, this particular marriage did not require a choice between affection and political expediency. Allowing the match would only strengthen the alliance to be cemented by the marriage already agreed between Brecon and Richelle. Rory could even live in Meara with his bride, as Rothana had pointed out.

By the time Kelson went forward to receive Communion, he had begun to sort out some of the issues he would need to address—though not yet in sufficient detail to discuss most of them with Nigel, when they were short on time. But when the Mass ended shortly thereafter, he felt he had begun to regain a measure of control over his life, despite Rothana's pronouncement of the night before. Refreshed, at least in spirit, he slipped outside with Dhugal immediately following Nivard's final blessing, and was there to waylay his uncle as the rest of the congregation came out of the chapel and began to disperse.

"Have we much business for the council meeting," he asked, as he and Dhugal fell in with Nigel, "or is it just documents to be signed and sealed?"

"Mainly that," Nigel replied. "If you like, I can brief you while we break our fast. It's a fine morning for a wander in the garden."

Very shortly, the three of them were strolling in the scent-laden garden beneath the great-hall windows, each with a tankard of nutty brown ale and a chunk of fine manchet bread smeared with butter and honey. They ate as they walked and talked, reviewing the business to be covered in the meeting to follow. Nigel was focused on business and breakfast, and did not seem to notice that Dhugal had dropped back to a discreet distance to give them privacy, and also to fend off would-be interruptions.

"There is one further matter that I'd like you to consider while I'm away," Kelson said, as they paused by a fountain to rinse off their hands. "I don't intend to bring this before the council until I return, but it's something you should be thinking about—especially if I shouldn't come back."

Nigel shook water from his hands, then wiped them back across his temples. Like most of the older men at court, he wore his black hair shorn to collar-length.

"Not a premonition, I hope?" he said lightly.

Kelson allowed himself a droll half-smile. "Not at all. But it *is* serious—and it bears considering, no matter what happens in Torenth. Are you aware that Rory fancies Noelie Ramsay?"

Nigel went suddenly very still, his expression of surprise swiftly shifting through consternation to indignation.

"If he's laid a hand on her, I swear—"

"Nigel, Nigel, he hasn't touched her, and he wouldn't," Kelson assured him. "He knows she's been discussed for me, and he's as bound by duty as the rest of us."

"Then, what in God's name—who told you that?"

"Rothana told me last night," Kelson replied, glancing away momentarily, "and I asked Rory about it this morning. Believe me, I'm not at all upset. I have no romantic interest in the girl."

"Well, you *should*!" Nigel retorted. "That's one of the best possible matches you could make, politically speaking."

"But there's absolutely no affinity to go with it, other than her mother's affinity for my crown." Kelson turned to sit down on the edge of the fountain. "Politically speaking, a match between Noelie and Rory would be just as good; it would still strengthen the Haldane match with Brecon. And, as Rothana pointed out, Rory could even live in Meara, provide a permanent Haldane presence; as king, I couldn't do that."

"That would present—its own difficulties," Nigel said stiffly, after a moment.

Kelson drew a slow, measured breath, quite aware that at least one of the difficulties to which Nigel was referring was one he had brought upon himself. And it traced back to Albin Haldane, and the treason of his father, who had been Nigel's eldest son, and should have been his heir.

So bitter had been the pain of that son's betrayal—whose name was rarely mentioned in his presence—that Nigel had set aside Conall's son in favor of Rory, who was his second son, and was grooming Rory to succeed him as Duke of Carthmoor. Nigel would not care to have his heir resident in Meara, half a kingdom away.

"I'm aware of some of the difficulties," Kelson said, "and we haven't time even to think of all of them, much less address them, before I leave tomorrow. And if, God forbid, I shouldn't return from Torenth, the match makes even better sense. But meanwhile, I should think that a great many of the issues important to the Mearans will already have been addressed in the context of last summer's negotiations.

"That should give you a starting point," he went on, rising. "In fact, it's just occurred to me that, since we *could* have a Haldane prince resident in Meara, we might want to consider giving the province viceregal status, down the line—which might placate the separatists. They'd see it as the next best thing to regaining independence as a sovereign principality." They began walking slowly back toward the great hall. "Of course, he's young yet. We'd want to give him several experienced men to advise him, in the beginning—let him ease into it."

Nigel slowly nodded, for the strategy Kelson had just outlined for Meara was sound, but he did not look particularly pleased.

"I shall abide by your wishes, of course—but you do realize, I hope, that by giving Noelie Ramsay to Rory, you're eliminating one of the best matches for yourself."

"But it's an even better match for Gwynedd, Uncle," Kelson replied with a grimace. "Isn't that what this is all about, since I can't marry the woman I love?"

"Kelson, you know I *am* sorry."

"I do—and if it were your fault, I might resent you for it; but it isn't." He heaved a heavy sigh and signalled Dhugal to join them. "But we'll speak more of royal brides when I return from Torenth. I've already been warned to expect another review of likely candidates when we stop at Coroth, on the way. Morgan tells me that Richenda has spent the entire winter collecting portraits, and Arilan apparently has a few new ones as well. I shall do my best to be attentive—for the sake of Gwynedd."

CHAPTER FOUR

I have peace offerings with me; this day have I payed
my vows.

Proverbs 7:14

That same morning, while the king and his uncle proceeded with the business of Gwynedd's royal council, Alaric Morgan, Duke of Corwyn, cast a sidelong glance from under his steel-lined cap at the two Torenthi emissaries riding beside him on the road from Desse to Rhemuth. Behind them, a mixed escort of royal Haldane lancers and desert-robed Moorish cavalry trotted two by two in apparent amity, horses fresh and restive, silent but for the jingle of bits and harness and the soft thud of steel-shod hooves on the unpaved road. From off the wide river rolling placidly to their left, wispy fog dissipated only gradually under a strengthening sun, promising a close, humid day.

Already, it was growing warm for Morgan's tastes, especially in riding leathers and light mail. Not a breath of air stirred beyond the faint breeze caused by their passage, and Morgan brushed at an irksome lock of pale, damp hair as he reined back a little to keep from crowding Saer de Traherne's bay, just ahead. Beside Saer, who was commanding the guard detail, a state herald on a grey palfrey had charge of a swallow-tailed pennon of Haldane crimson, the silk so limp that the crowned golden *K* cypher of Kelson's diplomatic service was all but invisible within its drooping folds.

Better suited to the still air was the triangular pennon carried by one of the Moors, riding directly behind Morgan's charges, with a stiffener fixed along its top edge, so that the black-and-white leaping-hart badge of Torenth was clearly readable against the field of *tenné*. The tawny orange was repeated in the feathered aigrettes affixed to the fronts of the Moors' white turbans, and in the tassels adorning the headstalls and reins of the Moorish steeds.

Thus far, their journey had been uneventful. The two envoys were Deryni, of course, as was Morgan, and thus capable of significant treachery if they chose to violate the truce mandated by the formal hostage status of their king. But though Gywnedd's dealings with the Deryni of Torenth had long been fraught with misdirection, deception, and outright treachery, Morgan thought it unlikely that this pair would attempt any overt offensive while on Gwynedd's soil. Not with Liam's return to Torenth imminent.

Of far more concern was the possibility that unknown agents might choose the occasion of Liam's installation to take their revenge on the king who had kept him in custody for four long years—for Kelson would be assisting at the ceremony and, of necessity, vulnerable, especially working within the unfamiliar context of another culture's magical symbolism, with himself and his supporters greatly outnumbered. The testing of Torenthi honor was always uncertain.

And the danger to Liam himself could be as great as any danger to his erstwhile protectors, if the rumors about the boy's uncles were true. And even if they were not—though Morgan suspected that they were—at the very least, the ceremonies were expected to be excruciatingly elaborate, alien, and long.

He glanced over his shoulder to smile at his stepson Brendan, who was serving as his page. Brendan gave him a grin. Morgan had debated whether to include the boy on this present errand, if only because of the physical pace—three trips back and forth between Rhemuth and Desse, in the pace of as many days—but Brendan had begged to come along.

At least any actual danger was likely to be minimal, despite their present company, for Brendan was part Deryni—only just eleven, but with well-developed shields and, thanks to his mother's tutelage, already competent well beyond his years to resist tampering by others of his blood, who might try to take advantage of his youth and his access to high-ranking individuals.

He was also keen to go to Beldour, though Morgan had thus far avoided giving him an answer. In support of his plea, Brendan had pointed out—quite reasonably, and without a trace of arrogance—that the Deryni skills he was learning from his mother might be helpful on the trip; for he was starting to develop a knack for Truth-Reading, and his youth and his status as a mere page would tend not to put people on their guard. But Morgan was not sure he was prepared to expose the boy to the dangers that accompanied such possibilities—or that Richenda would let him.

Morgan's horse misstepped, and he steadied it with hands and legs, returning his attention to the two bearded men riding beside him. The Torenthi delegation had arrived at Desse the previous afternoon, aboard a sleek Torenthi war galley under escort by Morgan's own flagship, *Rhafallia*. Morgan had been expecting the senior of the two men. Very early on in Liam's wardship at the court of Gwynedd, al-Rasoul ibn Tariq had been designated by Liam's regents as their official liaison between the two kingdoms, and he and Morgan had established a comfortable if guarded working relationship in the four years since.

But as Morgan noted the circling arm of Saer de Traherne, signalling to extend their pace to a canter, he reflected that he still knew little more about the cultured and exotic Rasoul than he had after that first dramatic introduction, when the Moorish lord had ridden his desert steed right into the great hall at Rhemuth, with a live cheetah sitting behind him on his horse's crouper. Focused and articulate, with all the glib facility of an accomplished courtier, the dark-skinned Deryni amused, informed, and sometimes vaguely threatened, according to his orders, but revealed little about himself and nothing of his master's mind save what he chose to disclose.

Apart from an apparently genuine affection for his young king, only one abiding personal interest had he divulged: a keen appreciation for fine architecture that bordered on the passionate. Himself responsible for the design and execution of several castles and fortified towns at home in Torenth, the keen-eyed Rasoul never failed to spend a portion of his visits to Rhemuth in exploring the architectural wonders of the city—and by speaking freely and at length on this one topic, he managed to avoid discussing anything else in depth. Between him and Morgan had grown mutual respect and even understanding of their respective positions, but there could not be true trust, given the masters they each served. Should political circumstances require it, Morgan had no doubt that Rasoul could be a formidable adversary, indeed.

Of more immediate concern, because he was still largely unknown, was the bearded younger man riding on Rasoul's other side: Count Mátyás, the youngest brother of the regent Mahael and, therefore, an uncle to the young king—and undoubtedly a Deryni of substantial ability. After Liam himself, only a second nephew and two brothers stood between Mátyás and the Torenthi throne—and kindred blood had never counted for a great deal in the wranglings of the House of Furstán. Though Mátyás was said to be without political ambition, his energies focused on a young family at home and on tending his vineyards, Morgan had his doubts that any Furstán could make such a claim. Acquisition and intrigue were in the Furstán blood, and came as naturally as breathing.

Mátyás himself seemed to convey nothing beyond mere self-assurance in his rank and station—though his black hair was braided and neatly clubbed at the nape in a warrior's knot, in echo of the very utilitarian mud-knots binding the tails of the Torenthi steeds, and Morgan had no doubt that he wore mail beneath his outer garments—as, indeed, did every man in the cavalcade. He rode like a warrior, too, relaxed but alert astride a close-coupled black barb, clearly taking in every detail around him; and Morgan reckoned that the aristocratic Mátyás probably could use the long, curved cavalry blade strapped beneath his left thigh—as he undoubtedly could use the powers brooding behind impenetrable shields.

Yet, for all the expected appurtenances of a powerful man come on an important diplomatic mission, Mátyás somehow was not what Morgan would have expected of a scion of the House of Furstán—gentler, perhaps, and apparently a man of faith. When he first stepped from the gangplank at Desse, inclining his dark head as Rasoul performed the introductions, Morgan had caught the blue glint of sunlight on a fine miniature icon of the Blessed Virgin on his breast, its rich enamels glowing like some rare jewel. And while the count now had tucked it inside his tunic, against loss or damage on the ride to Rhemuth, something in his manner suggested that its wearing and even its possession went beyond mere adornment or social convention. Morgan occasionally had seen Eastern patriarchs wearing two or three such icons, on visits to the Hort of Orsal's court, their oval frames adorned with rubies and rose diamonds and sometimes a pendant pearl.

The rest of Mátyás's attire likewise called to mind the opulence of far Byzantyum rather than the southron silks and flowing robes favored by Rasoul and the rest of their Torenthi escort. His wide-sleeved brocade coat of sapphire-blue was edged with fur and slit to the waist at sides and back, revealing glimpses at throat and wrist of a close-fitting, high-collared tunic of darker blue, lavished with gold bullion. And on his head, no graceful *keffiyeh* such as Rasoul wore, with its gold-wrapped cords suggestive of a coronet, nor the snowy turbans mostly covering the pointed helmets of their escort, but a tallish, flat-topped cap of close-clipped sable fur, aglitter at the front with a jewelled aigrette.

Ahead, Saer raised an arm in signal of another change of pace, and the riders dutifully closed down to a brisk walk, the horses snorting and blowing. Now less than an hour out of Rhemuth, they had passed through a forested area of sparse population to emerge on a stretch of road atop a slight embankment that skirted the river. A freshening breeze off the river hinted at a possible shower to break the sultry warmth. Morgan glanced aside, instantly alert, as Mátyás murmured something to Rasoul and then smoothly reined back and aside to change places with the other, so that he and not Rasoul now rode at Morgan's left knee.

"Methinks your King of Gwynedd rules a fair and pleasant land," Mátyás said without preamble, as his pale gaze ranged out across the river to the fertile fields beyond. "Tell me, why do they not plant vines along those slopes?"

He gestured toward the distant hills, and Morgan recalled the younger man's reported interest in viniculture. Morgan's own expertise on the subject extended mainly to the quality of wines he was served at table, for little of Corwyn was well suited to the growing of grapes, but the topic might well serve to draw out further insights regarding this Torenthi prince.

"I can't say that I know," he said. "I should imagine that something about the climate is not right—perhaps the sun's angle on those hillsides. Lord Rasoul has given me to understand that you are something of an expert in these matters."

Mátyás shrugged, a faint smile curving at his lips as he glanced at Rasoul, who nodded.

"Al-Rasoul is generous, as always," Mátyás replied. "My vineyards were long neglected, and I still have much to learn. The estate was a legacy from my late half-brother, the Duke Lionel. I believe you and he met, on at least one occasion."

Morgan stiffened slightly, for Mátyás must know full well that Morgan had been present when Lionel met his death—though it had been Kelson who killed him, as he also had killed Wencit and Bran Coris, the father of Brendan. Morgan tended to regard the slayings as mercy killings—or, at worst, executions—but Mátyás might not see it that way, especially if he knew that Morgan had shown Kelson the magical means for accomplishing the killings.

"The circumstances were regrettable, my lord," Morgan said carefully. "All of us who are bound to the service of our kings do our best to serve them with honor."

"So it would seem," Mátyás agreed. "And the Duke of Corwyn is widely held to be a man of honor, even in my country." When Morgan did not reply, he sighed and turned his gaze straight ahead, his head bobbing gracefully with the movement of his horse.

"You must understand, my lord, that I hardly knew Lionel," he said after a moment. "He was the son of my father's first wife, and went to court when I was still a weanling. That day with Wencit, he had the ill fortune to be on the losing side—and who can say that Torenth would be the better, if my king and not yours had prevailed?"

"Surely an unusual perspective for a prince of Torenth," Morgan observed.

Mátyás shrugged. "The past is as it was, and as was meant to be. He was my brother, but I can accord no personal blame to you or even to your king. It was Wencit who set out the terms of the fray, and his supposed man who set it all at naught."

"True enough," Morgan allowed.

"But, enough of this," Mátyás went on brightly. "I recall it to your memory only to reassure you that I bear you no ill will. The day was in God's hands—*insh'allah*, as my esteemed companion al-Rasoul would maintain: as God wills it. And it *did* gain me Komnéné." He sighed as he glanced out across the river again.

"How I do love that place," he confided. "Its river much resembles this one."

My wife and son are there. I love watching the vines grow, and the grapes ripen on the vines." He grinned almost boyishly as he glanced back at Morgan. "My wife ripens as well. She carries our second child."

"Then, congratulations are in order," Morgan said, himself smiling slightly at the other's obvious delight in fatherhood. "May I ask how old your boy is?"

"He will be three in a few months' time."

"Indeed?" Morgan replied, with a grin of his own. "Mine was three in May."

Mátyás cast him a thoughtful glance. "Then, perhaps one day they shall be friends."

"Perhaps," Morgan said neutrally. "I should hope they will never be enemies."

Mátyás eyed him speculatively, then gave a cautious nod.

"*Insh'allah*," he murmured almost to himself. "And what of Liam-Lajos? Shall he be friends with your Kelson and still remain the friend of his own people?"

"You shall see for yourself very soon," Morgan replied with a smile. "I think you will not be disappointed. Look ahead, just through the haze. You can see the towers of Rhemuth."

*T*hey clip-clopped into the yard of Rhemuth Castle early in the afternoon, after passing along the main thoroughfare of the city below. A courier had been sent ahead from the city gate as soon as their identity was ascertained, so servants were waiting to take the horses and see to the needs of the men.

"He's in the middle of court," Rory said to Morgan, bounding down the great-hall steps just ahead of Lord Pemberly, the deputy-chamberlain, as a pair of pages scurried forward to offer refreshment to the new arrivals—wine for Morgan, Mátyás, and Saer, and cool water for Rasoul, who never took alcohol.

Morgan drank deeply of his wine—a fruity Vezairi red of excellent ancestry, he was happy to note, with a glance at Mátyás—then wiped his mouth with the back of a hand as Pemberly elbowed his way past Brendan and the servants dealing with the horses.

"Welcome, my lords. Your Grace, would our guests prefer to go directly in to court, or to refresh themselves first, in the quarters we have prepared for them?"

"I see no need to delay," Rasoul spoke up, beckoning Rory closer. "Mátyás, I present to you Duke Nigel's eldest son, Sir Rory Haldane. Sir Rory, I would have you know Count Mátyás Furstán-Komnéně, one of the uncles of Liam-Lajos."

Rory gave the newcomer a smile and an easy neck bow.

"Count Mátyás, you honor our court. Your nephew has been an eager pupil—an excellent squire. And if I may say so, an engaging addition to the royal household. We shall miss him. *I* shall miss him."

"I see he has won at least one Haldane friend," Mátyás said with a faint smile. "Is he serving as squire today?"

"He is, my lord. King Kelson is investing a new baron. Would you care to observe? My younger brother is squiring with your nephew."

At Mátyás's look of inquiry, Morgan gestured toward the great-hall door in invitation.

"I shouldn't think they'll be long, my lord. We can watch from the back of the hall. I gather from Lord Rasoul that you wish no particular ceremony for yourselves."

White teeth flashed in Mátyás's close-trimmed beard, and amusement stirred behind the pale eyes. "Forgive me, my lord, but I doubt whether you can imagine the ceremonies we shall all have to endure, once we return to Beldour. No, we seek no ceremony here in Rhemuth, save what courtesy requires. But I *have* been instructed to make a presentation to my nephew. If you will permit . . . ?"

"Of course."

As Mátyás withdrew to speak briefly to one of the Moors waiting in the background, Rasoul followed where Rory was already leading, up the shallow stairs to the level of the hall. As the two disappeared inside, Morgan following with Mátyás, the Moors began to form up in a guard of honor, two of them unlashing a bulky bundle from behind one of the saddles.

The great hall was flooded with golden light from the range of long windows along the western side, beyond which lay the castle's formal gardens. On the dais far at the end of the hall, before an attentive assemblage of perhaps threescore men and women, Kelson sat at ease in the midst of a handful of his great lords of state, a jewelled circlet on his raven head and a naked sword across the knees of red riding leathers, listening as a herald read from an unfurled document. Duncan and Dhugal flanked him, the former clad in the purple of his episcopal rank, the latter tartan-clad and ducally crowned.

At the foot of the dais steps knelt the dark-haired figure of Jatham Kilshane, wearing a heraldic surcoat of scarlet, ermine, and gold. As Morgan glanced aside at Mátyás, he wondered what impression the Torenthi lord was taking from his first glimpse of the court of Gwynedd's sovereign.

The herald lowered his scroll, and Kelson swept a hand toward Jatham as he glanced at Dhugal, who moved briskly down a step to take the new baron's oath, his red hair and coronet sparkling in a beam of sunlight that fell upon the pair of them as Jatham offered his joined hands. Beyond the sweep of green, black, and white tartan brooched to Dhugal's right shoulder, two squires laden with regalia stood waiting in a glare of sunlight—Payne and Liam, looking remarkably alike in their crimson Haldane livery, Payne's clubbed hair glinting blue-black, Liam's lit with tawny highlights in the harsh sunlight. Behind them, Nigel leaned on the staff of a furled banner, with Janniver and Meraude watching from the slight recess of a long window behind him.

"There's your nephew, holding the cushion with the coronets," Morgan murmured to Count Mátyás. "From this far back, it's sometimes difficult to distinguish, when they're in livery. The other squire is Payne Haldane."

"Ah. And the young man in tartan?"

"Dhugal Duke of Cassan, the new baron's feudal superior," Morgan replied. "He is also the king's foster brother."

"I see."

". . . do become your vassal of life and limb, and enter your fealty, and do homage for the Barony of Kilshane and all its lands and folk . . ." Jatham was saying, his hands now set between Dhugal's.

As the oath continued, Mátyás turned in response to some whispered comment from Rasoul, making comment of his own. Morgan did not attempt to listen, satisfied to let his attention range restlessly across the hall, marking Kelson's immediate focus as Rory slipped to his side to whisper in his ear—and a subtly heightened vigilance on the part of Duncan, standing at the king's other side, as his blue eyes flicked out across the assemblage.

". . . pledge unto you and all your people the protection of Cassan and of our lord King Kelson of Gwynedd, of whom I hold," Dhugal was saying, "to defend you from every creature with all my power, giving loyalty for loyalty and justice for honor . . ."

Himself sweeping the assemblage, Morgan at once found the reason for Duncan's vigilance—a tall, black-robed figure melting back from the throng to glide purposefully toward the rear doors: the hieromonk Irenaeus, sent the previous winter to instruct Liam in Torenthi protocol and the specifics of ceremonial he would need for his enthronement. Arilan, in particular, had been none too happy about his arrival, for the hieromonk's secondary brief had been to examine Liam's orthodoxy—certainly diluted and possibly tainted by four years of exposure to Western religious observance; and the ongoing presence at court of a Deryni of Irenaeus's probable ability was always a danger.

Fortunately, Father Irenaeus had proven affable, intelligent, and not overly dogmatic, and appeared unalarmed by any deficiencies in his hostage king's spiritual state. Nor—so far as anyone could tell—had he ever crossed beyond the bounds appropriate to his calling; Father Nivard, who had spent much time with him, had declared him a very spiritual man.

The hieromonk nodded to Morgan as he approached—a dark-eyed, somewhat florid individual with grey speckling his long black hair and beard, the black veil of his flat-topped headdress billowing behind him. When he had quietly greeted Rasoul and Mátyás, the latter bending to kiss his hand in respect for his office, the three of them slipped back outside, presumably to organize the Torenthi presentation. Morgan gazed after them for a moment, then sent Brendan as well, ostensibly to offer any required assistance but also to observe.

Meanwhile, the ceremony of investiture was winding to a close, the new baron being dubbed by the king and invested with the symbols of his estate. As soon as Jatham and his new baroness had retired to the side of the dais, accompanied by the good-natured murmurs of the court's approval, Morgan strode boldly forward.

Kelson had noted his arrival well before Rory came to notify him, and gazed down the hall expectantly as Morgan approached, an aisle parting before him and a hush radiating outward from his path, for most of those present were aware of his recent mission. With a dip of his head for the sake of convention, Morgan continued up the dais steps in a few easy bounds, there dropping to a crouch at Kelson's right hand. Duncan and Dhugal had moved to the king's left, the latter now holding Kelson's sword, and both eased closer at Morgan's summoning glance.

"The man with Rasoul is Count Mátyás Furstán-Komnénë, a brother of Mahael," Morgan murmured, in response to Kelson's unasked question. *He is also,* he added silently, *the half-brother of Lionel, whom you killed with Wencit and Brendan's father. In fairness, he seems to bear you no ill will—though he made a point of letting me know that he knew.* "They've asked for no great formality," he went on verbally. "It might be politic to have young Liam receive them."

Inclining his head in immediate understanding, and hoping Mátyás would not become a problem, Kelson glanced beyond Morgan to where Liam waited beside Nigel, crooking a finger for the boy to join them. Liam came at once, dropping to one knee close beside Morgan, his back to the great-hall doors.

"Sire?"

Kelson smiled faintly as he leaned closer. "Liam-Lajos, King of Torenth, is it your pleasure to receive emissaries from your kingdom?"

The tone of the question had been deliberately casual, and audible only to those immediately around them, but Liam stiffened slightly, restraining an impulse to look back over his shoulder.

"Sire, must I?" he murmured. "I am still your squire for a few more days."

"And you are also their king," Kelson said quietly. "Do you not wish to accord them the courtesy of your recognition? They have come a very great distance to escort you home."

"Who are they?" Liam asked.

Kelson glanced at Morgan, who inclined his head to Liam.

"Your old friend Rasoul—alas, without his cheetah—and a Count Mátyás."

"Uncle Mátyás is *here?*" Liam breathed, his eyes widening.

"Aye. He seems pleasant enough," Morgan replied. "Is there something we should know about him?"

"No, sir, it's just that— Sire, this is most unexpected," he blurted, his gaze darting back to Kelson. "Here, before your court—I had not thought—"

"If you prefer me to receive them, I will do it," Kelson said. "We all know there will be a period of adjustment. But this might be an easy beginning."

Liam looked less than comfortable with the prospect, but he nodded dutifully as he swallowed and lifted his chin.

"I will be pleased to receive my envoys," he said formally. "Father Irenaeus has instructed me in the proper protocols."

"I doubt you'll need to worry about protocol," Kelson replied, smiling. "Apparently they wish no great formality. Now, stand here at my right hand."

Liam visibly braced himself, drawing a deep breath, but he managed to cover most of his nervousness as he obeyed. Morgan also rose, both of them turning to face down the great hall.

"Admit the emissaries from Torenth," Kelson said to the herald, rising to take the sheathed Haldane sword from Dhugal and cradling it in the crook of his left arm.

The order was passed. Almost immediately, the double doors at the end of the great hall swung back and white-robed Moors began filing in, two by two; but there were only five pairs of them, and with no accompanying flourish of kettle-drums or trumpets or any of the other embellishments of Oriental pageantry that sometimes had accompanied Torenthi embassies in years gone by.

Behind the white robes, and sweeping between them as the two files parted, came al-Rasoul ibn Tariq, his desert silks of amber and gold by now well familiar at court, followed closely by Father Irenaeus and a bearded, younger man who could only be Count Mátyás. The latter bore draped across one arm a gold-glittering swath of rich purple damask, and favored Kelson with a formal inclination of his head as Father Irenaeus bowed over folded hands and Rasoul made a more flamboyant salute, sweeping a graceful brown hand to breast, lips, and forehead.

"May Allah, the Compassionate, the Merciful, grant peace and health to all within this house," Rasoul said. "As ever, I bring greeting unto Kelson of Gwynedd from the regents of Torenth—the Lady Morag Furstána and my lord Mahael Furstán d'Arjenol. In addition, I bring especial greeting unto my sovereign liege lord and *padishah*, Liam-Lajos, whom I congratulate upon the attaining of his majority, and whose return is eagerly awaited by his loyal subjects." He bowed again to Liam.

"By my lord Kelson's gracious leave, I would also present the compliments of Count Mátyás Furstán-Komnéné, brother to my lord Mahael, who comes bearing gifts for their royal nephew."

Kelson nodded as Mátyás also bowed again, more deeply than before.

"We thank you, Lord Rasoul. As always, you are welcome at our court. Count Mátyás, as well: My compliments to your House. Liam-Lajos, you have our leave to receive your uncle's presentation."

Liam drew a deep breath and stepped forward, inclining his head as Rasoul, Mátyás, and Irenaeus all bowed deeply from the waist.

"My lord Rasoul, it is always good to see you," the boy said a little stiffly. "And Uncle Mátyás: I have not seen you in a very long time."

"The want has not been of my choosing," Mátyás replied, smiling faintly. "We have both of us been otherwise occupied, these past four years. But I begged Mahael to let me come to bring you home. I have missed you, Laje."

The boy's eyes had lost a little of their slightly haunted look as Mátyás spoke, and he even managed a weak smile at the old pet name.

"Thank you, Mátyás," he murmured.

"You would thank me more, I think, if I could spare you all the pomp and ceremonial that lies ahead. But Father Irenaeus tells us that you are well prepared. To that end, your lady mother sends this robe of state, that you may be fitly attired to enter your kingdom."

He shook out the folds of purple damask and fanned the garment on the steps before him—a long coat cut very like the one he wore, though edged with miniver and lavished with even more gold bouillon and jeweled buttons than his own.

"I did point out that such a garment would hardly be appropriate with squire's livery, or suitable for a sea voyage," Mátyás said, with an arch shrug at Liam's look of dismay. "But she did insist." He passed the collar of the coat to Rasoul, who gathered it back across an arm. "Meanwhile, this second token sent by your uncles Mahael and Teymuraz will perhaps prove more to your liking, and suitable for a wider variety of attire. They bade me help them select it from the treasury at Beldour."

From where it had been hidden, looped over the arm that had borne the robe, Mátyás produced a handsome circlet of beaten gold, nearly the width of a man's three fingers, set round with smoky balas rubies, baroque pearls, and chunky, rough-polished emeralds the size of a man's thumbnail.

"It is not the crown of Furstán—yet," Mátyás said, extending it in both hands, "but perhaps it will serve until you are girded at Holy Iób."

He had set one foot on the bottom step of the dais as he spoke, perhaps intending to come closer; but before he could ascend or Liam could come down to take it, Morgan briskly intervened, taking the jewelled circlet from Mátyás's hands and testing with his powers in the few seconds it took to pass the object up to Kelson.

It's clean, came Morgan's assessment, *but the giving of it is meant to be symbolic. Only you should convey any coronet to Liam, as your vassal.*

But Kelson had marked the symbolic intent even before Morgan pointed it out, and could hardly fault Mátyás for attempting to assert the independence of his prince, regardless of any resentment he might or might not harbor toward Kelson himself. He smiled faintly as his own quick probe confirmed nothing more sinister than a Christian blessing. Nor had he expected that there would be, for even Mahael would not be so bold as to attempt an attack on Liam or himself in full view of the court of Gwynedd, risking open and immediate war.

The count looked almost amused as Kelson passed the circlet on to Liam, perhaps having expected that his gesture would be thwarted. The boy smiled bleakly as he took the diadem with a whispered thanks, giving it a perfunctory glance, but he did not put it on.

"I thank you, Uncle. I shall wear this at a more appropriate time. I am—still in service as a squire today."

"Surely, your service has now ended, my prince," Rasoul said reasonably. "You are about to return to your own people."

Liam dropped his gaze, looking decidedly uncomfortable, and Kelson suddenly wondered whether the boy's reaction came of simple nervousness or something more.

"Perhaps we should continue this discussion in private," he said quietly, gently setting a hand on the boy's shoulder. "Clearly, this is a time of great change for Liam-Lajos. Gentlemen, perhaps you would be so good as to join us in the withdrawing room."

CHAPTER FIVE

That they may set him with princes, even with the
princes of his people.

Psalm 113:8

$\mathcal{K}$elson kept his manner casual and easy as he ushered Liam toward the side door, gathering Nigel and Dhugal with a glance as Payne scurried ahead to draw back the heavy drape curtaining the arched doorway. He hoped he was being overprotective, but he dared not assume that Liam's uneasiness was born of mere nerves. At least to Kelson, Count Mátyás was very much an unknown quantity—and he was Mahael's brother.

Glancing behind them, to a rising murmur of speculation as they left the dais, he saw Rasoul tossing the damask coat to Father Irenaeus, exchanging a glance with Mátyás as both of them followed; but since Irenaeus was not being included, Kelson signed for Duncan to remain as well, though Morgan was already bringing up the rear. He could feel Liam's growing tension under his hand as they came before the panelled room behind the dais, where he often held impromptu council meetings.

"Gentlemen, we'll join you in a moment," he said to Rasoul and Mátyás, handing his sword and coronet to Dhugal and gesturing for the pair to enter. "Alaric, perhaps you and Dhugal would be so good as to acquaint our guests with the proposed plans for this evening. Uncle Nigel, please attend us. . . ."

Rasoul and Mátyás had little choice but to comply, though they looked less than happy as Morgan ushered them into the room and Dhugal followed. As soon as the door began to close, Kelson drew Nigel and Liam into an alcove near the stair, standing shoulder to shoulder with his uncle to shield Liam from curious eyes, for there were servants and guards passing occasionally.

"*Now* would you like to tell me about Mátyás?" Kelson said, though he kept his voice very low. "Or is it something about the gifts? What is it, Liam? I have to know, or I can't protect you."

Liam ducked his head, nervously fingering the jewelled circlet still in his hands. The muscles worked in his throat, but no words came out.

"It isn't Uncle Mátyás, Sire," he finally managed to whisper, shaking his head. "He was my first tutor in the *ars magica*. I know he would never do me harm. And it isn't the gifts he brought; it's—what they mean, I suppose."

"Ah, that you must be a king now," Kelson guessed. "I hoped it was only that. But you *are* well prepared—or as prepared as we can make you. You've certainly had more preparation than I did."

"I know that."

As Liam briefly glanced up, sudden tears sparkled in his dark eyes—much to his mortification—and he angrily dashed at them with the back of a hand, looking away again. Smiling faintly, Nigel produced a square of fine linen and handed it to him, ever the attentive squire-master and surrogate father.

"Liam, you've been here four years," he said quietly, as the boy dabbed fiercely at the tears. "You've formed attachments. That's only natural—and proper. But you know it was never intended that you should remain here indefinitely. Your fosterage was meant to keep you safe while you grew into manhood and learned the skills needed by a king. You've now done both—at least as much as one can, at fourteen."

"And under the laws of your land and mine, that makes me a man!" Liam muttered, a mutinous tone to his voice, though he kept it low. "That means I can now make my own decisions about my future. It means that if I choose, I don't have to go back!"

"That's true, you don't," Kelson replied, with a glance warning the alarmed Nigel not to interfere. "Under law, you have reached your majority—which means that you could, indeed, refuse to go back; and under law, we'd be powerless to make you go.

"But also under law, if you weren't to go back, your uncle Mahael could and probably would declare the throne vacant, and install Ronal in your place. Your brother is only ten years old, Liam; hardly older than you were when Alroy died—and Mahael is next in line. With you out of the way, how long do you think he would let *this* brother live? And then, he'd be king."

Choking back a sob of denial, Liam ducked his head again, eyes squeezed shut as he drew a slow, steadying breath, even his surface-most thoughts suddenly hard-shielded. During his four years in Rhemuth, with cautious training from a handful of Deryni Kelson knew he could trust—for the boy must be able to protect himself when eventually he returned home—Liam had gradually allowed an occasional guarded rapport to develop between himself and Kelson, especially as he entered adolescence and his access to his powers deepened. Right now, though, his shields were impenetrable.

But Kelson could guess what was racing through Liam's mind. Soon after Alroy's death, the rumor had begun to circulate—along with another, current only among the more paranoid in Torenth, who held Kelson responsible—that Mahael had arranged the fatal riding accident that cost Alroy his life. Whether or not it was true, Kelson knew that Liam feared it was—though nothing could be proven. Despite the shields, Kelson could sense that the reminder about his brothers was helping Liam still his flare of rebellion, bringing him back to focus as he slowly exhaled.

"Mahael shall *never* be king!" he said flatly, steely determination in his gaze as he looked up at Kelson.

"Indeed, he shall not," Kelson agreed. "But to prevent that, you must go back."

"I know that!"

Liam's fingers were clasped white-knuckled around the jewelled circlet, but his declaration seemed to deflate what remained of his defiance. Exhaling with another heavy sigh, he glanced down at the diadem and made his hands relax their death-grip, lifting it slightly as he shook his head.

"I don't want this," he said softly. "I never wanted it. But I've got it. And I know I'll have to wear it, and wear the responsibilities that go with it, when—when I go home. I only wish . . ."

"What is it you wish?" Kelson prompted gently, when Liam did not finish the thought.

Sighing, the boy gave a resigned shrug.

"It little matters," he murmured. "I have duties to my people, to my House—and to deny those would be to deny who I am, who I was meant to be—or, who I became, once various relatives got themselves killed and pushed me that much closer to the throne of Furstán." He turned the circlet in his hands, plucking a bit of lint from the setting of one of the emeralds, allowing himself a faint, mirthless smile as he dared another glance at Kelson.

"I am—not yet back in Torenth, Sire. Tell me, do you think I might indulge one final whim of childhood, before I take up the crown that must be mine?"

Kelson smiled faintly, glancing at the gold in Liam's hands.

"That depends on the whim," he said quietly. "As a king, you're entitled to a few. What did you have in mind?"

"Well, I—wondered whether you might pretend, for just a while longer, that I'm still only a squire to the House of Haldane, and not yet the King of Torenth."

Kelson slowly nodded, for suddenly he realized that it was childhood itself to which Liam was saying goodbye—and goodbye to all his childhood friends and dreams, and all the life and security he had known here for the past four years. He glanced again at Nigel, who nodded minutely, then back at Liam.

"I suspect that's one whim we can indulge without any difficulty," he murmured. "Nigel, can you think of any reason he needs to be King of Torenth before we actually enter Torenthi waters?"

Nigel waggled a hand, yes-and-no. "It would probably be advisable for the King of Torenth to arrive at the court of the Hort of Orsal, since his official escort will be awaiting him there. But as I understand it, you'll be calling first at Coroth. I don't see any reason the King of Torenth needs to make an appearance there. In fact, I always find that my squires and pages benefit greatly from exposure to foreign courts—and I believe that Liam has not yet been to Duke Alaric's capital, have you, son?"

Liam shook his head, speechless at the unexpected reprieve.

"Well, then," Nigel went on, smiling as he laid an arm around the boy's shoulders. "It seems to me that this squire ought to have a chance to serve at the court of the Duke of Corwyn, if only briefly. And I don't believe that a coronet is part of a squire's livery," he added, with a glance at the circlet in Liam's hands.

"No, sir," the boy whispered, with a ragged grin.

"Fine. If you like, I'll see that it's packed with the rest of the state regalia until you need it. Anything else?" he asked, with a glance at Kelson.

"Not unless Liam would like to tell us what it is he really wishes," Kelson said "I think it does matter, even though he says it doesn't."

Liam ducked his head, but encouraged by Nigel's sheltering embrace, he dared to answer, though he could not bring himself to look up.

"I—I only wished that there were some way I could remain here until I reach the age for knighthood. I know that isn't possible, but it—would have been a great honor to receive the accolade from Duke Nigel. I mean no disrespect to you, Sire," he added hastily, with a quick glance at Kelson, "but I was present when Duke Nigel knighted you. That memory will be with me until the day I die."

"It is a day that I, too, shall never forget," Kelson said quietly, with a fond glance at Nigel, remembering that mystical moment when he had knelt transfixed before the descent of Nigel's blade on his shoulder. "Unfortunately, you're correct, in that you can't stay another four years; and I don't think that either Nigel or I could condone knighting you at fourteen. But you could come back when you're eighteen. I would be honored to be your sponsor, and I believe it would please my uncle greatly to bestow the accolade."

"If it would please Liam, and ease his mind concerning the future," Nigel said with a faint smile, "I would be willing to bestow a private and informal accolade tonight, before he leaves, as a promise that when he is of sufficient age and achievement, he may return for a proper ceremony. He *is* a king, after all; and the circumstances are unique."

Liam had turned to stare at him as he spoke, and blinked back new tears as he slowly shook his head in wonder.

"You would do that for me, sir?" he whispered.

"I would."

Briefly the boy turned away, indecision mingling with the joy and gratitude spilling from behind his shields. But when he turned back, in control once more, a renewed self-confidence marked his carriage. His solemn response carried the conviction of one who had taken yet another step along that sometimes uncertain road between childhood and maturity.

"You both do me greater honor than I could have dared to dream, by these expressions of your faith in me," he said carefully. "Trusting in that faith, I would not diminish it by taking up even the generous token you have offered, for I have not earned it. Being a king should make no difference in matters concerning the honor of a man.

"Therefore, I desire no promise save the pledge of your hand, Duke Nigel: that when I attain the customary age—*if* you still think me worthy—I may return to Rhemuth to receive from you the accolade of knighthood. I am—well aware that one of fourteen years is a man in law but not in fact; but you have given me the courtesy of treatment as a man and, I hope, as a friend. I shall treasure that always, whatever may come to pass when I return home."

"It is not only years that make a man," Nigel replied, clasping Liam's right hand in his. "I give you my pledge as you have asked—and I know that my king supports this pledge," he added, as Kelson laid his hand atop their joined ones. "If it were in my power, I would accompany you to Beldour, to be at your side as you take up your throne—but my place is here, to hold this throne for *my* king. Rest assured, however, that you *are* a knight in spirit, if not yet by accolade; and you shall be in my prayers as if you were my own son."

"Amen," Kelson murmured, grateful for the elegant resolution to this particular situation, but mindful that others had yet to be reassured regarding

Liam's status. "Much as I might wish to continue this discussion, however, I suggest that we ought not to keep Rasoul and Count Mátyás waiting any longer." Releasing their clasped hands, he glanced back in the direction of the door.

"Liam, I assume that you would prefer to keep our pledge confidential. I think I know how to explain our absence. Would you like a moment more? A Haldane squire should always convey dignity and serenity. You'll attend on me, when we go back in."

Liam nodded agreement and gave his eyes a last swipe with Nigel's handkerchief before handing it back to him, along with the coronet. Nigel received both with a little bow, smiling as he tucked the handkerchief back into his sleeve and looped the coronet over one arm.

In the space of those few seconds, as they composed themselves to go back in, Kelson concocted a plausible scenario to extend Liam's respite from kingship, mentally imparting the gist of it to Nigel in a tightly focused burst as he briefly touched the other man's shoulder while shepherding the two back into the withdrawing room. Nigel had gained much in Deryni ability, in conjunction with his stints of service as Kelson's regent and especially as king-apparent, and had been allowed to retain all of it following his return of the reins of power to Gwynedd's rightful king. His bemused approval set the seal on his nephew's intent—and carefully unfolded, the story would withstand Truth-Reading by either of their guests, while still preserving Liam's dignity.

"Gentlemen, forgive the delay, but it seems I was mistaken regarding the status of Liam-Lajos," Kelson said by way of preamble, as Dhugal admitted them and Morgan and the two Torenthi envoys rose. "Duke Nigel tells me that he had not intended that this squire should be officially released from his duties until the official departure from the Ile d'Orsal next week."

"May one ask why?" Rasoul said with a frown.

"Certainly," Nigel replied, taking up the agreed explanation. "It has long been my practice to give our squires and pages as much exposure as possible to a variety of court functions—especially courts besides Rhemuth, since this can teach important lessons in diplomacy. It had come to my attention that before meeting the official Torenthi delegation at the Ile d'Orsal, the royal progress will be calling at Corwyn, which I believe Liam-Lajos has never visited. It seemed, therefore, an ideal opportunity for him to acquire that additional measure of experience, before he must take up the full burden of his royal duties. I trust you will agree that such experience is particularly useful for a future king."

Rasoul and Mátyás exchanged bemused glances, and the latter inclined his head.

"My lord, I say this not in contradiction, but Liam-Lajos is not a future king; he has been king for nearly five years. Now he is of age, preparing to return to his own people, and should be accorded the courtesies due his rank and blood."

"And I would answer, in return, that he is presently accorded all the courtesies due a Haldane squire, which is a rank to which many young men aspire, whatever their blood," Nigel said carefully. "Time enough to be a king, when he has made the most of this important training."

Rasoul folded his arms across his chest, visibly impatient. "Has he not been a servant long enough?" he muttered.

"Ah, but a squire is not a servant, my lord," Kelson said easily. "He is a pupil— as I myself was, until the day I was knighted by Duke Nigel—and I was a crowned king."

"We do not crown our kings," Mátyás said pointedly.

"Not the way we do—no," Kelson agreed, searching for a way to shift the tenor of the discussion as he glanced back at Liam, for it was becoming clear that both men were more focused on the boy's rank than on his feelings. "You invest them, you gird them with the sword—I've had instruction from Father Irenaeus.

"The point is that once Liam-Lajos is acknowledged in his kingship, in whatever form is customary in Torenth, he will always be regarded as a king from that time forth. He can never be a boy again. Believe me, I speak from experience. Would it do any harm to let him be a boy for a few more days?"

As Rasoul and Mátyás exchanged dubious glances, Morgan cleared his throat, his expression suggesting faint amusement.

"Sire, may I speak?"

"Of course."

"And may I ask that Liam-Lajos be excused?"

Wondering what Morgan was about—and he dared not use his powers to inquire, in the presence of two Deryni of the caliber of Rasoul and Mátyás—Kelson feigned only casual concern as he glanced again at Liam. The boy stiffened slightly as he drew himself to attention, but his face betrayed nothing, and nothing escaped from behind his shields.

"Squire, please inform the lord chamberlain that I have no further business for the court," Kelson said, glad for the opportunity to release Liam from the tension that was building. "After that, you may proceed with your usual duties. And Dhugal—perhaps you would be so good as to inform Father Irenaeus and the captain of the Torenthi guard of honor that Lord Rasoul and Count Mátyás will join them shortly. Assure them that all is well."

Liam immediately made good his escape, Dhugal with somewhat less alacrity, for he clearly would have preferred to hear out the discussion. When they had gone, Kelson pulled out a chair near Mátyás, with a gesture inviting the rest of them also to sit—and curious how Morgan intended to turn the discussion. Nigel appeared as mystified as their two guests.

"Sire," Morgan said, as he sat beside Rasoul, "I was reluctant to speak in front of Liam-Lajos, for I wished not to cause him embarrassment. However, I find myself privy to information suggesting that he himself may have at least one personal reason for retaining his squire's status a while longer. If he truly desired early release, I have no doubt that Duke Nigel would grant it."

He managed to look somewhat tentative, and Nigel nodded impatiently.

"Understand that I speak now as a father," Morgan went on, "—which I suspect both our esteemed guests may appreciate. Count Mátyás tells me that he is soon to become a father for the second time, and Lord Rasoul, I believe, has rather a large family—though I am unacquainted with specific numbers."

Rasoul cast a bemused glance in Morgan's direction and raised an indulgent eyebrow. "Allah has blessed me with four sons and three daughters, mostly grown," he said blandly, "and I have six grandchildren as well. But do, pray, continue, my lord Alaric."

"I bow before al-Rasoul's superior experience of fatherhood," Morgan acknowledged, with a smiling nod in the Moor's direction. "But, returning to our soon to be ex-squire, your king: Understand that, officially, I know nothing of any of this, but my lady wife felt that I should be informed. It seems that my stepson Brendan, whom you both have met, has asked permission to host something of a farewell supper for Liam-Lajos and the other squires and pages, when the royal progress calls back at Coroth in a few days' time."

To Kelson's surprise, Morgan's declaration rang of nothing but truth, and could certainly explain some of Liam's attitude. He found himself beginning to smile as Morgan continued.

"It is meant to be a secret, of course," Morgan went on, "but apparently the word has spread among the boys, to the delight of those who are going along on the progress to Torenth and the envy of those who must remain behind. The guest of honor affects utter unawareness of the plans."

"I—fail to see what the taking up of his proper estate has to do with this—social whim," Mátyás said uncertainly.

"That's because your boy is only three," Morgan replied, sitting forward in his chair. "When he's older, it will mean a great deal to him to be included in the activities of other boys his age. And as for Liam-Lajos taking up his proper estate—well, our squires' training is such that I have no doubt Brendan can cope with entertaining fellow squires and pages; but entertaining a king might present an altogether more daunting proposition—for all of them. I—believe this may explain a great deal."

A faint smile flickered within Rasoul's close-trimmed beard, and even Mátyás seemed somewhat amused. Kelson, Truth-Reading Morgan as he was certain the others also must be doing, allowed himself to relax a little. Morgan's explanation cast additional light on the story Kelson himself had wheedled out of Liam—trepidations of a normal fourteen-year-old. Almost, he wished he could attend the affair.

"Were we ever that young?" Nigel said with a chuckle.

"We were," Morgan replied. "I believe your Payne may also be one of the ring-leaders." Nigel rolled his eyes. "I gather that all three boys have become quite close, through being thrown together in their various squiring capacities. I'm afraid you have only yourself to blame for that!"

Mátyás now was smiling faintly as well, and nodding his head.

"You are a perceptive man, my lord duke. It would seem that this imminent parting of Liam-Lajos from the company of his friends represents something of a personal tragedy in their young lives."

"It certainly does for Brendan," Morgan replied. "I may tell you now, Count Mátyás, that a friendship has grown between him and your king that is similar to the one we both wished for our own sons, earlier today. He desperately wishes to come along to Beldour, but I haven't yet decided to allow it. I—hesitate to expose him to what might prove more dangerous than any of us would wish, who care for Liam-Lajos."

The seamless shift from whimsy to the tension that was in the back of every-one's mind caught both Torenthis by surprise. Mátyás averted his gaze, and Rasoul leaned back in his chair, tracing patterns on the tabletop with a brown forefinger.

"My lord Alaric," Rasoul said carefully, "I must wonder what you are trying to tell us."

"Only that I am concerned for your king's safety," Morgan said quietly, glancing at Kelson. "I believe my king shares that concern."

"I do," Kelson said guardedly.

The safety of Liam-Lajos had, indeed, been a subject of growing concern and much discussion, as the time approached for his return to Torenth—though the question of whether to voice that concern to his own people had been reserved until they could obtain a better sense for the true alignment of Torenth's various political factions.

Of the two regents, Mahael was the far greater danger, though Morag, too, remained an enigma—working closely with Mahael but surely aware of the rumors concerning her first son's death. The brother between Mahael and Mátyás was totally unknown in Gwynedd, but probably in league with Mahael—as Morag herself might be, especially if, as sometimes was whispered in the gossip that filtered across the border, Mahael was seeking her hand in marriage.

Mátyás himself was a doubly unknown commodity. But since Morgan had maneuvered the conversation so that, if Kelson desired, their fears for Liam's safety could be broached, that very likely meant that his cautious assessment of Mátyás thus far was largely positive—if anything about the Torenthi political situation could be called that. Of Rasoul they need have no fears save that the interests of Torenth would always take precedence over those of Gwynedd—and for Rasoul, the interests of Torenth included the interests of Liam-Lajos, to whom he was fiercely devoted.

As, indeed, Mátyás appeared to be. At least Liam himself seemed to have no doubts regarding this favorite uncle, who had started him on his magical training—though he had truly been a boy when last they met, and much could have changed in four long years. Once again, Kelson wished he dared use his powers to consult with Morgan. But Morgan's expression, as their eyes briefly met, seemed to suggest that he might proceed with caution.

"My lords, these are not the circumstances under which I had intended to bring this up," Kelson said, "but given our discussion, this seems an appropriate time. I will be frank with you—and I invite you to read the truth of what I am about to tell you, for I hope and believe that all of us want what will be best for Liam-Lajos."

He tried to keep his focus on both Rasoul and Mátyás equally, but he sensed that Mátyás was the key.

"First of all, be assured that my only aim regarding Torenth and her king, for these past four years, has been to ensure that the boy receive the best possible preparation for taking up his kingship. I never asked for his wardship, but it was forced upon me when Wencit set forth the terms under which our own conflict was fought—and Count Mátyás, I regret the circumstances under which your brother and I met. It was none of my choosing. If you wish, I am willing to discuss the matter in private, but I will be blunt and say that I hope this long-ago connection will not adversely influence our present dealings."

Mátyás inclined his head neutrally, no flicker of passion stirring behind the pale eyes.

"Regarding Torenth itself, however," Kelson went on, "it was never my intention that Torenth should remain a client state of Gwynedd forever, and it is not my intention now, as Liam comes into his full inheritance. It is a sign of my faith in him that I now prepare to set him on his own throne, among his own people—not yet fully independent, for he is young, but if he is eventually to stand on his own, as is my intention, I am well aware that I must gradually begin loosening the reins.

"The doing of this thing entails no small risk, on my part and on his; but in the fullness of time, when I and my advisors deem him ready, I hope to release him from the homage he presently owes Gwynedd, and to release Torenth to full independence once more. Toward that end, I trust I may count upon you and other men of good will in your land to support him."

Rasoul's eyes had never left Kelson's as he listened; Mátyás kept his gaze averted. After a beat, Rasoul inclined his head gracefully.

"Tell me truly, my lord of Gwynedd, for I *am* Truth-Reading, as you did invite: Have I ever given cause for you to doubt my loyalty to my king?"

"None, my lord," Kelson said steadily. "And not only loyalty, but genuine affection. I merely wished to clarify my own intentions regarding him, and to voice my concerns for his safety."

"And also, perhaps, to sound out my esteemed colleague?" Rasoul ventured, with a sidelong glance at Mátyás.

"I have made my peace overture to Count Mátyás," Kelson said carefully, as Mátyás stiffened slightly. "That is a private matter between us, I think, but I say again that I would wish to clear the air of any rancor that might lie between us because of my role in the death of his brother. In truth, however, I am far more concerned about the plans of his brothers who are living than the one who is dead."

Mátyás looked up, sharp emotion in his gaze, though the flicker of passion quickly disappeared behind the bland façade of a practiced courtier.

"I have told the Duke of Corwyn that I hardly knew my dead brother," he said softly. "But mind how you speak concerning the living ones."

"I do not ask you to choose between them and me, Count Mátyás," Kelson replied. "But I would hope that you will always choose the welfare of Liam-Lajos over furthering the ambitions of any of his subjects, including your brothers. You cannot be unaware of the rumors that were rife following the death of King Alroy."

"That Mahael somehow was responsible?" Mátyás's retort was far milder than Kelson might have expected. "I recall that there were also rumors that the King of Gwynedd contrived the accident that cost the boy his life. I am quite aware of the truth of the matter."

"Are you?" Kelson said, though the words were not a question.

Mátyás did not answer, but he did not turn his gaze from Kelson's. After a moment, Kelson looked deliberately back at Rasoul.

"I fear that this was not, perhaps, the best time to discuss this matter after all," he said quietly. "I apologize if I have given offense. My concern was and is for your king. I shall continue to act in what I believe to be his best interests, to see him secure upon his throne. I hope that I may count on your support in that regard, and on the support of all his loyal subjects."

Rasoul inclined his head. "My lord of Gwynedd is a man of honor," he acknowledged. "Torenth thanks him for his support of her king."

Feeling suddenly weary of it all, Kelson got to his feet, the others rising as well, for the discourse clearly had reached an impasse that would not be easily resolved.

"You will wish to refresh yourselves before we dine," he said. "My uncle will see that you are shown to the quarters prepared for you. Meanwhile, I trust that you will not object if Liam-Lajos continues to function in his capacity as squire, until after the visit to Coroth?"

Rasoul looked pointedly at Mátyás, who appeared still somewhat out of sorts, but the count favored Kelson with a stiff nod of agreement.

"If he wishes it, my lord, I have no objection."

"Thank you."

Before the awkwardness of the moment could escalate again, Nigel swept one arm toward the door, inviting the two to accompany him. When they had gone, Kelson sank back into his chair, numbly staring for several seconds at nothing at all before glancing up at the man who had long been one of his own most important mentors, and remained one of his closest friends.

"I didn't handle that very well, did I?" he said quietly, hunching his shoulders as he rubbed at a dull ache at the base of his neck.

Smiling faintly, Morgan came to stand behind him, drawing him back to lean against his waist while he began massaging the tight shoulder muscles.

"You handled it as well as could be expected," he said, his thumbs working at the tension. "I'm still not sure of Mátyás's game, but nothing that was said here contradicted what passed between the two of us on the way here—and Liam does seem to trust him. See for yourself."

Kelson had already been prepared to ask for a sharing of the exchange, so he closed his eyes and let himself relax against Morgan, dropping his shields. The other's mental touch was gentle and sure, the information quickly imparted. A surge of renewing energy came with it, unbidden but welcome, so that as Kelson opened his eyes, he felt as if he were awakening from a sleep of several hours. He grinned and stretched as Morgan came around to drag a chair facing him, plunking down expectantly.

"You're very good at that," Kelson murmured. "I feel like maybe I can face Mátyás again, when we go down for supper. But you're right: He's still a giant question, even though my basic instinct is positive."

"He is still Mahael's brother," Morgan cautioned. "Nothing can change that."

"Nor could I forget it." Kelson rubbed at his neck again, more out of preoccupation than any lingering discomfort, and allowed himself a sigh.

"At least we seem to have gotten Liam something of a reprieve. Is that true, about Brendan's plans for a farewell supper?"

"Of course it's true," Morgan said with a smile. "I'd hardly dare to make up something like that, in front of two Deryni of the obvious caliber of Rasoul and Mátyás—though the plot isn't quite as advanced as I implied. But it *will* be. The part about the friendship among the boys is quite true, however, and Brendan does want to come to Torenth."

"Will you allow it?" Kelson asked.

"As I told Mátyás, I haven't decided. But I'll allow him to come as far as the Ile d'Orsal. That's safe enough. By then, I hope we'll have a better feel for what to expect in Beldour. Arilan should have further intelligence, when we reach Coroth, and I expect that Richenda may also have some additional information from her contacts."

"The Ile d'Orsal," Kelson murmured, grimacing.

Mention of the place had sharply reminded him of his more personal mission at the Orsal's court, bidden by Rothana, successfully suppressed in the tension of the afternoon, and not at all safe for *him*. Once again, the unbidden images of long-ago summers came surging into mind—of Araxie, who resided at the Orsal's court. And Kelson had promised to meet her, and to consider asking her to become his queen.

"What about the Ile d'Orsal?" Morgan asked.

Shrugging, Kelson shook his head, trying to look unconcerned.

"Oh, it's just that the place will be awash in preparations for my cousin's wedding next month," he said lightly, skirting as close to the truth as he dared. "Richelle and her sister are also the Orsal's nieces, you know. Once I show up, that atmosphere will only fuel speculation about my own eventual plans."

"I hardly need remind you that those plans are a topic of intense interest in a great many quarters," Morgan replied with a droll smile. "I will be bolder, still, and remind you that one of the candidates most highly favored for your hand will be attending the nuptials of Richelle and the estimable Brecon Ramsay—namely, his sister. Many are hoping to hear announcement of another royal betrothal, at the wedding feast."

Kelson managed a grim smile, for the matter of Brecon's sister, at least, was resolving happily for all concerned.

"Well, they may, indeed, hear of a royal betrothal in connection with Noelie Ramsay," he replied, enjoying Morgan's startled look, "but it will be with a different Haldane than they have in mind. It seems that Rory fancies her, and the feelings are reciprocated."

"*Rory* and Noelie?" Morgan arched a blond eyebrow, clearly surprised, but apparently taken with the prospect. "Indeed. May I ask who told you that?"

"It was Rothana," Kelson conceded. "She rightly pointed out that the political implications are little different than if *I* married Noelie—better, in fact, since

Rory can live in Meara. I've been thinking about it, since I found out. After he has a few years' experience, I thought I might make him my viceroy."

"I see," Morgan said. "In the short term, I would agree that this sounds like a promising notion, but—have you discussed this yet with Nigel?"

"Only briefly."

"Indeed. Need I point out that he very likely will not take kindly to the notion of having his heir live so far away? And what's to happen to Meara, when Nigel eventually dies and Rory must come home to rule Carthmoor?"

"I avoided getting into any of that, when we spoke briefly about it this morning," Kelson said uneasily. "It's occurred to me since, that I might revive one of the old Mearan titles for Rory—say, Duke of Ratharkin. That would be a fitting rank for my viceroy, and the Mearans would like it—that the title eventually would be vested in a son of Rory and Noelie."

"I think I see where this is headed," Morgan interjected. "If you're intending that Nigel should restore Albin to his place in the Carthmoor succession—"

"And why not?" Kelson retorted. "It should have been his, after all. He shouldn't be penalized for what his father did."

"I agree—and I know how you feel about the boy—but I don't think that Nigel will be easily won on this point. I suppose you *could* always create a new title for Albin, when he's older. That's assuming that he doesn't end up in the Church, as his mother plans."

"That's another battle to be won in the future," Kelson murmured. "Rothana and I had words about that, too."

"I can imagine." Morgan sighed. "Well, one battle at a time. The council won't be pleased, since they wanted *you* to marry Noelie, but I'm happy for Rory, especially if it's a match of true affection. I had no idea."

"Nor did I. But someone might as well be happy." Kelson heaved a heavy sigh, suddenly weary of the entire subject. "Dear God, all that talk of sons, earlier, was *so* depressing. Once Dhugal and Liam left, I was the only man in the room who doesn't have any."

Morgan leaned back in his chair, eyeing the king with sympathy.

"You have it within your means to change that, whenever you choose to do so," he said. "You know I try not to bring it up—you get enough of that from everyone else—but it *is* time you took a queen."

"I know," Kelson said. "But the right queen won't have me. Alaric, what am I going to do?"

"I cannot answer that for you, my prince," Morgan said, with genuine regret. "Only you can make that decision."

Kelson nodded bleakly, but he was not yet prepared to share with Morgan what the "right queen" had proposed to him.

"I know you're right," he said softly. "I just—"

He sighed and got wearily to his feet, retrieving his coronet and the Haldane sword that Dhugal had left lying on the table.

"I'll be in my quarters, if anyone should need me."

"Is there anything I can do?" Morgan asked.

Kelson shook his head. "I wish there were. I'm afraid this is something only I can resolve."

CHAPTER SIX

*And he that honoureth his mother is as one that
layeth up treasure.*

Ecclesiasticus 3:4

*K*elson tried to sleep in the several hours before he must contend again
with his Torenthi guests—not a state affair, but formal enough, for
most of the court residents in Rhemuth would be present for this last such
appearance of the king before his departure on the morrow. He lay with his eyes
closed, but he only drifted, periodically jerked back from the brink of true slum-
ber by snatches of dreams, fragmented glimpses of possible calamities whose
details remained always just beyond ken, though most of the players were all too
familiar.

Not surprisingly, young Liam was usually one of them. The boy's momentary
reticence before his own envoys, while awkward at the time, was certainly understandable at fourteen, as was a certain amount of anxiety. Nonetheless, that incident plus the ensuing somewhat testy exchange with Rasoul and the still
unfathomable Mátyás had left Kelson uncertain as to whether Liam was really
ready to face the challenges that lay before him when he returned to his own land.
The boy's revealed maturity regarding knighthood was somewhat more reassuring.

In theory, at least, both Liam's potential and his preparation were far better
than Kelson's had been at the same age, for all Liam's training and experience of
the past four years had been geared toward a definite time when he must func-

tion as king; but the challenges facing the boy were also greater. Daunting enough was the very process of taking up his kingship, especially in its more eso- teric aspects, in a ceremony of installation and magical confirmation in which Kelson himself would have a small part—and from which he hoped to prevent anything from going dreadfully awry. Father Irenaeus had briefed him in the gen- eralities of what to expect, but *practicum* rehearsals would follow once they actu- ally reached Beldour.

The structure of the rite was of great antiquity, formal and stylized, its outward symbolism couched in a mythology now only dimly remembered, expressed in rit- ual drama and a sequence of magical trials whose successful completion would aug- ment and complete the empowering begun in a similar but far simpler ritual enacted shortly after Liam's ascension to the throne. The boy's youth had precluded his undergoing the entire ceremony at that time; so though he had been girded with the sword on the New Year's Day following, as was customary, receiving most of the outward forms of a traditional enthronement, the full substance of his assumption of power had been reserved for this second ceremony, at his coming of age.

Under ordinary circumstances, this final enabling should be accomplished with little possibility of mishap. Given adequate preparation and support from the ancil- lary participants in the ceremony, the procedure should present only a vigorous but largely token testing to be endured by a king well capable of withstanding the stress. The ritual ordeals guarding Gwynedd's kingship in a mystical sense were far younger and far simpler, and sprung from different needs and perspectives; but it was Kelson's understanding that all such tests were, at their heart, also part of the means whereby previous capacities were at the same time stretched and strengthened to accommo- date more concentrated reservoirs of power. Though that first inrush was likely to cause a certain degree of discomfort, variable according to the inherent strength and preparation of the individual, the chances of any lasting injury were only slight.

Any real danger lay in the principal's vulnerability in that instant just before the power began to flow, when all defenses must be laid aside in order to allow the influx. Should a supporter in the ritual falter in his duties—or worse, take advantage of the principal's helplessness during that critical stage—the consequences could, indeed, be deadly. This made it a matter of no little concern that Liam's uncle Mahael was almost certain to be one of his chief supporters, with his own priorities and agendas.

That, no doubt, was why Mahael also drifted in and out of Kelson's troubled dreamscapes, even though Kelson had never actually met the man: a murky, brooding presence whose face he could never quite see clearly, sometimes resem- bling an older, more devious Mátyás and sometimes a muddled composite of the slain Lionel, who had been Liam's father, and the sly and treacherous Wencit, both of whom Kelson had been obliged to kill. Sometimes Kelson sensed a second presence behind Mahael's—perhaps the other brother, Teymuraz, whom he also had never met. Whatever the true alignment of the three Furstán brothers, Kelson had no doubt that they represented varying degrees of potential threat to Liam.

The boy's mother also figured in Kelson's troubled reveries, and was not above suspicion. That face, at least, was known, from the several months she had spent under house arrest at Rhemuth, following the seizure of Liam as hostage. Though co-regent with Mahael, as she had been for the dead Alroy, her eldest son, the true degree of collaboration between the duo remained unclear, as did any part Morag herself might have had in Alroy's death.

Even if Morag were entirely innocent of Alroy's blood, Kelson did not see how she could fail to be aware of the rumors regarding Mahael's involvement. Her continued silence on the question might bespeak an abysmal unawareness of the truth—or a blind refusal to deal with it; or tacit support of the dynastic ambitions of her brother-in-law, regardless of their cost; or some other game as yet unguessable. That a mother might have countenanced the killing of her own son seemed incredible; but so long as the question of Alroy's death remained unanswered, Kelson could not rely on any normal assumption regarding the Princess Morag Furstána.

Mingled with these images of menace were gentler visages as well, no less alarming for being no danger in the same sense, but emblematic of his thwarted yearnings for some measure of fulfillment that answered only *his* needs, *his* longings.

Rothana, her dark eyes filled with tears, turning her face away from his . . . The slain Sidana, drowned in her own blood, limp and lifeless in his arms . . . A jumbled succession of other female faces, dark-haired and fair, echoing the endless parades of marriageable hopefuls that were constantly thrust upon him by a host of the well-meaning . . . or the galleries of painted likenesses that his council set before him with increasing urgency, begging him to choose, to marry, to provide an heir . . .

And ever among them, at the same time elusive and oddly tantalizing, a fairhaired girl with a face little more distinct than Mahael's, though something in the eyes somehow reminded Kelson of his aunt Sivorn. . . .

After a while, he abandoned any real attempt to either sleep or put his worries from mind, and gazed up unseeing at the underside of the canopy above his bed, mentally reviewing the likely course of the evening and the departure on the morrow, liking none of it, only adding to his unease. When Ivo at last came to dress him for the evening's social duties, he felt little more rested than when he had lain down, and certainly no more reassured.

But the evening went well enough. To honor Torenth, he wore the fine enamelled cross that Rasoul had presented to him on the occasion of his knighting four years before: the gift of Liam's regents, and blessed by the Torenthi patriarch. Rasoul noted the courtesy at their first exchange and made comment to Count Mátyás. The younger man smiled faintly, touching the icon hanging on his own breast as he made Kelson a slight bow.

Seated at Kelson's right hand, between him and Morgan, both Mátyás and Rasoul proved mannerly if sometimes distant table guests, dutifully commending the quality of the fare, the comeliness of the ladies, and offering gracious toasts to the prosperity of both lands; and only twice did any of Kelson's lords bring their daughters or sisters to be presented to the high table. All things considered, Kelson could hardly have wished for more.

Even Liam could have little cause for complaint, for the decision of the afternoon was allowing him to retain the relative anonymity afforded by squire's livery for at least a while longer. Initially self-conscious, he waited upon the king and his two countrymen with competence and a growing confidence as the evening progressed, while Payne and Brendan did the same for their fathers and the remaining guests seated at the high table.

Other squires and pages of the court attended to the rest of the hall. All of the boys performed their duties with diligence, determined that their Torenthi guests should carry away glowing reports of the grace of King Kelson's court. And whenever a lull in service permitted them to congregate in the antechamber behind the dais, they whispered and snickered among themselves like the boys they still were, though the sharp eye of Lord Pemberly, the deputy-chamberlain, ensured an appropriate level of decorum.

The array of other guests dining in the great hall included some of the most illustrious names in Gwynedd, many of them not normally resident at court, summoned to serve on the regency council over which Duke Nigel would preside during his royal nephew's absence from capital and kingdom. Assisting Nigel, and maintaining Deryni links with the king and his party, would be Bishop Duncan McLain—to be sorely missed on the mission to Torenth, but Kelson dared not leave his regent without the protection of at least one powerful Deryni, much though he would have wished Duncan's company and counsel along with that of Morgan and Dhugal. The young Deryni priest, John Nivard, would also provide Deryni clout, if necessary.

Nigel would be further assisted by his wife, the astute and level-headed Meraude, whose brother Saer would be accompanying the king. Queen Jehana had also returned to take up her rightful place on the regency council. Likewise, Thomas Cardiel, the Archbishop of Rhemuth, had agreed to make himself available on a regular basis; he was seated tonight just beyond Nigel and Archbishop Bradene, far on Kelson's left side.

Kelson had even called his most senior duke out of semiretirement: Ewan, the grizzled and irascible Duke of Claibourne—at nearly sixty-two, still Marshal of Gwynedd, though his eldest son and heir, Earl Graham, had been taking on increasing responsibility for management of the family interests in Claibourne for close to a decade, and was ready to step in when required. These days, the old man only put in the odd appearance at court, usually in the summer; but his mind was as sharp as ever.

Given that the king's plans regarding Liam had been known for more than a year in advance, and Ewan's eldest grandson, Angus, had been scheduled to be knighted the previous Twelfth Night, the duke had travelled south the previous autumn by easy stages, there to winter at Rhemuth Castle, serve as a sponsor for young Angus at his knighting, and stay on as a member of the regency council. Since the knighting, Angus and several of the other young men dubbed at the same time, including Rory, had been serving as Ewan's aides—and his legs.

This combination of rank, office, and physical limitation, then, had given Ewan and his grandson places at the high table tonight, just beyond Rasoul. At one point, over joints of wildfowl and a pottage of dumplings and legumes, young Angus boldly engaged a somewhat amused Count Mátyás in well-mannered but occasionally vigorous discussion regarding the relative merits of Kheldish garrons versus the steppe ponies of distant Östmarcke. Lest discussion become too heated, Ewan and Rasoul kept attentive vigil from either side, as did Morgan and the king himself, all of them exchanging the occasional indulgent glance; but the conversation never crossed the boundaries of courtesy. From what Kelson could gather, only catching snatches from behind Mátyás, Angus fared surprisingly well against a man probably a decade his senior, at an age when even two or three years more experience could mean a great deal. Or perhaps it was Mátyás's forbearance.

The evening's lone note of discord, which Kelson had known was probably unavoidable, came when, partway through the last course but one, he turned in response to an approach at his left elbow to see his mother's chaplain, Father Ambros, who bent with a whispered request that he please join her briefly down in the garden. Kelson had been all too aware of her presence in the hall earlier in the evening—not at his left side, where protocol would have suggested, but seated at the far left end of the high table, flanked by the two archbishops—and as far as possible from the two Deryni seated at Kelson's right. He had not noticed when she made her quiet departure, but he had hoped he might be spared the personal interview that now seemed inevitable.

Making his excuses to Mátyás and Rasoul, Kelson followed Father Ambros down the stair at that end of the hall, emerging in the cloister walk that skirted

the garden. It was twilight still, on this mild midsummer evening, the air heavy
with the scent of roses and jasmine, lilac and lavender. Gravel crunched under
their boots as he and Ambros headed deeper into the garden, bypassing a tinkling
ornamental fountain to branch off down a side path.

His mother was waiting in one of the rose bowers with the black-robed Sister Cecile, the white of her royal widow's mourning as stark as the garb of a
novice nun, save for the plain circlet of gold set over her close-pinned white
wimple. Jehana of Bremagne once had been a beautiful woman, but the harsh
religious disciplines to which she had subjected herself in the decade since her
husband's death, in expiation of what she regarded as the taint of her Deryni
blood, had left her gaunt and fragile, looking haggard far beyond her nearly
forty years.

"Kelson, my son," she said, a hesitant smile lifting bloodless lips as she
absently looped a string of coral prayer beads several times around one thin wrist.
Beside her, Sister Cecile dipped him a curtsy, eyes averted, and then slipped past
to join Father Ambros, the two of them moving just out of earshot but still in
sight, though they turned their backs.

"I cannot stay long," Kelson said a little stiffly. "I have guests waiting."

"I have been waiting, too," she said, offering her cheek for his kiss. "I trust you
did not plan to leave tomorrow without a proper farewell."

He sighed as she drew him into the bower to sit beside her on the stone
bench.

"I would have seen you after Mass tomorrow," he said. "I was afraid we might
quarrel. I know that you don't approve of my going."

She glanced away uneasily, hugging her arms as if against a sudden chill,
though the night was warm. The prayer beads dangling against her robes looked
like blood in the twilight.

"It is not your going of which I disapprove—though that will be danger
enough. It is your participation in the boy's ceremony of installation. Nigel tells
me that you mean to take an active part."

"You mean, I think, a *magical* part," he said quietly.

"If we discuss that, we *shall* quarrel," she whispered.

"Mother, I am what I am—and Liam is what he—"

"He is a Furstán, and Deryni, and the enemy of Gwynedd!"

"He is a fourteen-year-old king, as I once was, and he will be surrounded by
his enemies, from among his own people, some of whom may try to take his life!
He is also—though I never asked for it—my vassal. I cannot stand by and watch
him slain."

"Oh, by all means, save him, so that he may return one day to destroy
you!"

He bit back an angry retort that only would have pulled them deeper into dissension, for this was an argument both long-standing and unlikely to be conceded by either side. Drawing a deep breath, he looked out across the darkening garden to where the chaplain and Sister Cecile had turned at the sound of the raised voices, though he doubted the actual words had been distinguishable. Not that Father Ambros, as the queen's confessor, must not have heard it all before, at least from her perspective.

"We wished not to quarrel," he said quietly. "I will not discuss this further except to say that both Liam and I have very powerful enemies, who will use every resource available to *them*, to see us overturned. While it is possible that eventually he might turn out to be one of those *I* need to watch out for, I would like to think that in these four years at my court, we have managed to break some of the old patterns of enmity between our two lands, and begun to establish some groundwork for peace in the future. I have no designs on any lands beyond our eastern borders, and Torenth need not look west. We can coexist peacefully, and begin to rebuild some of what was lost after the Restoration."

"But, they are Deryni—"

"So am I, Mother!" he retorted. "Even if I didn't have that blood from *you*—regardless that you refuse to acknowledge it!—I feel more and more certain that my Haldane powers come from Deryni sources."

"Accursed powers," she muttered.

"No, the *powers* aren't accursed!" he replied. "They simply *are*. It's what one does with *anything* he has—how one *uses* one's power—that makes him accursed or not. And I intend to use some of mine to make certain Liam gets properly installed in his kingship, able to wield *his* power for the betterment of his kingdom—as I have tried to do for Gwynedd, and as I will continue to try."

She turned her face away, rebellious still, one hand nervously fiddling with the coral beads wrapped round the other wrist.

"I did not think I could sway you," she said after several long seconds. "You are stubborn, as was your father—and Alaric Morgan encouraged both of you."

"Had he not encouraged *me*," Kelson replied, "we should not be having this conversation, because both you and I would have perished at my coronation. The powers that he and Duncan helped me secure are what have kept me alive, what helped to save you, and what are enabling me to keep moving Gwynedd forward. The progress is slow, but now, after nearly two hundred years, there's actually a chance of peace between us and Torenth—but only if I can keep Liam alive for long enough. If one has been given the power to assist such a purpose, doesn't one have an obligation to use it?"

"Peace is a gift," she finally conceded, her head bowed over her beads, "but not, I think, at the price of one's immortal soul."

"And *I* think," Kelson countered, "that the state of my immortal soul is not something that you have any right to judge."

Another silence fell between them, and after a moment Jehana sadly shook her head and lifted it to look out over the garden.

"I know you must go," she murmured. "I know the duty of kings, and I know that you value the oaths you have sworn to your vassal. Might I—ask a favor, since you stop first at the Ile d'Orsal?"

"What favor?"

"Oh, nothing so onerous as what undoubtedly awaits you in Beldour." She gave him a wan smile as she produced from within one sleeve a flat packet of folded parchment, sealed with scarlet wax that bore her crowned *J* cipher.

" 'Tis but a missive that I would have you deliver to your aunt Sivorn," she went on. "Women's gossip, mostly: trifling details of gowns and jewels and flowers and such, for the wedding of your cousin Richelle. But I know that the subject of weddings gives you no pleasure."

"I am well enough content regarding *that* wedding," he said pointedly, his tone making it clear that he did not wish to discuss any other. He particularly did not want to discuss or even to think about the wedding plans of Richelle's sister.

Jehana sighed and shook her head, pretending to study the inscription on the outside of the letter.

"You little reckon what you miss," she mused. "It was good to winter there. The Orsal keeps a laughing, happy court, teeming with young children—and with all his brood, plus his sister's younger four, how could it be otherwise? Seven, he has now, and soon another! When you are there, you must be sure to notice his eldest girl, now that she is grown. Elisabet, she is called—a lovely—"

"Mother!" he said sharply.

"Well, a mother cannot but try," she replied with a shrug and a wan smile. "All apart from Gwynedd's need for an heir, I would have grandchildren to dandle on my knee. Failing that, however—" She raised the letter in her hand, to silence the new protest on his lips.

"Nay, I will not say it. I ask only that you give this to Sivorn, for I do miss her company. All the winter long, she and I did spend many a happy hour in contented stitchery, with her girls and the ladies of her brother's household, sewing the garments for Richelle's wedding finery. Pray God that you may live to see it worn, at summer's end. And since the wedding will bring the sister of her bridegroom to Rhemuth . . ." she added, with a hopeful tilt of her head.

"Mother . . ."

"I know, I know. What I do *not* know is why you object to *that* match," she went on. "An alliance with Noelie Ramsay——"

"Mother!"

She lowered her eyes and extended the letter wordlessly.

"Is there anything else?" he asked, though his tone was less harsh than he had feared, as he took the letter and slipped it into the front of his tunic.

She shook her head, not looking up. "Nay, only——" Impulsively, she unwound the prayer beads from her wrist and cupped them in one hand in timid offering. "Will you, for my sake, carry these on the day you stand protector with the King of Torenth? Mayhap the prayers that accompany them may offer *you* some protection."

Resignedly he held out his hand to receive the beads, briefly seeing a stream of blood spill from her hand to his. Among the beads twinkled a thumbnail-sized rondelle of enamelled gold that reminded him of the icon Count Mátyás was wearing—except that when he bent to look at it more closely, he saw that the glitter of blue enamel on gold was not the Blessed Virgin, but a wing-graced being with hands upraised in benediction, the palms set with twin flecks of some opalescent gemstone that somehow caught the light and almost seemed to glow from within.

Caught in the compass of the beads themselves, he could feel the quiet thrum of power, somehow akin to the tinkling laughter of a sunlit freshet, clean and potent. He wondered if she guessed what she had just handed him: an artefact undoubtedly of Deryni origin, its reservoir of grace augmented through her own devotion.

"It was my mother's gift before my first Communion," she said a little nervously at his guarded look of wondering question. " 'Tis said in Bremagne that coral gives healing and protection. The figure on the medal is meant to be my guardian angel. I—would have her guard *you*, my son—for I know I cannot sway you from what you feel you must do."

Her eyes were bright with tears as she blurted out the last, her lower lip trembling, and he took her hand in his and gently kissed it before easing to one knee before her, knowing that it was love that moved her in her ignorance, and love that impelled her concern.

"Mother, try to understand this, at least," he said gently, not releasing her hand. "When I came to my own throne, you hazarded life itself in my behalf. Now I must do the same for Liam."

"But, why?" she whispered.

"Because I am his overlord and protector, and sworn to defend him," Kelson said. "That is not a vow I take lightly. Nor, I promise you, do I receive your gift lightly." He closed his hand around the beads she had given him. "May I ask, as well, a mother's blessing?"

Releasing the hand he still held, he bowed his head very deliberately, closing his eyes as he felt the hesitant brush of her hands on his hair and then a firmer pressure that, unbeknownst to her, was a pressure of loving spirit as well as flesh, to which he gladly yielded, so that he might drink in its benison.

"Beloved son, you who are bone of my bone and flesh of my flesh," she whispered, "may God grant you wisdom and discernment and strength and mercy, to withstand the wiles of evil and stand steadfast in the Light. And may He bring you back safely to me," she added, "for I do love you so. *In nomine Patris, et Filii, et Spiritus Sancti.* Amen."

"Amen," he repeated, touching the handful of beads to his lips and then lifting his eyes to hers.

Openly weeping now, she clasped his face between her hands and bent to press her lips to his forehead. In answer, he slid his arms around her waist and clung to her for a long moment, his head against her lap. He had not realized until this moment just how anxious he really was, about what he must face when he went into Torenth—or how much this woman's blessing meant, to set him on that road.

But he dared not linger, for either his sake or hers. His duties recalled him, as they always would; and the morning would come all too swiftly. After hugging her closer for just a moment more, he drew back from her and got to his feet, keeping one of her hands in his, bending then in a courtly kiss, his lips only lightly brushing her knuckles.

"I must go now," he said. "I shall send back regular reports. You will not reject them if they come by less than ordinary means, will you?"

She stiffened slightly, pulling her hand from his. "By means of Duncan McLain?" She did not dignify the Deryni bishop by any title, deeming him damned for even being Deryni, much less having accepted the ordination then forbidden to those of his race.

"In part," he conceded. "I know you would prefer not to deal with him. You will also prefer not to be reminded regarding Transfer Portals—but they exist. There is one at Dhassa, there are several here, and there will be more at Beldour, I have no doubt—though whether access will be possible, I know not. At very least, I should be able to send messengers by land, as far as Dhassa, and from there—"

She had closed her eyes as he spoke, resistance back in every line of her taut body.

"Mother, I have never flaunted what I am, and I promise you that I never shall, unless I must, for I would not offend the sensibilities of those of my subjects who have yet to accept that the power of the Deryni is benign. But it will be important that Nigel, at least, receive news in a timely fashion. If I can, I will send to him, and you may inquire of him, if you wish to maintain the fiction that you must not involve yourself in such matters."

He did not stay to hear any answer or protest she might offer, only inclining his head in leave-taking and turning to make his way back, lightly fingering the prayer beads she had given him before slipping them inside his tunic as he crunched his way back along the garden path. Back inside the great hall waited the first of the men with whom he must treat regarding Torenth—whether friends to be won or enemies to be overcome, only time would tell.

CHAPTER SEVEN

*I am become a stranger unto my brethren, and an
alien unto my mother's children.*

Psalm 69:8

*T*hree days later, Kelson watched silently beside Morgan on the afterdeck
of the Caralighter ship *Rhafallia*, elbows braced against a forward rail as
the first of the twin lighthouses guarding the mouth of Coroth Harbor gradually emerged from the haze lightly veiling the Corwyn coast. High above,
perched in the fighting castle atop the ship's single mast, a lookout with the
green cockade of Morgan's sea service in his cap kept watch ahead, occasionally calling course adjustments to the helmsman manning the great starboard
steering rudder. The ship's painted sail had been loosely furled, the bright
color-pennons of Royal Gwynedd, Royal Torenth, and Corwyn trailing limp
from the top-rigging, for the modest breeze of the morning had fallen away
utterly by noon.

Now the measured splash of oars marked their progress rather than the rattle
of canvas, unrelieved by any of the sea-chanteys the men sometimes sang to set
the rhythm and relieve the boredom of a long haul. From behind them came the
rhythmic splash of a second set of oars, subtle reminder of the sleek Torenthi galley ghosting in their wake.

Kelson glanced back at the following ship, noting the bright-clad knot of
nobles lounging beneath a green-striped canopy amidships, then returned his
attention to the distant lighthouse, where crimson smoke had just begun to billow

from atop its fire-platform. Far forward in the bow of *Rhafallia*, watching beside Brendan and Payne, Liam suddenly pointed at the beacon with a cry of delight. Simultaneously, the first dull clang of the bell-buoys at the harbor mouth began to reach them, underlined by the long-drawn note of a horn, repeated several times and then answered on a lower note.

"Always a welcome sound," Morgan murmured, his gaze flicking down to the main deck, where Dhugal and Saer de Traherne were leaning against the port rail to better observe the approach through the harbor mouth.

Kelson only nodded, turning his gaze to the lofty towers and battlements of Coroth Castle thrusting upward from behind the more domestic bustle of the harbor's town. No fond sailor at the best of times, he had remained doubly uneasy since leaving Desse, never able to put from mind the presence of the Torenthi war galley that accompanied them—though, at least, fair winds had enabled them to make the journey in less than half the time it would have taken overland. Only today had the wind failed them.

There were children scrambling on the twin jetties of tumbled granite block that guarded the harbor mouth, waving and shouting with excitement as *Rhafallia* glided between—waving, too, at the foreign war galley following behind. Some of the sailors on both ships waved back. Kelson winced as the keel of *Rhafallia* scraped its length along the lowered harbor chain, just before they gained the more open water of the harbor proper.

"We'll soon be ashore," Morgan said, smiling faintly at the king's grimace of distaste.

"Is it that obvious?" Kelson replied.

"Not to anyone else."

They had come down to join the others by the time the two ships bumped gently alongside the main quay. There, reception parties were taking position before both ships: smart detachments of armed men in Morgan's livery. Farther back, Kelson could see two mounted officers amid a score of green-liveried men holding horses obviously intended for the new arrivals. Beyond, men in the livery of the town guard lined the mouth of the street leading up toward the castle.

As dockhands hefted a gangplank into place and crewmen secured it, the officers dismounted and one of them lifted down a bright-haired girl-child of about five. The child immediately wiggled from his grasp and bolted in the direction of *Rhafallia*, dodging among the forest of moving horses' legs with reckless abandon, her keeper jogging after her somewhat less handily.

"Pardon me, Sire," Morgan murmured, grinning single-mindedly as he slipped past Kelson to intercept his daughter.

"Papa!" she squealed. "Papa! Papa!"

Laughing, Morgan bent to receive her embrace, staggering a little under its force. Hugging her close, he scooped her off her feet and twirled her around in equally delighted reunion as she showered him with a flurry of exuberant kisses.

"Papa, you're home, you're home!"

"Why, Poppin, I do believe you've missed me," he answered, bestowing a kiss of his own on her nose. "Look who else is here. Have you a hug and a kiss for your godfather?"

As she twisted in her father's arms and saw him, Kelson grinned and held out his arms to her, feeling deliciously foolish—and happy—as she squirmed from Morgan's grasp to his, to renewed squeals of delight.

"Briony, my goodness, haven't you grown?" Kelson exclaimed, when they had exchanged enthusiastic kisses. "What a nice welcome!"

"I rode on Uncle Séandry's big horse!" Briony announced, settling happily into the king's arms as her father moved briskly on toward the Torenthi ship. "Can I ride home with you?"

"Why, of course you can."

As Liam and the other squires streamed past Kelson and his armful of small child, her youthful, blue-cloaked keeper caught up with his charge, rolling his eyes in mock exasperation as he sketched the king an apologetic bow.

"I apologize for the assault, Sire," he said with a grin. "Welcome to Coroth. Would you like me to take her?"

"No need," Kelson replied. "I expect that 'Uncle Séandry' could use a bit of a respite from this young lady."

"Uncle Séandry" was Sean Seamus O'Flynn, the Earl of Derry, once Morgan's aide and now his trusted lieutenant in Corwyn—and apparently as smitten with the charms of the ducal daughter as her father and Kelson himself. As they made their way back to the horses, Briony chattering happily about the excitement of the ride down from the castle, and the ships, and the exotic visitors disembarking behind them, Kelson found himself remembering the first time he had ever met the young earl: perched wide-eyed at his father's knee to watch as Morgan brought the just-knighted Derry before them to exchange the oaths whereby Derry entered the Deryni duke's personal service.

Though silver was beginning to thread the curly brown locks clubbed back in a warrior's knot, Kelson suspected that the white belt knotted about Derry's narrow waist was the same with which he had been knighted, more than a decade before. Only etched around the bright blue eyes could one find hint of the ordeals suffered by Derry in service of overlord and king, at the hands of a man who had been kinsman both to Mátyás and to young Liam, for whom horses were now being brought up.

Derry's easy manner turned momentarily to wariness as he saw the pair, but he did not falter in courtesy as he saw his lord's guests mounted. As Kelson swung up on his own mount, he found himself wondering, as often in the past, what lingering terrors might haunt Derry's dreams—and wondered anew whether Derry was strong enough to deal with those terrors if they reawakened in Torenth, for he knew Morgan wished to bring him along.

But under the hazy sunlight of these southern skies, such worries seemed somehow distant and diffuse. With Briony in the saddle before him, Kelson rode beside Count Mátyás, who paid indulgent court to Morgan's daughter and made courteous small talk as they passed through the streets of Corwyn's capital. Behind them, Rasoul kept up a running dialogue with Morgan regarding the architectural features of the town, which he had never visited before. Father Irenaeus rode beside Dhugal, the pair followed by Saer with Liam and the other royal squires and pages, and a mixed escort of Corwyn and Torenth men.

Richenda, Morgan's duchess, was waiting to greet them as they rode into the castle yard, with the three-year-old Kelric on her hip and a warm welcome for her husband, the king, and their noble guests. Of the principals among the new arrivals, only Mátyás was unknown to her; she had met Rasoul several times at court, over the past four years.

As had Bishop Arilan, who was standing farther up the stairs with Coroth's own bishop, Ralf Tolliver. As the two came down the steps and Rasoul gracefully performed appropriate introductions regarding his two countrymen, Kelson thought he detected a faint bristling on the part of Arilan; but wariness was only to be expected from one with powers similar to those of their guests and, therefore, well aware of potential dangers. Besides, there was no opportunity to inquire further, just then.

Meanwhile, the bustle attendant upon Morgan and his reunion with his young family left Kelson feeling more than usually wistful regarding the domestic emptiness of his own life. Briony favored him with another emphatic kiss before letting him hand her back into her father's outstretched arms, and beyond the pair he was aware of young Brendan making a beeline for his little half-brother, drawing Liam and Payne with him. As the brothers embraced, obviously devoted to one another, and the four boys headed off toward the stables, Kelson found himself looking for traces of Albin Haldane in the sunny-natured Kelric, and had to look away, blinking away the beginnings of tears.

Fortunately, the children were little more in evidence for what remained of the afternoon and evening, for the squires and pages had duties to perform before being released to the farewell supper being held in Liam's honor. Arilan, too, disappeared—gone with Tolliver to hear Evensong at the cathedral down in the town, Morgan's chamberlain told the king—thereby precluding any immediate inquiry regarding his reaction to their Torenthi guests. But the king did find opportunity to reassure himself regarding Derry.

While Richenda entertained Rasoul, Mátyás, and Father Irenaeus with refreshments and a leisurely stroll through the ducal gardens, Dhugal absenting himself to oversee the squires and pages, Kelson withdrew with Morgan and Derry for an ostensible briefing on recent intelligence gleaned from Torenth. En route to Morgan's library, where they intended to work, he silently advised Morgan of what he had in mind.

During the Mearan wars of several years back, making the most open use yet of their Deryni powers, he and Morgan had succeeded in persuading certain royal scouts to allow direct reading of their intelligence reports by means of magic, thus bypassing the intervening filter of interpretation, misremembering, or omission of important details. Even before that, Derry's utter trust in Morgan and his magic had allowed him to accept magical enhancements unthinkable in most humans—and perhaps had made him more vulnerable, when eventually taken prisoner by Wencit of Torenth.

Only Morgan perhaps knew the true extent of what Derry had suffered during those days and nights he lay captive in Wencit's prison; and since escaping Wencit's clutches, only Morgan had he willingly, and always reluctantly, allowed to touch his mind. Though Morgan had satisfied himself that all the bindings set by Wencit had been severed with his death, Kelson could not help wondering whether the scars from those bindings might still hamper Derry, if only because he believed they did.

"You've done good work," Kelson said, when Derry had finished his briefing. "There's just one other thing. I'll be blunt and ask whether you're sure you're up to the strain of going deep into Torenth with us."

Derry had risen to roll up the map he had used as part of the briefing, and faltered just slightly before continuing with his task, not looking up.

"I'm fine," he murmured.

"Derry, you needn't come along on this mission, if you aren't entirely comfortable with the notion," Kelson said.

"Sire, I shall never be entirely comfortable about anything to do with Torenth," the earl said quietly, slipping the map into a stiff leather tube. "But if I allow nightmares to interfere with my duties, then Wencit has won after all, hasn't he?"

Morgan raised one blond eyebrow, the grey eyes narrowing. "I thought you said the nightmares had stopped—years ago."

"They did," Derry replied, though a trifle too quickly for Kelson's taste. "But lately, knowing I'm about to go back into Torenth, I—sometimes still wake up in a cold sweat. I suppose there are some things that one can never really forget—even with help," he added, with a nervous glance at Morgan.

"Perhaps I ought to have another look," Morgan said quietly.

Derry shook his head vehemently, though he managed a taut ghost of a smile. "I do appreciate the offer, but I think I've had enough of other people inside my mind to last a lifetime. It's nothing like it once was—truly, it isn't."

"It wasn't an offer; it was a request," Morgan replied, with a sidelong glance at Kelson, who nodded. "In fact, it was a statement of intent."

Derry's head snapped toward Kelson in mute, panicked appeal, looking as if he might bolt.

"I'm sorry," the king said softly. "I'm afraid I have to insist—unless, of course, you prefer to stay behind. We must be certain. I saw your reaction when Count Mátyás and the others were disembarking this afternoon."

Shivering, Derry turned partially away from them, his arms clasped to his shoulders, not seeing what lay before physical vision.

"I know that he can't touch me now," he whispered. "He's dead. I *know* that. And I know up *here*"—he tapped a finger to one temple—"that what he did to me—and made me do—was no fault or failing of mine. But something in *here*"—he jabbed a hand at his stomach—"still cringes from the very thought of ever being touched that way again. It isn't either of you; it's that touching—by *anyone*. . . ." He shivered again and sank back onto his chair.

"Anyway, it wasn't Count Mátyás who spooked me this afternoon. At the time, I didn't even know who he was. I suppose it was Liam. I *know* he's just a boy, and was only a small child when Wencit died. But he's still Wencit's nephew, his sister's son. And Wencit put his stamp on everything he touched . . . including me," he added, almost in a whisper.

"Wencit wasn't *that* powerful," Morgan muttered.

Derry shook his head in emphatic denial. "You don't know that! You weren't there. You don't know what it was like, when he—forced his thoughts into mine, into the deepest recesses of who I am, and—made me believe, made me feel, made me betray . . . It was slimy, filthy, a—a violation even worse than—than the most revolting physical rape you can possibly imagine . . ."

As his voice choked off on a sob and he buried his face in one hand, Morgan quietly rose and came around behind his chair, gently but firmly clasping the taut shoulders and drawing Derry back against him, damping his distress and starting to invoke the triggers that would ease him into trance. Under any other circumstances, Kelson would have offered assistance, but he could sense Derry's shrinking resistance to even Morgan's touch, and knew he dared do nothing that might disrupt the fragile rapport the Deryni lord was teasing out. He knew that Morgan would never force the issue if it meant actually hurting Derry—not without cause beyond mere curiosity—but he was acutely aware of the halting nature of Morgan's progress.

Eventually Derry ceased resisting, as Kelson had prayed he would; and there followed a long stillness in which Kelson knew the other was probing deep into Derry's memories, looking again for any lingering taint of compulsions Wencit might have left. But the duke's soft sigh as he emerged from his own trance, leaving Derry quietly immersed in healing sleep, confirmed Kelson's hope that the other had found no serious cause for concern.

"If there's something still there," Morgan murmured, coming around to sit again, "it's beyond my detection. Someone better skilled, more formally trained, might be able to go deeper and find something—Arilan, maybe. But that assumes there'd be something to find, which I don't think there is—something potentially dangerous enough to warrant compelling such an intimate intrusion. His rape imagery isn't far off, even for what I just did. If anyone else were to try it . . ."

Kelson grimaced and shook his head, reminded anew how easy it was for those of their kind to become casual about the power they could wield so easily, against others unable to resist—how easy to justify, especially in times of stress. Hearing Morgan liken it to physical rape, he found himself flashing on unbidden images from his own meager insights in that regard—secondhand, and filtered through Rothana, but far more potent than he ever would have dreamed; for she had compelled him to absorb the full spectrum of fear and helplessness and violation that she gleaned from probing Janniver's memories, while seeking out the identity of her assailant.

The terror and despair of Derry's ravaging must have been infinitely worse: a violation of his innermost soul, utterly helpless before the will of Wencit of Torenth. But beyond rooting out the compulsions he had set, and blunting the memories of that ordeal, Morgan dared do little more. For good or for ill, Derry's experience had contributed to who he was, at all levels. To strip away all traces of that experience would leave him less than whole, more damaged than before.

"I certainly wouldn't force the issue," Kelson said quietly. "And most assuredly, not by Arilan. Besides, Arilan didn't seem any too sure himself about Furstáns. Did you see his expression when we rode into the yard this afternoon? I don't know whether it was Mátyás or Father Irenaeus to whom *he* took exception."

"I think we're all being spooked by the thought of what *any* Torenthi Deryni might do," Morgan muttered. "But if you're going to let Liam return to his kingdom—and I think you must do that—then we have to trust and hope that his champions will emerge to help him take up his throne and keep it. Reason might suggest that you keep him safe with you in Rhemuth for another few years; but as he himself pointed out, and by the reckoning of our kingdom as well as his own, the law says that he's a man at fourteen, and at least theoretically capable of functioning as king."

Kelson exhaled with a gusty sigh. "You don't need to convince *me*," he replied. "Here sits a man who had to do exactly that. And when I'm not letting my imagination run rampant, I confess that, within the bounds of caution, I'm inclined to trust the three Torenthis we've got with us right now. I think they genuinely care for the boy."

"Mátyás is still Mahael's brother," Morgan pointed out.

"I could hardly forget that," Kelson replied. "Speaking of whom, I suppose we ought to rejoin the good count and his companions. And I believe Derry was to take over from Dhugal, to keep a weather eye on Brendan and his squires' supper. What's your decision on allowing him to come with us to Beldour?"

"I think he would be devastated if I asked him to stay behind—despite his fears," Morgan replied. "Excluding him would confirm in his mind that he isn't to be trusted—and there's absolutely no evidence to suggest that."

Kelson nodded. "I agree. And facing up to his fears may well allow him to finally exorcise the last of his demons. Wake him up, then, and we'll say no more about it."

Half an hour later, Kelson was sitting down to the obligatory evening meal with their Torenthi guests, taken in Morgan's ducal council chamber rather than the more impersonal great hall. To fill out the numbers of what all hoped would be an informal affair—their last before embarking upon the series of state functions requisite to Liam's state return to Torenth—Morgan had invited several of his senior household officers. Bishops Tolliver and Arilan were also in attendance, returned from their devotions in the cathedral; but Arilan seemed little fortified by his meditations, and retained a measure of the wary reserve glimpsed during his initial introduction to Mátyás and Father Irenaeus—and it had to be one of them to whom Arilan was reacting, for he knew Rasoul from previous encounters over the past four years. Richenda, as the sole woman present, managed to give the affair a softer edge than might otherwise have been expected.

Fortunately, the evening ended early, partly through expected awkwardness and partly because of the morrow's departure. When leave had been taken, Rasoul and Mátyás were shown to quarters prepared for them in one of the castle towers, with Saer deputized to keep casual watch through the night and ensure their continued good manners. Father Irenaeus elected to sleep aboard the Torenthi galley, conveyed thence by the guard detail accompanying Bishop Tolliver back to his episcopal palace.

When the rest of Morgan's officers had also gone, leaving only Arilan with the king, Dhugal, Morgan, and Richenda—who had already warned Kelson to expect at least a brief discussion of bridal candidates—Kelson set aside his coronet and sat back in his chair with a weary sigh, watching while Dhugal cleared away the last of the meal's debris from one end of the table and Morgan produced a decanter of sweet Fianna wine. As the latter was poured into tiny silver cups and Dhugal pushed them before each place, Richenda pulled off her circlet and veil and loosed her red-gold hair, giving it a shake as she settled contentedly into the chair closest to Kelson.

"So much for social obligations," she said, twisting her hair back into a loose knot and securing it with a pair of golden pins. "At least everyone was well-behaved."

"I have hopes that will continue to be the case," Kelson replied, considering how to sound out Arilan. "It's probably as well that Liam was otherwise occupied this evening. I wonder how Brendan's supper went."

Morgan snorted softly and sat on the other side of the king. "With the feast he ordered up, they should all be groaning in their beds."

"Not drunk, I trust?" Arilan said, though his expression proclaimed this the least of his fears.

"Oh, Derry had his orders," Morgan assured him. "Our young charge is well prepared, I think."

Richenda chuckled lightly, shaking her head. "He has become quite the young man, hasn't he?—for all that he would remain a boy for a while longer. When he rode into the yard with Brendan and Rory, I scarcely recognized him. Can he really have grown so tall, just since Michaelmas?"

"He has grown in strength as well," Arilan murmured. "His shields are those of a man. Is that the work of the monk—Father Irenaeus, was it?"

"In part." Kelson set down his wine, choosing his next words carefully. "The good hieromonk seems to be precisely that: good, both in virtue and in ability. I almost trust him. I am—somewhat inclined to trust Mátyás as well," he added, watching for a reaction from Arilan.

The Deryni bishop sat back in his chair, his manner taking on a faintly guarded edge.

"Beware of any Furstán, Sire," he said. "And as for the monk—never forget that it was Mahael who sent him."

"Actually," Morgan said, "it was the Patriarch of Torenth who sent him."

"On Mahael's instructions, you may be sure."

"Yes, on Mahael's instructions," Kelson answered, "or at least his recommendation. But his credentials came directly from the Patriarch, who I very much doubt takes instructions from Mahael. Unless Irenaeus is far, far more skilled than I believe him to be—and far more devious—I do not think his brief runs beyond giving his prince the instruction needed for the ceremony of installation—which is of considerable complexity, as you must know."

"I am quite aware of the complexities," Arilan replied. "And of the opportunities for things to go wrong—and for them to be *made* to go wrong."

"If that is intended," Kelson replied, "I cannot think that Irenaeus is any part of it. I have several times observed his celebration of the sacred offices, the better to understand what we will be witnessing in Beldour. He strikes me as a man of genuine piety, without guile. Do you assume that he would hold his vows less sacred than your own?"

"I merely point out that he is Deryni, Torenthi, and favored of Mahael," Arilan said mildly. "On those points, I assume nothing."

"And *we* have assumed nothing," Morgan said a little sharply. "Do *you* assume that we simply gave him free rein with the boy, as soon as he arrived at court? Of course we did not. Both of us interviewed him quite extensively, before allowing him access to Liam, as did Duncan. All of us Truth-Read his answers—and found no deception. One of us was always present when he worked with Liam, save for pastoral converse."

"I'm certain you mean that to be reassuring," Arilan said a little testily. "However, I should not have to remind a Deryni how easily those of our kind can abuse such a position of trust—*especially* a priest."

Kelson allowed himself an exasperated sigh, wondering how they had gotten into an argument about Irenaeus.

"Why are we bickering among ourselves?" he muttered. "Denis, I will not deny the distant possibility that treachery might be his eventual intent—but subtle treachery requires time, of which he had little. And as for more overt treachery—well, I believe Liam strong enough, both in moral and magical strength, to resist any meddling within the context of holy offices."

"You clearly hold a high opinion of the boy," Arilan said. "He still is the nephew of Wencit and Mahael."

"And of Mátyás," Kelson retorted, going on the offensive. "Earlier, when I indicated that I was somewhat inclined to trust him, you side-stepped comment. Instead, you diverted us to a discussion—nay, almost an argument—about Father Irenaeus. And yet, when Rasoul first introduced Mátyás this afternoon, your reaction seemed to evidence not hostility, but surprise and . . . what?"

Arilan leaned back in his chair, eyes averted, one fingertip methodically tracing the rim of his cup for several seconds.

"There may be . . . grounds for guarded hope in that regard," he said quietly.

Kelson sat back abruptly, casting questioning looks at the others, but got only varying reactions of bewilderment, wariness, and speculation.

"What are you saying?" he asked softly. "What does that mean, 'guarded hope'? He isn't—surely you're not implying that he's—a member of the Camberian Council?"

Arilan shook his head, smiling faintly but not looking up, no doubt well aware that all of them would be Truth-Reading his response.

"I may not answer that," he replied.

"But, you do know him?" Morgan ventured.

Again Arilan shook his head. "I have never met him before today."

Which was precisely true, Kelson knew. Which meant that Mátyás could not be a part of the Council, despite Arilan's refusal to answer the direct question. Kelson had no doubt that selected members of the Council besides Arilan would be at Liam's enthronement ceremony in Beldour, at least unofficially, to monitor the proceedings. But what Mátyás's role in all of this might be, Kelson had no idea.

Was Arilan simply being cagey, or was he trying to tell them something without violating the letter of his oaths to the Council, which they always had been given to understand were formidable. Kelson knew of at least two former members who had circumvented their oaths—both of them now dead, though apparently not through the direct consequences of their disobedience. Of the present Council, he had met only three other members besides Arilan, and could not imagine any of them aiding a Furstán against Gwynedd.

But if Mátyás was *not* a member of the Council, why was Arilan at such pains to protect him, and what was he hiding?

"I must ask you to clarify what you've just told us," Kelson said carefully. "I will not command it, because this obviously has something to do with the Council, even if Mátyás isn't a member—and I accept that you mayn't tell us that he is or isn't. But you've made a point of reminding us about the treachery of Furstán blood— yet now you suggest that there might be cause to trust this particular Furstán."

Arilan cast a furtive glance at Morgan, Dhugal, and Richenda before returning his gaze to the king.

"That would be an overstatement," he said. "Let us merely say that I am . . . aware of certain . . . connections he has with Deryni of another powerful family. I may not disclose that connection without leave, and it is no guarantee of his intentions. It had not occurred to me that he might be part of this delegation. Nor had I considered that he might be involved in Liam's enthronement; he is said to be not at all political. But his powers undoubtedly are formidable."

"Do you have reason to suspect that he would support his brothers in whatever treachery they might be planning?" Dhugal asked.

"Let us simply say that the thought had never crossed my mind that Mahael's youngest brother would *not* support whatever might further the fortunes of the Furstán family—until I considered this connection, and its possible influence. It now becomes clear that nothing is clear, and that Mátyás is now even more an unknown quantity: undoubtedly powerful, if he chose to play political games, yet never has there been any hint of political ambition on his part. Some men really *are* content to tend their vines and lead a quiet life—as he was at pains to reassure us over supper."

"I detected no false note in his remarks," Morgan said quietly.

"Nor did I," Arilan said. "But we must wonder why he made such a point to tell us. To put us off our guard? If so, in what direction? Our assumption would be that he will support Mahael and Teymuraz in whatever it is they plan, if he were to become involved at all; I think he cannot be neutral, else he would not have agreed to act as his brother's emissary in this matter."

"Perhaps," said Richenda, "his declaration about the quiet life is meant to reassure us that he *would* take Liam's part against his brothers, in the interests of a continued quiet life. Perhaps it was even a veiled offer to ally with those who will be supporting Liam in the taking up of his throne."

Arilan shook his head. "I cannot say. He could be a powerful ally or an implacable foe. At this point, either is possible."

"Well, that's a better position than before," Kelson murmured, "with at least the possibility of an ally in the Torenthi camp."

"A possibility isn't good enough," Morgan retorted. "How can we find out? This—connection you spoke of: Could they confirm or deny?"

"Once I have made contact—perhaps. Whether they *would* confirm or not might be another matter. But I can do nothing until Beldour—or perhaps the Ile d'Orsal." He sighed. "Eventually, I must persuade the Council to allow a Portal here at Coroth."

"You set up a temporary one at Llyndruth Meadows," Kelson reminded him. "Could you not do the same here?"

"Not now," Arilan said. "The energy expense would be too dear, with what may lie ahead—and we will be at the Orsal's court tomorrow. It is possible that I may be able to access a Portal."

"Is the Orsal part of the Council?" Richenda asked, flashing him a smile of mock innocence as he looked at her sharply.

"You know I may not answer that. But another contact will be able to instruct me regarding Portal access. And if circumstances do not permit it, the query can wait until we reach Beldour. Whatever Mátyás's political alignment, I think he will make no move before the ceremony—and a full week has been allowed for rehearsals: plenty of time to deal with Mátyás, for good or for ill."

CHAPTER EIGHT

The daughters of kings are in thy honour.

Psalm 44:10

*A*fter the somewhat taut conversation regarding Mátyás, and with the hour growing late, Kelson had hoped to escape the threatened nuptial discussions—especially in light of his secret and reluctant mission at the Orsal's court. He wondered if Richenda knew about Araxie, for he knew she was a student of Rothana's uncle Azim. But Arilan, once he had agreed to consult with his private contacts, seemed determined to proceed with a review of matrimonial prospects—if only the ones that might suit Liam.

"I accept that perhaps this is not the best time to discuss your own prospects, with Liam's enthronement still ahead of you," the Deryni bishop said. "But I assure you that his marriage will have been a topic of increasingly lively speculation among his own people, as the day of his return draws near."

Kelson briefly closed his eyes, girding himself for many of the same old arguments.

"Denis, he is only fourteen," he muttered.

"True enough," Arilan replied. "But like yourself, he is a king with a succession to secure. His marriage will be a high priority, once he settles back into his own court—and no amount of dithering on your own behalf is going to change that."

"I am not dithering!"

"You're dithering," Morgan said blandly. "But we'll let that pass, under the circumstances. Denis is right, however: If you won't talk about your own marriage prospects, we at least need to talk about your rival's, before you fling him back among his own countrymen—and countrywomen."

Kelson sighed and picked up his cup, draining it in a single draught, then rolled its chill silver against his forehead, desperate for some stalling tactic, well aware that discussion would not stop with Liam. He was not ready to tell them of Rothana's proposition, and certainly could not yet bring himself to talk about Araxie, who they thought was beyond consideration.

"I'm sorry," he murmured, not looking at any of them. "I know I *am* going to have to talk about it eventually. It isn't easy to accept that I can't marry the woman I love. That said, however, it would be nice to at least *like* whatever woman I do marry."

"Kelson, you know our sympathies are with you," Richenda said softly. "And you know that I *have* tried to change Rothana's mind. Repeatedly."

Kelson bowed his head into one hand, covering his eyes, elbow propped on the table. "I do know that," he whispered, "and I do appreciate your efforts. She—has her own logic, and I—can't gainsay it, much though I dislike her conclusion."

"But you must respect it," Richenda replied, "and you must accept it—and accept that she has reasons that even she may not be able to articulate clearly at this time. However much you may feel betrayed by what she did, in marrying Conall—or however much she may *think* you feel betrayed—her own feeling of having betrayed *you* overwhelms it all."

"But she didn't—"

"Of course she did not. But you must recognize that her love for you also became bound with your love for Gwynedd, whose bridegroom you were long before Rothana came into your life." She gestured toward the two rings on his hand, the signet of Gwynedd and Sidana's ring. "It was for Gwynedd that she let herself be persuaded that marriage with Conall might preserve at least part of the dream that you and she shared for Gwynedd—and what she does now, she also does for the sake of Gwynedd. And again for the sake of Gwynedd, *you* must go forward with your dream—but with another queen at your side."

Kelson was nodding by the time she finished, eyes closed and lips tightly pressed together, knowing it was true, no matter the pain that admission cost. After a moment of taut silence, he allowed himself a heavy sigh and made himself look up at Richenda.

"I know that you're right," he said quietly. "And I do appreciate what you're trying to do—all of you." He drew another deep breath and exhaled gustily. "Very well. Trot out your candidates, for me and for Liam. But I make no promises."

For answer, Richenda rose to fetch from the sideboard a small wooden chest, which she set on the table before the king. Inside were more than a score of miniature portraits and sketches, which Richenda laid out on the table and proceeded to identify by name and lineage. Kelson suppressed a groan as he saw their number.

As the arguments for and against each candidate were offered, one person or another always managed to find serious fault. Arilan judged one candidate of insufficient rank for the King of Gwynedd. Dhugal declared another too boring—he had met her. Morgan opined that a third was, in fact, rather older and plainer than depicted—and dull, to boot, though the political alliance would be acceptable.

"That presumes that I'd find dull children acceptable," Kelson pointed out sourly. "Since I'm under the impression that the purpose of this exercise is to produce suitable heirs, I hardly think that the lady can be considered a serious contender. Nor would I inflict such a bride on Liam."

When a likeness of Noelie Ramsay came up—an exquisite miniature painted on ivory, of a handsome young woman with soulful eyes and masses of dark hair—Kelson fell suddenly silent.

"Yes?" Richenda said hopefully.

"No," Kelson replied.

"Well, you certainly don't want Liam to marry her," Arilan muttered. "Her dowry will include considerable land in Meara. You can't afford to give Torenth a foothold on your western border."

"I don't intend to do that," Kelson said.

As he glanced at Dhugal for support, he decided to reveal at least a part of what had come of his disastrous meeting with Rothana. Some semblance of a plan had begun to take shape in the past days, at least regarding Noelie and Rory, and tonight seemed as good a time as any, to try out his proposal on his closest advisors.

"Actually," he said, "I have another match in mind for the lady."

Arilan looked immediately at Dhugal, obviously mistaking Kelson's previous glance for intention.

"Surely not—"

"Good God, no!" Kelson said quickly, as Dhugal shook his head in alarm. "It has never even been discussed. No, the lady's heart lies elsewhere."

"Ah, a love match," the bishop guessed, as Richenda cocked an eyebrow in question. "With whom?"

"My cousin Rory."

The name silenced Arilan, and elicited a thoughtful nod from Richenda, but their expressions told Kelson that both of them immediately saw at least some of the positive implications. Dhugal and Morgan, of course, had already known.

"I'm glad I see no disagreement," he said mildly. "It was Rothana who brought the prospect to my attention. It seems that when Noelie and her family came to court last summer for her brother's betrothal, she and Rory formed an attachment. Rory had backed off from the relationship, because he knew the council was hoping *I* would marry Noelie—but that's never been a possibility, so far as I'm concerned. I could never marry into Meara again."

Richenda nodded slowly, smiling faintly, and Kelson found himself wondering how much she knew about Araxie. Arilan looked decidedly uncomfortable with the notion.

"I would be interested to know what Nigel thinks of this idea," the bishop said. "Or have you told him yet?"

"I told him," Kelson said, "and I postponed any further discussion until I return. I've asked him to consider any potential problems that might be attendant upon such a match, and to come up with suggestions for resolving them. I also pointed out that *I* do not intend to marry Noelie Ramsay, regardless of what else might be decided, so he might as well let Rory be happy."

"That is an admirably generous statement," Richenda said neutrally. "And I can see immediate benefits to Gwynedd. Unlike you, Rory could live in Meara, and provide a permanent Haldane presence there. And their issue, along with the issue of Brecon and Richelle, would ensure that Haldane interests and that last link with former Mearan sovereignty are forever merged."

"It did seem to *me* to be a happy and peaceful resolution to a very long-standing problem," Kelson agreed, bracing himself for reaction to his next proposal, which addressed the probable source of Arilan's misgivings. "I've—suggested to Nigel that, eventually, I would like to make Rory my viceroy in Meara. I've already agreed to confirm Brecon as Earl of Kilarden, on the day he marries Richelle, so Rory will need a superior Mearan title—perhaps Duke of Ratharkin."

"That would eventually give Rory two ducal titles," Arilan pointed out.

"True enough," Kelson agreed. "But only if he retains Nigel's Carthmoor succession—which shouldn't be his anyway." He drew a bracing breath. "There's no question that the title rightly belongs to Albin, once Nigel is gone. To that end, as part of the marriage settlement, I propose to ask that Nigel restore the boy to his proper place in the succession. Rory will still have a dukedom, so this doesn't change the expectation he gained when Nigel first passed over Albin—and he doesn't even have to wait for his father to die."

"It seems a fair resolution to *me*," Dhugal said, with a glance at Morgan, though Richenda looked immediately dubious.

"Nigel will never agree," Arilan muttered. "And even if he does, I believe Albin's mother will have something to say about the matter. Everyone knows she intends him for the Church."

"His mother has enough to say about her own life—and mine," Kelson replied. "If Albin himself chooses the religious life for which she's trying to groom him, I'll accept that, if it's his decision; there have been Haldanes in the Church before. But I want him to have the options of choice that should accompany his royal birth."

"Kelson—" Richenda reached out to adjust one of the portraits on the table before them, not looking at him. "Kelson, she will not thank you for this."

"And I do not thank her for clinging to her stubborn pride, when I have told her that I bear her no resentment for having married Conall!" Kelson retorted. "Nor do I thank her for presuming to make this decision on behalf of her son— who should have been *our* son!"

"Kelson—"

He shook his head, all his tight-reined pain and frustration suddenly erupting.

"Do not press me in this, Richenda, for I can be as immovable as she," he warned. "She *shall* yield in the matter of Albin, if I—if I have to seize the boy and bring him up myself! I cannot force her to marry me, but I can and will ensure that Albin Haldane shall have the inheritance that should be his!"

"And how will you do that?" Morgan said quietly. "Will you force Nigel to agree? I suppose you could. You *are* the king—and with powers that lesser mortals can scarcely imagine, much less comprehend. No wonder they fear us. At very least, you could certainly throw Nigel in prison, strip him of his title, bestow it upon Albin. Not even Rothana could stop you from doing that, if you chose. You might even be able to force her to marry you. But you will do none of these things."

Kelson had whirled to stare at Morgan as he spoke, all the color draining from his face, and he slowly collapsed back into his chair, feeling suddenly light-headed, shocked at how easy it might have been, to step across that line into prideful power, no matter how righteously intended.

"He—he *must* agree," he whispered. "He must do it for Rory, so that he may wed where his heart desires, not as duty compels. And *she* must agree, for Albin's sake, so that *he* may be free to choose according to his heart—as I would wish, for my own son." He paused to swallow. "And I—I must . . . do as Rothana bids me do, and marry . . . elsewhere. . . ."

And marry the bride she has chosen for me, he added in the grieving loneliness of his own thoughts.

In the awkward silence that fell among them, Morgan exchanged troubled glances with Richenda, who slowly reached out to cover Kelson's hand with hers.

"Kelson—there is something you should know," she said tentatively. "Something that may give you some measure of comfort. I am not certain that even Rothana is wholly aware of it as yet—at least not consciously.

"You spoke of her pride as the impediment to your marriage: her refusal to forgive herself for losing faith, for believing you dead, for marrying Conall. Perhaps it *was* pride, in the beginning. But not now."

"Then, *what?*" Kelson asked.

"I think," she said, "that it is not just marriage with you, but marriage itself, that now seems inappropriate."

"I don't understand," Kelson whispered, stunned. "What are you saying?"

Richenda sighed, briefly glancing at all of them before returning her attention to the cheerless tracing of her fingertip on the table.

"At the risk of sounding callous, I must point out her condition when first you met her, my prince. Quite bluntly, she was under vows of religious obedience, vows of service. Caught up in the stirrings she felt for you, she decided to set aside her vows—which she had every right to do, for they were not yet permanent—and was prepared to turn her life to service as your queen—a Deryni queen for Gwynedd. Then, believing you dead, she still was prepared to take on that life of service as Gwynedd's queen, but at Conall's side rather than yours—because the work was and is important. Once you returned, and he died as he did, all of that changed."

"Gwynedd still needs a queen," Kelson said numbly. "*I* still need a queen."

"No one would dispute that," Richenda replied. "But Rothana is correct in pointing out that, in the eyes of many, *she* is no longer as acceptable a choice as she once would have been. Your queen should be a woman above reproach, without a past; she has borne the child of an executed traitor—a stigma very difficult to erase, as I have cause to know full well. It is a burden that is not eased by the fact that this child could become a serious threat to the very throne you and she would protect."

"*Any* child could become a threat to my throne," Kelson said bitterly. "We cannot know the future. And the other could be overcome; *you* have overcome it."

"Albin is not the most compelling part of the dilemma," Richenda replied. "Nor is the traitorous betrayal of her late husband. But given these impediments, either of which might be overcome singly, we must return to that first, inescapable part of the equation—which is her long-term commitment to a life of service."

"No!" Kelson blurted. "Her commitment was to *me*! It is our love that is the inescapable part of the equation. She loved me! She *still* loves me! She told me so, but a few short days ago!"

"Kelson, Kelson, my dear, sweet prince . . ." Richenda twined her fingers together, daring to meet his eyes. "I am searching for words that will not cause you further pain. Please believe that these past three years have not been any easier for her than for you. She still loves you, of *course*—and once loved you in a way that bade her put aside her holy vows to God, out of love for you and for the chance to make a difference as Gwynedd's queen.

"Believing you dead, she still put aside her vows, for the sake of the love you had shared—and again, to serve Gwynedd—and married Conall."

"I never blamed her for that," Kelson whispered. "Everyone had good reason to believe me dead; and if I *had* been dead, and she Conall's eventual queen, she would have been in a position to fulfill many of the same dreams that she and I had shared. That is truly what I would have wished."

"And if you *had* been dead, that is precisely what would have happened," Richenda said, "though God knows how Gwynedd would have fared, under Conall's rule. But you weren't dead. You came back—and suddenly, everything changed."

"Would she have preferred that I hadn't come back?" he said bitterly.

"Of course not. But everything *had* changed. She had left behind a long-cherished vocation to become wife, widow, and mother in the space of less than a year. And in the aftermath of such change, as she has searched her heart for a future, and pondered meanings in all that has transpired, she has come to realize that it was always the notion of service that called to her—first, simple service to God, and then that more specialized service to Gwynedd and to our Deryni race, which is no longer possible in the way she had planned. It was never just marriage with you, or even marriage at all, which called her, much though she does love you—and content though you both might have been, I think, had things not happened as they did.

"But things are as they are, and nothing can change that. The impediments do stand, to her being queen: widow of a traitor, mother of a potential rival to your throne. And meanwhile, there is still great service that she may do for Gwynedd *and* its king: no longer by becoming the physical mother of your heirs—for Albin's very existence has already complicated *that* succession for you—but by becoming a spiritual mother for the heirs of Gwynedd—especially Gwynedd's Deryni heirs."

"I still don't understand," Kelson said dully.

"Try, my prince. Think where she has passed the nearly three years since Albin's birth. She has been with the Servants of Saint Camber. Do you truly understand what it has meant, that you and Dhugal found their village?"

Kelson only looked at her, for he had no idea where her question was leading.

"Think of it, Sire. For nearly two centuries, they have lived apart from the rest of Gwynedd, humans and Deryni, side by side, and perhaps blended now, so that there is very little difference. You experienced their power; you, better than anyone in this room, know how much we might learn from them. How much have they preserved of Saint Camber's own wisdom?

"We are beginning to catch glimpses, as they assist in the reinstatement of his shrine in Rhemuth—and that, Rothana assures me, is only the beginning. Think how much more they could do, if they had the patronage of someone of her stature: a trained Deryni with important connections in lands where Deryni are still honored for their talents; a royal princess in her own right, mother of a future priest or bishop—or a royal duke, if you prefer—who could help them carry on their work."

"She could do that as queen," Kelson said desperately. "God knows, theirs is a good and worthy cause—but she need not immure herself to do this. She could be the royal patron of such a place, and support its work, and *still* be queen beside me, and the mother of future kings. Another could take up this work with the Servants!"

Richenda sadly shook her head. "Sire, she is proposing to give her life's service for the future of *all* the people of Gwynedd, not just its king. You have heard, I know, of the ancient *scholae* where those of our race once taught and learned the *ars magica*, even the gifts of Healing. They did not have to stumble upon these talents half-blind, as Alaric and Dhugal and even I have done. With the help of the Servants, it is in Rothana's mind to establish a new Deryni *schola*: a safe refuge where Deryni may learn to use their gifts. In all this land of yours, there is no other so well suited to do this—and even so, teachers will have to be brought in from outside Gwynedd; already, Azim has been to Saint Kyriell's to assess their needs.

"Reassembling the lost knowledge will be an enormous undertaking, for our numbers have never been great, even in Torenth and other lands where Deryni were never persecuted—and our influence has always been vastly disproportionate to our numbers." She flashed him a forbearing smile. "By the time of the Interregnum, much of the higher knowledge had become the domain of scholars or opportunists; and the advent of Deryni persecution, so soon after the Restoration, destroyed the formal institutions of Deryni learning as well as thousands of individuals. The promulgation of the Laws of Ramos crippled and all but destroyed us as a race, and the simultaneous sweeping away of the great Deryni healing and teaching orders meant that most of our formal knowledge was lost—though it *can* be recovered, in time.

"The task will not be completed in our lifetimes—and it will *never* be completed, if it is not begun. But Rothana proposes to begin it—a task requiring total commitment. You, in turn, need the total commitment of a full-time queen and mother of your heirs. I honestly do not see how the two may be joined."

Kelson found himself reeling under the onslaught of revelations Richenda had offered, and he briefly lowered his head on his arms, fighting back near-nausea. With the gradual abatement of the sick churning in his stomach came a calmer, more resigned acknowledgement that the logic—Richenda's *and* Rothana's—was sound—alas, all too sound. Now he began to understand his last conversation with Rothana, and the proposition she had offered him—and with that understanding finally came reluctant acceptance—and a numb resignation to the fate she had decreed for him—which, given everything Richenda had outlined, perhaps was, indeed, best for Gwynedd, in the end.

Schooling his expression to one of stolid calm, he raised his head and glanced at his silent companions, surreptitiously wiping his sleeve across damp eyes as he turned his gaze across the portraits of prospective brides still spread on the table before them. He could not yet bring himself to confide the commission with which Rothana had charged him, regarding his cousin Araxie, but he decided he might take temporary refuge in at least pretending academic interest in their interrupted discussion of bridal candidates. His eyes lit on the miniature of Noelie Ramsay, now happily out of contention, and he reached out to turn it gently face-down on the table.

"We can put this one aside, I think," he said quietly, pulling closer two ink sketches beside it. "Did someone say that these are the Hort of Orsal's daughters?"

"They are," Richenda said, as if the preceding outburst had not taken place. "The older girl is called Elisabet. She is said to be quite stunning. I am told that the sketch does not do her justice. You may judge for yourself tomorrow. Also, her younger sister, Marcelline—just on the brink of womanhood, and perhaps more suitable for our younger bachelor king, in a few years' time. Both would make worthy consorts."

"And that one?" Kelson asked, with a gesture toward the miniature of a pretty brunette.

"Ursula, a granddaughter of one of the Howiccan princes," Arilan offered. "She is rich, accomplished, politically acceptable; the line is healthy."

Only half listening, Kelson sat back and allowed them to rattle on about the latest spate of candidates, taking faint consolation in the knowledge that Rory, at least, might achieve a match of potential happiness. His own happiness no longer seemed an issue; Richenda's revelations had left him in something of a state of shock. The notion of actually giving up Rothana still made him heartsick; but as the voices of the others droned on, examining the virtues and foibles of various "suitable" bridal candidates, including several he had never heard mentioned before, he found his attention wandering . . . and found his gaze occasionally lighting on a portrait already set aside with that of Noelie Ramsay: the painted likeness of his cousin Richelle, the sister of the bride Rothana had chosen for him, who was already contentedly betrothed to Brecon Ramsay and, therefore, out of the marriage race.

There had never been a companion portrait of the younger Araxie, whose "imminent" match with a distant Howiccan prince had been rumored for several years. Nonetheless, Kelson found himself taking repeated glances at the likeness of the raven-haired Richelle, who favored her Haldane blood.

And much against his will, he found himself superimposing on those classic features the gamin, pixie face of a much younger girl, with straggly blond braids and pale eyes—an annoying yet engaging child with whom he had played in the gardens at Rhemuth. . . .

CHAPTER NINE

Let no man despise thy youth.

I Timothy 4:12

The morning dawned fair and bright for the crossing to the Ile d'Orsal, with a steady crosswind all the way. As the towers of Coroth disappeared into the coastal mist behind them, far beyond the following galley, Kelson tried not to dwell on what lay ahead, both in Torenth and, more immediately, at the Orsal's court. After he had retired at last from the bridal deliberations of the previous night, ghost-glimpses of Araxie intruded on his dreams. Grimacing, he ran a finger inside the neck of a crimson Haldane tunic whose collar was just a bit too tight.

At least Liam himself, standing at the rail between him and Morgan, seemed somewhat more resigned to what was unfolding. In understated acknowledgment of the role he must now assume, the boy had put aside his Haldane livery in favor of a plain white shirt belted over black breeches and boots, with his squire's dagger thrust through the back of a knotted sash of tawny silk. His full sleeves billowed in the breeze as he leaned against the rail at Kelson's side and squinted against the bright sparkle ahead. Since setting sail from Coroth, something in his manner, his poise, even a subtle shift to his way of phrasing, suggested a greater self-confidence than Kelson had noted hitherto, as if his last supper with his fellow squires and pages the night before had somehow been a rite of passage into manhood, helping him put his childhood behind him.

The blue water of the Great Estuary became gradually murky as they sailed between the Tralian headlands and the jutting upthrusts of basalt that were the Ile, roiled by the spill from the great River Thuria, whose tributaries served land-locked R'Kassi and all but one of the Forcinn buffer states. The wind held steady, funnelled by the high cliffs, so that even when they passed beneath the green-and-white striped pharos guarding Orsalis Harbor, they were not obliged to resort to the oars.

Liam watched unspeaking as the Orsal's great, three-tiered summer palace of Horthánthy came into view above the busy port, ranging his gaze over the port's defenses with a tactician's air of calculation before returning his attention to the palace: an exuberant array of graceful open arches and slightly domed roofs, soft verdigris against the chalk-white summit.

"The king's palace at Beldour has rooftop gardens such as those," he said to neither Kelson nor Morgan in particular, noting the greenery projecting above the topmost balconies. "The color is different, though—a sort of milky blue, that bit more intense than the sky on a clear day. I've not seen that color in all of Gwynedd."

"And you've obviously missed it," Kelson replied, smiling faintly as he watched Liam. "Aside from the dangers, I expect you'll be glad to be home."

Liam ducked his head, momentarily an awkward boy again. "Nothing will be the same," he murmured. "Nothing."

" 'Tis the way of the world," Morgan said quietly. "*Nothing* stays the same. But that doesn't have to be a bad thing. As king, you can make a difference."

"Perhaps," Liam replied, looking dubious. "But not for a while yet. Not until I wield the full power of Furstán."

Pensive, his manner inviting no further exploration of the subject, he ranged his gaze out ahead. Off to the right, an anchored row of black war galleys caught his eye: six sleek coursing ships moored side by side like a floating platform, mast-heads streaming tawny pennons ensigned with the white roundel and black leaping hart of Torenth. Along the decks of the galleys, their crews were lined up smartly beside the oars, which were shipped upright in salute, like black, spiky insect legs.

As a single, warbling trumpet call floated across the chop, Liam straightened and then moved apart from Kelson and Morgan to stand alone by the starboard rail, shading his eyes against the glare, gazing out at the black ships that obviously had come to be his escort home. In the bow of one of the ships, Kelson caught the glint of sunlight on brass as they were scanned by a man with a spyglass, who closed down his glass and turned to give an order as *Rhafallia* began crossing their bows.

In perfect unison, the six crews sank to one knee and raised both palms in

salute, like priests giving benediction, breaking into a deep, rhythmic chant—
"*Fur-stán-Lajos! Fur-stán-Lajos!*"

Liam stiffened as he realized what they were chanting, understood what they
were doing, tight-reined emotion flickering briefly across the guarded features.
Slowly he lowered the hand he had lifted to shade his eyes. Slowly he drew himself to attention. And as he, too, thrust his palms upward, returning their salute,
the chanting shifted to a roar of wild and spontaneous cheering and ululation,
some of the men now brandishing curved daggers or whipping off hats or head-
shawls to flap at him in welcome.

Ragged cheering continued as *Rhafallia* sailed past the galleys, Liam occasionally saluting them again—even moving to the stern so they could see him longer.
The cheering only died away when *Rhafallia* turned into the wind and dropped
her sails a few cable-lengths from the quay, a crewman in the bow tossing out a
line so a pilot boat could take them in tow.

The boy was flushed and bright-eyed as he came back to Kelson and Morgan,
occasionally grinning when he would glance astern at their escort galley, now also
in tow, and the black ships beyond.

"They knew me!" he said breathlessly. "They gave me salute as *padishah!*"

"They did, indeed," Morgan said, smiling, "and so you are."

"I know I am, but—until now, I am not certain I truly believed it. I have spent
nearly a third of my life away from my kingdom."

Kelson, too, ventured a faint smile as he turned away to watch the distance
close between ship and quay, breathing a silent prayer that Liam would, indeed,
be a *padishah* his people would welcome.

Order quickly emerged from the seeming chaos that always greeted an
arrival at Orsalis Port, as the *Rhafallia* bumped gently against the bustling dock
and crewmen began securing lines ashore. Scores of brightly clad onlookers
milled behind a mostly amiable cordon of port constabulary, hopeful of catching a
glimpse of the visitors. Children with wooden flutes played a piping welcome as
they disembarked.

The Orsal's chief chamberlain was waiting at the foot of *Rhafallia*'s gangplank
to greet them: Vasilly Dimitriades, well known to both Morgan and Kelson from
previous visits, a smiling, stick-thin individual in sea-green robes and an office-
chain of golden cockleshells, who alternated between bowing and beaming as
Rasoul and Mátyás joined them and courtesies were exchanged. Vasilly then
began directing his master's guests, by twos, toward a string of small, brightly
canopied carts, each one little more than an upholstered double chair atop a pair
of wheels, drawn and pushed by teams of liveried runners. Liam had never seen
such conveyances, and looked less than certain as Kelson headed him toward the
second one. A guard captain was waiting expectantly with the crew of the first

cart, presumably to ride with the chamberlain for the trip to the summit. Kelson mounted the second cart without hesitation, and its burly brakeman held out a hand to assist Liam as well.

"They rarely take horses up to the palace," Kelson explained, patting the seat beside him as Morgan and Brendan got into the third cart. Rasoul and Mátyás were shown to the fourth, and the others paired off in succeeding ones. "Remember that this is the Orsal's summer residence. Protocol is relaxed, and there's rarely much urgency about getting from port to palace. In truth, there's rarely much urgency about *anything* at the Orsal's court, as you'll see," he added with a chuckle. "In any case, you surely don't fancy walking up *that*, do you?"

Liam's glance upward at the steep road snaking toward the palace apparently convinced him that the carts were, indeed, probably a superior form of transport—and riding with Kelson would keep at bay the question of Liam's precise status, fellow king or still royal squire. Clambering up onto the seat, he kept a nervous grip on the chair arm at first, as the carts began moving across the esplanade in colorful procession and then took to the narrow road, but he soon relaxed and let himself be caught up in Kelson's running commentary on the view and what they might expect during this brief visit to Kelson's old ally.

What they did not expect was treachery. The attack came when they had nearly reached the palace gate, just at the last but one of the sharp switchbacks, where the edge fell away to their left in a breathtaking vista to the rocks and the sapphire depths below. With nary a hint of warning, the man between the pulling shafts suddenly stopped and whirled to thrust the shafts sharply over his head, tipping the cart backward to tangle both Liam and Kelson amid the cart's silk canopy, through which the brakeman began stabbing viciously with a long dagger.

Liam somehow managed to scramble clear—on the side toward the sheer plunge to the rocks below—and only saved himself by grabbing frantically for a handful of the canopy's fringe, the fingers of his other hand clawing for a handhold in the rocky ground as Kelson struggled to squirm out from under the hampering silk and avoid their attacker's blade.

Meanwhile, the lead man was wrenching the pulling shafts toward the cliff face, eyes wild and glazed, to pivot the cart and begin pushing it toward the edge, putting his shoulder into the effort, kicking at the scrambling Liam to loose his precarious hold on survival. Kelson, still entangled in the canopy, felt a glancing blow along his ribs, but the pain at least enabled him to locate his attacker. Twisting desperately, he managed to roll out from under the canopy and catch the brakeman's wrist as he drew back his dagger to plunge again.

The man outweighed Kelson by half again, and heaved himself atop his intended victim with a *whoof!* that all but crushed the breath from the king's lungs as they grappled for the blade. At the same time, Kelson could feel the crackle of powerful shields surging around him, probing for an opening in his psychic defenses, just as the deadly steel was pressing ever closer to his breast.

Then, all at once, a flailing whirlwind of Haldane livery was hurtling onto the back of Kelson's assailant—young Brendan Coris, clinging like a limpet with his strong legs locked around the man's waist, throttling the king's attacker from behind and gouging at his eyes while Morgan threw himself nearer Liam, just catching a fistful of the boy's shirt and holding him fast as the cart flipped over them with bruising force and tumbled over the edge, to the sound of splintering wood as it shattered on its way to the rocks below.

Somehow, the lead man managed not to go over with the cart, though he teetered precariously on the edge. His crazed glance frantically sought his colleague, but the venture clearly had failed. Having yanked Liam to safety, Morgan was scrambling to the assistance of Kelson and Brendan, still grappling with the brakeman, and Rasoul and Mátyás were within a few strides of joining in the fray, with murder in their eyes, followed by an eruption of others from carts farther back.

With dawning terror in his eyes, the lead man hurled himself over the edge, his thin wail of despair ending abruptly in a meaty *thunk*. Simultaneously, with a violent lurch that all but threw Brendan over the cliff after him, the brakeman twisted his wrist and, using Kelson's strength as well as his own, wrenched the blade around and drove it upward through the roof of his own mouth.

Abruptly, it was over. The man collapsed with a little grunt, a look of startlement on his face, all at once a dead weight on Kelson's chest, with Brendan's live weight squirming to scramble clear. As the king heaved at the body to shift it off of his, Morgan's hands were assisting, and then Liam's and Brendan's. Rasoul and Mátyás had reached them by then, but Kelson warned them off with a glare, breathing in great gasps as he struggled to his knees and set his hands to the dead man's temples, forcing his mind past fast-disintegrating shields.

He let Morgan join in, but they found only the chaotic remnants of a complex suicide-trigger and accompanying mind-wipe, willingly accepted, to ensure against betrayal of the man's superiors, if he were taken. Of those superiors' identity, they could find no trace. He expected it would be the same with the other man, who had gone over the cliff.

"Laje, are you injured?" came Mátyás's sharp inquiry, as Kelson surfaced somewhat jerkily from trance.

"Nay, I am unharmed. But the king—"

Kelson lifted his head to see Liam and Dhugal peering at him anxiously, Brendan helping the latter to also keep Rasoul and Mátyás from coming any closer. The Torenthi pair looked grim, and Rasoul's thin lips tightened as he glanced over the edge of the cliff. On the rocks below, amid the smashed debris of the cart, lay the broken body of the man who had flung himself after it rather than be taken, impaled on one of the cart's broken shafts.

"Lord Vasilly is making arrangements for retrieval of the body," Dhugal said, gesturing downhill. "And he's already sent a man ahead to alert the Orsal."

Nodding his acknowledgment, Kelson drew a deep breath and let Morgan help him to his feet, his nod of thanks to young Brendan delivered with gritted teeth as he winced from a sharp twinge in his side. Fortunately, no blood came away when he probed gingerly at the hurt, though he was sure he would have a goodly bruise as reminder of his narrow escape. He could only suppose that both he and Liam had been meant to perish.

The question now arose as to possible complicity by Rasoul or Mátyás, though both men looked genuinely shocked and outraged. He eyed them guardedly, noting that Arilan had worked his way to Dhugal's side, close behind the Torenthi pair, his face unreadable.

"Quite obviously," Kelson said with pointed care, "I do not know whether this attack was meant for me or for your king—or maybe both of us." He gestured toward the shaken Liam, still catching his breath between Brendan and Morgan. "But you will understand that I must ask both of you whether you had any hand in this, or any foreknowledge."

"I am a diplomat, not a master of assassins," Rasoul said quietly. "Tell me truly, my lord, for your life may depend upon it: Did the blade draw blood?"

He gestured toward the long dagger still embedded in the dead man's mouth, but Kelson shook his head.

"You suspect poison?"

"It would not be out of character," Rasoul replied. "May I?"

As he gestured toward the dagger again, Kelson gave a clipped nod and stepped back while Rasoul bent to the blade, bracing a boot on the body to dislodge it. When the Moor had sniffed cautiously along its length, then held it briefly to the light, he dropped it into the dust beside the dead man with a gesture of disdain, dusting his hand against a thigh. Liam was staring at him, wide-eyed.

"*Was* it poisoned, Rasoul?" he asked.

"No, my prince—thanks be to Allah. But if these men had succeeded, you would have been just as dead."

"You never answered my question," Kelson reminded him. "Have you any knowledge of this?"

Smiling faintly, Rasoul held out his open palm, inviting Kelson's touch.

"Read the truth of my words, my lord," he said softly. "I swear to you, by the beard of the Prophet, that I had no part in this, nor any foreknowledge. Nor would I have allowed it, had I known."

It was the answer Kelson had hoped to hear. And with his hand on Rasoul's, and Truth-Reading to a level the Moor had never before allowed, he could detect no trace of guile; nor had he expected to, for he and the Torenthi ambassador had developed a semblance of guarded trust over the years of their association, approaching friendship. No, what had just occurred was not Rasoul's way. Whether it might be Mátyás's way remained to be seen.

Lifting his hand from the Moor's, Kelson shifted his gaze to Liam's uncle with somewhat less confidence.

"And, you, Count Mátyás—I must be blunt and ask whether you can also assure me that you knew nothing of this attack."

"Under the circumstances, the question is a reasonable one," Mátyás said carefully, though he did not offer physical contact the way Rasoul had done. "But I tell you truly that I had no knowledge of it or part in this. I certainly could have countenanced nothing that would put my nephew at risk."

Kelson gave Mátyás a cautious nod, knowing that Mátyás himself must be well aware that Morgan and Dhugal and Arilan—and probably Brendan, as well—were likewise reading the truth of his words. A glance at Morgan and the others confirmed their agreement that in this, at least, both Mátyás and Rasoul appeared to be innocent. But while *this* uncle might be innocent of what had just occurred, Kelson could not discount the persistent whispers regarding Mahael, the eldest of the three uncles, long rumored to have been responsible for the death of Liam's elder brother. More than ever, he was convinced that Furstáns were little to be trusted.

Farther downhill, he noted that Derry had taken charge of the contingent going to retrieve the body from the rocks below. At the approach of the Orsal's chamberlain, Kelson gestured toward the men who had been propelling the cart bearing Morgan and Brendan, indicating that they should take charge of the other body at his feet.

"My lord," said Lord Vasilly, "I cannot explain what has happened here. I thought I knew that man." He jerked his chin toward the dead brakeman, being hefted onto a cart. "And Gaetan, the man who fell to his death, was a trusted retainer of many years' faithful service. I can only think that he must have been forced to do what he did. My lord Létald will be mortified at this breach of hospitality."

"I put no blame on Létald or on you," Kelson assured him. "However, I think that I should prefer to walk the rest of the way, if you don't mind."

The chamberlain could not but agree. Sending his own cart on ahead, Vasilly trudged along with them in silence, leading the august foot assemblage that included Kelson, Morgan, and Liam, along with Rasoul and Mátyás. The cart bearing the body of the assassin came just behind, Arilan swinging up at the last minute to conduct his own quiet investigation as the procession wound up the final approach to the Orsal's summer palace. Brendan retired to the next cart, now riding nervously with Dhugal.

Preceded by the captain's news, and given the manner of their entry into the palace yard, they received quite a different welcome from that customary at the court of Létald Hort of Orsal. Indeed, upon hearing of this attempt on the lives of his important guests, the Orsal had sent his multitudinous family inside, and awaited the visitors' arrival amid a military guard of honor—quite at odds with his usual style. Looking cross and appalled, his grey hair dishevelled, he came down the broad steps of the palace in a flurry of jade-green silk, flanked by two huge Tralian pikemen.

"My lords, I know not what to say," he declared. "Tralia offers profound apologies to Gwynedd and to Torenth." He bowed jointly to Kelson and to Liam. "I cannot explain what has happened, but I assure you that measures will be taken to discover who was responsible. Please—come inside and take refreshment. My lord Alaric, it is good to see you as well."

Létald conducted the principals straightaway to a private reception room, where cool ales and refreshing sherbets were quickly produced, along with a collation of bread and cheese and fruit. There he listened avidly as Kelson, then Liam and Morgan, gave their accounts of the attack, even asking for Brendan's impressions, after being told of the boy's boldness in coming to his king's defense.

Kelson began to relax a little as he watched Létald listen, for he could entertain not the slightest doubt regarding the loyalty of his old ally. A normally jolly, moon-faced man of some fifty years, with sea-green eyes that crinkled at the corners and a fringe of close-trimmed, grey-speckled hair, Létald rarely displayed such intensity. His well-manicured hands bore rings on every finger, glittering as he handled the dagger wielded by the unknown Deryni assailant, and the silk of his gown protruded slightly over a well-fed torso, but any inference of softness in the man known as the Hort of Orsal would have been mistaken.

His preferred style referred to his lordship of the strategically powerful Ile d'Orsal, above whose port this summer palace of Horthánthy perched. But he was also Prince of Tralia and High Prince of the Forcinn buffer states, of which Tralia was one, exerting personal rule over a sovereign principality the size of Cassan. His overlordship of the Forcinn gave him influence over lands as extensive as Meara and the Connait combined. Long a trading partner with Torenth, Corwyn, and, therefore, Gwynedd, his family had dominated trade in the Southern Sea for generations—a force always to be reckoned with, in the politics of the Eleven Kingdoms.

"I am profoundly disturbed that such treachery could have surfaced here in the bosom of my court," Létald told them, when all had offered their accounts of the attack and Arilan had reported his lack of success in ferreting out anything else from the dead Deryni or his accomplice. "I have not had the pleasure of prior acquaintance with Count Mátyás," he said, with a nod toward the Torenthi prince, "but I have always known my lord Rasoul to be a man of honor, even if I have not always agreed with the policies of his sovereigns or their regents."

Liam was seated between Kelson and Brendan, dust-streaked and silent, picking nervously at one of the torn wrist ties of his once immaculate white shirt. Father Irenaeus, tight-lipped and silent until now, flicked a troubled glance first at the young king, then at Rasoul and Mátyás.

"I fear these are difficult times, my lord Létald," he allowed. "Most in Torenth rejoice that their *padishah* is to return to his homeland at last, after so long an absence and so long a regency. While all his loyal subjects should welcome such a homecoming, it cannot be denied that much will change, as he assumes his personal rule."

Taken at face value, the statement seemed merely to state the obvious. Coupled with the glance at Mátyás, however, it stopped just short of pointing out that among the things that would change the most was the regency to be dismantled upon Liam's return. Kelson cast a covert glance at the priest, then at Mátyás, wondering whether he was catching the hint of criticism because he himself suspected Liam's uncles. Rasoul looked thoughtful. Mátyás was giving studious attention to a goblet of blown glass between his hands, eyes lowered, apparently choosing to ignore the implied suggestion. Arilan's gaze was more frankly appraising, his response all but confrontational.

"An interesting observation," he said after a beat, "but what happened a little while ago was clearly meant to kill my king as well as yours. Of course, both deaths would profit those who have prospered during this long regency in Torenth. Is that not so, Count Mátyás?"

Mátyás set down his goblet with care, his dark eyes lifting coolly to Arilan's. "As both the reverend fathers have said, the *padishah's* return will change a great many things. In general, however, his people will welcome a return to direct rule. Regencies are sometimes a necessity, but I think they rarely reflect the best governance for a kingdom, however benign they may be. My nephew is young, and will require guidance initially, but I think he has been well prepared to take up his estate—for which I, at least, thank you, my lord." He nodded in Kelson's direction. "I hope he may depend upon me to render whatever assistance I am able."

"Your gratitude is noted, Count Mátyás," Morgan said smoothly, before Kelson or Arilan could respond. "However, I believe that all of us find it greatly troubling that at least one of today's would-be assassins was Deryni—and not just Deryni, but of sufficient training and commitment to protect his identity, and that of those who sent him, by the most sophisticated and deadly measures. I fear it does point to his probable origin among your own people—and quite likely at a very high level, for I am given to understand that, even in your land, such skills are not altogether common."

"Indeed, they are not," Létald agreed gruffly, "and that troubles me greatly. How came such a man into my household, Lord Rasoul? It is a serious breach of diplomatic privilege."

"My lord, I cannot account for what has happened," Rasoul replied, with a lifting of open palms to underline his disclaimer. "You have the most profound apologies of Torenth. Please be assured that I shall take up the matter with my superiors immediately upon our arrival in Beldour."

On this note of uneasy rapprochement, they continued to speculate for a while longer, no one quite willing to make specific accusations regarding the attack—for Mátyás's brothers, if not Mátyás himself, were still highly suspect—until Morgan tactfully suggested that a period of rest might benefit all concerned.

"I, for one, will welcome the opportunity to bathe and be rid of these soiled clothes," he said, with a faint smile, plucking at a fold of his dusty tunic. "And if Létald has laid on the usual festivities that accompany a state visit to Horthánthy, we shall all be glad of a nap before supper. He dislikes having guests fall asleep at his table."

"I do, indeed," Létald agreed, nodding toward Liam as he rose. "I look forward to offering more appropriate Trailan hospitality to our distinguished young guest," he added, tendering the boy a reassuring smile.

Kelson was only too happy to agree, emotionally wrung out and beginning to ache from his exertions of the past hour, following without demur as Létald himself escorted him and Dhugal to the quarters they would share for their brief visit. The royal squires, Ivo and Davoran, were there already, unpacking fresh clothing from a pair of leather-bound chests brought up from the ship, and servants were topping up a hot bath set before an arched window looking seaward, where a cool breeze stirred the gauzy hangings swagged back from the arch. Kelson began stripping off his filthy clothes as soon as Létald and the servants had withdrawn.

"I wonder whether Morgan still thinks that Mátyás isn't in league with his brothers," he said from inside his tunic, as Dhugal helped pull it off over his head. He flinched as the other prodded disapprovingly at the now livid bruise purpling his ribs, and handed off the tunic to Davoran.

"I dunno," Dhugal replied. "Mátyás isn't saying all he knows, but I think he was as shocked as anyone, that you and Liam were attacked. If you'll sit down, I'll see if I can't heal that for you."

Himself fingering the bruise, and little minded to object, Kelson let himself be directed to a bench nearer the tub. There, after Davoran had pulled off his dusty boots, Dhugal crouched beside him to cup one hand over the bruise, his other hand lifting to fold across Kelson's eyes as his patient exhaled on a long-drawn sigh.

"That's good," Dhugal murmured, healing ease already stirring beneath his hands. "Relax and let me work on this. When I'm done, you'll want a hot soak and a good nap."

Dhugal's ministrations helped; the hot bath helped even more, unknotting aching muscles and sluicing away the dust and grime of the road. When Kelson at last lay down to rest, reclining drowsily on pristine bed linens, he let himself be lulled by the reassuring domestic sounds of his squires chattering softly in the next room, now attending to Dhugal's ablutions and continuing their preparations for the evening.

But as he drifted on the edge of sleep, his thoughts began to flit unbidden toward the part of the evening for which there could be no adequate preparation: the inevitable meeting with his cousin Araxie.

CHAPTER TEN

. . . *As a bridegroom decketh himself with orna-*
ments, and a bride adorneth herself with her jewels.

Isaiah 61:10

*A*t least Kelson did not dream, when he eventually fell asleep for a while. But resigned awareness of the duty before him was the first thing that came to mind when the squires woke him to prepare for the evening's reception and feast, never far from consciousness as he let them dress him in rustling silks of Haldane crimson. After binding his Border braid with cord of gold bullion, they brought out the heavy jewelled circlet he would also wear for Liam's installation—heavy like the burden he carried in his heart, as he settled this emblem of his rank and duty on his brow.

Dhugal, meanwhile, had arrayed himself with sober care, a swath of dark McLain tartan brooched to the right shoulder of a tunic of slubbed black silk, shorter than Kelson wore, over black hose and short boots. A black ribbon tied his Border braid, and a duke's golden coronet circled his brow, further binding the copper-bronze hair.

Neither he nor Kelson wore a sword, but both belted on silver-mounted border dirks, at once highly decorative and more functional at close quarters than a longer blade. In less uncertain times, both would have been confident of their safety beneath the roof of Létald Hort of Orsal; but after the afternoon's attack, not even the Orsal could be certain that his guests were safe.

Morgan was with the page sent to fetch them at the appointed hour, clad in forest-green silks and similarly armed, and accompanied them downstairs, where music and laughter met them well before they actually reached the reception hall. The Orsal's line had always been prolific as well as exuberant. Accordingly, the arched reception hall was bursting at its seams with von Horthy children and cousins and other shirttail relatives as well as court retainers, all eager to welcome the royal visitors and greet old friends, all looking forward to the festivities of this brief visit, before the royal party embarked upriver on the morrow.

Létald's customary ebullience seemed to have been little affected by what had happened earlier, though Kelson was quite certain that their host would have made additional security arrangements in the intervening hours—there *were* more guards than usual, and less visible measures no doubt in force. Flanked by his two dukes, and preceding Liam and *his* noble escort, Kelson let himself be swept up, at least for a time, in that unique intermingling of exotic panoply and jovial informality that characterized the Hortic court, summer or not, somehow making of a full state reception a reunion of old acquaintances, even those not met before.

"Be welcome to my court!" Létald declared, sweeping an arm grandly to encompass his immediate family, who still numbered nearly a score. "Welcome, all! My beloved Niyya begs to be excused from this official greeting, for she soon will be brought to bed of twins—*very* soon," he added, miming the greatness of his wife's belly. "God willing, however, she will join us at table a little later. Standing is not easy for her, in these final days before her confinement."

Kelson inclined his head in bemused acknowledgment as Létald rattled on.

"Meanwhile, with joy I present to you my children. They do grow when one feeds them, Sires, but what is a father to do?" Létald rolled his eyes in mock despair as he drew a stocky, self-conscious teenager into the embrace of one arm, then brought forth another child, and all the many others, introducing each by name, for Liam's benefit. "Here is my second son, Rogan, whom Duke Alaric will remember far better than he or Rogan wishes, I feel sure—though he's a good lad, a good lad. I have heeded your suggestion, Alaric, and Rogan is happily pursuing academic endeavors with the scholars." He tousled the boy's hair with obvious affection.

"And Cyric, my heir, who is soon to enter a period of service to his maternal uncle, the King of R'Kassi—a very fine appointment!" A taller, fairer youth of about Liam's age moved forward at his father's gesture, exchanging handshakes first with Kelson, then with Liam, as his father swept a ripely attractive teenage girl into the embrace of the arm that had just released Rogan.

"And here, my eldest daughter, Rezza Elisabet—who goes very shy when any marriageable bachelor visits her father's court—and the twins, Marcel and Marcelline," he went on, jutting his chin at a smiling boy and girl dressed very similarly, "and little Aynbeth, who is six, and dear Oswin, the apple of his father's eye—"

The introductions were whirlwind and almost overwhelming, a kaleidoscope of eager faces and chattered pleasantries and gem-bedecked garments in every jewel-tone imaginable. At some point, amid the flurry of other greetings and introductions, Kelson's great-aunt Sivorn—who was also Létald's sister—approached to offer him her cheek and then shoo forward a giggling handful of his younger cousins, who swarmed around him to bestow and receive dutiful kisses.

Two older girls held back to wait their turns, both of them lightly veiled in the Eastern fashion and wearing the silver circlets of princesses, but he knew the darker one with teasing eyes to be Richelle, even if her gown of Haldane crimson had not marked her out, radiant with excitement over her coming nuptials. He avoided taking any proper look at the second, but he was left with an impression of pale hair and an emerald-green veil and gown and the fleeting press of soft lips to his cheek, through the veil.

That he dared not dwell on such impressions was as well, because there was Liam to formally present to Létald and his court, in his newly attained status as a king now legally of age and about to be acknowledged in his own kingdom. Now apparently reconciled to his royal status, the boy was even wearing the jewelled circlet Mátyás had brought from Beldour—though not the full-sleeved robe of purple damask. Instead, he had chosen a close-fitting tunic of heavy bronze silk, the parting gift of Nigel and Meraude. It made him look the prince he was, a young man Kelson suddenly was not sure he really knew.

Liam's countrymen, Rasoul and Mátyás, remained politely in the background as their young liege exchanged courtesies with Létald and his family. Though they were clad in the same court finery they had worn in Rhemuth, Kelson was suddenly struck by how much more alien they seemed than even as recently as this morning, their Deryniness far more obvious than it had been in Rhemuth. Farther back in the hall, Father Irenaeus had his head bent in conversation with another bearded priest in flowing black robes, yet even he seemed somehow more sinister than he had during those months at Kelson's own court.

Was it merely their growing proximity to their own homeland, Kelson wondered, and increasing distance from his own? Or were their two lands really that different? He feared that they might be, and that the differences would only become more glaring as they moved on into Torenth itself. (Would Liam, too, become a stranger?) None of the three had put a foot wrong for the entire length of the journey thus far—in fact, all had been surprisingly forthcoming in the wake of the assassination attempt; but all were at once Torenthi and Deryni—a combination often proven dangerous in the past, even in a court like the Orsal's, where being Deryni was little remarked upon unless one of that race overstepped the boundaries of good guestship and courtesy.

Clearly, the incident of earlier in the day had done precisely that—though, to Kelson's surprise, it seemed not to have damped the festive atmosphere in Orsal's hall that night. Almost, he could keep at bay the private concern that had haunted him increasingly in the past several days: that niggling awareness of an impending domestic mission for which he could summon little enthusiasm.

But it came to the fore in a manner he could not avoid when, midway through the feasting, he and Ivo Hepburn, his duty squire of the evening, withdrew in search of the privies; Morgan had forbidden him to leave the hall unattended. They were on their way back, in an unaccountably empty stretch of corridor, when a tall, black-robed figure loomed suddenly before them, of whom only a pair of black eyes could be seen within the swath of a black *keffiyeh*.

A gesture from a dusky, powerful hand, one forefinger laid vertical where lips would be behind the veil, seemed to freeze Ivo in place, hand on the hilt of his squire's dagger and lips just parting in surprised question. Kelson, too, had started back in reflex wariness, shields instantly flaring, but he made himself relax at once. He had been expecting the contact, sooner or later.

"Have we business, Kelson of Gwynedd?" a low voice inquired, as the hand released a fold of the headdress to reveal a long, aquiline nose and a close-clipped black beard.

"Prince Azim." Kelson barely mouthed the name as he inclined his head in taut greeting, for Azim ar-Rafiq was Rothana's uncle, brother to her father and a prince in his own right—and a high-ranking member of the mysterious desert brotherhood, the Knights of the Anvil, of whom Kelson knew very little besides their name. That Azim might be trusted was beyond question—Morgan's wife had trained with the Deryni mage, as had Rothana; but Azim's mission was little to Kelson's liking.

Azim glanced pointedly at Ivo, obviously imparting some silent command, for the squire immediately closed his eyes, breathing out in a soft sigh as his hands fell to his sides. Kelson controlled a shiver as the black gaze returned to his, though he knew that neither he nor Ivo were in any danger.

"I shall be brief," Azim said softly, compassion in the dark eyes. "Believe that I grieve for you, my prince, but my niece bade me tell you that she has provided for you and your land as best she can. Later tonight, if it is your will, I am instructed to take you to a place where you may speak privily with the Princess Araxie, your cousin. You know my niece's wishes in this matter. She prays that you will do as your good duty to Gwynedd bids you."

Kelson drew a deep breath and let it out slowly, tempering his reply with the duty that bore more heavily upon him with every heartbeat.

"I am at your disposal, my lord, and that of your niece," he said softly. "Will you come for me, or shall I meet you at an appointed time?"

"I shall fetch you, my prince, after you have taken your leave of the Orsal's table," Azim murmured with a bow. "Until then."

Kelson was hardly aware of his departure; almost, the Deryni mage seemed to vanish into thin air, right after brushing Ivo's temple with a feather-touch that Kelson knew would erase the squire's memory of the encounter, even as it released him from the control Azim had brought to bear. Ivo's soft gasp brought Kelson himself back to full awareness, suggesting that he, too, had been somewhat entranced—though, unlike Ivo, Kelson knew he would remember what had passed between himself and his dark-clad visitor. His pulse was still pounding as he and Ivo made their way silently back to the hall, much relieved to regain the relative anonymity of the crowd—for he could cope with merely being on display.

He had been seated at Létald's right hand, between him and the heavily pregnant Princess Niyya, with Liam on Létald's other side and Létald's eldest beyond Liam. Létald had withdrawn down the table to exchange pleasantries with Derry and Bishop Arilan, and Cyric had his fair head bent to listen to Liam, lips upturned in apparent amusement at some anecdote the younger prince was relating. Behind the pair, and included in their camaraderie, Brendan and Payne had drawn up stools to join them. Liam had long since put aside the jewelled diadem worn earlier for the formal reception and entry in to supper, and seemed to be enjoying himself.

His Torenthi countrymen likewise seemed absorbed in the festivities of the evening, the day's earlier tensions largely dispelled. Rasoul sat on Princess Niyya's other side, making idle discourse on the delights of large families, with the others of the royal party ranged across the rest of the top table and high along the two tables set angled from the ends. Kelson spotted Sivorn and her husband, Baron Savile, seated near Count Mátyás, but none of Sivorn's children had made an appearance at supper, for which he was profoundly grateful.

Lest he arouse comment or offend his host, Kelson dared not make too precipitous an escape, little though he was looking forward to its reason, but he caught Dhugal's eye shortly after returning to table, only nodding slightly to indicate that the expected contact had taken place. Thereafter, he bided his time, watching the assorted entertainments as further courses were served, half-listening to Niyya and Rasoul, chatting with Létald when he returned, waiting for the opportunity to retire gracefully. He accepted greetings and a glass of wine from Lord Rather de Corbie, an elderly, bandy-legged little Tralian courtier whom he knew from Morgan's court, but he hardly touched his cup as he and the man exchanged courtesies.

When, after another quarter-hour, Létald's princess quietly bade them good night and slipped off to bed, while acrobats tumbled and sprang to the music of flute and drum, Kelson seized that opportunity to take his leave as well, pleading fatigue of the journey and entrusting Liam to the company of Létald and the Torenthi lords. Dhugal would follow shortly, bringing Morgan with him, for Kelson knew he ought not to embark upon his reluctant mission without at least informing Morgan.

Accompanied by Ivo and Davoran, his other squire, both of them chirpy and cheerful after what was, for them, the excitement of the evening, Kelson reached the relative refuge of his assigned quarters without incident. Two of his Haldane lancers were on duty outside the door, but adjusting their memories would present no problem when the time came to go with Azim. Inside, he bade the squires help him change his court robes for a short silk velvet tunic of drabbed claret, its only adornment a tracery of bullion-embroidery on the standing collar—far better suited to skulking among the shadows than rustling Haldane crimson, its color reflecting both his rank and his state of mind regarding this latest foray toward matrimony. Giving the squires permission to wait until morning to pack for their departure, he sent them off to bed in the adjoining room with a command to sleep and hear nothing, and followed a few minutes later to reinforce the command.

Dhugal had not yet arrived when Kelson came back into the room. Impatient, the king picked up the formal coronet he had worn to supper, hefting it in his two hands. The circlet was of hammered gold, studded with jewels, and heavy. The prospect of putting it back on was less than attractive, but he needed to make it clear that any offer he might make to Araxie would be as king, not as an offer of the heart. He set the coronet on the mantel as Dhugal slipped into the room with Morgan right behind him. Morgan looked mystified, and gave the king a strange look as he sat where he was directed.

"Is something wrong?" he asked, taking in the change of attire and the king's taut expression.

"That depends on your definition of 'wrong,'" Kelson replied. He sighed and bowed his head, leaning one forearm along the edge of the mantel, not looking at Morgan. "You'll recall the conversation we had about Rothana, back in Coroth?"

"Yes."

"Well, I wasn't entirely forthcoming about my last conversation with *her*, the night of Jatham and Janniver's wedding." Kelson looked up, but not at either of his companions. "Not only has she not changed her mind about marrying me, but she's picked the woman she does want me to marry. I'm to meet her shortly."

Morgan gasped audibly, though he regained his composure almost at once, glancing first at Dhugal, then back at the king.

"This is hardly something anyone would make up," he said softly, "so it must be true." He drew a deep breath and let it out slowly. "How do you feel about the prospect?"

Kelson wearily shook his head. "Numb. Resigned, I suppose. Alaric, she sprang all the arguments on me that I can't refute. Most telling is the fact that I daren't wait much longer to provide an heir—not with Liam going back to his own kingdom."

"And who is her choice?" Morgan asked.

Kelson set both hands on the mantel and glanced up at the chimney breast as he gave a heavy sigh.

"Someone I can't possibly quibble about—other than on the grounds that I love someone else. From a dynastic and political perspective, she's even more suitable than Rothana."

"And she is——?" Morgan persisted.

"Duke Richard's younger daughter, my cousin Araxie."

"Araxie? But, isn't she——"

"No, she isn't," Kelson said impatiently. "That's what everyone thinks, but apparently it's been a deliberate smoke screen, concocted for Cuan and his cousin, and then encouraged by Rothana while she set this up. According to her, Araxie has simply been acting as the go-between—so there are no legal impediments of pre-existing contract, no adverse political implications, and our blood relationship is distant enough that a dispensation can be easily arranged. Not only is she a Haldane, she's part Deryni from her mother's side—in short, everything a Haldane king could want in a queen. Except that I don't love her."

"Do you think you might learn to love her?" Morgan asked quietly.

Kelson shrugged and poked distractedly at a rivulet of molten wax running down a candlestick on the mantel. "I have no idea. I haven't even seen her since we were both very small—at least not to talk to."

"Did you at least *like* her, in those days?"

"I suppose so. I certainly didn't *dis*like her. That's hardly a recommendation for marriage, though."

"Not for most men, no," Morgan agreed. "Unfortunately, as we've acknowledged before, the King of Gwynedd is not 'most men.' " He sighed wearily and rubbed between his eyes with thumb and forefinger. "Well, I don't suppose it can be any worse a situation than Sidana. You've done this before, out of duty."

"That was before I fell in love," Kelson murmured. "If I had never known what it was like——"

A quick rap on the door cut him off in midsentence, and he whirled in near panic.

"Dear God," he whispered, as Dhugal glanced to him for instructions. "Tha' has to be Azim. Alaric, come with me to meet her. Both of you, come with me—please. . . ."

At Dhugal's questioning look, Morgan slowly nodded, rising as the younger duke headed for the door and the king nervously straightened his tunic. The tall black-robed man who entered at Dhugal's bidding was well known to Morgan, being tutor to his wife, and merely raised an eyebrow when he saw Morgan with the king.

"This becomes increasingly a family affair," he said. "And I welcome your presence, my friend, for I have news to impart to his Highness before we embark upon our other mission that will be of interest to you as well."

"What news?" Kelson asked impatiently.

"Only a hint of vague warning as yet, my prince," Azim replied. "But it may well relate to what occurred earlier. I am advised, by a source I may not name, that serious mischief may be attempted when young Liam-Lajos is enthroned."

"Mischief of what kind, and from whom?"

"Oh, Deryni mischief—and deadly, to be sure—but I am not yet prepared to name names. Suffice it to say that I would not put too much faith in family loyalties."

"Mahael," Morgan muttered under his breath.

Azim inclined his head minutely. "That is as may be. However, I have neither proof nor particulars, as yet."

"Would you advise that we not go on to Beldour?" Kelson asked.

"No, you must go. Liam is of age, and must be presented to his people. In general, they welcome his return. We must pray that he will be able to hold his throne, once you have set him upon it."

"That presumes that he *and* Kelson will live long enough for that to happen," Morgan said. "What's to prevent another incident like today?"

Azim shook his head. "More subtle measures are contemplated. Another such overt attack would be seen as treason and an act of war against Gwynedd, especially did it occur when you have passed into Torenth, as you will tomorrow.

"No, I think it likely that today's essay was but a hopeful trial, with little real expectation of success, meant to be perceived as the work of independent dissidents who could not be traced back to Beldour. You may be certain that the perpetrators were to die, whichever way it came out. But had it succeeded, the ceremony shortly to be enacted at Torenthály would have been the girding of yet another minor king, rather than the confirmation of one come of age. There are those who would welcome that—as, indeed, they would welcome your death."

"Mahael would welcome both," Morgan whispered.

"I have not said it," Azim replied. "But if he was, indeed, responsible, he will now bide his time until he may take more subtle action. His nephew's homecoming is an occasion of great joy to the vast majority of the people of Torenth, and he will not risk being perceived for what he is. Too many tongues still wag regarding the circumstances of young Alroy's death."

"Will they not wag if he moves during the ceremony of investiture?" Dhugal ventured. "Will *that* not be perceived as treason and an act of war?"

"It will," Azim agreed. "But if, thereby, Mahael can manage to seize the full power of Furstán, who can gainsay him? He would then be king by right of power, not merely regent."

"*What* am I walking into?" Kelson muttered.

"A dangerous situation," Azim replied. "But you have always known that. Nonetheless, you have a duty to your vassal, Liam of Torenth." He paused a beat. "And tonight, I think you have a somewhat more immediate duty to Gwynedd—closer to the heart."

The deft shift back to the reason for Azim's presence came as something of a shock, refocusing all Kelson's earlier apprehension.

"Closer to the Crown, perhaps," he managed to murmur. "You know where my heart lies, Azim."

"I do, my lord, and I am sorry for it."

When he said nothing more, Kelson breathed out in a long sigh and glanced at Morgan and Dhugal, both watching him impassively, then gave a determined nod as he took his circlet from off the mantel and set it on his head.

"Very well. Let's get on with it, then."

He saw his aunt Sivorn first, as he came into the room where Azim took them. She was warming her hands before the fire when he entered, her finery of earlier in the evening shrouded under a long, filmy wrap, for the night air was chill this close to the sea. Her veil had fallen back from a plaited coronet of pale blond hair that shimmered like molten gold in the firelight. She turned as he approached, silently holding out her hands to him. He took them and kissed each in turn, then stepped back to look at her.

"I've brought the Dukes of Corwyn and Cassan," he said by way of explanation, as she glanced beyond him in question at Morgan and Dhugal. "They're the only ones I've told."

She smiled faintly. Up close, even by firelight, she looked older than he had remembered, from his glimpse of her at court and at table.

"I remember the Duke of Corwyn from many years ago," she murmured. "Richard thought him among the most promising of the squires at court—an expectation more than fulfilled, I think, for it is said you owe him your crown."

"And my life, several times over," Kelson said.

"And I have heard of the Duke of Cassan—and his father," Sivorn went on

"Tell me, Kelson, did you think you might need Deryni support, to speak with my daughter?"

She was still smiling as she said it, but Kelson found himself dropping his gaze.

"Forgive me," he whispered. "I mostly have vague recollections of playing together, as small children. But that was a very long time ago, and my heart—is not entirely free."

"Kings' hearts are rarely free," she replied, her pale eyes searching his face. "Nor are queens'. But Haldanes have always known their duty."

He nodded mutely.

"Araxie is waiting for you in the next room," Sivorn said quietly. "I shall remain here with your companions."

CHAPTER ELEVEN

Search, and seek, that she may be made known unto
thee.

Ecclesiasticus 6:27

$\mathcal{K}$elson tapped on the door Sivorn indicated, then slipped inside. Far on the other side of the room, a slight, bright-headed figure was standing in the shadows of the window embrasure, a fringed shawl of heavy striped silk clutched close round her shoulders. A thick plait of pale gold spilled over it, falling nearly to her waist.

Her head turned as he entered, the pale oval of her face emerging from the dimness as she came to meet him in the brighter light before the fireplace, where candle sconces and several lanterns of pierced brass cast a golden glow. There she dipped in graceful curtsy, right hand pressing the silk to her heart. Her eyes, as she rose to meet his wary gaze, were a pale, clear grey, very like his own. She was far prettier than he had remembered or dared to hope.

"You've—grown up," he said lamely, at a loss what else to say.

"So have you." A ghost of a smile quirked at one corner of full, rosy lips. "I think we both have changed a bit since we played together all those summers ago."

He managed a cautious nod, feeling as gawky as any green squire newly come to court.

"You weren't at supper," he ventured.

"No, it seemed—less than wise, under the circumstances. I—suppose you've become accustomed to having people try to kill you."

"One lives with it," he conceded with a faint smile. "Or doesn't. I'm afraid it's one of the obligations one accepts along with the privileges of a crown."

"Like the obligation to contract a suitable marriage."

"Yes," he said, after a beat. "You—didn't you have *two* braids then, rather than one?"

Her nose briefly wrinkled in a grimace of indignation. "Yes, and horrid Conall used to pull them and try to make me cry. He only succeeded once— and I kicked him more times than that! But usually Richelle would come to my rescue—or you would."

"I had forgotten that," he admitted with a sickly attempt at a grin. But he had flinched at her mention of Conall—willful even then—and she looked away in momentary embarrassment.

"Forgive me. I shouldn't have mentioned Conall."

Nervously she gestured toward a bench before the fire, sitting on one end without looking to see whether he followed—which he did, but only slowly. She kept her eyes averted as she leaned forward to pitch a few sticks onto the flames.

"I fear my poor mother must have despaired of me," she went on, dusting her fingers against her skirts as she sat straight again. She was wearing the gown of green she had worn earlier in the afternoon. "Richelle was the proper little princess, but somehow I always managed to get my face and gown dirty by midday. I was forever rescuing some kitten up a tree, or racing about on my pony, or playing with Uncle Brion's hound puppies in the stable yard."

Kelson only nodded as he let himself sit down gingerly beside her, acutely aware of his mission.

"Araxie, I didn't come here to talk about the past."

"I know that. But perhaps we need to talk about some of the past before we can talk about the future—about your future and my future. Perhaps it only delays the inevitable, but we *are* people, as well as being royal."

Her comment made him realize that she was as nervous as he; and it suddenly occurred to him to wonder whether she, too, was having to put aside a longing of the heart in order to serve a duty of blood.

He glanced distractedly at the fire, forearms resting on his knees, twisting at Sidana's ring on his little finger, beside the larger signet that bore his Haldane arms as king. He did not travel with the Ring of Fire, which had helped seal his kingship; that was safely in Nigel's keeping back in Rhemuth, should the worst happen and he not return from this mission.

"We're both bound to duty, aren't we?" he said softly. "You know that I married once for duty."

"Yes. Your silken princess—Sidana of Meara. We heard that she was young and fair, and even that you had come to love her."

He lowered his gaze, trying not to remember all the blood, as Sidana lay dying in his arms.

"She was—very fair," he whispered. "And very brave. I—can't honestly say that I exactly loved her . . . but I had made up my mind to *try* to love her. I respected her greatly, for having the courage to agree to a marriage that should have resolved the old enmities between our two lands. In time, I think a kind of love might have come—or at least a fondness, an agreeable partnership."

He shook his head, remembering. "But it didn't happen. I told myself, in those early days after her death, that I *had* loved her—or at least that I would have loved her, had she lived—and I used that as an excuse not to let myself be pushed into another match that answered only political expediency. And when I met Rothana, falling in love with her was the farthest thing from my mind."

"She is—quite extraordinary," Araxie murmured, not looking at him.

Kelson lifted his head to study her profile against the firelight, her fair beauty so unlike Rothana's.

"Has she spoken much of me?" he dared to ask.

Araxie smiled faintly, eyes averted to the graceful hands folded in her lap. "She has given a most excellent account of the King of Gwynedd, and his honor, and his gentleness, and his need for a queen to rule beside him," she said. "Of Kelson the man, she has said but little. I think it must be very difficult to sing the praises of one's beloved to another, weighing hopes of persuasion against fears of loss."

"Then, she does still love me," Kelson ventured.

"Oh, aye, there can be no question of that," Araxie replied, "and shall, I think, until the day she dies. And learning the depth of her love, as it gradually was revealed to me, I shrank from what she asked for a very long time."

Her fingers had begun to pleat folds in the fabric of her skirt, and she made herself release them and gently smooth the wrinkles.

"But she has proven steadfast in what she asks of me . . . and the wisdom I have gained in these past months of study with Master Azim and others has persuaded me that this compromise may well be a good choice for Gwynedd, given the circumstances. I can only hope I may prove worthy to stand in her stead—if that is your wish as well, my lord."

As she settled the striped shawl more closely around her shoulders, biting at her lip, Kelson let his eyes close momentarily, jaws clenched against his sorrow as he made himself swallow.

"A king's duty can be a very weighty thing," he finally said, choosing his words carefully. "And yet, I would not have you think that any reluctance on my part comes from any failing on yours. Rothana has—made the decision she has made—with what she believes is a far greater good in mind than the happiness of mere individuals. She has been bred to her duty, as I to mine and you to yours, and it seems this is the path she has judged best for all concerned." He glanced up at Araxie. "Unless, of course, contrary to what I was told, your heart is, indeed, linked to Cuan of Howicce, as popular rumor would have it. Or to some other . . ."

An ironic smile touched her lips as she lightly shook her head. "There is no other, my lord. And as for rumor, let us not allow *that* to color what little freedom such as you and I might have, regarding whom we wed. Cuan is a sweet boy—and if my little brother had lived, I would like to think he might have been like Cuan."

"Then, you think he does care for Gwenlian?" Kelson said. "After all, by marrying her, he would inherit both crowns if Colman dies without issue."

"I assure you, the match is one of desire as well as expediency," Araxie said with a smile. "As for Colman, may he receive his just due, for his callous treatment of the Princess Janniver. After nearly four years, no honest court in all the Eleven Kingdoms will yet entertain any offer of marriage with Llannedd. That will pass, in time," she conceded, "for some woman or some court will eventually judge a crown worth the sacrifice of honor. But meanwhile, Colman grows no younger, a proper heir no nearer, and Cuan and Gwenlian can afford to bide their time."

Kelson smiled despite his own predicament, almost pitying Colman. "I see that if you and I should wed, fair cousin, I would gain a fierce and compassionate champion. But justice has been done, in this case—and I was glad to be its instrument in part. Only a few days ago, I gave Janniver in marriage to a far more worthy husband than Colman of Llannedd."

She cast him an amused glance, truly smiling for the first time.

"So we had heard, my lord. Word of the marriage reached us two days past, and has provoked much gleeful gossip among the ladies of my uncle's court. Further rumor has it that, in honor of this match, you have created a bold new Baron of Kilshane, who is more than worthy of his royal bride."

Chuckling despite their own plight, Kelson returned his glance to his hands, slowly shaking his head. "The outcome is, indeed, fortuitous for both of them. They seem very happy. Would that—that our own situation could be resolved so agreeably for all concerned."

She turned her gaze back to the fire, silent for a long moment, then spoke softly.

"My lord, I will speak plainly, for one of us must. I must further confess that Rothana's proposition has greatly colored my outlook, these past months. As a Haldane, I have always known that political expediency would govern at least a part of the choosing of my husband, just as you have always known that such considerations would govern your own marriage. If such a match does not produce the grand passion both of us would prefer, at least we are of common stock, you and I, with common goals. And when I was very small, I confess I did adore my brave and dashing cousin Kelson. Perhaps we could build on that."

He rose abruptly and began pacing before the fire, silent for a long moment as his mind raced over everything she had said. He found himself confused but also gently touched by her clear and simple faith that together they might fashion a life from the shards of what might have been. And as he turned to glance at her, pale head bowed before his indecision, he began to draw upon an inner strength that might just be sufficient to sustain him, if he offered her his hand and crown.

"Araxie, he said quietly, keeping his gaze steady as she lifted her eyes to his, "in honor I must tell you two things before I ask you a third. First, I can never stop loving her, whatever else might grow between you and me. Having said that, however, I wish to assure you that I would never, *ever* allow that love to compromise the faith and honor I shall owe to my queen."

He paused to swallow, fearing to see denial in her eyes, but she only inclined her head in acceptance, blinking back tears.

"The second thing concerns her son, Albin," Kelson said steadily. "Had—things been different, Albin would have been *my* son as well—and for that reason, he will always hold a special place in my heart, even though there can be no question that my own sons will always take precedence in the succession.

"Unfortunately, as you are no doubt aware, Ro—his mother has expressed profound concern that others might one day try to use him against me, and for that reason intends him for a life in the Church. I maintain that the boy must have the right to make his own choices concerning his life. I intend, therefore, to make certain proposals to his grandfather, my uncle Nigel, whereby the boy would be restored to his proper birthright. In time, I believe Nigel can be persuaded to agree to these proposals, and I have hopes that eventually she will agree as well. Is this—acceptable to you?"

She nodded, again blinking back tears. "It is a kind and generous thing that you propose, Sire," she whispered. "His mother and I have come to regard one another almost as sisters, in these past months, and I would welcome whatever role you deem appropriate for her son. He is a lovely child."

Drawing a deep breath, Kelson turned to face her squarely. "Then, we come to that third thing, which I must ask you, rather than tell you, because it is *her* wish—and because I know she desires it out of the same love and duty to Gwynedd that I believe you share." He sank slowly to one knee before her.

"Araxie Haldane, I cannot promise you the same sort of love I hold and will always hold for Rothana, but I give you my word, as king, as your kinsman, and as a man, that I will do my utmost always to treat you with honor, with respect, and with affection. Having heard this, will you do me the very great honor of giving me your hand in marriage, to be Queen of Gwynedd beside me, and mother of my sons?"

Tears were running down her cheeks—and making his own vision waver—but she conjured a brave smile as she placed her hand in his.

"The honor is mine, Sire, so to serve my country, my king, and my House," she whispered. "And perhaps, in time, if God is kind, we may recover a little of that carefree fondness we used to share when we were children together. I think that would not be deemed disloyal to—to joys of the past," she added softly.

For answer, unable to speak, he lifted her hand and pressed it to his lips, his face averted, shuddering a little as her other hand lightly brushed his head. But then he let himself sag against her knee in sheer relief as her hand continued to stroke his hair, for the deed was all but done.

"I am told," she said softly, after several seconds, "that at times such as this, it is sometimes customary among Deryni to—share a certain level of rapport. I have been instructed in the procedure, and I am willing to attempt it, if you will be the guide."

He found himself stiffening at the offer, wondering whether it had been Rothana or Azim who had given the instruction, and knew he could not yet face that intimacy, no matter Araxie's willingness or her ability. Gently, though, lest she take it as rejection, he lifted his head from her knee, closing her hand in both of his and bending to kiss it again.

"Dear cousin, you truly have the heart of a Haldane," he murmured, "but I think that might not be wise at this time."

"But Rothana said—"

"Rothana may dictate only *some* of the terms of this match," he said firmly, retaining her hand as he half-rose to sit beside her. "Believe me, I mean no reflection on you. What she has taught you can create a powerful bonding, as she has cause to know full well. But I think it might be best if you and I get to know one another as people first, after so many years apart. Better to reserve that other intimacy for marriage."

She pressed her lips together and looked away for a few seconds, pulling her hand from his, then bravely lifted her chin to face him again, a tremulous smile on her lips.

"In fact," she said, "I think I may be relieved you said that. This particular marriage is going to present its own set of challenges, as it is. Best not to take on too much at once."

He shook his head and found himself returning her smile. "As I said, the heart of a Haldane—and a mistress of understatement. You'll do well in politics."

"You may be pleasantly surprised at the schooling I have gotten from Uncle Létald," she returned tartly.

"Surprised? I very much doubt it. I don't know him well, but my father was in awe of Létald—and of *his* father. Political savvy is in the von Horthy blood, I think." He sighed and released her hand.

"That being said, I suppose we ought to discuss the first of the political practicalities, before we part tonight," he went on, glancing at her. "I—think it wise if no public announcement is made of our intention until after I return from Torenth. Especially after today, it will be clear to you that my mission there carries no small degree of risk—not from Liam himself, I think, for I am reasonably certain of *his* loyalty, but I cannot say the same for all his subjects. Once it becomes known that you and I intend to marry, it is almost inevitable that you will acquire at least some of my enemies. I should prefer not to have my focus diffused by having to worry about you, when I should be worrying about Liam."

She nodded, clearly aware of the concerns he had outlined.

"I quite agree. For entirely different reasons, I think it equally advisable to delay any public announcement until after my sister is wed. Not only is she the elder of us, but you will not wish to detract from the importance of the Mearan marriage, and the alliance it represents." She cocked her head at him. "Which raises another question. Many have speculated that you might marry Brecon's sister, to put a double Haldane stamp on the Mearan alliance. In light of what we've just agreed, that obviously won't happen."

"Ah, but there *will* be a double Haldane alliance," he retorted with a grin. "It will simply involve a different Haldane. It seems that our very discreet cousin Rory formed an attachment with the fair Noelie Ramsay last summer, when she came to Rhemuth for her brother's betrothal to your sister."

"*Did* he?" Araxie looked pleased.

Quickly Kelson related the essentials of the revised Mearan arrangement, and the accommodation he hoped Nigel would accept.

"That's what I was thinking of earlier, when I told you that Nigel might be persuaded to let the succession return to Albin." He allowed himself a sigh. "It was a genuine pleasure to tell Rory that I'd found a way to reconcile the prompting of his heart with the needs of state."

She glanced at her lap, lips lightly compressing, and Kelson suddenly realized what he had said.

"Araxie, I'm sorry," he said. "I didn't mean that the way it must have sounded."

"I understand," she said, lifting her chin. "Just because there isn't anyone else for me, though, please don't forget that, by marrying you, I'll be closing *myself* off to the likelihood of ever knowing the kind of love you've felt for Rothana. It isn't necessarily any easier for me, Kelson. Only different."

He nodded regretfully, determined not to let himself forget that again.

"I'm truly sorry," he murmured. "I *am* aware of the sacrifices you'll be making—and I have no right to assume that your sacrifices will be any less than the ones I'm forced to make."

"Perhaps we should talk about possible dates, then—at least for the betrothal. So far, we've mostly talked about things that *aren't* possible."

Numbly he glanced at his hands, at the rings on his fingers.

"Well, I suppose we could set the betrothal for—Christmas Court?"

"Half a year from now," she said quietly. "And when, for the wedding?"

He looked up. She was gazing into the fire.

"Perhaps—next spring, at Eastertide?"

She turned to look him squarely in the eyes. "My lord," she said quietly, her tone softening the formal address, "I quite agree that the public announcement must be delayed until after Richelle's wedding. But I must warn you not to let delay build false hopes. *She isn't going to change her mind.* Not when she's chosen her successor, and persuaded me to accept her choice—and persuaded you to agree to it. And the fact remains that Gwynedd still needs an heir of your body."

The stark logic of her statement was inescapable—as was his sudden, sick recognition that a part of him still *was* hoping that Rothana might yet relent. But that was not going to happen, especially given what Richenda had told him the night before. Abruptly he wanted it all to be over, decided, done.

"You're right," he said decisively. "I shall make the public announcement at Richelle's wedding feast, after I've announced Rory's betrothal. Shall we marry at Michaelmas? That's hardly two months later, and only three months from now. Can a queen arrange a wedding and a coronation in that short a time? Can your *parents* bear to see two daughters married in the space of six weeks?"

She was staring at him in astonishment, her mouth agape, and he knew he must look and sound like a madman.

"Kelson, we don't have to do it *that* fast—"

"I think perhaps we do. You're right, it's pointless to hold out false hope—and once we've gone and done it, maybe we can get on with our lives. Making the public announcement at Richelle's wedding feast is excellent timing. And in the meantime, I—I am prepared to plight my troth to you tonight, before witnesses."

"Tonight?" she whispered. "Are you sure?"

He drew a deep breath and forced himself to meet her gaze squarely, remembering his conversation with Azim.

"Araxie, anything could happen in Torenth. I could even die. What we do here tonight won't change that, but I feel that I ought to make this at least semi-official, before I go. Rothana and I had made no formal promises, and I—shall probably regret that for the rest of my life."

"Would it really have made any difference?" she asked. "She still would have thought you were dead—and she still would have done what she felt was best for

Gwynedd. And we still should be in our present situation. You mustn't torture yourself further over what wasn't meant to be."

"I'm sorry," he whispered. "It would have given me some measure of comfort, if that was to be the only time we stood before God and declared— But if you don't want to do it yet, if you'd like more time to think about it . . ."

"Good gracious, it isn't that!" Araxie declared. "I've had months to think about it, to get used to the idea. I just thought you might need more time. But if you wish to do it tonight . . ."

He nodded slowly. "I think we should," he said. "If I cannot promise you my heart entire, at least you should have my unqualified friendship, sealed before God and witnesses, as befits my intended queen. We mustn't let ourselves find excuses to avoid doing what we know must be done. So if you are willing . . ."

"I am willing," she whispered, and gently set her hand on his.

CHAPTER TWELVE

If a man commit himself unto her, he shall inherit her; and his generations shall hold her in possession.

Ecclesiasticus 4:16

s Kelson re-entered the room where he had left Morgan and Dhugal with Azim and Araxie's mother, all four of them rose, anticipation writ upon each face, though no one said a word. Without speaking, Kelson crossed directly to Sivorn and made her a stiff little bow.

"My lady," he said quietly, "it is my honor to inform you that your daughter Araxie has graciously consented to become my wife. With your permission, I should like to formalize the betrothal before a priest, before I leave for Torenth. May I send Duke Alaric to fetch Bishop Arilan?"

Sivorn gave him a searching glance, then dipped in a deep, graceful curtsy. "Sire, you honor my daughter and your House," she murmured. "If you prefer, however, we may delay this until your return from Beldour. I am aware of the gravity of your mission there."

Kelson very nearly smiled, finding it strange that, after years of being urged to marry, he now was being invited to delay.

"I am grateful for your concern, but I think it best that this be done tonight— perhaps in my quarters. For honor's sake, I would make my promises before God and witnesses—but not before the possibly public scrutiny of the Orsal's chapel."

"Sire," Azim said, "I am obliged to point out that excessive movement to and from your quarters may well be noted, despite my best efforts to the contrary.

Might I suggest that you consider, instead, the private oratory adjoining these apartments?"

"Point taken," Kelson agreed. "However, I—do wish to return briefly to my quarters." He drew a resolute breath. "Very well. Alaric, please ask Arilan to join us here in an hour's time. Aunt Sivorn, Araxie's sister may join us—and you may invite your husband and Létald, if you wish. For now, however, I would prefer to keep this private beyond that."

"As you wish, Sire. We shall await your return."

Desperate to escape, Kelson allowed Azim to escort him and Dhugal back to the quarters allotted them. The Deryni mage agreed to return within the hour. When the door had closed behind him, Kelson gave his coronet into Dhugal's keeping and took momentary refuge before a little shrine niche set into one wall, sinking onto its prie-dieu with face buried in his hands, fighting back the tears as he mourned what he had done—and was about to do. As king, he knew he was making the decision that best served Gwynedd—for Gwynedd must have a worthy queen, and Kelson the king must always take precedence over Kelson the man.

But Kelson the man grieved for what now would never be; grieved for what another's duplicity, coupled with cruel happenstance, had changed beyond redemption, forever denying him the woman whose touch had stirred unfathomed and now unfathomable depths of possibility. With God's grace, he prayed he might at least find contentment with Araxie; but his heart declared that there would never be another like Rothana.

He heard Dhugal cough, and knew he dared not long indulge in self-pity. Raising his head at last, he dashed at his tears with the backs of his hands. As he did so, light glinted on the rings on his left hand—on Sidana's ring, next to his Haldane signet, yet another poignant reminder of what he was about to do.

For a long moment, as he turned it to the light of the votive candle that burned before the little shrine, he thought back on what the ring had symbolized, over the years: the tiny Haldane lion engraved in the flat oval pared from along the thickness of the golden band. From within that remembrance came sure and certain knowledge of what he must do before he made any further vows before God.

"Dhugal?" he called, as he pulled the ring from his finger.

Dhugal came at once, from where he had been waiting silently just inside the door, clearly reluctant to intrude on the king's private grieving.

"Sire?"

"Not 'Sire,' for what I need from you now," Kelson said. "Dealing with this requires the assistance of a brother, not a subject. I should have destroyed it after Sidana's death—and I certainly never should have given it to Rothana."

Dhugal eyed it and Kelson appraisingly, then dropped to his knees beside the king.

"What are you going to do?" he asked.

"Hopefully, just melt it down." Kelson cast a speculative glance at the little tabernacle within the aumbry niche, shaped like a golden church and resting on a fine cloth of embroidered silk. Turning back the edge of the cloth, he saw that the niche itself, though lined with wood, had a stone floor. "Ah, good."

As he laid the ring on the stone, Dhugal eyed him dubiously. "What do you want *me* to do?"

"Just stand by, I think. When Arilan had this made, he told me it was of Deryni crafting—which means that melting it down may not be as simple as one might hope. This is one of those spells I only know in theory, from my Haldane empowering, so don't be surprised at anything you may see or hear."

As Dhugal nodded and set one hand on the king's forearm, Kelson drew a deep breath and exhaled gustily, then crossed himself and laid his cupped hands to either side of the ring, focusing his intent and entwining it with a whispered invocation.

"Holy Lord," he breathed, "I here offer up the shattered dreams symbolized in this ring of gold, which was born of fire, forged in power, given and received in hope. Now send forth Thy mighty archangel, holy Michael, to purify with fire, that new dreams may answer old, and new hope kindle from the ashes of the past. Amen. Selah. So be it. *Veni, Sanctus Michaél.*"

So saying, he invited the presence of elemental Fire, visualizing the fiery archangel—stiffened as he sensed a presence suddenly towering behind him, simply *there*, which swept invisible pinions around his shoulders and cupped fiery hands beneath his own, though the fire neither burned nor could be seen. He heard Dhugal's faint gasp, but the other's clasp on his forearm held steady.

"*Fiat!*" Kelson whispered, never wavering.

The fire now bulging visibly upward between his palms resembled handfire, but he knew it was far more than that. Holding his focus, he turned his cupped hands to compress this supernal fire over the ring, containing its power within the compass of his two hands and molding it downward. He could feel a semblance of heat as the ring began to smoke and then to glow—red-gold, white-gold, its rising temperature distorting the air around it.

Closing his eyes, Kelson began drawing from deeper within his reservoir of Haldane power—willed the refining fire to burn away all dross, all imperfections, all former associations, to cleanse all pain—at last sinking back on his heels to breathe out with a slow sigh, the spell's course run. When he opened his eyes again, the ring had become a flat roundel of molten gold, like a thin, new-minted coin, shimmering slightly in its own heat.

"*Jesu,*" Dhugal breathed, only then releasing Kelson's arm, as the king reared back onto his knees to look.

"Well, it appears I did melt it, didn't I?" Kelson said, with a ragged grin. Of the tiny rubies that had been the lion's eyes, he could see no trace. "Now we'd better pick out something to replace it."

Leaving the remains of Sidana's ring to cool, he sent Dhugal to fetch his jewel casket from the room where the squires were sleeping, summoning a bright sphere of handfire as Dhugal set the casket on the table and opened it. His mother's letter to his aunt Sivorn lay atop the contents, and Kelson handed that to Dhugal before lifting aside the padding that normally protected the jewelled circlet he had worn earlier.

Beneath, amid a sparse assortment of personal items and another, simpler circlet, his chancellor had packed a selection of trinkets intended as guesting tokens, in case the king should wish to bestow gifts in the course of his visit. From among these he must select something suitable to give to Araxie: something to symbolize new hopes, new associations, new loyalties—and sufficiently anonymous that she might wear it safely in his absence without betraying their connection prematurely.

He laid aside the enamel cross he had worn at his final court in Rhemuth and began rummaging amid the coral prayer beads his mother had given him, fingering through the smaller items in the bottom of the casket. He examined and discarded an emerald and several rubies; pondered a band of granulated gold encrusted with golden cairngorms; held to the light another ring set with a limpid sapphire, water-pale, polished en cabochon like the moonstones on either side; eliminated a dusky baroque pearl that would have suited Rothana, but not Araxie . . .

Then his fingers disturbed a tangle of three narrow rings with no stones at all, one each of yellow, white, and rose-gold, the three of them intertwined. Intended to be worn together, the rings had been the gift of Father Irenaeus, a memento of the first time Kelson had witnessed the Eastern manner of celebrating the Eucharist. Irenaeus had told him that such rings symbolized the Trinity, and were sometimes given in the East as wedding tokens.

As Kelson weighed them in his hand, to a faint, musical chiming of the three, it occurred to him that they might also symbolize the lives being bound together by what he was about to do—for Rothana would always be there, in the marriage, along with Araxie and the memory of Sidana, no matter what he did.

"I think not," Dhugal said quietly. "No one would miss the symbolism, who knows the background of this betrothal."

Kelson bowed his head, closing his hand on the triple-ring, silencing their music.

"I hadn't thought to give it to Araxie," he said. "She doesn't need reminding, any more than I do."

With a shake of his head, he poured the triple-ring back into the jewel casket and took up the sapphire again.

"This one, I think." He did not add that the cloudy moonstones flanking it were the color of her eyes. "Sapphires symbolize fidelity—and I *will* be faithful, once I make my vows. And I'll—speak with Arilan about having a new ring made for the wedding."

"An excellent choice," Dhugal said, taking the ring and slipping it onto his little finger for safekeeping. "Do you wish to change clothes, before we go back?"

Kelson shook his head.

"Why don't you wash your face, then, and we'll get on with it. There's no point prolonging this."

A quarter-hour later, again wearing the gemmed circlet of his rank, Kelson once again made his reluctant way to Sivorn's apartments, Dhugal at his side. Azim had done his work well, because they passed no one. Without comment, he showed them into the adjoining oratory, which as yet was peopled only by a silent procession of long-faced saints painted life-size on the walls all around them. The wavering light of a dozen hanging lamps of polished brass shimmered across the gold leaf adorning the images, lending them a semblance of life. Above the little altar table with its gilded tabernacle, a sweet-faced Queen of Heaven gazed down with compassion from a painted triptych, flanked by adoring angels and balancing a big-eyed Child on her knee. A hint of frankincense hung on the air.

Azim left them briefly amid the hushed beauty of the place, but returned almost immediately to admit Morgan and Arilan before withdrawing again. Kelson straightened as the two entered, inclining his head to the Deryni bishop in formal greeting.

"Thank you for coming," he said quietly. "I apologize for the lateness of the hour."

Arilan nodded and handed off a bound book to Dhugal, divesting himself of a dark, hooded cloak. Underneath, he had donned a white surplice and stole over his bishop's cassock of purple, with his bishop's cross bright against the snowy linen.

"I cannot imagine that this is any sudden whim, so I wonder why you did not see fit to mention it last night," he said, taking back the book from Dhugal. "When did you decide to do this? I approve of the choice—who could not?—but we all might have avoided some of what obviously was a painful charade."

Kelson lowered his eyes, vaguely aware of Morgan in the shadows behind Arilan, likewise removing a cloak that concealed attire appropriate to the betrothal of a king.

"Believe me, I would have preferred it otherwise," he said quietly. "But last night, it had not yet been decided. Rothana told me, on the night of Jatham's marriage to Janniver, that she had chosen me a bride. I've thought about it, I've prayed about it—but even when I went to meet Araxie tonight, I wasn't sure that I was actually going to ask her."

"You're about to make promises before God," Arilan said. "Do you intend to keep those promises?"

Kelson swallowed and slowly nodded, still not meeting Arilan's gaze. "I must. For the sake of Gwynedd. I require an heir. I daren't put it off any longer.

"Besides, nothing is going to change. Rothana has made up her mind, and she's offered me her own choice to take her place. It's—an astute match. No one in Gwynedd can possibly object. And I—was fond of Araxie, when we were children. Perhaps we can learn to be fond again."

"Perhaps you can," Arilan replied. "It is more than many kings and queens are given. And you know that I *am* sorry about—the other brides that might have been."

"I do know that," Kelson whispered. He found that he had been toying with the remains of Sidana's ring, which he had brought along to return to Arilan. Abruptly he offered the bright circle of it on his open palm: the coin of his sorrow.

"Know this for a token of my commitment in this decision, now that it has been made," he said quietly. "It used to be Sidana's ring." *And Rothana's*, he added to himself. "I thought it best not to keep it, since I'm about to make new promises. I'll need something different made for—for my queen."

Nodding, Arilan took up the flat roundel of gold and slipped it into some inner recess beneath his surplice.

"We can discuss that later," he said, not unkindly. "Meanwhile, we probably ought to review the ceremony briefly. It isn't a long one—which is probably a mercy for all concerned."

They had read over the simple ceremony and settled on a tentative date for the eventual marriage when another tap at the door heralded the arrival of the bride and her family.

Sivorn came first, now with the bright coronet of her hair covered by a veil, followed by her brother Létald and Araxie's stepfather, Baron Savile. As Sivorn came to kiss Kelson's cheek, Savile and then Létald offering him neck bows, Araxie and her sister slipped into the room, arm in arm, both of them cloaked. Azim brought up the rear, quietly closing the door and remaining there with his back against it.

At Arilan's bidding, Sivorn and her husband and brother came to stand beneath the gaze of the Virgin presiding from the eastern wall. As Richelle helped Araxie shed her cloak, Kelson and his party moved into place as well, Morgan opposite Araxie's parents and Dhugal standing as Kelson's supporter. It was

Richelle who brought her sister beside the king, as Haldane-dark as Araxie was fair, and then backed into position beside Dhugal.

Araxie had not changed her gown of forest green, but in token of her maidenhood, she had loosed her pale hair to cascade down her back in a molten ripple of silver-gilt, confined across her brow by a deeply chased circlet of emerald-set gold. She gave Kelson a hint of a nervous smile before turning her attention to Arilan, dutifully kneeling with the rest of them as the Deryni bishop invited all to join him in prayer.

"*Adjutorium nostrum in nomine Domini,*" he began, also turning to face the east.

"*Qui fecit caelum et terram,*" came the ragged reply.

"*Domine, exaudi orationem meam.*"

"*Et clamor meus ad te veniat.*"

Our help is in the name of the Lord . . . Who made heaven and earth . . . O Lord, hear my prayer . . . and let my cry come unto Thee . . .

"*Dominus vobiscum.*"

"*Et cum spiritu tuo.*"

"*Oremus.*"

He led them then in a whispered recitation of a *Gloria*, a *Paternoster*, an *Ave*, and then another *Gloria*, after which he turned to face them again, bidding them rise. As intended, the conjoined prayers had helped to still and focus all present. The lamplight gilded Araxie's face and hair as Kelson helped her to her feet, but he released her hand as soon as they were standing, resolutely fixing his gaze on the back of the Gospel book Arilan hugged to his chest.

"Beloved in Christ," the Deryni bishop said, "I believe none of us can be unaware of the circumstances that have brought us here tonight, and for what purpose. I have served the House of Haldane for many years now, through many trials, and—save for one tragic example—I have never found a Haldane wanting in honor, duty, or courage."

He drew breath to continue, and Kelson closed his eyes briefly, knowing that Arilan referred to Conall—without whom so much might have been different, for so many.

"The road that has led us here has not been easy for anyone," Arilan continued, "and no one can promise that the way ahead will not be difficult as well. All marriages present challenges; this one will present more than most. But whatever the future may hold for these two Haldanes, whatever sacrifices may be required, I have no doubt that with good will—and with the honor, duty, and courage that are characteristic of their House—something good can be made of the circumstances; and I am persuaded that this will have been a wise decision for Gwynedd."

He turned his gaze on Araxie. "My lady, because of the upcoming nuptials of your sister, and the uncertainty regarding the next few weeks in Torenth, the king proposes that your vows specify only that the marriage shall take place before the turning of the year, though I understand that Michaelmas has been suggested as a suitable date. Is this agreeable to you?"

As she dipped her head in silent assent, he smiled gently and held the Gospel before her, watching her place a steady hand upon it.

"Araxie Léan Haldane, before God and these witnesses, do you here promise and covenant to contract honorable marriage with Kelson Cinhil Rhys Anthony Haldane, before the turning of the year, according to the rites of our Holy Mother the Church?"

She glanced at Kelson, composed and serene as she said quietly, "I do so promise and covenant, here before God and these witnesses."

As she drew back her hand, Arilan turned his gaze toward Kelson, who set his own hand upon the holy book as Araxie had done, feeling somehow insulated and distant as Arilan spoke again.

"Kelson Cinhil Rhys Anthony Haldane, before God and these witnesses, do you here promise and covenant to contract honorable marriage with Araxie Léan Haldane, before the turning of the year, according to the rites of our Holy Mother the Church?"

Kelson could feel his heart thumping, and a sick, tight sensation in his chest, but his voice was no less steady than Araxie's had been, as he, too, repeated, "I do so promise and covenant, here before God and these witnesses."

"Amen," Arilan murmured, taking the Gospel from under Kelson's hand. "Have you a ring to seal the covenant?"

At Kelson's nod, the bishop opened the book and extended it. Detached now, Kelson received from Dhugal the pale sapphire set in its band of gold and laid it on the illuminated page, watching numbly as Arilan signed above it with a Cross, then set his hand atop it in blessing.

"Lord, we pray Thee to bless this ring, given and received in fidelity. May he who gives it and she who wears it walk always with Thee in honor and friendship, and may it become a symbol to sustain them as they continue about their work in Thy name. *In Nomine Patris, et Filii, et Spiritus Sancti, Amen.*"

The blessing had been apt, Kelson thought, as Arilan held book and ring toward him, speaking not of love, but of fidelity and honor and friendship. He supposed that was deemed sufficient for a king.

Feeling numb inside, he took Araxie's left hand in his and slipped the ring onto her wedding finger. It was very big on her hand, and she forced a faint smile as she closed her fingers to keep it in place, so trusting. . . . Kelson could not but feel like an utter cad.

"Now give me your right hands, and kneel for God's blessing," Arilan said, passing his book to Dhugal.

Rock-steady now, for that first, inexorable step now was taken, Kelson set his right hand in Arilan's left, still curiously detached as the bishop likewise took Araxie's hand and joined them. Together they knelt, leaning on the bishop's hand for balance. Beyond Araxie, the king could hear someone softly sniffling; he thought it might be Sivorn. Beside and behind him, both Dhugal and Morgan were close-shuttered against any contact of mind to mind.

Bowing his head, Kelson let the familiar words of blessing wash over him all but unheard, for his own prayer was not to God but to Rothana, wordlessly begging her forgiveness, grieving for what might have been. Arilan's murmured "Amen" jarred him back to the present, but not wholly to reality, for a part of him seemed to watch from somewhere outside his body as he exchanged a chaste kiss of peace with Araxie and accepted the quiet good wishes of those who had witnessed the betrothal.

Very shortly, pleading the lateness of the hour and the need for an early departure, he bade all a gracious good-night. Morgan said nothing as he, too, prepared to leave with Arilan, only touching Kelson's hand in an instant of shared compassion as he and the Deryni bishop took their leave and departed. Kelson let Azim escort him and Dhugal back to their quarters, sinking mindlessly into a chair when Dhugal had closed the door.

"Are you all right?" Dhugal asked quietly.

Kelson merely shrugged and set aside his coronet. "No. But thank you for standing by me."

Dhugal ducked his head. "I wish I could have spared you this. It isn't what either of us ever dreamed. I know what it has cost you."

"Do you?" Kelson whispered, though it was more a dull statement than a question, and required no reply.

*A*nd in the shadows of another part of the castle, Denis Arilan waited for approaching footsteps, stepping into view as Azim came around a turn in the corridor, having seen Kelson and Dhugal safely to their quarters.

"I need a word," he said, his face taut in the torchlight.

Azim cast an appraising eye beyond and behind, then inclined his head.

"You knew!" Arilan whispered. "You arranged it. You lied to the Council!"

Azim shook his head, setting a hand on Arilan's forearm to draw him closer, his whisper even softer.

"I did not lie—how could I, before them? I simply did not speak. Until tonight the arrangement was but an aspiration of my niece. Kelson might not have agreed. That he did ensures that full Deryni blood will sit upon the throne of Gwynedd—for I am convinced that Haldane blood will prove to be Deryni."

Arilan drew a deep breath.

"You tread very close to the line, Azim," he murmured. "You well know that Kelson's marriage has been a primary concern of the Council for some years—long before *you* became a part of it."

"And the Council, in its wisdom, does not always hold the answers," Azim retorted. "We were at deadlock. Rothana could not be moved. That being the case, something else had to move. By having her present a viable compromise, the king now has moved. Gwynedd must move ahead, if the balance among the Eleven Kingdoms is to be maintained."

Arilan breathed out in a long, tempering sigh.

"The Council should be told."

"The Council cannot be told at this time, for we have no direct access," Azim returned. "Without doubt, there is a Portal here, but I have yet to locate it. Nor am I minded to inquire of Létald—unless it is your wish to tell him of our connection with the Council."

"There are other ways," Arilan replied.

"Yes, but news of this sort, without the means to respond to the myriad speculation it will raise, would only foster debate that is neither necessary nor productive."

"You assume they will disagree," Arilan muttered.

"I doubt not that some of them may—which is all the more reason *not* to tell them until Liam-Lajos is safely installed on his throne. The Council tends to lose its focus when dealing with too many things at once. Time enough for Gwynedd's succession, when Torenth's is secure."

Arilan breathed a heavy sigh, forced to concede that Azim probably was right. Though only a few months seated on the Council, the desert prince already had gained a keen appreciation of its shortcomings as well as its strengths. And for now, the coming encounter in Torenth was, in truth, far more important than what had been done in the last hour, or even that afternoon.

"Should they not at least be told of today's attack?" he asked.

"To what purpose?" Azim retorted. "Can they prevent another one?"

"*We* must," Arilan said. "Do you think it was the uncles?"

"Who else?" Azim countered. "However, I do not think it was the one in our midst. As for the ones in Beldour . . ."

The lift of one black eyebrow said all that was needful. Arilan found himself suppressing a shiver of dread.

"I could wish that you were travelling with us," he said.

"I shall be but a day behind you," Azim said. "Perhaps not even so long as that. The ship from Nur Hallaj is expected but a day hence, and I must await my brother's instructions. The king will be safe enough until he reaches Beldour. By then, I will hope to have joined you."

"Very well," Arilan murmured. "I see that you cannot be moved. But God help us. God help us all."

CHAPTER THIRTEEN

For thou wilt light my candle: the Lord will enlighten my darkness.

Psalm 18:28

$\mathcal{T}$he next morning, while the king's party prepared for a noon departure from the Ile d'Orsal and Kelson himself tried to put from mind what he had done, others back in Rhemuth were discussing the general subject of nuptial intentions, as yet unaware of the decisions made the previous night.

"I confess myself quite as much amazed as you must be, to learn of Rory's interest in the Ramsay girl," Meraude remarked to Jehana after Mass and break-fast, as the two of them stitched companionably in Meraude's sunny solar. "I hon-estly have no idea when he had time to make such an attachment. The Mearans were only here for a fortnight."

Jehana kept her gaze fixed on the curly leaf she was outlining with careful stem stitches. She was still mulling the implications of Nigel's disclosure to them in the previous hour, and nursing a faint disappointment of her own, for she had hoped that Kelson might choose Noelie Ramsay as his queen.

"From what Nigel said, Rory is very earnest about the proposition," she offered. "But I don't suppose one can truly object when a match is from the heart, as well as satisfying needs of state. That happens seldom enough in royal matches. You and I were fortunate."

"Yes, we were," Meraude replied. She stopped stitching, in fond reminis-cence. "Well I remember the first time I ever set eyes on Nigel. It was the same

Twelfth Night when he was knighted, that year of the rebellion in Eastmarch. You and Brion were only a year married, and I had come to court with my brother Saer to take up an appointment in the household of Queen Richeldis. I was just fifteen. And Saer was three years younger, beginning service as one of Duke Richard's squires at the same time. He was so proud. . . ."

Smiling wistfully, with a hint in her manner of the young girl she had been, Meraude shook out her length of thread, letting the needle dangle as the silk uncoiled.

"I remember standing with the old queen's other ladies-in-waiting, off to one side, so very new and overwhelmed. It was *nothing* like anything I had experienced at home in Rhendall. You and Brion seemed like a pair out of legend—it was clear you adored one another. And when Nigel came to kneel before you, to receive the accolade from his brother's hand . . ."

She shook her head and sighed. "I think my knees went a little wobbly as I gazed at him, and my heart skipped a beat. All that long winter and spring, I prayed he'd notice me—as did every other eligible lady at court, and a few who weren't at all eligible. And I shed romantic tears with the rest of them when he and the other fine young men rode off to war with Brion and Richard and the others—and secretly wept more tears into my pillow on many a night, especially when periodic reports would arrive on the progress of the campaign. I was terrified that he wouldn't come back—and that he wouldn't notice me, if he did.

"He did come back, of course, having truly won the spurs he'd been given at his knighting—and amazingly enough, he *did* notice me. After that, I don't think either of us ever looked seriously at anyone else."

Jehana, too, had stopped stitching as Meraude spoke, remembering her own life at that time, before Brion's forbidden magic had driven a wedge between them. She still had loved him—always—but their relationship had never been the same, once she learned the true circumstances of that Eastmarch campaign, and the encounter with the Marluk, and how her beloved Brion, with the help of the half-breed Deryni Alaric Morgan, had kept his throne by means of forbidden magic. Nor had the pair of them spared her son, who even now was sailing toward what could be his death by that same magic—and worse than mere death of his body: the death of his soul.

Meraude seemed to catch an inkling of her sorrow, and reached a hand across to touch hers in compassion.

"Dear Jehana. We all share your worry for Kelson."

Jehana shrugged and laid aside her needlework. "He is his father's son in his stubbornness," she said. "Would that I could change him. But if I could, perhaps he would not be the effective king he has been. I only pray that he has not overestimated his abilities—or underestimated his enemies."

"Do you truly think that Liam will prove to be an enemy?" Meraude said thoughtfully. "I don't. He's a good boy, Jehana. He has had firm, careful guidance these past four years, away from the influence of the court of Torenth. Nigel says he is one of the finest squires he has ever trained."

"But, what if we have only trained up a cuckoo in our nest?" Jehana replied. "Will he turn on those who trust him, when he has settled back with his own people? Things are very different in Torenth, Meraude. When I was a girl in Bremagne, Torenthi courtiers sometimes came to my father's court. They always used to frighten me. At the time, I hardly knew why. Now, I know all too well."

"Because of their magic?" Meraude asked quietly.

Jehana managed to turn her shiver into a shrug, but she could not mask her distaste.

"I'll tell you what," Meraude said brightly, stabbing her needle into her work for safekeeping and pushing back her embroidery frame. "Let's be properly meddlesome mothers and go down to the library for a while, shall we? If my son is bent on marrying this Mearan heiress, I should like to know a bit more about her family. I'm certain Nigel already knows all the gory details, since he helped arrange the marriage contract between the girl's brother and Richelle, but I didn't pay a great deal of attention at the time. After all, it wasn't a child of *mine* who was proposing to marry with Meara."

She rose and gestured for Jehana to put aside her own sewing. "Leave that and come along. We'll have a peek at what Nigel rather annoyingly refers to as the stud book. It will be pleasant to reassure myself that my potential grandchildren won't have extra toes, or tails, or both eyes in a common socket."

"Meraude!"

"Well, there's no danger of *that*, of course; the two families aren't at all related. But I'm mightily curious to see who'll be added to our extended family. Please come," she said, holding out a hand.

Meraude's cheerful approach to the proposition at least held promise of diversion, so Jehana reluctantly agreed. Ten minutes later, she was hanging back somewhat behind Meraude as the latter pushed open the door to the library.

"Father Nivard, are you here?" Meraude called, glancing around and then entering.

Jehana followed somewhat more timidly. The room was whitewashed, flooded with light from two tall, west-facing windows, and deserted. Between the windows, whose heavy red damask drapes were swagged back behind iron finials, a wide reading desk displayed a variety of open books and unfurled scrolls and leaves of parchment, bespeaking research in progress. A heavily sculpted fireplace dominated the wall on the left, breaking the expanse of bookshelves and scroll-cases and pigeonholes lining most of the rest of the walls. A painted interlace design of mostly blues and greens arched above the fireplace and the windows, the green picking up the paving of greenish Nyford slate inside the embrasures and on the windowsills.

"No one seems to be here," Jehana said cautiously. "Good heavens, it's been years since I've been in this room."

Smiling breezily, Meraude led the way in, slipping behind the desk to cast an eye over the books and documents spread thereon.

"Has it really? I thought this was one of Brion's favorite rooms."

"Oh, it was. Perhaps that's why I've avoided it since he died."

"Well, there's no better place, if you want to vet prospective brides," Meraude said brightly, settling down in the chair behind the desk to look more closely at a genealogical chart laid out on vellum. "It appears that Father Nivard was researching the same thing. Here's the Ramsay lineage, all sketched out. Nigel must have put him to work on it."

Jehana came over to cast her gaze briefly over the chart, then stepped up into the airy brightness of the left-hand window embrasure where, in the first several years of her marriage, she and Brion sometimes had spent idyllic summer afternoons, reclining lazily amid hillocks of fat cushions while they read to one another from verse and legend and sipped at chilled wine and sometimes took their pleasure of one another. Sweet memories of the place came flooding back, making her ache for his caress as she had not in all the nearly eight years of her widowhood, but also enfolding her like a mantle of comfort and peace.

She felt her breath catch in her throat, and she glanced down into the stable yard below, to distance herself a little; but to her surprise, the old memories no longer brought pain, as they once had done; merely fond nostalgia. The difference surprised her, for always before, such thinking had only stirred up old sorrow for his loss—and her fears, now that he was gone. She let a little of the sweetness linger as she stepped down out of the embrasure and allowed her fingers to brush along some of the volumes shelved near the fireplace, remembering the pride her husband had taken in the royal collection.

It was not all Brion's work. Assembling the library had been the work of many Haldane kings and princes. King Donal, Brion's father, had achieved scholarly competence in several areas of interest, despite an active and successful military career, acquiring many of the volumes and documents now deemed among the rarest in the royal collection; and even before Donal's time, the royal library at Rhemuth had been said to house one of the finest collections of ancient texts in all the Eleven Kingdoms.

Brion had been more partial to the arts of war and diplomacy than those of the written word, but he had continued the family tradition of literary acquisition; and unlike many a predecessor similarly drawn to more active pursuits, he had even made the time to read many of them—though he had never been a scholar, and subtle learning had always come hard for him, and he had been impatient to sit for as long as a scholar should have done.

Still, if only in his somewhat limited fashion, Brion had loved learning, and instilled a love of learning in his son, and spent many a contented hour here. As Jehana wandered along one of the bookshelves nearer the fireplace, fingering a ragged-looking volume here, brushing the dust from a scroll-case there, she noted some of the titles that had brought her husband pleasure: *Carmena Sancti Bearandi*, a favorite of hers as well, written by one of Brion's distant ancestors.

And on another shelf, some of his favorite military treatises: *Historia Mearae, Liber Regalis Gwyneddis, Bellum contra Torenthum*, a bound volume of *Reges Gwyneddis post Interregnum*. Seeing the latter, she wondered who would eventually add an account of Brion himself to the chronicle of post-Interregnum kings. He had been a good and a wise sovereign, for all that his dabblings in forbidden arcana had imperiled his soul, and she hoped the historians would be kind to him.

Sighing somewhat wistfully, she turned to survey the rest of the room. Meraude was still bent avidly over the Mearan genealogy, tracing out lines with a careful finger as she consulted one of the open references. More bookshelves lined the wall opposite the fireplace, beyond Meraude, with a further band of the painted interlace running above, just beneath ceiling level. To the left, hard in the corner of the room, another red damask curtain of lesser proportion than the window draperies suggested the presence of a garderobe beyond, though she remembered none in this room.

Mildly curious, she walked over to the curtain and drew it back. The cubicle beyond was the standard L-shape of most garderobes, with the latrine shaft cut into the outer wall, but the stonework looked new, neither plastered nor whitewashed. She would have given it no further notice, deeming it an alteration made by Kelson in the years since his father's death—except that, as she let fall the curtain, her eye caught just an impression of an arched opening in the wall common to whatever room lay beyond the library.

Memory could supply no immediate recollection of what that room might be, nor of any passageway between the two. Puzzled, she caught back the curtain again and looked more closely. There was, indeed, a keystoned arch set into the wall, but it was filled with cut-stone. Probably an architect's ploy to relieve weight on the wall, then, meant to be plastered over; she was sure there had been no doorway here in Brion's time. But when she reached out absently to touch the stones, just before turning away a second time, her hand encountered—*nothing*.

Only barely did she suppress her start of surprise—though what had made her even try to touch it, she had no idea. Cautiously she reached out again, recoiling when, in that split second before she could actually jerk back her hand, her fingertips seemed to disappear into the very stone, as if they were penetrating fog or smoke.

She clutched clenched fingers to her suddenly pounding heart—though they did not hurt—willing herself not to panic. Thoughts of *what* and *why* and *how* tumbled together with the certainty that magic was responsible for the illusion, but oddly enough, her usual reaction of fear and distaste was mingled with a dispassionate curiosity. She could not fathom the purpose of any magic so oddly cloaked—in a garderobe, of all places!—but the fact that it had to be of Kelson's doing gave her odd reassurance.

She considered whether she might have imagined what she felt—or had not felt—whether the emotion of returning to the library for the first time since Brion's death might have triggered her imagination; but when she contemplated touching the wall again, she could not bring herself to do it. She *was* certain, however, that the garderobe had not been here in Brion's time—though it appeared to be a perfectly ordinary privy. The niche in the outer wall was, indeed, real, as was the wooden seat set atop the latrine shaft. And it certainly smelled like a privy.

"Meraude?" she said over her shoulder, in an admirably calm tone. "Could you come here a moment?"

She backed out of the niche and held the curtain aside as Meraude came to peer past her, half a head shorter than she.

"What is it? Are you ill?"

"No, I'm fine. I just don't remember this being here. Would you please touch that wall?"

Meraude looked at her strangely, then reached out and touched the wall.

"What's wrong with the wall? Jehana, it's just a new garderobe. I think it was built over the winter. Father Nivard probably got tired of going down the hall. Or maybe Kelson did. Actually, if you'll pardon me, I think I'll use it myself," she added, slipping past Jehana with a grin and pulling the curtain back into place. "Did I tell you that I think I may be pregnant again?"

Her announcement left Jehana standing in stunned bemusement as Meraude chattered on from behind the curtain about when a baby might come, and how nice it would be for little Eirian to have a playmate—she was hoping for another little girl—and then whether Nigel eventually might be persuaded to let her bring Conall's former leman and her daughter into their household.

"The child *is* our granddaughter, after all," Meraude said, as she came out from behind the curtain and gave her skirts a shake. "From what I've been able to learn of the mother, she's a rather fetching country maid—sweet and unassuming. Vanissa, she's called. If she's suitable and willing, I thought I might make a place for her in my household, perhaps as a seamstress."

She hooked her arm through Jehana's and began drawing them both toward the door. "Conall did provide for them, of course—his daughter will never go hungry—but I would so love to have my granddaughter here at court, where I can watch her grow up. She'll be nearly three, by now—just a year younger than Eirian—and I've already missed so much of her life!"

Jehana made vague agreement that little girls were dearly to be cherished, pushing back bittersweet memories—all too few—of the longed-for daughter who would have been Kelson's sister—born too soon to live more than a few hours. And after Rosane, there had been no more children, either sons or daughters. . . .

"I don't expect it to be easy, of course," Meraude went on. "You know how Nigel feels about anything to do with Conall. And the child's name doesn't help: the mother calls her Conalline. Understandable enough, I suppose, from her point of view, but it's unfortunate. Still, if I can get Nigel to accept *her*, maybe he'll soften his attitude regarding little Albin. He does love little girls—he positively dotes on Eirian. . . ."

Only when they had gone, Meraude chattering happily and Jehana in something of a daze, did Father Nivard emerge from the room beyond the Veil, briefly survey the materials on his desk, then disappear behind the Veil again.

*J*ehana spent the remainder of the day in somewhat distracted conspiracy with Meraude, watching the four-year-old Eirian play in the garden with the cook's cat and her litter of kittens while mother and aunt contemplated strategies for softening Nigel's attitude regarding his grandchildren. In the course of the afternoon, Jehana learned that Meraude had actually discovered the whereabouts of Conall's daughter and her mother, with the connivance of Rory, and was contemplating a casual ride in that vicinity in the very near future.

"It's fortunate that the child was a girl," Meraude observed, as she wound yarn onto a ball, from a skein Jehana was holding. "With the benefit of a gentle education, the natural daughter of a prince can hope to make quite a good marriage. After all, blood is blood, especially when it's royal. And if I could once move her and her mother to court, and Nigel got used to seeing the child with Eirian before he realized who she really was, I think he'd come around. I thought I might ride out to have a look at the pair of them in the next few days. I don't suppose you might consider coming along? I'm not very good at plotting behind Nigel's back, and I should welcome the company of a sympathetic co-conspirator."

On that, at least for the moment, Jehana declined to commit herself, much though her heart went out to both Conall's children, for any eventual placement of little Connaline at court would pave the way for Albin to join her—along with his very dangerous mother, for whom Kelson still was pining. While Jehana could not fault the young woman for attempting to keep her son from becoming any kind of threat to Kelson's throne—and even felt pity for her treatment at Conall's hands—Rothana still was Deryni.

True, her return to a religious vocation seemed genuine—though Jehana still had her doubts about whether a Deryni could properly have a religious vocation, notwithstanding that both civil and canon law now recognized the clergy status of men like Denis Arilan and Duncan McLain. Rothana's place among the Servants of Saint Camber was not bound by traditional religious vows, however, for the Servants themselves were not a traditional religious order. In fact, Jehana had suspicions that they, too, were Deryni, or at least tainted by the Deryni, since they called themselves in honor of the long-discredited Deryni saint, even now being restored to respectability, and by her own son.

But at least Rothana's affiliation with the Servants kept her far from Rhemuth most of the time. And her intentions for a religious life for her son, coupled with Nigel's adamant refusal to acknowledge the boy, meant that mother and son probably would remain safely tucked away with the Servants, notwithstanding Kelson's contrary wishes for both of them. Jehana little cared how Rothana brought up her child; but if Meraude succeeded in making a place at court for little Conalline, Albin might be next—which, inevitably, would bring his mother to court more often. And until Kelson was safely wed to a proper queen, that presented an ongoing danger.

Jehana supped quietly with Father Ambros and Sister Cecile that evening, as was her usual custom; but after evening prayers, as she prepared for bed, she found herself again considering her experience in the library that morning. She had not allowed herself to think about it earlier, refusing to let it intrude on the more pleasant distraction of discussing children, which she loved; but now, as she let a maid brush out her hair, the soothing monotony of the ritual let her relax, and the memory came drifting back—but not, strangely, in any threatening way.

"Thank you, Sophie, you may go," she said, when the maid had finished brushing, and had plaited her hair in a loose braid.

The girl dipped her a quick curtsy and departed, leaving Jehana to sit for a long moment gazing into her mirror. She would be forty in a few months' time. Even in the candlelight, she looked her age. There was very little grey yet threading the auburn hair—mainly, a faint frosting at the temples that was not at all unattractive—but the fine lines around the smoky green eyes told of the toll the years had taken since Brion's death. She was not so painfully thin as she had been, a few years before, so that she no longer had to bind a ribbon through her marriage ring to keep it from slipping off her finger, but there still was not enough flesh on her bones.

She pinched at her hollow cheeks to bring some color to them, then made a face at herself—she who, at home in Bremagne, had once been regarded as a great beauty. Then she shook her head and turned away with a sigh. After a moment, following another, more resolute sigh, she rose and wrapped herself in a dark cloak over her night shift, pulling up its hood to hide her bright hair. Before leaving, she took up a lighted candlestick from her dressing table, pausing to look down the corridor in both directions before emerging, the candle's flame shielded behind one hand. Her soft-soled slippers made no sound as she padded softly to the turnpike stair at the end of the corridor to descend several flights.

She was not sure what she planned to do. Quite probably, the library would be locked at this hour. And she certainly did not wish to rouse Father Nivard, whom she suspected of being Deryni. Even were she so disposed, she had no idea where his quarters lay. What both frightened and drew her was the knowledge that she herself might have the resources to deal with the lack of a key.

The thought of actually doing so sent a thrill of fear and guilt through her, and she closed one hand around the little crucifix she wore around her neck as she emerged at the level where the library lay and peered cautiously out of the stairwell. The corridor was sparsely lit by a torch at either end, but as deserted as the one she had just left, for the hour was late, and this area housed no living-quarters.

Breathing a tiny sigh of relief, she continued on toward the library. The door was closed and locked, as expected, but at least no light showed beneath it. She glanced again in either direction, then continued on a few paces, looking for a door to the adjacent room, but there was only the arched outline of a doorway now blocked up, just visible in the wavering light of her candle.

Then, it must be through the library, if she meant to carry through with her intention; but she *must* have a closer look at that very strange arch beside the garderobe. Returning to the library door, she again cast a guilty glance toward either end of the corridor, then crouched down and set her candlestick on the floor, laying her hands on the lock as she took a deep breath, asking God's forgiveness for what she was about to do. It was one of the less alarming of the abilities she had discovered within herself in the past few years—the power to move small objects simply by willing them to move—and she told herself that tonight's indulgence was in a good cause.

As the tumblers of the lock shifted beneath her hands, she rose to ease the door softly inward, knocking over the candlestick in her hurry to slip inside before someone came. The mishap extinguished the candle, but she snatched it up with a little gasp and scurried into the sheltering darkness of the room. Time enough to find flint and steel when she was sure no one had seen her. Pulse throbbing in her temples, she closed and locked the door, then pushed back her hood and turned to stand for a long moment in utter darkness, back pressed against the solid oak, feeling lightheaded and almost giddy as she strained her ears for any sound.

None intruded, save the pounding of her heart. After a moment, she recovered enough presence of mind to finger her candle and candlestick, making sure the two were still secure. The room was pitch-black, but she remembered its layout well enough to make her way carefully across it, half a step at a time, until she fetched up gently against the writing desk and then edged far enough around it to reach up and gently move aside the drapes in the left-hand window embrasure. The moonlight flooding into the room revealed that someone—presumably, Father Nivard—had returned to the room since her visit of the morning, for the books on the desk were now stacked neatly, scrolls rolled up, the vellums gone. She glanced nervously in the direction of the presumed garderobe, but its curtain still obscured whatever might lie beyond, besides a privy.

In the semidarkness, she could not find flint and steel. For that, too, she had a remedy, reluctant though she was to use it. But having come so far, she was not ready to abandon her mission simply because of timidity. If she could justify tampering with the door lock, she supposed that relighting her candle was not apt to damn her any more irrevocably than what she had already done.

Schooling herself to a calm she did not feel, she pulled the drape back into place, lest her light be seen from the stable yard outside, then gathered her intent and passed her hand over the candle in her other hand. Flame smoldered and then caught at the candle's tip, settling to a cheery, reassuring flame. Her sigh of relief nearly blew it out again, but she shielded it with her hand until it steadied, then moved over to the suspect corner, where she carefully pulled back the curtain and swagged it behind the iron finial on the wall.

By candlelight, the wall that was common to the next room still showed what appeared to be a blocked-up doorway filled with cut-stone; but when Jehana turned her head to let it slip into peripheral vision, she caught an impression of an open archway with perhaps another dark curtain on the other side.

She turned her head toward and away from the wall several times, trying to discern more as she wavered between the solid image of stone, when she looked at it head-on, and the ghost-ripples of dark archway that could only be glimpsed indirectly, now certain that the wall was some kind of illusion. She reached out to touch it—controlled her instinct to flinch and draw away when her fingers encountered nothing—then pushed slightly.

The fingers seemed to sink into solid stone, but she felt nothing. She drew back and examined her fingers, waggled them experimentally, then set the candlestick on the edge of the latrine and again cautiously reached her right hand into the wall, this time turning her head so that she might catch some impression of where she was reaching. This time, her fingers did, indeed, touch the fabric she had glimpsed before.

She closed her eyes briefly, allowing her hand to close on a fold of that fabric—*real, real!* a part of her mind gibbered—but then she opened her eyes again and shifted her hand to the right, searching for the edge of the curtain. Finding it, she gently drew it toward her until her hand and part of the curtain emerged from the "solid" stone. The red damask was the same as the garderobe curtain and the heavy drapes over the long windows. It crossed her mind that Father Nivard's quarters might lie beyond the curtain, but she thought that unlikely. A sidelong glance into the room beyond suggested the dark shapes of more bookshelves— perhaps an annex to the main library, then.

She dared not give herself time to consider too fully what she was about to do. Not releasing the fold of curtain in her right hand, she leaned back with the other to pick up her candlestick, then drew a deep breath and ducked her head as she turned and shouldered the curtain aside, sheltering the candle behind her body as she pivoted through the archway and into the room beyond. Thankfully, it did appear to be very much like the one she had just left, with bookshelves lining the wall common to the corridor, on the right, and a reading table hard against the far wall. Indeed, no more than an adjunct to the main library.

But, why the elaborate measures to hide it? The range of bookshelves had been built right over where the door to the corridor should have been—which meant that the only way into the room was the way she had come, guarded by magic. If this was, indeed, an extension of the library, it followed that whatever was contained here was not for the eyes of just anyone. And only Deryni works were likely to fall into that category.

Kelson, Kelson, what have you done? she whispered to herself, releasing the curtain as she approached the bookshelves immediately to her right, holding her candle closer as she scanned a finger along a row of books. None of the titles were familiar, but a few caught her eye:

Haut Arcanum . . . Liber Ricae . . . Codex Orini . . . Annales Queroni . . .

Her finger stopped on the latter, and she pulled it from the shelf with a mixture of fascination and dread, opening it at random.

"*Always in mind should be this precept,*" she read softly aloud. "*That the Healer' magic must respect the free will of his patient as a sacred trust. Yet sometimes may a mind be so sorely wounded that no willing access may be gained. Then must he make insistent ingress into that mind, even in the face of resistance, easing pain and making whole, and with reverence and due care—*"

Both taken aback and intrigued, for this clearly was a Deryni text—and one suggesting a moral dimension that she had not hitherto considered—she glanced

around for a safe place to set the candle and started toward the reading table—
and stumbled amid a faint tingle of power at her feet.

She caught her breath and stepped back in alarm, and the tingle stopped.
Looking down for an explanation, she saw that the flagstone on which she had
trodden looked just like the others around it—except that it seemed to be the
only square one—yet she knew what it was, by some deep-seated surge of recognition that she could not begin to explain. Nor, once she began to breathe again,
did she even feel inclined to further retreat. She could still sense the tingle of
power, right at her toes, but it neither threatened nor horrified. On the contrary,
it fascinated.

A Transfer Portal. As she gazed down at it, faintly agleam in the light of her
candle, she had no doubt that was what it was—and far more potent magic than
any she had dared to summon tonight. She had not wanted to hear, when Kelson
told her that he meant to use such Portals to send home reports during his
absence, but this, almost certainly, was one such that he meant to use. Which
meant that Father Nivard, as keeper of this place, probably was Deryni, as she had
feared.

And yet, even that did not alarm her as it once would have done. Could it be
that repeated exposure to the forbidden made it somehow less repellent? Certainly, it could not mitigate the inherent evil of such things. And yet . . . and
yet . . .

Held from further flight by a strange fascination, intrigued by the Portal despite
her aversion to any taint of magic, she even found herself wondering what it would
be like to use one—though she quickly stifled that speculation with a deliberate
recalling of other magic she had once tasted, all too horribly. It had begun at Kelson's
coronation, when the Deryni sorceress Charissa had used her terrible powers first to
blast Jehana into an awful limbo state, from which she could do nothing to protect
Kelson; and then Charissa had attacked Kelson himself. Jehana's joy at her son's eventual victory had been soured by her fears that the victory might have been bought at
the price of his soul, for her own forced taste of magic had been bitter, revolting.

She winced at the memory—far worse than more recent memories of what
she herself had done since that time—and different, she suddenly realized. For
she had begun to discover that her own power, stirred to wakefulness that day,
was within her, whether she willed it or not, and it *could* sometimes be used for
good cause. Once, in Kelson's absence, it had enabled her to warn Nigel of a
planned attempt on his life. And for many years, she had experienced flashes of
unexplained insight that she now knew were called Truth-Reading, by the Deryni.
And she certainly had not scorned using her undoubted powers to come here
tonight.

Nor would the gentle allure of the Portal at her feet be dispelled. The power glittering there, just beyond sight, seemed to beckon gently—not the seductiveness of temptation, to be denied whatever the cost, but the wistful calling of a friend—benign and reassuring, surely not evil.

Like one in a trance, she found herself sinking to her knees to lay aside book and candle, setting her hands flat on the square stone. The song it began singing softly to her soul seemed gradually to surround her with peacefulness, poignant and joyful, like kneeling in a chapel in the Presence. The sheer wonder of it made her weep, like being reunited with a loved one after a long absence.

She lifted her hands in awe, turning her palms to stare at them in the candlelight, suddenly beginning to comprehend who and what she was—no monster or creature of evil, but one gifted with powers she could choose to use for good. She cupped her two hands together and willed the power to manifest, caught her breath in silent delight as a firefly-flicker began to glow between her hands, cool and golden.

"Dear, sweet *Jesu*," she breathed, as she raised the growing sphere of handfire before her face—and in that instant, caught sight of the dark silhouette of the man sitting far back in the embrasure of the room's single window, only just visible in the light of her candle and the light she had called forth.

She muffled a wordless cry as she reared back from him, the handfire dying, nearly overturning her candle in the course of scrambling to her feet, clutching her cloak around her and at the same time wiping her palms guiltily against her skirts. Had he seen?

"Who are you?" she demanded. "What are you doing here?"

Only the man's hairless head moved, dipping in apology.

"Please forgive me if I startled you, my lady—or, should I say, Your Majesty?" His voice was soothing and gentle, somehow lower than she had expected. "I assure you, I am but a harmless scholar, come to use the library. The king gave me leave."

"The king? But . . . Well, you should have spoken up!" she blurted. "You frightened me half to death. And you still haven't told me who you are. And why are you here at this hour, lurking in the dark?"

"I fear I must have dozed off," he said somewhat sheepishly. "I confess that Kitron sometimes puts me to sleep—though that is, perhaps, a blessing, in these twilight years of my life. I am called Barrett. And I do beg your pardon if I gave you a fright. May I suggest that the fright is mutual?"

Barrett. The name meant nothing to Jehana. And if he had, indeed, been asleep, could it truly be that he had seen nothing?

"Well, that still doesn't explain what you're doing here at this hour," she said, trying to regain her composure. "The library was closed and locked, and——" she glanced guiltily at the archway. "How did you even get in here?"

He chuckled gently and shook his head, beginning to roll up the scroll in his lap. "How did *you?*"

"Why, I——I had a key!" she lied. "Don't be impertinent. What were you reading, anyway?"

"Kitron, as I said. Do you know his work? This is a very recent find——far more accessible than his *Principia Magica*. But I question his premise regarding the origins of the Healer's *Adsum*. He and Jokal both credit Orin, with influence from several lesser Lendouri masters, but I've always preferred Sulien's exegesis. Of course, if we had more than fragments of Orin's original texts . . ."

She stared at him aghast, hardly able to believe what she was hearing.

"What?" she whispered.

"I'm sure your own selection will provide more lively reading," he went on, continuing to roll up his scroll. "May I ask what it is?"

She felt her cheeks burning with embarrassment, and she glanced furtively at the book still on the floor before her.

"I——don't recall. I was just browsing. I didn't even know this room was here. I——why am I explaining? I don't have to justify myself to you. I think you'd better leave."

"If you wish," he replied, rising. "But I must ask you to stand clear of the Portal."

She gasped and scuttled backward at his movement, stifling another gasp as she was brought up short against the bookshelves behind her. How had she not anticipated that he had to be Deryni——right here in the palace, and apparently with Kelson's sanction!

"How dare you come here?" she whispered. "Stay away from me!" she warned, as he laid his scroll on the seat and began moving toward her.

"I mean you no harm," he said quietly. He came to the edge of the window embrasure and stopped, sinking to steady both hands on the stone to either side as one foot probed for the step-down onto the floor, but he did not look down. In a shocked rush, Jehana realized that it was because he could not see anyway. His gaze was fixed quite unfocused in her direction.

"You're blind!" she blurted.

"I am," he agreed, "though not so blind as some. My sight was the price I paid to ransom the lives of many children."

"To ransom children?" she repeated stupidly. "Who would demand a man's sight, to ransom children?"

"Those more blind than I am now," he said gently, as he found his footing and stepped down, then straightened before her. "That was long ago. They were not ordinary children, and I was not an ordinary man. One does what one must, to save the lives of little ones."

But before he could continue, a soft light flickered between them, and then another old man in flowing black scholar's robes was standing on the Portal square, a scroll tucked under one arm. He and Jehana gasped simultaneously as they saw one another, but his reaction echoed only her surprise, not her alarm. She shrank even harder against the bookcases behind her, considering a dash for the safety of the curtained doorway that led back into the main library.

"Good God, what is *she* doing here?" the newcomer demanded of Barrett, eyeing Jehana as he backed protectively toward his friend. "Do you know who that is?"

"We've made informal introductions," Barrett replied, his tone easy and soothing, aimed at disarming Laran's hostility. "Since I know of only one woman the king specifically granted access to this room via the Veiled doorway—and I assume the Duchess Richenda to be safely in residence in Coroth—this lady had to be the one woman in the world related to the king by blood, for whom specific authorization would not be necessary." He smiled disarmingly in Jehana's direction. "I apologize if I misled you, my lady, but it had not occurred to me that you would enter here—or even that you could. I have no wish to cause you distress. We shall leave immediately."

"You're Deryni," she whispered. "*Both* of you are Deryni. Sweet *Jesu*, how long has this been going on? Coming and going at will, right here in the palace!"

She shrank back as Barrett merely moved closer to the newcomer and took his arm—contained a little gasp as the latter glared at her, just before the pair of them vanished in a faint flash.

Then she was alone with her candle and her fear, blinking into soft silence, trembling in after-reaction. Numbly, mechanically, she picked up the book she had discarded and replaced it on its shelf. She did not dare to chance a look at the one the man named Barrett had left on the window seat. When she had returned to her quarters, she knelt long beside her bed, but prayer would not come. At last she fell asleep on her knees, forehead resting against the edge of the bed—and dreamed of the man with the emerald eyes, silently reaching out to her, almost as if the emerald eyes could see. . . .

CHAPTER FOURTEEN

He believeth not that he shall return out of darkness,
and he is waited for of the sword.

Job 15:22

 $\mathcal{T}$ hat same day, while Jehana made her first foray to the library with Meraude, Kelson and his party sailed for Torenth, now the guests of Létald
Hort of Orsal aboard one of the ships of his coastal fleet, capable of penetrating
farther upriver than Morgan's *Rhafallia*—even as far as Beldour itself.

Many of the Orsal's family had accompanied the royal party down to the
quays to see them off—most of them, save Létald's pregnant wife. Araxie was
among them, standing between her mother and her sister and dutifully waving a
brightly colored kerchief with the other women as the ships set sail.

The departure was more festive than Kelson might have expected, given the
previous day's attempt on the lives of two kings, but Létald seemed very sure of
what he was doing. As they moved away from the quay, the green sail of Létald's
caïque, the *Niyyana*, caught the wind and bellied above them, bringing to life the
white sea-lion emblem of Tralia painted on the canvas; his personal colors
streamed from the masthead with those of Gwynedd and Torenth. A pair of
Tralian war galleys waited to pick them up as they skimmed between the black
galleys drawn up in salute, perhaps in pointed statement that Létald would not
countenance another breach of hospitality to guests under his protection. It
occurred to Kelson that only on that stretch of road between port and palace
could such a breach have been even contemplated—and to ensure that there

would be no repetition, Létald had caused every member of staff accompanying them on the journey to be re-vetted during the night.

"I cannot think that anyone will dare to breach the peace again," he told Kelson, as *Niyyana* and her escort cleared the pharos and headed north, the black ships falling in behind. "Leastways, not while we are at sail. I don't know Count Mátyás at all, but Rasoul has always played honest with me, and it's he who now heads this Torenthi delegation. I cannot hold him or Torenth responsible for yesterday, but if anything goes amiss from those"—he gestured toward the ships ranged around them—"he risks war with me. But I cannot answer for Beldour."

Kelson only hoped that Létald was right about Rasoul. Here in Tralian waters, it was easy enough to posture bravely; and for a time, once they started upriver toward Beldour, they would still be skirting Tralian territory, for the river was Létald's northern boundary with Torenth.

But if both Létald and Azim were mistaken, and more overt treachery should surface before they reached Beldour, the six black galleys were more than enough to easily overwhelm any physical resistance by Létald's much smaller party. But as Létald had said, to do so was to risk war with Tralia as well as Gwynedd. No, they were safe enough until they reached Beldour.

Accordingly, having taken all due precautions, Létald seemed determined to put aside further worry and enjoy the journey, anxious that his guests should do the same. Kelson could not but admire his aplomb—though perhaps that came of living cheek by jowl with Torenth for centuries. Létald had even allowed his eldest son and heir, Prince Cyric, to join the royal party as planned, nominally commanding the second of the Tralian vessels—further evidence of his confidence that nothing further would happen.

After consulting with Morgan, Kelson asked Bishop Arilan to travel aboard Cyric's ship with Derry Brendan, and Payne, to keep all of them that bit removed from constant contact with the Torenthis—who, save for Liam, were dispersed among the black galleys. Liam seemed more restless than the previous night, but Kelson ascribed the tension more to growing excitement rather than to any real fear.

They sailed northward, close along the coast of Tralia, with a fair breeze, entering the broad mouth of the River Beldour in the long twilight of the summer evening to anchor still in Tralian waters, but within sight of the domed city of Furstánan, nestled in the haze of the far Torenthi shore. As Rasoul and Mátyás came aboard Létald's vessel to dine with the royal party, the distant city began to twinkle with silvery flashes like spangles on a veil.

"Furstánan sends her welcome with mirrors," Rasoul told them, jutting his bearded chin in that direction as Kelson and his intimates lined the port rail with

Liam to gaze and point. "They know that we bring Liam-Lajos home. After dark, you will see far greater spectacle."

"Are those also part of the welcome?" Kelson asked, indicating the scores of small boats sailing toward them, each bearing a torch in its bow.

"Yes, we will see increasing numbers of them, the closer we get to Beldour. That is part of the reason for the black ships."

Indeed, the black galleys had deployed around the three Tralian vessels, and would allow the smaller boats no close approach, so the smaller craft gradually turned around and went back, the brightness of their torchlight seeming not to diminish for a long time, for as their distance increased, so did the darkness. As the sun sank behind the distant headlands of Corwyn far behind them, Liam gazed unspeaking at the receding boats and across to the darkening line of the far Torenthi shore. After a while, Kelson moved closer beside him. The others had drifted safely out of earshot.

"You've been a long time away from home," he observed, as Liam glanced aside at him. "I'm sorry for that."

Liam smiled bleakly and returned his gaze to the distant shore. "I think it was not entirely your choice," he said. "My uncle Wencit will have had much to answer for, when he met his Maker. And had I not spent these last four years safe at the court of Gwynedd, I think it entirely possible that my fate might have held a fatal accident like my brother's."

"Are you saying it was no accident?" Kelson asked.

"No more than yesterday's attack," Liam said with a shrug, "and I have no proof."

Chilled, Kelson, too, turned his gaze toward the distant city. "Have you any suspicions?"

"Yes."

"Mahael?"

"Yes," Liam said, after a slight hesitation.

"Any others?"

"Maybe my uncle Teymuraz."

"What about Mátyás?"

Liam shook his head quite emphatically. "No. Mátyás loves me. Of that I am certain."

"Enough to stand against his own brothers?" Kelson countered, turning to regard the boy, who looked at him long and searchingly, then slowly nodded.

"Even so," the boy said softly. "Mátyás would never betray me."

Behind them, a sudden, collective gasp whispered among the others gathered on the deck of the *Niyyana*, and both young men looked back in inquiry, then turned again to gaze out at the distant Torenthi shore. A steadily growing light had begun to play above the city's cupolas and domes, pale and rainbow-hued, shimmering in a larger dome of iridescence like an illuminated soap bubble. Kelson, too, gasped as he saw it, but Liam only laughed softly in delight, grinning as Mátyás came to join them and sweeping an arm in the direction of the display.

"Is all of that for me, Uncle Mátyás, or do they do this every night?" he asked.

Mátyás nodded amiably to Kelson and leaned against the rail to Liam's other side, relaxed and easy in a plain silk tunic of deep blue, his dark head bare. "They do it on the eve of every Sabbath, my prince, to herald the Lord's day; but tonight, they do it in your honor—for you are their lord in this world."

"*Who* does it, Count Mátyás?" Kelson asked.

"Why, the holy monks and sisters of Saint-Sasile," Mátyás replied. "It is part of their ministry, to give witness to the glory of God through perpetual prayer and through this visible manifestation of their devotion. They are Deryni, of course. But perhaps you think it a frivolous use of our powers."

"Not at all," Kelson said carefully, eyeing Mátyás with closer interest. "If, as I believe, such powers come from God, Who is Lord of Light, then what better way to acknowledge Him?—and in a way that gives public witness to His beauty and power." He shrugged wistfully. "Would that my own people believed that."

Mátyás allowed a faint smile, glancing down at his interlaced fingers. "Your people have much to learn, I think. And perhaps mine have much to learn from yours. You are not as I imagined, Kelson of Gwynedd—though Rasoul has insisted from the beginning that you are a man of faith and honor."

"Lord Rasoul is generous," Kelson replied. "But it is, indeed, my intention always to keep faith with my friends." He paused a beat. "I would have Gwynedd and Torenth to be friends, Count. There is no reason our two lands must continue to be at enmity with one another."

"I fear my brothers would not agree," Mátyás said, his tone betraying nothing.

"No, they would not," Kelson said quietly. "And had it been up to them, I think your nephew would not have spent these past four years at my court." He allowed himself a careful breath, declining to mention the attack of the previous day. "But inasmuch as the choice of these present circumstances was given to none of us—not to me, not to you, or to your brothers—I think that you, at least, can appreciate the merit of allowing Liam-Lajos a chance to gain a better understanding of his neighbors to the west before he comes into his personal rule—something not enjoyed by any other King of Torenth in recent memory."

Mátyás smiled faintly, slowly nodding. "Boldly spoken, my lord. And I, at least, do not question your wisdom in this matter. Nor—and I will be more frank than, perhaps, my brothers would wish—nor do I think that dwelling on the long-ago claim of Festillic pretenders to your Crown serves any useful purpose.

"Let it have died with Wencit," he went on, turning his gaze out wearily to the rosy light still glowing above the city. "It has been more than two hundred years since Imre and Ariella passed from this mortal sphere. It has been a hundred since the death of the last Festil in the direct male line, on that bloody battlefield at Killingford, when so many good men of both our lands died—and for what?"

Liam had gone very quiet, wide-eyed and tight-wound as Mátyás spoke, drawing back a little from between his uncle and Kelson, his dark gaze flicking appraisingly at Rasoul. The Moor's dusky face was unreadable. Mátyás continued to gaze out across the water.

Kelson studied all three of them for the space of a handful of heartbeats that seemed like thunder in his ears, wondering whether he was hearing only what he wanted to hear or whether he was detecting a subtle attempt on Mátyás's part to offer solidarity, at least in Liam's cause. He had been Truth-Reading as Mátyás spoke, and could detect no hint of any attempt to mislead, and yet . . .

"Indeed, for what did so many good men die?" he repeated, hardly daring to breathe for fear of breaking the spell. "You will appreciate, I think, that we of Gwynedd regard the Festillic interregnum as an unfortunate period of foreign occupation, ended when Deryni led their own to throw off the invader's yoke. Much that was less than noble came after that, but I would venture to suggest that subsequent confrontations have amply demonstrated that my people will not bow again to foreign domination. Alas, many suffered and died needlessly in the demonstration. I would have no more young men slain in furtherance of this old and worn-out contention."

"In this, I daresay we agree," Mátyás said mildly, not looking at Kelson as he gestured toward the city, where the dome of light was dimming. "But I see that our celestial display has run its course for the evening. That being the case, shall we see what delicacies the good Prince Létald has provided for our enjoyment?" He set a hand on his nephew's shoulder. "Pray, be free to join us, Kelson of Gwynedd. I think you shall always be welcome at my table," he added as he brushed past the king, so quietly that Kelson could not be certain he had heard correctly.

The king found no further opportunity to draw out Mátyás that evening, though he later informed Morgan and Dhugal of the conversation, when Mátyás and Rasoul had returned to their galley and the others aboard the royal caïque had mostly bedded down for the night. Sitting far forward in the bow of the ship, under a canopy of stars, the three linked together in magical rapport, for the subject matter was too delicate to chance eavesdroppers, always a possibility in such close quarters.

He and Liam spent a long while together after supper, just standing at the rail, Kelson pointed out, after the three of them had pooled their knowledge of Mátyás in light of the conversation Kelson reported. *I would be very surprised if they were not in rapport. Mátyás seems to genuinely care for the boy; I think he honestly does have Liam's best interests at heart. But whether he would stand against Mahael and Teymuraz is another question entirely. I just don't know.*

Do you think we should tell Arilan about this? Dhugal ventured.

Morgan's psychic equivalent of a snort was almost audible.

What, and have him start playing word games again, dancing around the subject?

Perhaps not yet, Kelson allowed, taking the middle ground. *But if this peace overture comes to have a bearing on what may happen in Beldour, I think there will be time enough to consult him. I know that part of my wariness comes of Mátyás's being kin to Wencit and that line—though, as even he pointed out, any Festillic claim to Gwynedd is so watered-down by now that it hardly bears thinking about.*

Then, perhaps we wait for Mátyás to make his next move, Morgan replied. *We have several days until we arrive at Beldour. Who knows what may develop in that time?*

*T*hey sailed again as soon as the predawn doldrums gave way to morning breezes, each of the Tralian ships flanked by a pair of black galleys, the Torenthi flagship whispering half a ship-length behind and to the left of Létald's vessel. Rasoul, Mátyás, and four Torenthi guards of honor had come aboard before the morning's sailing, the latter to take shifts by pairs as the day wore on, and various of the ranking nobles of both parties took turns attending on the two kings.

Now that they were entering Torenthi waters, the royal party took up daily station beneath a purple canopy of state stretched over the dais on the caïque's afterdeck. Set apart from the bustle of crew and servants, the platform became their observation post by day, where they took their ease amid plump cushions and balmy breezes, sipped cool sherbets, and sampled exotic fruits. By night, they slept beneath the stars, which seemed more numerous than Kelson had ever noted at home in Gwynedd.

Not for generations had a Haldane king penetrated so deeply into Torenth. It seemed very different from Gwynedd. True to Rasoul's predictions, small sailing vessels and transport craft now sallied forth from the villages and settlements strung along the riverbanks on both sides as they pressed eastward, though the black galleys kept the smaller craft at a distance. The occupants of these vessels cast brightly colored wreaths and garlands upon the water to herald Liam's coming—or sometimes to salute Létald, while they yet skirted Tralia along the south bank—so that often the royal flotilla glided through a veritable floating garden.

The vistas of the distant shore changed almost hourly, golden beaches and craggy cliffs giving way to gentle green meadows and fields and the occasional walled town sprawled at water's edge, each with its domed churches and minarets glinting amid gabled rooftops and pointed towers. By the end of the second day, they had left behind the last of Tralia's fertile fields and gently rolling hills and were pressing deeper into Torenth, with the first purpled slopes of the mountains of Marluk beginning to thrust upward to their right.

The newness and the variety of the passing landscape provided reasonable diversion for the first day or two, with Liam eagerly pointing out features of his homeland to anyone who would listen; but even he had begun to lose enthusiasm by the end of the second day. By the third, when no wind came at dawn and the crews of all the ships must take to their oars, their progress slowed and, with it, the passage of the hours. After the first day of this, the ships began to exchange a few passengers among them, to lend variety to conversation.

Noon of the third day found Kelson leaning against the starboard rail in something approaching boredom, with Dhugal on one side and Létald's son, Prince Cyric, lounging on the other, his back to the river and his face upturned to the sun. Despite the lighthearted introduction Létald had given his heir at Horthánthy, the Tralian prince was of an age with Kelson and his foster brother, well prepared for his future role, and evidenced little interest in the unfolding countryside, for he had travelled widely with his father in the buffer states and along this very river, which was Tralia's common border with Torenth, and had even been to Beldour. This particular trip marked his first official diplomatic mission, as one of the Tralian observers at Liam's enthronement, but it soon became clear that Cyric's personal focus was less diplomatic than matrimonial.

"They say that it rarely gets this warm in Gwynedd, and that the weather is always a safe topic for discussion," he remarked by way of preamble, turning his face toward Kelson and blinking in the strong sunlight. "That's boring, though. I don't suppose you could be persuaded to talk about the subject of marriage instead?"

Kelson gave Cyric a wry look that did not require accompanying words, to which the Tralian prince only shrugged and grinned sheepishly.

"I know, it must become tiresome. But I must confess that I share a certain measure of your disgruntlement, if for different reasons. Unlike you, I am eager to marry."

Dhugal snorted, not looking at Kelson. "The last I heard, there was no shortage of eligible princesses."

"No shortage at all," Cyric agreed. "But alas for me, most of them would far rather live in hope of the hand of the King of Gwynedd than hear the suit of a mere crown prince of a Forcinn state. Frankly, I wish that your esteemed foster brother would make up his mind, so that the rest of us can get on with our lives."

Kelson had known Cyric since childhood, though not well, but the long acquaintance still had left an easiness between them that allowed so bold a statement. Since leaving the Ile d'Orsal, Kelson had tried to put Araxie from his mind, preferring not to think about that situation while he dealt with the potentially more deadly problem regarding Liam; but he well knew what Cyric was trying to say. The Orsal's line were a hot-blooded and passionate lot, inclined to marry young and breed prolifically. Only lately had Kelson begun to be aware that his own reticence regarding marriage was beginning to affect the matrimonial plans of those of lesser station.

"Was there any particular princess you had in mind?" he asked, faintly amused, and keeping his tone casual.

Cyric gave an exaggerated yawn behind one languidly raised hand and turned to gaze down at the oars moving with hypnotic rhythm beneath them, trying not to look like he really cared.

"Well, my Haldane cousins are already spoken for," he said airily. "Richelle will be married to Meara by the end of summer, and I expect that Araxie will marry Cuan of Howicce; they've been courting for ages. I'd briefly considered *his* cousin, the Princess Gwenlian—but she'll be Queen of Llannedd if her brother produces no male heir, and that would present problems for *me*. I'll be Prince of Tralia one day, so I couldn't live with her in Llannedd; nor could the Queen of Llannedd live here in Tralia.

"Actually, I was thinking of Noelie Ramsay—unless, of course, you're looking in that direction. That's what they're saying: that you're waiting for her brother and Richelle to wed, and that a betrothal will soon follow."

"Is that what they're saying?" Kelson said, feeling faintly sorry for Cyric, who would end up with none of the ladies he had named.

Cyric ducked his head, suddenly embarrassed. "Now you think I'm foolish," he murmured. "Actually, there *are* several lesser ladies I could become fond of—but it's as easy to like a rich wife as a poor one. You aren't going to give me any hint, are you?"

"Sorry," Kelson said, with what he hoped was sufficient finality. "I must see Liam safely enthroned first. After that, I'll worry about getting married."

As soon as he could, he found excuse to leave both companions and move far forward onto the prow of the ship, where he gazed long into the lazy curl of wave folding back from the bow, trying to visualize Araxie's face but seeing only Rothana's.

The afternoon stretched on, close and oppressive, with no breath of air and no prospect of any, as the oarsmen kept a steady rhythm, to the slow, even beat of the pace drums, throbbing like the heartbeat of the land. After a while, Kelson rejoined the others under the state canopy to pick halfheartedly at bread and olives and sip at chilled Fianna wine, but it was too warm to eat. Off to their left, the southernmost reaches of the great fertile crescent that was the Torenthi heart-land stretched northward in a great, rolling plain of undulating wheat and grain, all hazed in the summer heat. During the hottest part of the afternoon, Kelson sprawled with the others amid the piles of cushions beneath the purple canopy and tried to doze, while servants stirred the still air with feathered fans.

Not until dusk did a faint breeze begin to rise—enough to begin easing the oppressive heat, and to raise sail, but not enough to let the oarsmen stand down. Nonetheless, their silent convoy made far better progress in the several hours before the lowering darkness obliged them to halt for the night.

They dropped anchor mid-river, off a substantial walled town that soon spawned a fleet of tiny, torch-lit boats bearing singing occupants. The very tone of the chanted song conveyed unmistakable joy and welcome, even though Kelson could understand not a word. Somewhat revived by the growing breeze, Liam leaned eagerly over the starboard rail beside Kelson, gazing longingly at the spec-tacle of little boats, occasionally raising his arms in salute as garlands of flowers again were cast upon the waters.

"The song is one of welcome and blessing," he confided, grinning as he acknowledged the wave of a particularly fetching girl in the bow of one of the lit-tle boats, who tossed out a garland of pale blossoms and shiny leaves. "I confess, I know it by the tune, not the words, at this distance, but—" He bit at his lip to stop it trembling. "I had not realized how much I missed home," he said more softly. "I only hope I may live to be their king in fact."

"And for many a year," Kelson said quietly, echoing a Torenthi phrase taught him by Father Irenaeus. "Liam—we *shall* see this through, you and I—trust me."

"I do," Liam murmured, ducking his head. "I only hope that trust may be enough."

They fell silent at that, watching together as torches gradually lit the town walls like a necklace of topaz as the twilight deepened. With the black galleys standing to, the little boats did not approach too closely or stay too long, but Liam's delight at their gesture was evident. They watched until the last torch had disappeared into the darkness before the town, only then turning to rejoin the others.

The creak of rigging and the gentle slap of wavelets against the ship's hull hovered on the water like ghost-whispers as the party aboard the *Niyyana* settled for a quiet supper—their last such meal before reaching Beldour the next after-noon. On this occasion, Rasoul and Mátyás did not join them, permitting Liam to share a final evening with his friends from Gwynedd. One of Létald's sailors brought out a mandolin, and songs of Torenth and Gwynedd as well as Tralia floated out into the darkness; but even cooled by the continuing breeze, Kelson slept badly that night, his dreams permeated by the increasingly alien images of the river—and imagination supplied more threatening glimpses of what might lie ahead in Beldour. The next day would see their arrival at the Torenthi capital, and unmistakably within the sphere controlled by Liam's uncles.

The morrow dawned cooler than any thus far, with a welcome breeze promising both milder temperatures and swifter progress. With the sails bellied by a goodly wind, the oarsmen were able to abandon their rowing benches and deploy along the decks, ready to serve as the honor escort intended.

Just before noon, the three royals withdrew briefly below deck to dress for their arrival. Kelson's lightweight Haldane silks glittered with gold embroidery as he emerged into Torenthi sunlight, the scarlet a subtle contrast to the royal purple Liam wore; in compliment to Torenth, he had donned again the enameled cross sent him upon the occasion of his knighting. Though he and Létald both wore jewelled diadems, Liam had donned a flat-topped black hat similar to the one Mátyás usually wore, with a rich starburst of jewels affixed to the front and pendant jewels dangling past his ears on either side. Rasoul and Mátyás came aboard the royal caïque at midday, accompanied by an honor guard of six white-robed Moorish warriors, and stood to either side of three chairs of estate now set beneath the caïque's rich canopy, where Kelson King of Gwynedd and Liam-Lajos King of Torenth took places flanking Létald Prince of Tralia, whose ship it was.

Beldour lay at the confluence of two of the three great rivers serving Torenth: the mighty River Beldour and its lesser tributary, the River Arjent. Shortly before the first spires of the Torenthi capital came into view, as they passed beneath the cliffs of Anowar, thrusting upward to their right, men ranged along the cliff edge began sounding welcoming blasts on long, curled horns of brightly glinting brass. Rasoul pointed out, interspersed among the men, the source of an eerie yet melodious ululation interwoven amid the trumpet calls.

"Such welcome is custom among desert tribes and the women of the steppes," Rasoul told them, directing Kelson's gaze to the veiled women, brightly dressed in every shading of the rainbow. "It is said to be a woman's mystery."

As the royal flotilla rounded the cliffs, a long row of gilded and canopied state caïques parted before them, manned by smartly liveried oarsmen who raised their oars in salute, then fell in on either side of the *Niyyana*, rowing to the rhythm of shimmering bells rather than pace drums. In their wake, swarming outward from increasing signs of habitation along both river shores, came growing numbers of smaller boats, their occupants singing and waving scarves and branches and casting garlands on the water to welcome home their king.

Adjusting sail, the black galleys drew ahead to form a phalanx like an ebon arrowhead, clearing the way before them. Beyond the galleys, rising boldly from both banks of the river, the first of Beldour's domes and minarets and blue-black battlements thrust boldly upward against a pale cerulean sky, gleaming in the summer sun.

"There's that blue I told you I had missed," Liam said to Kelson, pointing out a domed building crowned with a gilded cross, poised at the edge of a spit of land that jutted into the river from the right. "The blue of the dome comes from glazed tiles—if we were closer, you could probably see that each one bears a golden star of six points. The wash of blue on the walls is more delicate. It's like the blue on your *panagia*, Uncle Mátyás: the blue of Mother Mary's mantle, or maybe angels' eyes. . . ."

The comment conjured an image for Kelson of the medal on the coral prayer beads, and the flecks of gemstone in the hands of the angel—and he found himself wondering if the medal might have been crafted here in Torenth, where the things of heaven and earth seemed to blend more seamlessly than in Gwynedd, and wondering how the beads might have come into the hands of Jehana's mother, who had never told her daughter of her magical heritage. . . .

He cast his gaze farther ahead toward Beldour itself, where more and grander domes of the milky blue were scattered amid the darker profusion of towers and spires and arches.

"The blue *is* distinctive," he said. "It seems to be mostly confined to domes and the buildings beneath them. Are those all churches? Most of them seem to have crosses."

"Say, rather, that the color is reserved for holy buildings," Rasoul replied. "Domes also adorn the prayer halls of the Prophet and parts of some royal palaces. The color, of course, has a celestial connotation, and its use is regulated. The best of it is enriched with ground lapis lazuli, which makes it quite costly; the veins of gold in the lapis impart a luminous quality not otherwise obtainable. It is believed that something in the makeup of such pigment is conducive to carrying the energy of our powers, as you saw that night off Saint-Sasile. When you look upon Hagia Iób, you will see the finest example in all the known world."

"Hagia Iób—isn't that outside the city?" Kelson asked, recalling his briefings with Father Irenaeus.

Mátyás smiled, inclining his head approvingly. "You were an attentive pupil, my lord. Hagia Iób is at Torenthály. You will see it in a few days, when we begin rehearsals for the *killijálay*."

"I look forward to it," Kelson replied.

"Is the welcome as you had envisioned it, my prince?" Mátyás asked, for Liam was grinning, and the state caïques that had replaced the black galleys as close escort were allowing the smaller vessels to approach more closely.

"Almost," Liam said softly, lifting his face toward the distant city.

They fell silent as Beldour grew before them, its ramparts all but luminous in the later afternoon sun. Rasoul kept up a running commentary on the city's architectural features as they approached what he informed them was Old Beldour, on the river's left bank. Beyond, the great stone arches of a formidable bridge spanned the river, linking Old Beldour with the more recent parts of the city.

"The Cathedral of Saint Constantine," Rasoul said, pointing out an enormous complex of sparkling blue domes and milky blue walls near the water's edge before them, like jewels heaped by a giant's hand. "And beyond, Furstánály Palace, the principal residence of the *padishah*, where you will be lodged. We will land at the Quai du Saint-Basile, there before the cathedral plaza."

CHAPTER FIFTEEN

*He hath delivered my soul in peace from the battle
that was against me.*

Psalm 55:18

During the four days it took Kelson and the Torenthi party to make their
slow way upriver toward Beldour, Jehana's unexpected encounter with
Deryni in her son's library had prompted much prayerful contemplation and
deliberation. The very next morning, following a night of little sleep, she
returned early to question Father Nivard about the secondary library—and the
man she had met there.

"He said his name was Barrett," she told him, somewhat indignantly. "After
discovering that adjoining room, I don't suppose I was surprised that he proved to
be Deryni—and right here in the palace! But the room itself, the entrance to it—
when I was here yesterday with Meraude, she couldn't even see that there was an
archway there! Surely you know about this!"

Nivard had risen from his chair behind the writing desk when she entered,
laying aside his quill. He listened with little outward reaction, only lowering his
eyes briefly at her direct question.

"I know about it, my lady."

When he did not say more, she stared at him, then looked away with a sinking feeling, twisting nervously at the marriage ring on her left hand.

"You're Deryni, too, aren't you?" she said quietly—a statement, not a question, as she regarded him sidelong.

He only inclined his head slightly, the wise sea-green eyes not leaving her face. She looked back at him, drawing a cautious breath, a little surprised that she felt none of the outrage that would have greeted this admission only a few months earlier—though, indeed, she had suspected, all along. But she had always liked the young priest, who was only a little older than Kelson, and found that she could not bring herself to despise him.

"This . . . Barrett," she said after a moment. "Besides being Deryni, who is he, to merit such access to my son's library?"

"A scholar," Nivard said simply.

"A scholar," she repeated. "But—he is blind."

Again Nivard inclined his head. "It is possible for some Deryni to compensate for physical blindness. Reading requires . . . a great deal of concentration and skill. And it is very tiring." He smiled faintly. "I expect that is why he fell asleep. That *is* how you found him, isn't it?"

"Yes, I—does he do that often?"

"More often than he would like," Nivard allowed. "But his studies give him great pleasure in this, the winter of his life."

"You know him, then," she said.

At his confirming nod, she swallowed with an effort, her gaze darting again to the curtain covering the strange archway into the library annex.

"And—what of that doorway? Why could Meraude not even see it, yet I could?"

He studied her for a long moment, then gave a faint shrug. "Do you really wish to know, my lady?"

"I—yes, I do."

"Very well. There is a—magical veil set in place to obscure the opening. Those of the king's blood may pass, and such others as he gives leave, like myself; but no others."

"And does this Barrett have such leave?"

"No, he does not."

She simply blinked at him in amazement for several long seconds, but she quickly grasped the implications.

"Then, he may come and go only by means of . . . the Portal there," she ventured.

Nivard nodded silently, studying her with compassion and frank appraisal.

"If you wish, my lady," he said quietly, "I shall attempt to explain the king's rationale for the arrangement. But if you would rather not hear it, I shall, of course, respect your wishes. Please believe that I am sensitive to your fears and apprehensions in this regard, having myself lived for many years in fear of being discovered for what I am. I assure you, I did not lightly enter my present state and situation. But your son may be quite the most remarkable individual of his generation. I would say this even if he were not my king and my patron."

When he did not continue, only gazing at her neutrally, Jehana found herself sinking straight-backed onto a stool before Father Nivard's writing desk, for something in the young priest's manner was both compelling and reassuring—and it was clear that his respect and admiration for Kelson were genuine.

"Do you wish me to continue?" he asked gently.

"I—do," she whispered.

He nodded and also sat, both hands resting easy on the writing table before him.

"First of all," he began carefully, "allow me to reassure you that only a very few Deryni know of the Portal in the next room, and they bear no ill will toward any of your family. Though we believe the Portal has been there for a very long time, its existence had been largely forgotten until relatively recently.

"When it was rediscovered, the king carefully considered the implications—for, as you quickly realized, it was a means by which Deryni who knew of its location could come and go as they pleased, here in the heart of an area private to him and his most trusted associates: a serious breach of security, should a Deryni hostile to Gwynedd's interests discover its location and determine to use it against us."

Jehana found herself nodding in agreement, though strangely without any particular sense of being threatened by this notion, for the very existence of the Veil across the access doorway was proof that Kelson had taken responsible measures to guard against such intrusion.

"Duke Alaric has reason to believe that the danger was more than theoretical," Nivard went on. "I am told that the sorceress Charissa gained access to this room on the night before the king's coronation—and the Portal would have provided the means. Yet the king was reluctant to simply destroy it, for creating a Portal requires considerable effort; and properly used and safeguarded, it provides a valuable link with other locations similarly equipped." He paused a beat. "You *are* aware that there are other Portals to which your son has access?" he asked.

She dipped her gaze uneasily, staring at her fingers entwined in her lap, and managed a taut nod, though she did not speak.

Nivard nodded carefully. "There was also the happy circumstance of the Portal's location, immediately adjacent to the library—which meant that, with appropriate precautions, the library could be extended to include that room, and to make certain . . . specialized reference volumes available to outside scholars."

"You mean . . . *Deryni* scholars, don't you?" she said softly. "It had—never occurred to me that there were such things."

Nivard ventured a tentative smile. "If we knew more of our powers and how to control them, my lady, there would be less cause for fear from those who do not have them. Even during the worst of the persecutions, the mind was a place where even a Deryni could still be free. Honest scholarship leads to understanding—and only by abolishing ignorance may we hope to live together in peace as we once did." He paused a beat. "The Church did not always teach that our magic was evil; I think you know that."

She swallowed down the lump rising in her throat, remembering the words she had read the night before, of the almost holy admonition to accompany the employment of one's gifts with reverence and the utmost respect for the free will of others. . . .

"Then, men like Barrett may come and go at will, by means of—that Portal?" she dared to ask.

He inclined his head. "Yes, but its location is not lightly shared. Are you— aware of the conventions of Portal use, my lady?"

She shook her head, wide-eyed.

"Do you—*wish* to be aware?"

At her very faint and tentative nod, he raised an eyebrow and went on.

"In order to use a Portal, one must learn its coordinates, the unique characteristics that make it different from any other Portal. This is best done in person, at the location, though occasionally it is possible for a skilled practitioner to show a Portal location to another with sufficient clarity that the location could then be accessed.

"And of course, one must also know the location of another Portal where one wishes to go." He cocked his head at her wistfully, a touch of kindly challenge in the sea-green eyes. "I don't suppose you would like a demonstration? I know of two other Portals here in Rhemuth."

She could feel the color draining from her face as she quickly shook her head.

"I do beg your pardon," he said hastily. "That was impertinent of me."

"No, no, not . . . impertinent," she found herself murmuring, even as she rose and began edging toward the door, and escape. "But I—I have other duties to attend to, Father. If you will excuse me . . ."

But even as she fled down the corridor, seeking the refuge of her apartments, she found herself re-examining his offer—and wondering more about the mysterious Barrett, who was blind, and Deryni; and wondering what it would actually be like, to use a Portal. . . .

She surrendered the rest of the morning to a relaxing bath, thinking back on her astonishing encounter with Father Nivard as Sophie washed her hair. Noontime found her walking in the sunny garden orchard with Sister Cecile and Meraude, while the former read her breviary and the latter selected ripe fruit, and Jehana herself still mulled the mystery of what Nivard called the Veil.

Nivard had said that "those of the king's blood" might pass—which, besides herself, she took to mean Haldane blood, and in the collateral line as well, since Kelson as yet had no children. Which meant that Nigel also could pass—but not Meraude, who was not Haldane, and, indeed, had appeared to touch only stone, when Jehana bade her test the wall of the garderobe. But Rory and Payne could pass . . . and presumably, the dead Conall's children, Albin and Conalline.

Which made her think more about Meraude's intention to seek out little Conalline and her mother—and made her accept without demur when Meraude again broached the subject later that afternoon.

"It's a perfect time to do it," Meraude told her, as she and one of her maids helped Jehana change her habitual white garments for one of her own gowns, more suitable for riding. "Nigel has gone off with Bishop Duncan to look at something down at the basilica, and then I expect he'll stay to supper with the archbishops. And Rory has said he'll go with us. It was he and Payne who found the girl, and they're both quite smitten with their little niece. Apparently the child is an angel."

Half an hour later, they were riding out of the gates of Rhemuth with Rory and an escort of two Haldane lancers, Jehana mounted on a smooth-gaited bay palfrey a shade lighter than the gown she wore, and with her auburn hair braided and neatly bound under a neat white kerchief, looking more a servant than a queen beside Meraude's royal blue. Indeed, she had asked that no mention be made of her rank once they reached the cottage, for this was an affair of Meraude and Nigel's family, and ought not to be influenced by whatever awe a queen's presence might inspire in a simple country girl.

The day was sunny and pleasant, not overly warm, and to Jehana's surprise, though she had not ridden for some time, she found herself enjoying the outing, even requesting a faster pace once they had made their sedate way through the streets of Rhemuth. Rory happily obliged her, glad to see her smile, and their journey passed in half the time allowed, as they interspersed gentle canters with the more sedate walks he had expected.

The cottage where he took them was sited at the edge of a broad meadow, small but tidy—cut-stone with a thatched roof, and a small barn built onto the back and a tiny garden to one side, in full summer-flowering, though the neatly trimmed hedges ringing the garden sported laundry spread to dry in the afternoon sun. As the five of them rode closer, a slender, kerchiefed figure in aproned blue skirts and a laced bodice over her shift stood up from among the flowers to peer at them, one hand shading her eyes. Then, after wiping her hands on her apron, she bent to scoop up a small child and brace it on her hip as she came before the cottage to await their arrival.

"God give you grace, my lady," Rory called, as they came within hailing distance. "I've brought some visitors."

The girl bobbed a quick curtsy, looking a little frightened, but the child in her arms crowed delightedly at the arrival of the newcomers and held out chubby arms in greeting. The little girl had the mother's fresh coloring, but the glossy brown hair was a shade lighter, and sprang in little ringlets framing her face. The mother's eyes were brown, but the child had eyes of Haldane-grey like her father's—Conall's child, without doubt, and by the shape of her mouth as well, though at least she had not inherited the straight black hair that was also such a Haldane hallmark.

Meraude exchanged glances with Jehana as they drew rein, but she looked a little relieved. Neither spoke as Rory and one of the lancers helped them down from their horses and the other lancer unfastened a satchel from his saddle.

"Mother, this is Vanissa," Rory said, "and the child is Conalline. Vanissa: my mother, the Duchess Meraude, and her companion."

Vanissa's eyes got very round, and she sank trembling to both knees, head bowed over the child she held tightly to her bosom.

"Dear child, you mustn't be afraid," Meraude said immediately, coming to gently take the girl by the shoulders and raise her up. "I have only come to meet my granddaughter. What a pretty child! She does have her father's eyes, doesn't she?

"Did he ever mention that he had a little sister? My daughter is just a little older than yours. It's a charming age, isn't it? But I've found, after raising three sons, that daughters provide their own delights—very different from boys."

As Meraude chattered on, soon putting the wary Vanissa at her ease, they moved back to the garden, where Rory and one of the lancers spread their cloaks on a grassy space beneath an apple tree and then withdrew to wait with the horses. The two royal ladies settled on the cloaks with Vanissa and her child, whereupon Meraude proceeded to produce an assortment of foodstuffs from the satchel they had brought, along with more tangible gifts: a soft doll and a necklace of pale coral beads for Conalline, and several lengths of fine woollen cloth for her mother. Vanissa fingered the cloth with shy gratitude but only nibbled at the dainties Meraude offered, clearly nervous, but Conalline happily sampled the gingerbread and sweetmeats and soon let herself be lured into her grandmother's lap to have the beads fastened around her neck.

Jehana, too, found herself warming to both mother and child, again recalling the infant daughter she had lost, and soon found herself following Meraude's lead, making occasional comments that would help draw out the shy Vanissa. The girl seemed mannerly enough, if lacking in sophistication, but gentle-natured. And a quick perusal of the cottage, when they took the gifts and remnants of food inside, preparatory to leaving, revealed her to be a tidy housekeeper.

"Child, I have something to propose to you," Meraude said to Vanissa from the open doorway, eliciting a darting look of dread as the girl turned around from putting things into a cupboard.

"Oh, madame, I beg you, do not take away my baby!" the girl cried, looking stricken.

"Good heavens, I don't intend to do any such thing!" Meraude reassured her. "But I *would* like to offer a proposal that might make all our lives far happier. My son provided for you; this I know. And if you wish to continue here, I shall not stand in the way of that. But I would wish to provide more for my granddaughter. I should like to see her have the advantages of her royal blood, to be educated as a lady, to make a good marriage."

Little reassured, Vanissa scooped up the child and clutched her to her bosom. "You *are* going to take her away!" she said accusingly.

"If you're willing, I propose to take *both* of you away," Meraude said calmly. "I am offering you a place in my household."

"What?" The girl stared at her in shock.

"I am offering you a place," Meraude repeated. "I cannot say exactly what position might suit you, but I am willing to give you every opportunity to be trained for whatever gentle occupation you might fancy, provided that you are honest and loyal to my House."

Vanissa's jaw had dropped as Meraude spoke, and she recovered herself enough to set little Conalline on the floor and put her doll in her hands, sending her off to play with a gentle push.

"We would live at court?" she whispered.

Meraude inclined her head, smiling faintly. "Conalline is the great-grand-daughter of a king. With the right advantages, she could have quite a promising future. I would propose to educate her beside my own daughter." She paused a beat. "You, too, may avail yourself of the royal tutors, if you wish. You could learn to read and write—and if you are clever and diligent, I think you might make a comfortable life for yourself. You might even marry."

Vanissa sank down on a stool by the fireplace, both hope and disbelief on her face.

"To live at court," she breathed. "Perhaps to marry . . . Madame, I know not what to say. Never, in my most foolish dreams . . ."

"There *is* one thing you should know, before you give me your answer," Meraude said gently. "Understand that I bear you no enmity for your relationship with my son—in truth, I think you probably had very little control over what happened between the two of you; Conall could be very . . . persuasive. But my husband, Duke Nigel, for all his even-handedness regarding the kingdom and his duties to King Kelson, has been unable to accept that Conall, in the end, went against everything he had been taught of duty and honor, and died a traitor's death."

Vanissa bowed her head, her fingers clenching in the folds of her apron.

"They—chopped off his head," she whispered.

Meraude closed her eyes briefly, shivering slightly, and Jehana laid an arm around her shoulders in comfort.

"Best not to dwell on that, child," Meraude whispered. "*I* dare not. You do not know the half of what my son did, that he should deserve to die, but none of it was your fault or that of either of his children." She paused a beat. "You did know that Conall married, and that a posthumous son was born to his wife, six months after your own child?"

Vanissa nodded. "The Princess Rothana—and her son is called Albin. But I never expected Conall to marry me. Princes do not wed country girls."

"No . . . they do not," Meraude said quietly. After a moment, with a bleak glance at Jehana, she went on.

"Be that as it may, because of his shame at our son's betrayal, my husband will have nothing to do with anything of Conall's—to the extent, even, of passing over Conall's legitimate son in the ducal succession. He has only seen the boy a few times—and those, by accident, and only from a distance—so I don't know what his reaction will be to Conalline." She glanced at the child, playing on the hearth.

"At least she doesn't look so distinctively a Haldane; little Albin is the image of his father. What I'm hoping is that, by the time he finds out who she is, my husband will have become accustomed to seeing her playing with our own Eirian, and will have come to accept her. It—ah—might help if she weren't called by that name. Has she a second name?"

"It's Amelia," Vanissa whispered, looking up at her. "For my grandmother."

"Then, perhaps you would not mind if she went by that name, from now on?" Meraude asked. "Assuming, that is, that you're willing to take this slight gamble: that you and she can win over my husband before he finds out who you are. Nigel can be a very stubborn fool when he wants to be, but I do love him dearly."

Vanissa managed a faint smile. "The ordinary folk speak of him with respect and affection, my lady. And Jowan, the squire who usually came with Conall—he was devoted to the duke." She lowered her eyes. "Jowan must be a knight by now. He was very kind and courteous. He always made me feel like a lady."

"Jowan?" Meraude's brow furrowed. "Oh, dear, I'm afraid he—died, child."

"He died?" Vanissa looked briefly stunned, but she quickly composed herself, only looking down again. "May I—ask how it happened?"

"I fear he was drowned, in the same accident that we thought had claimed Kelson and Dhugal."

"Drowned." Vanissa shook her head regretfully, her reaction betokening,

Jehana thought, more than mere affection for the dead Jowan. "I am very sorry to hear that. He was a gentle young man."

"Yes, he was." Meraude grimaced as she glanced at Jehana. "Will you come back with me to Rhemuth, then?" she asked. "You need not give me your answer right away, if you would like some time to think about it."

Bravely lifting her chin, Vanissa rose and came to kneel meekly before Meraude, trembling hands demurely folded.

"My lady, you have made me a most generous offer, not only for my daughter but for myself. I accept and thank you, from the bottom of my heart—and Conalline thanks you."

"Make certain it is *Amelia* who thanks me, child," Meraude returned with a smile. "We must, all of us, begin getting used to her other name. Come, come, get up," she said, helping Vanissa to her feet. "Perhaps we'd best give you another name as well; Nigel knows the name Vanissa. Have you a second name, or any preference?"

"My confirmation name is Mary," Vanissa ventured.

"Always a good name," Meraude agreed, "but perhaps a more distinctive form, betokening your aspirations. How about Maria?"

Vanissa nodded slowly. "I could answer to that—yes. Maria." She smiled, and Jehana could see how Conall might have been charmed by her. "Thank you, my lady."

"Good, it's settled, then," Meraude said. "How soon would you be prepared to make the move?"

"Whenever best pleases you, madame. We have but little that I would wish to bring along."

"Then I shall give you a day or two, while I make definite arrangements," Meraude said, with a pleased glance at Jehana. "We shall wish to choose an appropriate time for your arrival, when my husband is occupied with other concerns. My son Rory assists me in this conspiracy, as you know, being also enamored of his first niece. I shall send him with a cart in a few days."

CHAPTER SIXTEEN

For their feet run to evil, and make haste to shed blood.

Proverbs 1:16

"So, little brother, how did you find Kelson of Gwynedd?" Mahael said to Mátyás, seated across from him at a meeting after supper the evening of their arrival, when their young nephew had been received in state and he and their foreign visitors all had retired gratefully to the quarters assigned them.

The middle Furstán brother, Count Teymuraz, sat to Mátyás's left at the small round table, between him and Mahael. To his right were Counts Branyng of Sostra and László of Czalsky, both of them of an age with the two older brothers, both of them highly accomplished Deryni mages. All of them would be participating in the enthronement of Liam-Lajos, in little more than a week's time.

Mátyás smiled faintly, but did not look up from paring a long, careful spiral of skin from a firm Vezairi apple.

"He is sensitive, well educated, a born leader of men. He seems both loved and respected by his folk. He is very fond of Liam-Lajos, and Laje of him."

"What of his power?" asked Teymuraz.

"You would do better to ask the man who tried to kill him at the Ile d'Orsal."

"*What?*" Mahael blurted. The other three looked similarly astonished.

"Dear, dear me," Mátyás said, looking up blandly. "I had assumed that at least one of you would know that. The man was Deryni. There was also a human, but when their mission failed, both of them killed themselves rather than be taken. That was fortuitous—at least for those who sent them—but the attempt itself was foolish. Laje might have died as well, and *we* were being blamed. Not by name, but the insinuations were plain. Fortunately, al-Rasoul is one of the finest assets of this kingdom. No one was willing to cross the line and make accusations."

"Probably because no one could prove anything," Branyng said. "I assume that death-triggers had been set, and mind-wipes."

"Compulsions rather than triggers, but the result was the same," Mátyás allowed. "And the memories had been erased. That bespeaks considerable skill on the part of whoever sent them. A bishop called Arilan probed both bodies, but nothing could be learned."

"Then, it was well done," Branyng said. "I wish I could take credit for it."

"Better to take credit for successes, dear Branyng," László said with a grim smile. "And one would wish that, if the venture had to fail, the perpetrators had at least elicited a response that would tell us something more about our foe. Mátyás, was the attack magical or merely physical?"

"I cannot say."

"Then we still know little of Kelson's power."

"By all accounts, it is formidable," Mátyás replied.

"Yet he did not read the bodies himself," Mahael observed. "Curious. Perhaps he has not the skill."

Mátyás shrugged and returned his attention to the ruby spiral growing under his knife.

"Perhaps he does not. Or perhaps it is simply that the skills of our race are not used so openly in Gwynedd. Truth-Reading is common, and commonly accepted, for the most part, but I saw little evidence of any overt Deryni presence at his court, though all close to him were well-shielded, as was he. What skills he possesses, however, he blends seamlessly with more usual human talents. He is a shrewd judge of character, for all his youth, and shows a keen understanding of human motivations. If Laje has paid attention during his sojourn in Gwynedd, it is likely that he has learned something useful of statecraft."

"Do I detect a note of admiration?" László asked, arching a grizzled eyebrow.

"Merely an acknowledgment of what is," Mátyás replied, pausing to lip a slice of apple off his knife. "Do not underestimate this Haldane, László of Czalsky. He has sent us back a king who is well prepared for his royal duties."

"Prepared for Gwynedd's idea of a king," Teymuraz said, with no little contempt. "Did Father Irenaeus give you any idea of his preparedness in other areas?"

Mátyás shrugged again. "Very little. He was more concerned to report on Laje's spiritual fitness—which he assures me has not been seriously compromised by his time spent in Gwynedd."

"I do not care about the state of his soul!" Mahael muttered. "Did he say nothing of the boy's powers?"

"Nothing."

"Then we can *assume* nothing. Branyng, what progress with the boy's mother?"

Branyng, who fancied himself irresistible where women were concerned, leaned back in his chair to preen, fiddling with one of his braided sidelocks.

"The Dowager Duchess Morag is greatly flattered to be courted by a younger man. She would have made a formidable queen, had we queens in this land. But she hardly knows this son. The youngest is now her favorite, and will claim her loyalty, if she most choose between them. It is a point to be kept in mind, on the day."

"Indeed," Mahael replied, with a slow, lazy smile. "Very well, then. Now that Mátyás has returned to us, allow me to acquaint you with further details of my plans."

_K_elson's first day in Beldour was appointed for acquainting him and his party with the sights of Old and New Beldour, with Rasoul and a count called Branyng to serve as guides. While they were thus engaged, Létald determined to begin meeting with other official observers arriving from the Forcinn, for all of Torenth's neighbors to the south were well aware of the instability inherent in Liam's return, concerned that even a partial hand-over should proceed as smoothly as possible. Liam appeared briefly to observe the departure of his royal visitors, but in the company of mother and brother and uncles, and looked like he would have preferred to come along.

The day grew progressively warmer as Rasoul led them on a whirlwind tour along the walls of the old city, past the cathedral, then across the arched stone span of St. Basil's Bridge for a quick turn through the Great Market Place, the Queen's Zoo, and around the University of Beldour. They returned at last at midafternoon, for refreshment amid the tiered hanging gardens, where the court was gathering.

There, high above the city, where tinkling fountains delighted eye and ear and cooled the sultry breezes, a silken canopy marked the place where Liam and his brother sat to receive their noble guests, under the watchful gaze of uncles, their mother, and several dozen of Torenth's senior nobility. Many foreign delegations had already arrived, and were sampling a sumptuous array of cooling libations and culinary dainties laid out beneath the shade of fragrant lemon trees.

Létald, who knew and was known by most of those present, betook it upon himself to escort Kelson among them and make introductions, on behalf of the Forcinn States. Dhugal and Morgan accompanied them, the latter keeping a wary eye out for Brendan and Payne, who had been asked by Liam to attend him close to the royal pavilion; for the young king was already feeling the effect of isolation from others of his age. Kelson had observed the abiding camaraderie among Liam and the two younger boys during the journey from Rhemuth, and wondered whether a time of squireship might be feasible for Brendan at the Torenthi court, if he managed to get Liam through this alive.

Kelson found that he recognized few of his fellow visitors by sight, though most of them could hardly be unaware of who he was. He did know Bahadur Khan, King of R'Kassi, of whom Létald had spoken in Horthánthy—the uncle with whom Létald's son was soon to begin service. The Hortic heir was at his uncle's side as his father brought Kelson to exchange greetings, and would return with him to R'Kassi, after the inauguration at Holy Iób. Kelson had bought horses from Bahadur. And Isarn of Logréine was often at the court of Gwynedd, promoting the premium wines produced by his tiny principality.

Kelson was somewhat surprised to find several of his own western neighbors represented as well: Gron, Grand Duke of Calam, on behalf of the Connaiti Council of Sovereign Princes, and even a deputy of Colman King of Llannedd. Later he saw Azim amid a handful of other nobles from the desert principalities, startlingly clad in the royal blue of Nur Hallaj rather than his customary black, for he was standing in for his brother, Prince Hakim. Azim touched his right hand to his heart as their eyes met, inclining his head slightly in response to Kelson's nod.

As Létald worked them closer to the royal pavilion, Kelson gathered both his dukes closer to his side. Their reception was cordial on Liam's part, but only barely civil on the part of the courtiers surrounding him, save for Rasoul; Mátyás was not in evidence. Morag had absented herself on seeing the approach of the man who had slain her husband and her brother. The eldest uncle, Mahael, tendered Kelson a frosty bow but only the barest words of formal greeting before returning to his conversation with another Torenthi noble.

No less disquieting was Liam's brother: an intense, wary ten-year-old little resembling his elder sibling, bright-haired among the dark heads of his Furstáni kin. Well shielded in his own right and by the uncle hovering close at his side—the one called Teymuraz—young Ronal Rurik gave Kelson dutiful salute exactly according to the degree required, but soon let himself be drawn away in his uncle's charge. Watching them go, Kelson reflected that the boy probably had good cause to be wary—though fleeing *with* Teymuraz rather than *from* him was probably not as safe as Ronal Rurik believed. But Kelson had hardly expected any different behavior.

That afternoon, Kelson observed little that *was* expected. Things were, indeed, different in Torenth, and he was struck repeatedly with how much he had to learn. One of the day's more poignant lessons came later in the afternoon, as he was exchanging obligatory courtesies with a somewhat condescending pair of

Torenthi courtiers presented by Father Irenaeus. Dhugal was still with him, but Morgan had drifted off to confer with Derry and Arilan and Saer de Traherne.

Later, Kelson could not have said why his attention wandered just then; only that he became fleetingly aware that Liam was walking utterly alone with Mátyás, their two heads bent in private converse, for the brief span that it took to cross from a flower-twined pergola to a sun-dappled pool with fat carp lazing just below the surface. Seated farther along the marble edging of the pool, more than one guest had found a cool refuge to sit and rest aching feet.

Even then, obliged to make at least a pretense of following the conversation with Irenaeus and his countrymen, Kelson would have paid the royal pair little mind—except that something in the intensity of their brief exchange struck him oddly as having far more import than idle chatter, even though the encounter seemed superficially casual.

It was enough to make him gaze distractedly after them as Mátyás continued on past the pool to join a knot of his countrymen. Liam, in turn, made his way casually in the direction of a dark-haired little girl of perhaps six or so who was crouched expectantly between Brendan and Payne at the far side of the pool, all of them gazing into the pool as she let the end of a long blue-black braid trail in the water, hands poised to either side. She pounced just as Liam reached them, plunging both hands into the water to scoop up one of the golden carp, holding it aloft with a squeal of triumph and spraying herself and both young admirers.

Accompanied by whoops of merriment, both Brendan and Payne tried manfully to catch hold of the slippery fish as it flapped and wiggled and struggled to escape, and even Liam belatedly joined in, though without effect. The splash of the carp's return to the pool gave all four of them a not unwelcome shower, and Payne very nearly tumbled in after it.

"What a charming child," Kelson remarked to Father Irenaeus, as the little girl and all three of her companions dissolved into peals of laughter. "It appears she has captivated both your king and a pair of my pages."

Irenaeus stiffened slightly, looking almost embarrassed, and the two courtiers exchanged uneasy glances.

"She is the Princess Stanisha, sister of the *padishah*," said Count Ungnad, the older of the two Torenthi courtiers.

"His sister?!"

"The posthumous daughter of Duke Lionel," Count László said frostily. "I believe you may take credit for the fact that she never knew her father."

Kelson imagined he could feel his face going scarlet. No one had ever mentioned any posthumous child of Lionel, whom Kelson had been obliged to kill

Not even Liam had seen fit to mention her—though, in truth, she would have been barely walking when last he saw her.

"I did not know," he said quietly. "It has never been my intention to deprive children of their fathers. Please God, there soon will come a time when no child will lose a father betimes, because of war between our two lands."

Father Irenaeus closed his eyes and nodded, tight-lipped, crossing himself with sober deliberation. "May God receive your prayer with favor, my lord," he breathed, "and grant its speedy fulfillment."

Kelson mirrored the priest's sign of blessing with a whispered "Amen," and the two Torenthi counts somewhat belatedly followed suit.

*T*he long, sultry afternoon dragged gradually into dusk. As Kelson and Morgan stood leaning against one of the stone railings, gazing out over the dimming city, Liam came casually to join them.

"I hope you have enjoyed yourselves today," he said, though something in the young king's manner suggested that the statement was not altogether casual.

"Thank you, we have," Kelson replied. "And you?"

Liam shrugged. "There is much to occupy my mind, much to learn, much to think about. Count Berrhones has asked that we begin rehearsals immediately for the *killijálay,* so we go tomorrow to Torenthály and Holy Iób. He is to be master of ceremonies, and he takes his responsibilities very seriously. I believe he fears that outsiders will not easily adapt to our ways."

"I hope that I may not be taken altogether for an outsider, Liam," Kelson said quietly. "I have paid careful heed to Father Irenaeus's instruction."

Liam managed a smile that was almost convincing. "I have little fear in that regard, my lord. It will be a great comfort to me to have you participate in my enthronement—despite what my uncles may say."

"I must confess that their reception has been . . . guarded," Kelson replied, "though that was no more than I expected. Is there something else that concerns you?"

Liam looked away, his dark gaze flicking out over the city. "All shall be well," he murmured. "You must trust me in this."

But when Kelson attempted gentle exploration of this enigmatic statement, Liam would not be drawn out. He dined with them a little later, accompanied by Mátyás and inviting the company of several nobles whom Kelson had not met earlier—Káspár of Truvorsk, and Erdödy of Jandrich, both of them dukes, and a count's son called Makróry of Kulnán—but there was no opportunity to speak again in private. Neither of the other uncles was present. Afterward, Dhugal remarked that Liam had seemed almost at pains to ensure that no private exchange was possible.

*T*he next day marked the first of many rehearsals for *killijálay*. At midmorning, a procession of state caïques took the royal party upriver to Torenthály, country seat of the Furstáns and site of Hagia Iób, that jewel among churches, where Kings of Torenth had been girded with the sword and enthroned since time immemorial. The purple-liveried oarsmen of the lead vessel rowed to the shimmer of bells to set the pace—a festive sound, but one that discouraged conversation, and which slowly built on the tension as the complex came into sight.

Unlike other churches Kelson had seen en route to Beldour—and there had been many—the clustered onion domes of Hagia Iób were clad with burnished gold, almost blinding in the summer sun as the royal party disembarked at the ceremonial quay and made their way on foot up the straight, cobbled Avenue des Rois. Save for the covered entry porch, which was gilded like the domes, the rest of the building was covered with the same gold-starred blue tiles of which Rasoul had spoken on their journey here; the high, narrow windows set around the base of the principal dome were limned with gold. The structure itself was somewhat smaller than Kelson had expected—though he reminded himself that Hagia Iób was not a cathedral but a memorial church and place of ceremony.

Passing from the heat outside, through the building's gold-cased double doors, was like stepping into another world. The vestibule within was hushed and cool—welcome respite as servants there divested them of boots and shoes and put upon them soft slippers of felt, for the inlaid floors and carpets within were too precious to walk upon shod. The walls and vaulted ceiling were clad with more of the blue tiles; and here, close at hand, Kelson could discern the shimmer of gold in the glazing, making the tiles almost glow in the light of handfire streaming from a pierced lantern.

Beyond another set of even grander double doors lay a broad, long nave surmounted at the transept crossing with a vast and lofty space beneath a dome that seemed to stretch very near to heaven. The murmur of many softly echoing voices met them as they entered the church, for several dozen men, lay and clergy, were already assembled for the rehearsal. Conversation quickly died away as those waiting melted back against the walls, a lingering echo of their converse continuing to reverberate within the vast dome crowning the nave.

But it was not the dome to which the eye was immediately drawn, but what lay beneath it: the black tomb of Furstán, for which the great church had been built, final resting place of this almost legendary founder of the Torenthi royal house, whose black sarcophagus was the focal point for the transmission of Furstáni kingship.

Kelson could sense its potency as he approached the relic, walking between Liam and Holy Alpheios, the grey-bearded Patriarch of Torenth, who had come to give them welcome. Kelson stopped when they stopped, rendering a respectful inclination of his head when Alpheios and Liam bowed deeply from the waist and crossed themselves in an expansive gesture that swept from brow to floor and then, as they straightened, from right shoulder to left in the Eastern manner. Early during Liam's sojourn at the court of Rhemuth, the boy had shown Kelson how, in token of the Trinity, the thumb was held pressed to the first two fingers of the right hand, and the two remaining fingers were folded into the palm, denoting the dual nature of Christ, both God and man. He had further explained that the sweep of the hand from forehead to floor was intended to encompass all of the worshipper's being in the gesture of reverence—a symbolism that appealed to Kelson's aesthetic sense, even though the custom was alien to his own tradition.

The form of the tomb thus saluted was likewise outside his previous experience, the top peaked along its length like the roof of a long, narrow house. Rough-hewn from a matte-black granite, the sarcophagus itself was encased in a framework of fretted silver inlaid with bits of onyx, delicate tracery as fine and fragile as a spider's web. Spears of sunlight from a series of narrow slits high in the dome pierced the incense-laden air to cast a constant dappling of illumination on the silver. But what pulsed deep within the relic's heart was something more than merely mortal, akin to the glimpses Kelson sometimes had been vouchsafed when meditating in the Presence of the Blessed Sacrament, or when he had felt the touch of Saint Camber.

"Here lie the bones of my distant ancestor, the great Furstán," Liam informed him, indicating the tomb but carefully avoiding physical contact. "It is said that his spirit attends upon the empowerment of each new king who follows him. I felt a whisper of his touch when I was girded with the sword, at the New Year after my brother died; but in a few days' time, I shall feel his full embrace."

At Kelson's faintly wide-eyed glance, Holy Alpheios squared his shoulders.

"You are advised not to scoff at our ways, Kelson of Gwynedd," he said, softly enough that none but Liam and Kelson could hear him. "Torenthi tradition stretches back to a time when Gwynedd was but an outpost of Empire—and your Deryni folk have been long apart from the magic of our race."

The patriarch's rich basso seemed to have come from some deep wellspring of confidence and spirituality—a most powerful Deryni, beyond doubt—and Kelson acknowledged that potency with a respectful bow.

"I assure you, All Holy, that I do not scoff," he said quietly. "I am eager to learn more of your ways. Father Irenaeus spent many an hour instructing me in the history of your people and your practice of our mutual faith. External differences are but illusion. I come into this house of God with humble heart and the utmost respect."

Some of the tension had left the patriarch's face as Kelson spoke, and he favored the visiting king with a thoughtful bow in return.

"That was gracefully said, if its source was a truly humble heart," Alpheios allowed, a hint of a pleased smile twitching his silvery beard as he lifted a hand toward a black-robed monk waiting just beyond earshot. "Pray, allow Father Károly to conduct you to a suitable vantage point. I fear that, even having been instructed, today's proceedings may appear somewhat bewildering; I confess *myself* sometimes somewhat bewildered, when Berrhones begins barking orders," he added with a sidelong glance toward the elderly courtier consulting a sheaf of parchment pages, blessedly out of earshot.

"But Father Károly will attempt to explain what is happening, and to answer any questions you may have," Alpheios went on. "I am certain that Father Irenaeus will have told you that Torenth observes somewhat different external ritual from that to which you are accustomed. But as you say, these differences of practice are but illusion beside true faith."

Deeming a bow to be sufficient reply, Kelson let himself be swept into the guardianship of the self-effacing Father Károly, who ushered him to the north side of the soaring nave where Father Irenaeus was pointing out architectural symbolism to Morgan, Dhugal, and Arilan. As Kelson exchanged social courtesies with Father Károly, he found himself pondering what Alpheios had said, wondering whether he had detected a note of guarded acceptance in the patriarch's manner.

Very soon, the sound of Count Berrhones' staff rapping on the floor gathered all the milling nobility and clergy into places that suddenly looked very planned, indeed, and the rehearsal began. Since Torenthi custom was to stand throughout religious observances, seats being provided only for the elderly and infirm, Kelson and his party stood throughout the long rehearsal that followed, with not even a wall to lean against.

At least it was cool in the lofty church. While Kelson watched Liam process toward the shimmering black silhouette of Furstán's tomb for at least the third time, preceded by his mother and brother and Mahael and surrounded by his other two uncles and Counts László and Branyng, whom they had met the previous afternoon, he found his gaze ranging somewhat restively over the rest of the church's interior, letting his thoughts wander where they would, hoping he might connect with any scrap of insight that might help him to understand this alien land.

He tipped his head backward to gaze upward at the high-arched ceiling of Hagia Iób. Father Irenaeus had told him that the inside of an Eastern church was meant to pattern the image of God's kingdom on earth, the lofty dome enfolding the sacred space like a loving embrace. The underside of this dome was washed with the same celestial blue he had seen elsewhere, and gilded and painted with holy images: the four Evangelists in the four quarters, and Christ reigning in majesty from the center.

Looking east, Kelson found further rich feast for the eyes. Rather than the customary rood screen, choir, and high altar that he would have expected in a Western church, a gilded and painted icon screen divided the nave from the sanctuary that lay beyond a pair of open gates in the center. Through that opening, dimly lit by a hanging Presence lamp, Kelson could see a square altar draped with golden brocade, the cloth richly worked on its front with jewels and embroidery, on which stood a golden tabernacle shaped like a miniature castle, and a massive seven-branched candlestick. Before the tabernacle lay what, by its jeweled cover, Kelson assumed to be the Book of the Gospel.

"There the Word of God lies enthroned before the Lamb of God," Father Károly whispered, noticing the direction of his gaze. "The icon behind the great candelabrum on the altar is that of Christ in Glory—and were you to look directly above the altar, from inside the sanctuary, you would see the Theotokos with the Christ within her."

"*Theotokos*—that means Christ Bearer," Kelson said, remembering his instruction from Father Irenaeus.

"It does, my lord," Father Károly agreed eagerly, his eyes lighting as he directed the king's gaze to further details. "The icons to either side of the royal gates are the Theotokos holding the Christ, and the glorified Christ Himself, showing that all of creation falls between these two events, of His coming as the Savior born of Mary—the Theotokos—and His coming as King and Judge, at the end of time." He glanced at Kelson in question and sudden misgiving that he had presumed too much. "Do you wish me to identify the other images on the iconostasis?"

"Not at this time, I think, Father," Kelson replied with a light shake of his head, though he smiled as he said it. "I expect that the Holy Alphheios would prefer that I pay attention to the rehearsal. Can you tell me anything about something called 'moving wards'? I've heard them mentioned several times this afternoon."

Father Károly blinked at him, then shrugged.

"They are a difficult magical working, employed almost exclusively during *killijálay*, but there is no secret to their existence or their general function. A Moving Ward requires four practitioners of a high degree of magical competence. They are sometimes referred to as the Pillars of the Realm. They surround the *padishah* in correspondence to the great archangels of the four Quarters, and raise a sphere of protective energy around him.

"That part is relatively easy," Károly conceded, "though the four require great stamina to maintain their warding for the requisite time. It is not a task for old men. To make of this Ward a Moving Ward, the *padishah* himself must integrate the energies of the four, and henceforth controls it. Some say that the four holy archangels actually overshadow their human representors during the most solemn part of the *killijálay*—but I do not believe this myself."

"Interesting," Kelson murmured, and fell largely silent throughout the rest of the rehearsal, wondering what constituted the "most solemn part" of the *killijálay*, and from what the *padishah* needed protecting, and whether angelic forces did, indeed, overshadow the *padishah*'s four mortal guardians.

When the rehearsal finally ended, a full four hours later, Kelson had expected that all the participants would be whisked back to Beldour aboard the same caïques that had brought them from the capital. But as he, Morgan, and Dhugal shuffled toward the great doors with all the others, already anticipating the blast of heat outside, Liam drew them aside to point out a particularly fine mosaic of Holy Wisdom set in the church's north wall.

When, at last, they emerged into the sunlight, Kelson was somewhat taken aback to see the forecourt deserted, the last of the rehearsal party boarding the ships tied up along the quay, where cooling refreshments awaited them. The state caïque carrying Liam's mother and brother was already in mid-river, and more were pulling away from the quay, including the one carrying Arilan, Saer, Létald, and the remaining Forcinn observers. Aboard another of the ships, even now casting off its mooring lines, Kelson could just make out Mahael, Teymuraz, and others of the Torenthi entourage.

Only Liam's own vessel remained moored at the center of the quay, its crew aboard and a dozen attentive Circassian guards drawn up smartly before the gangplank. Their captain, one hand on the hilt of his curved sword, had been speaking with Count Mátyás, and gazed back toward the *padishah* and his party as the count trotted briskly back up the cobbled avenue to join them.

"I ordered the others to go ahead," Liam said, as Mátyás drew near. "Before we go back, I thought to show you the Nikolaseum, and perhaps my brother's tomb." He gestured up the extension of the Avenue des Rois that ran past the north side of Hagia Iób, toward a vast walled necropolis that, on their approach to Torenthály, he had identified as the burial place of the Furstán kings. "Some of the tombs are very beautiful. It will not delay us long."

"Is it safe?" Morgan said uneasily, for the other caïques were rapidly disappearing downriver, leaving only Liam's ship with its guard complement—and Liam and his uncle Mátyás. Dhugal, too, looked less than comfortable with the arrangement.

Mátyás smiled faintly and gestured toward the silent necropolis. "Only the dead live here, Duke Alaric. Surely you do not fear the dead?"

Kelson sensed Morgan about to argue the point, but something in Liam's taut eagerness—and an edge of carefully veiled apprehension—persuaded him that the diversion was very important to the young king.

"No, we don't fear the dead," Kelson said easily, cutting short any comment of Morgan's. "Duke Alaric is solicitous of my safety, as Count Mátyás is solicitous of yours, Liam. I think we should not linger overlong, or those appointed to protect both of us will become anxious, but, pray, tell us more about this Nikolaseum while we walk. . . ."

Liam seemed palpably relieved as they set out along the extension of the cobbled avenue, leading them through a purple-tiled ceremonial arch and heading toward a fine, seven-tiered temple of alabaster set amid lesser tombs and a sea of azure pyramids that echoed the blue of Hagia Iób. Mátyás raised a hand toward the Circassian guards and signalled two of them to attend, though at a discreet distance. As they approached the tomb along a lesser avenue shaded by stately cedars, the young king spoke with passion of the valiant but ill-fated Prince Nikola, beloved younger brother of the future King Arkady II, who had fallen in the Battle of Killingford a century before.

"He died saving Arkady's life," Liam told them, as they mounted seven pristine white steps to enter the cooler shade of the building's entrance. "After Arkady became king, he built the Nikolaseum to honor his brother's memory. It is regarded as one of the wonders of the Eastern world."

They stood aside briefly in the doorway so that the Circassian guards could duck ahead of them for a quick look inside, confirming that the place was empty, but the pair immediately retreated to the avenue below, given leave by Mátyás to wait in the shade of one of the cedars. Flanked by Morgan and Dhugal, Kelson moved a few steps farther into the building and stood aside, still a little sun-blind, letting his eyes adjust to the dimmer light.

Inside, the structure belied its external form of seven tiers, encompassing a single vaulted chamber clad with the same star-studded tiles of sacred blue that adorned the domes of ecclesiastical buildings. On a raised dais in the center, lit by a silvery glow that intensified in response to a gesture from Mátyás, lay King Arkady's memorial to his slain brother.

"Come," Liam said softly.

The prince's effigy, recumbent on a bier of black basalt, was slightly larger than life-sized, carved of a single block of rosy Carrolan marble that gave the flesh a blush of seeming life, as if the slain prince only slept. The veining of the stone lent texture and contrast to the sculpted folds of the cloak in which he was wrapped from throat to ankle. The face was serene, handsome, even beautiful. Nikola had been only twenty-six when he died.

A carved stack of three battle drums guarded the foot of the bier, draped with a pair of crossed standards bearing the leaping hart device of Torenth, bright with paintwork on the carved alabaster. Beside the bier knelt a cloaked and hooded figure carved of tawny stone, its face buried in its hands and a jewelled crown lying discarded beside it. A fine sword, ornately wrought of gold and silver, was leaned against the other side of the bier so that its jewel-studded hilt projected as a sign of the Cross before the bowed head of the grieving Arkady.

"Prince Nikola died for his king," Mátyás said softly, from behind them. "I would die for mine."

CHAPTER SEVENTEEN

Cast in thy lot among us.

Proverbs 1:14

$\mathcal{K}$elson turned to regard Mátyás, oddly unalarmed. Dhugal had snapped his head around in surprise, suppressing a startled gasp, and Morgan looked poised to spring between his king and Liam's uncle, a hand on the hilt of the dagger at his waist—but Mátyás stood reassuringly motionless, hands empty and easy at his sides. As Kelson cocked his head in question, both arms lifting slightly in signal for his companions to hold back, Liam seized one hand in passionate entreaty, though his voice did not rise above a whisper.

"Sire, I beg you! Hear him! He has brought me warning of mortal danger—treachery planned for the *killijálay!* There is a chance it can be thwarted, but we must have your help!"

Liam's breathless plea sent a chill through Kelson as he thrust his free arm across Morgan's chest, blocking any further move against Mátyás, shifting his gaze urgently between the two Torenthi princes, sensing Dhugal's concern.

"*I would die for him!*" Mátyás repeated, his voice but a whisper in the taut stillness.

"Do you trust him?" Morgan said to Kelson, his voice barely audible.

"He would never harm me!" Liam declared. "At least hear him—please!"

Kelson's gaze fastened on that of Mátyás, at the same time using his physical link with Liam in desperate attempt to detect any trace of duplicity. He could find none.

"What is it you have to say to me, Count Mátyás?" he said quietly. "You ask much."

"And must ask still more," the other replied. "Please! I—dare not speak of this here. I must ask you to come with me. Let the Lord Dhugal remain here to keep the guards from asking awkward questions—though I promise you, we shall not be long."

"And where is it you propose we go?" Kelson asked.

"A Portal lies there at the head of the effigies," Mátyás replied, gesturing. "I dare not give you our destination, but I offer you this Portal's location. It might serve as an escape, if the *killijálay* goes completely wrong and at least some of us are fortunate enough to survive."

"You offer us a Portal location within Torenth, but to use it, you are asking us to open our shields to you."

Mátyás's pale eyes closed briefly as he breathed out a long sigh in an apparent bid for equanimity. "Your caution, where I am concerned, is not unreasonable. Will you allow Laje to bring you through? I accept that this presents no guarantee that he and I are not joined in some conspiracy against you, to compass your deaths by treachery—or that I will not move against Dhugal in your absence, before coming to aid Laje against you. If you fear that, then I shall go first. But if you cannot yet trust me, at least trust your vassal Liam-Lajos, who has sworn faith with you, before God. Please, I *beg* you!"

Kelson slowly turned his gaze on Liam, who now was trembling with the tension of the moment yet with shields all but transparent, utterly convinced of the sincerity and truthfulness of his uncle's words. Contact with Morgan likewise confirmed the Deryni duke's reluctant willingness to accept Kelson's judgment in the matter—though Morgan remained unconvinced regarding Mátyás. Dhugal, he knew, would abide by whatever instruction Kelson gave him in the matter.

"*Someone* must trust, if we are ever to end what brought Nikola to his death," Kelson murmured, glancing at the carved figures of Nikola and the grieving Arkady. He lowered his hands and moved warily toward the head of the bier, and was reassured to feel the tingle of a live Portal centered on the marble floor slab immediately adjacent to the bier.

"May we?" he asked Mátyás, indicating the Portal and including Morgan and Dhugal in his glance.

At Mátyás's clipped nod, Kelson drew both companions to his side and knelt to lay his hands flat on the white marble, Morgan and Dhugal crouching beside him. When they had set the location into memory, and while they continued pretending to do so, the king reached out in link with Morgan and Dhugal, mind to mind.

Am I mad to trust him? he asked them.

As you say, my prince, someone must trust, came Morgan's steady reply.

Dhugal?

It appears that I get the easy part, Dhugal responded, adding a physical grin to the impression of resigned amusement he sent. *I only need to keep the guards at bay.*

If we should not return within half an hour, or if anything else should go amiss, Kelson cautioned, *go first to Rhemuth and warn Nigel that we may have met with treachery, then return here and try to find Arilan. But I pray this will not be necessary.*

Drawing breath to ready his focus, Kelson set a hand on the edge of Nikola's bier and got to his feet, Morgan and Dhugal also rising. Liam was watching them avidly, Mátyás with bowed head beside him, one hand clasped around the icon on his breast. Dhugal gave them a nod.

"It appears that I'm seconded for guard duty," he said lightly, gesturing toward the sun-flooded doorway of the place. "Count Mátyás, have you any particular instructions regarding our friends outside, or are they likely to stay where they are?"

Mátyás breathed out softly as he looked up. "They have already satisfied themselves that this place presents no physical danger. Unless some sound of alarm were to summon them, or we should be out of sight for a very long time, they will not attempt to intrude on the private nature of our visit. We shall endeavor to return before our absence can arouse concern."

"Then, I shall pass the time in contemplation of Prince Nikola's memorial," Dhugal replied with a fleeting smile, "and remain in the vicinity of the entrance— just in case their curiosity should overwhelm their sense of decorum."

Mátyás nodded his gratitude, swallowing visibly, then moved briskly around the other side of the memorial, to take the place of Kelson and Morgan on the Portal slab.

"Laje, I shall await your coming," he said with a taut glance at Liam—and disappeared in the blink of an eye.

Breathing a guarded sigh, Liam moved into the space Mátyás had just vacated and held out both his hands with palms upturned, his gaze locking with the king's.

"We must not waste what time we have," he said. "I assure you, I am able to do this," he added, with a glance at Morgan. "I have never done it with more than one other, but the difference is negligible, and I am familiar with our destination."

Without hesitation, now that he had made up his mind, Kelson stepped forward and put one hand in Liam's, followed a heartbeat behind by Morgan.

"Do it," Kelson murmured, closing his eyes and dropping his shields—and opening to Liam.

In that taut eternity between one heartbeat and the next, before the earth shifted beneath their feet, he felt Morgan likewise lowering his shields. The instant of momentary vertigo and then disorientation ceased immediately as Kelson opened his eyes, Morgan still at his side and Liam still before him—but no longer in the Nikolaseum.

A whiff of ancient incense and the honey-scent of good beeswax candles tickled at Kelson's nostrils as he drew his first breath in this new place. They were standing in a rear corner of what seemed to be a tiny jewel of a chapel. The wavering light of scores of office lamps lent an illusion of near-life to the jewel-toned mosaics covering the walls and the inside of the modest dome.

Lamps set with ruby and emerald and sapphire amid their golden filigree hung from golden chains fixed to the vaulted ceiling. Long-faced saints and gilded angels gazed out from the painted panels of the iconostasis. The ones to either side of the doors to the sanctuary beyond—what Father Károly had called the royal doors—were entirely encased in jewel-studded silver, except for the faces. The doors themselves were closed, but were only partial doors, closing the icon screen from a height of shoulder to knee.

"Come away from the Portal," Liam whispered, drawing the pair into the center of the room. "It is not permitted that you may know of this one's location."

Morgan stiffened, but that had been the arrangement. Kelson touched his elbow in reassurance as they followed Liam into the center of the little chapel, searching the shadows for some sign of Mátyás. Kelson could detect none, but the place gave no hint of danger; rather, a sense of peaceful calm and true holiness, for all that the outward form of it seemed strange to his senses. Liam turned briefly toward the iconostasis, making a profound reverence toward the holy icons, then turned back to his companions, venturing a faintly nervous smile.

"Mátyás has gone to tend the Wards guarding this place, for the safety of all of us. I trust that you will not object?"

Kelson found himself thinking that now was a little late to object, if Liam had led them into a trap, but he only inclined his head in answer. Almost immediately, he felt the Wards rise up around them, solid and competent, focused energy soaring upward along the walls to arch over and under them in a protective sphere, squared to the shape of the chamber.

Then Liam was stepping to one side as movement stirred in the shadows beyond the arched doorway of the iconostasis. As Mátyás emerged, pale hands parting the double gate and then closing it behind him, his enameled icon of the Blessed Virgin glowed like a bright jewel on his breast.

"I thank you for trusting me in this," he said quietly. "I assure you that I appreciate the act of faith it required. I shall be brief, for I would not have any of us missed. I shall understand if you have reason to question what I am about to tell you."

"What is this place?" Kelson asked.

"What it appears. A private chapel. *My* private chapel. Actually, it is one of several that are private to me."

"In Torenthály?" Kelson asked.

"No, nor even in the region of Beldour. I assure you, however, that I would not deceive you in this place. But my brothers would deceive you even in Hagia Iób—and intend to do so. And they intend to betray our king. I cannot allow this."

"Go on."

Mátyás inclined his head. "They believe me a part of their plot. Teymuraz and myself and the two counts called László and Branyng are to serve as Moving Wards for the enthronement of Liam-Lajos, as Father Károly perhaps will have explained. It is a high honor, and requires considerable ability. The task of the Moving Wards is to guard the king-to-be on the way to his inauguration, and to protect him during those vulnerable moments prior to taking up the full power of Furstán.

"But Mahael has wielded part of that power during his tenure as regent, and is loath to give it up. It is his intent to mind-rip Laje rather than diminish his own influence. Ronal Rurik either will be killed in the confusion, or will shortly meet an 'accident' such as befell his brother Alroy Arion. Either way, Mahael shall be king."

"And what of Morag's part in all of this?" Kelson asked. "Was she a party to Alroy's death, and does she now countenance the murder of her two remaining sons?"

"No, to both questions," Mátyás replied. "But though she has shared in her sons' regencies, a woman may not take up the power of Furstán. Not that she *could* not, if she chose—as one might expect of the sister of *Wencit ho Phourstanos*. But without that power, she would be no match for Mahael wielding the additional focus of a Moving Ward."

"And Ronal Rurik?"

Mátyás shrugged in dismissal. "He is a boy of ten, and shares no part of Furstán's power. Laje was permitted to assume at least a portion of that power, when he was girded with the sword. But he will be obliged to set it aside and open himself unreservedly before attempting to receive the fullness of his heritage. And in that moment, he will be utterly vulnerable."

The duplicity of the plot was no less than Kelson might have expected of Mahael; and by no skill that he knew to apply was he able to detect any hint that Mátyás's own revulsion for the plot was anything less than genuine. Liam himself had gone white during the recitation, tight-jawed but utterly focused on his uncle. A glance at Morgan confirmed a similar reading of the count's truthfulness.

"What is it you propose?" Kelson asked.

Mátyás folded his hand around the icon hanging from his neck, his lips momentarily tightening, looking distressed.

"To save my king, I must betray my brothers," he said softly. "Before God and the Blessed Virgin, I swear that it was never my ambition to become caught up in the power struggles that have destroyed so many of my kin. Duke Alaric, I spoke truly when I told you that my greatest contentment is to tend my vines and care for my family. I long to see my young son grown to manhood, and to know the child yet in its mother's womb. If I fail in what I propose, I shall see none of these things."

"Indeed, you shall not," Morgan muttered through tight jaws, "for if you play us false in this, I shall slay you myself, though I must come back from hell to do it!"

"I hope to spare you that journey," Mátyás said with a faint smile. "In truth, I would be false to no one, but my brothers have been false to their own blood, and slain the last rightful king, and would slay another—him whom I love even as Arkady loved Nikola. Whether I will it or no, I must involve myself in affairs of state, lest my brothers seize the power that is not theirs to hold, and in doing so, deny Laje his chance to enjoy at least a part of what I have known: to live in love and contentment in the joy of wife and children, to turn his birthright toward peace. . . .

"I think this can be given him," he went on, with more determination. "My abilities are not inconsiderable—and far greater than my brothers are aware. But I cannot do this alone."

"But it *can* be done?" Kelson asked.

Mátyás nodded. "I believe it can. But it will require risk and boldness on your part as well."

"What is it you propose?"

"I shall ensure that Count László is unable to take his part in the Moving Ward—never mind how. Laje will then propose that you take László's place. Nay, he will insist upon it."

"Will you kill László?" Morgan said quietly.

Mátyás looked away, suppressing a grimace. "I have never killed before—but he is plotting to kill my king. Death is a fitting fate for traitors."

"And for your brothers?" Kelson asked.

"I would hope for judicial execution, if we are successful," he said, lowering his eyes. "Thus should traitors meet their end. But if I must slay them myself, in direct defense of my king—so be it. I hope I may have your support."

"Father Károly said that working in a Moving Ward requires considerable training," Kelson pointed out. "Nor is such a working within my previous experience or even the tradition in which I have been taught."

Mátyás nodded. "I understand that. Competent instruction can be obtained, and from a source you may trust. The expenditure of power is considerable, but it is said that you derive formidable resources from your Haldane potentials. I believe you may be equal to the task."

"And then what?" Kelson asked. "Will my mere presence in the Moving Ward prevent your brothers from making the attempt on Liam?"

"I doubt it," Mátyás replied. "But together, you and I should be able to protect Laje long enough to allow his assumption of his full power—and then you and I and Laje can overcome them."

"Or," Morgan muttered, "you and your brothers could overcome two troublesome kings, and eventually rule all the known world—for I think Mahael's ambitions do not stop at Torenth's borders."

"If I am lying to you—and to Laje," Mátyás said, "then perhaps that is true. But I am not lying."

They returned to the Nikolaseum very shortly, lest their absence be noted. Dhugal had no suspicious behavior to report on the part of their waiting guards, and no one else had approached along the Avenue des Rois.

Because they were on public view again, once they emerged from the Nikolaseum, they did not attempt to brief Dhugal regarding what had taken place—though, clearly, neither Kelson nor Morgan had come to any harm. The guards who rejoined them as they walked briskly back toward the waiting royal caïque were not Deryni, but there were Deryni among the vessel's officers.

Not until much later that night, after a tedious state dinner in the presence of Mahael, Teymuraz, and the treacherous Counts László and Branyng, was Kelson able to share with Dhugal what Mátyás had told them. Dhugal remained dubious, even though he understood why the king had tentatively agreed to the plan.

"I suppose it's occurred to you that Mátyás might have figured out a way around being Truth-Read," he pointed out glumly. "Even if he's telling the truth, even if he can do what he says he can, are you capable of learning what you need to know—and quickly enough—to function usefully in a Torenthi ritual?"

"I don't know."

"No, you don't. Kelson, they do things differently here, starting with the way they cross themselves. What you're describing will require serious cooperation, not to mention trust—and initially, it's going to be you and Mátyás against Mahael and Teymuraz and their crony—what's his name, Branyng? Even Mátyás admits that he isn't sure the two of you will be strong enough to stop them."

"We'll have Liam on our side," Kelson pointed out.

"Yes—if and when you get him far enough through the ritual to be effective. It sounds like the ritual strips him bare before it tops up his power. And the imagery of the magic is all . . . different. And what if Mátyás *is* lying, and this is all a setup to kill *you*, not Liam—or to kill you *and* Liam?"

"I asked Mátyás that very same question," Morgan replied. "It could very easily be a double-cross on either or both their parts."

"It could be," Kelson agreed. "But I don't think it is."

"*You don't think*," Dhugal repeated sourly, emphasizing all three words. "That's a pretty big gamble, Kel—maybe as big as any you've ever taken."

"I know that," Kelson whispered. "But I can't just abandon Liam to the less than loving intentions of his uncles. Not if I'm to provide him with the protection I promised when we exchanged oaths of fealty. To do less would be to betray my own oath—to lessen my honor as a man, as a king. We can only pray that Mátyás is, indeed, genuine—and take what precautions we can, in case he isn't."

"I wonder whether we should consult with Arilan about this," Morgan ventured. "Or maybe Azim."

"I think I'd prefer to wait until we've seen whether Mátyás really is prepared to sacrifice Count László," Kelson replied. "And maybe not even then. I want to get a further feel for how our enigmatic count holds up under pressure."

"There's still a great deal of scope for interpretation, regarding what he's told us," Morgan said thoughtfully. "I find myself returning to his assertion that he's never killed before—which could simply mean that he's never soiled his own hands. Truth-Reading wouldn't detect the nuances, if he'd ordered others to do his dirty work."

"Do you think he has?" Kelson countered.

Morgan considered for a moment, then slowly shook his head.

"Actually, I don't. I can't tell you why I feel this way, but I think that the face he's shown us—and Liam—is that of an honest and honorable man, who genuinely abhors the violence of the past. He must be walking an incredible tightrope."

"But, what if you're both wrong?" Dhugal asked.

"I suppose we'll only know that as the future unfolds," Kelson replied. "Based on our conversation today, however, I think we can safely assume that the untimely demise of Count László any time in the next few days will probably be the work of at least one of the Furstán brothers. If it's only Mátyás, we may, indeed, have an ally.

"But if either of the others seems even remotely involved, then this whole situation becomes even more delicate than we feared—because it means that we never won over Liam at all, and the old hostilities between Gwynedd and Torenth are set to flare up all over again."

CHAPTER EIGHTEEN

Many mighty men have been greatly disgraced.

Ecclesiasticus 11:6

With no general rehearsal set for the following day, the guests of Torenth were at leisure through the morning. Though Count László was not in evidence, no word had yet come of any change in his fortunes. At the invitation of Liam himself, Kelson and Dhugal and Morgan sampled the delights of the royal baths, deep in the bowels of the palace, seeking refuge from the heat.

In the afternoon, duty required their appearance at yet another state reception for prominent guests arriving daily for the coming *killijálay*. This one was to receive Prince Centule of Vezaire and the Crown Prince of Jáca, Prince Rotrou, representing two of the Forcinn States. Rotrou had brought his daughter, the Princess Ekaterina, a dark-eyed beauty who caused Dhugal to take sharp notice.

"I wonder why no one sent you *her* portrait," he murmured aside to Kelson.

"Just keep your mind on business."

"I am," Dhugal replied. "But I can look, can't I?"

As they now knew was customary in the summer heat, the reception was held in the shady tranquillity of one of the tiered gardens, where guests could stroll beside the fountains and ponds and catch the cooling breezes, sampling dainties from the royal kitchens and quaffing chilled wines, all to the accompaniment of harp and lute filtering from a ladies' bower. Kelson had already paid his respects to the new arrivals and to the sovereign Princess of Andelon, a handsome, serene woman whom he believed to be a distant relation of Rothana, though he was reluctant to ask. Before introducing them, Rasoul had told him that the Princess Sofiana was reckoned to be one of the most powerful Deryni in the Forcinn, and had married her children into most of the royal houses of the East.

Indeed, she seemed to be on cordial terms with nearly everyone present. In addition to her husband, a mild-mannered gentleman dressed in the Jácan fashion, with absolutely impenetrable shields, she was accompanied by their younger son and his wife, the latter clearly with child.

"Andelon is a prosperous state," Count Berrhones told them later, as he brought wine for Kelson and Dhugal, "and Sofiana is both subtle and adroit—her father's daughter, in every respect. He was a very great prince. It is said that she married the Lord Reyhan for love, since he has no wealth to speak of. An elder son will inherit—the Prince Kamil—but Prince Taher is believed to be her favorite. A daughter is consort to the Crown Prince of Nur Hallaj—whose sister, I believe, is known to you."

Which was the link Kelson had been trying to remember. The Crown Prince of Nur Hallaj was Rothana's brother.

A little later, as the gathering began to disperse, because of the heat of the afternoon, Rasoul came with an offer to escort a leisurely ride-out beyond the city walls, into the cooler refuge of the nearby hills—also an opportunity to escape the press of so much protocol, at least for a few hours. Though the prospect was tempting, Kelson tried to stall. Formal obligations of the day satisfied, the royal uncles and Count Branyng were preparing to retire with Liam for a practice session with the Moving Ward, as soon as Count László made his appearance. But László still had not arrived.

The reason soon became clear—if there had been any doubt in Kelson's mind, as the day wore on—as an excited verbal exchange suddenly erupted beneath the trellised arches far across the lawns, ruffling the tranquillity of the terraced garden. Though the circumstances were not immediately clear, the flurry of activity soon spawned a grim-faced senior courtier and a nervous and perspiring man in the livery of the city guard, followed purposefully by an older man of imposing dignity whom Kelson knew to be the Grand Vizier of Beldour, in charge of security for the city.

Kelson, in the company of Dhugal, Morgan, and Derry, had been discussing the proposed ride-out with Rasoul, Father Irenaeus, and a facile young man named Lord Raduslav, grandson of the Count Berrhones. But conversation ceased and all eyes turned in the direction of Liam and his uncles as the liveried messenger abased himself at their feet and began gasping out his news.

King Kelson's Bride   199

"*What?*"

Mahael's bellow carried to every corner of the garden precincts, and his red face bore witness to his outrage and consternation. Both Irenaeus and Lord Raduslav immediately drifted in that direction, lingering nearby until Mahael, his brothers, and an apparently distressed Liam disappeared into the palace with the vizier and the messenger. Father Irenaeus followed after them, but young Raduslav returned to report breathlessly to Kelson and his companions.

"A thousand pardons for the temporary abandonment," he said, nodding to Rasoul. "It seemed prudent to find out what has happened."

"Yes?" Rasoul said impatiently.

Raduslav rolled his eyes. "It now becomes clear why our naughty Count László has not yet made his appearance. Not an hour ago, his lifeless body was pulled from the river, nude save for a woman's veil tightly knotted around his throat."

Rasoul likewise cast his eyes heavenward and sighed, saying nothing. Kelson exchanged glances with his companions.

"Count László had—how shall I put it?—prodigious appetites," Raduslav explained. "At this time of year, lovers often take their dalliance under the stars, in small boats, some of which are quite lavishly appointed. Alas, I fear László may have offended one too many jealous husbands."

His tone suggested that the manner of László's death came as no great surprise, nor was entirely undeserved, but Kelson found himself wondering whether a jealous husband had, indeed, had any part in Count László's demise—and what part Mátyás might have played in the affair.

"Duke Mahael seemed particularly upset," he observed. "Was Count László a close friend?"

"Far more than that," Rasoul offered. "He was the fourth part of the Moving Ward, one of the Pillars of the Realm. My lord Mahael will not have been pleased that he now must replace him."

"Exactly," Raduslav agreed. "Already, they argue over who should take his place. I could not hear the *padishah's* remark, but his uncles seemed not to be pleased. I would not wish to be present for the clash of wills no doubt in progress."

Kelson lingered in the garden for some time, listening to speculation among the others present, but the brothers did not emerge—though Azim did, to whisper in the ear Rasoul bent to hear him. Very soon, in an apparent bid to divert attention from this evidence of disharmony within the Torenthi royal house, Rasoul again announced his willingness to conduct at least some of the royal visitors on the proposed ride-out from Beldour—an offer that Kelson now was ready to accept, for it appeared that no additional news concerning László was likely to be soon forthcoming. In case it should, he left Morgan behind with Létald and Arilan and a knot of Forcinn observers, and took Dhugal and Derry with him.

Somewhat to his surprise, Prince Azim was among those who joined the expedition into the hills; and when they stopped to rest and water their horses, after a long gallop up a grassy hillside, Kelson found himself adroitly drawn apart by the Deryni mage, who led the way toward a pool formed by a spectacular waterfall. When the horses had drunk, and they had led them into the cool shade of a sprawling pine, Azim lifted his saddle flap to adjust a girth strap, glancing at Kelson across the high-cantled saddle between them.

"Are you aware of the suggestion that Liam-Lajos has made to his uncles?" he asked, so softly that Kelson could just hear him above the sound of the rushing water.

"I've heard nothing," he said truthfully. "But I take it that you have."

Azim smiled at him faintly across his saddle. "From mere danger to mortal peril, my prince. He wishes you to take László's place in the Moving Ward."

Kelson feigned innocence of any such notion, merely blinking at Azim. "Me?"

"It seems you have gained his trust," Azim said neutrally, watching him closely. "The elder brothers are adamant that this must not be allowed, but the youngest counsels indulging the young *padishah*—who *will* have his way, it seems."

Kelson only shook his head lightly, in apparent bewilderment. "You sound very certain of that. How do you know such things?"

"I have my—informers," the other replied gravely. "And you need not play coy with me, Kelson of Gwynedd. You but waste both your time and mine. If you are prepared to trust me in the matter of your future queen, you must trust me in this. Are you able for the task that Liam-Lajos proposes to ask of you?"

"Suppose you tell me," Kelson countered. "*Am* I able? Can you teach me?"

Azim inclined his head. "I can. And I must, it seems. They are saying that young Lajos will not be moved, once his mind is set. He is very like his father in that regard. As for you, my prince, I think you are, indeed, able for the task. The question is, are you willing?"

"I have little choice, if that is what Liam wishes," Kelson replied, looking down toward the pool, where Dhugal and Derry were watering their horses— and casting the occasional glance in his direction. "If he is bound to me as vassal, I am equally bound as his overlord. I am aware that the prospect of his enthronement has caused him great anxiety. He has—even confided his uncertainty to me regarding his uncles' intentions."

Azim also turned his face toward the pool, allowing himself a small sigh. "My prince, I think it is a very important thing that you do, in aiding Liam-Lajos in this way," he said softly. "God grant that you may both survive it."

Kelson glanced at him sharply, daring to probe gently at Azim's shields but getting nowhere. "Azim, are you trying to warn me about Liam's uncles?" he whispered.

"I think that anyone who underestimates the guile of the elder brothers Furstán is very foolish, indeed," Azim said enigmatically.

"And what of the youngest brother, and Liam himself?" Kelson pressed.

"I have said all that I may," Azim replied. "But you would be well advised to consider carefully what I have said," he added, before turning his horse's head to lead it back toward the others, leaving Kelson wondering just what kind of warning—or reassurance—he had been given.

*T*he king told Morgan and Dhugal of the conversation later that evening, secure within the wards they had set to guard his quarters against Torenthi spying, but the pair were as mystified as he. Azim's specific exclusion of Mátyás from his warning about Liam's two elder uncles did seem to suggest, by default, that Mátyás was to be trusted; but was a default endorsement sufficient, when dealing with the present threat, which grew more complicated—and more dangerous—almost by the hour?

Morgan, who knew Azim far better than did Kelson, could offer no explanation for Azim's apparent involvement in the thick of Torenthi politics. He could only agree that if Liam did, indeed, ask Kelson to replace László in the Moving Ward, the king had no choice but to accept—and no choice but to accept Azim's assistance in learning how to carry out that task. Kelson slept badly that night, aware that whichever way the next day went, he was being led—or pushed—into a situation not entirely of his choosing or within his control or competence.

The next morning, while he prodded at a headache and they awaited instructions regarding the day's schedule, he was hardly surprised to find his presence requested by one of Mahael's liveried retainers, to attend a select Torenthi court in one of the small withdrawing rooms deep in the heart of the palace. He took Morgan and Dhugal with him, and found Azim, Arilan, and Létald waiting for him outside the door. By their expressions, they already knew what was about to be asked of him. None of them looked happy.

Inside, a determined-looking Liam was sitting beneath a state canopy—not precisely holding court, but clearly asserting his authority. No one else was seated—though that was fairly common in Torenthi court protocol. Mahael, Tey-muraz, and Mátyás were clustered to one side of Liam's chair, looking mostly sour and dissatisfied.

The Patriarch Alpheios stood at the other side, leaning on a pastoral staff shaped like a *tau*, his deep purple robe touching a somber note amid the other fin-ery of the court, a black veil trailing from the back of his flat-topped hat. An ornate pectoral cross and two *panagia* adorned his breast. Kelson noticed that Mátyás also wore his enamelled icon of the Blessed Virgin, and touched it lightly, in an apparently idle movement, as his eye briefly met Kelson's.

"The court of Torenth greets Kelson of Gwynedd in Christ's love," Alpheios said, as Kelson and his party entered the room and the door closed behind them. Kelson gave a nod of acknowledgment both to Liam and to the patriarch, and his companions offered more formal salute. "I am instructed to make certain inquiries regarding your willingness to assist the *padishah* in a delicate matter."

Kelson inclined his head in Alpheios' direction, now quite sure what he was about to be asked.

"As his feudal superior, I am always eager to learn how I may assist Liam-Lajos in the performance of his duties, Holiness."

"Torenth thanks you," Alpheios replied. "Perhaps you will have heard, then, that a valued member of the court of Torenth passed away yesterday: our dear Count László of Czalsky. He shall be greatly missed on his personal merits, for all did esteem him highly; but his demise at this time carries unfortunate and serious official repercussions as well, for he was to have served as one of the Moving Wards for the *padishah's* enthronement. To stand as a Pillar of the Realm at *killi-jálay* is deemed one of the highest honors that the House of Furstán can bestow, but great skill is required to serve in this capacity. It is the desire of the *padishah* to offer you this honor—that you take the place of Count László—but he will understand if you prefer to decline, not having experience of this function, nor familiarity with our ways."

Kelson favored the patriarch with a respectful bow. Probably on the instruc-tion of Mahael, Alpheios had phrased the invitation to offer him no graceful way to decline without greatly losing face—which could mean that Kelson's presence in the Moving Ward was precisely what Mahael wanted. But Kelson had to believe that neither Liam nor Mátyás had lied to him. He dared not decline the offer probably so dearly won by the young king.

"I appreciate your concern for our differences, Holiness," he murmured, choosing careful, courtly words to convey his answer—and careful, also, to avoid any deviation from literal truth, for he had no doubt that every Deryni in the room was reading him for any trace of the lie.

"In fact, I had been informed of Count László's demise—and had learned that Liam-Lajos desired me to assist in this capacity. I have taken the liberty of seeking counsel of Prince Azim, who is more conversant than I with the requirements of the function and who also has some acquaintance with my own abilities." Azim bowed as Kelson gestured in his direction, one hand to his breast. "He has assured me that, under his tutelage, I can learn the necessary skills to serve in this capacity. In addition, perhaps you would be so kind as to lend me the services of Father Irenaeus or Father Károly, to give me further instruction regarding the ceremonials customary in your observances; for I desire to fulfill my part in this very important event in Torenth's history in the reverent manner you would wish."

He sensed a collective sigh of relief breathing through the room—but whether it was from gladness that he would relieve them of this momentary stutter in expected protocol and procedure or from expectation that he would fail, he could not tell.

That very afternoon, Kelson began private instruction with Azim. He had never worked directly with the Deryni master, whose training came by way of the Knights of the Anvil and disciplines once practiced by the Knights of Saint Michael, back in the time of Saint Camber; but he knew that Azim had taught both Richenda and Rothana. (He had also contributed to Araxie's training, but Kelson tried to put that awareness from his mind, lest he be distracted from the task at hand.) By unspoken and mutual agreement, nothing of past affiliations was allowed to intrude, for both of them were well aware how much Kelson had to master, and in so little time. Nor was the possible deception of Mátyás and of Liam himself in the developing scenario ever mentioned.

"Balancing the energies will not be your concern," Azim told him, while they rested between sessions involving the visualizations Kelson must master, as representative of the Western Quarter. "Liam must blend the contributions of the four of you to stabilize the sphere of protection. While he does this, you must merely hold steady with the image you project—but you must hold it for two periods of approximately two hours: first, for the journey between here and Holy Iób, and then during the *killijálay* itself, which may be shorter, but will certainly be more intense, however things transpire. You will have a respite of no more than a quarter-hour between the two."

"Will that be long enough to recover?" Kelson asked.

"It must be long enough. Fortunately, by assigning you to the West—which is exceedingly appropriate, given Gwynedd's position relative to Torenth—they have also given you what is perhaps the least demanding of the four positions—the sphere of Gabriel, whose patron is Our Lady."

"This is the *least* demanding?" Kelson murmured, rubbing at his temples.

204 ﾞ KATHERINE KURTZ

Azim gave him a brittle smile. "Aye, the North is most difficult, perhaps; Uriel is the least understood of the archangels. But Mátyás is competent to mediate in that Quarter. The most dangerous is the South, where Teymuraz will wield Fire—for *Micháel Archangelos* takes precedence for the purposes of *killijálay*.

"But I can teach you much of that aspect, in what time we have before us," Azim went on. "You are an apt pupil. Being familiar with Fire's attributes, you may be able to minimize whatever trickery Teymuraz might have in mind. In the East, Branyng could also present formidable opposition, should the brothers decide to turn against you. He will have the might of storm behind him." He shook his head. "All are powerful positions."

"But each wields power that must be channelled in Liam's cause," Kelson replied, drawing himself up for yet another attempt to increase his staying power for the required visualization. "If I can, I must help to ensure that precisely that happens."

In the beginning, he had been able to hold his focus for barely ten minutes. By the following morning, he could hold it for an hour—and for three, before the day was out. With Azim's help, he slept like a dead man that night, but he awoke clear-headed, as Azim had promised.

Later that morning, Azim brought Father Irenaeus, Father Károly, and an elderly gentleman called Janos Sokrat to assist him. All had experience of Moving Wards, though such were usually the province of younger men—and these greybeards had not the endurance to maintain one for as long as would be required of Kelson. Janos, the most accomplished of them, had milky cataracts over both eyes, and walked with the aid of a young boy, but his mind was razor-sharp, his visualization of Uriel, in the North, a tower of anchoring strength for the balance of the Ward the four of them began rehearsing. Father Károly took charge of the South, and Father Irenaeus did a credible job in the East, with Azim himself assuming Liam's role for the rehearsals, blending the energies seamlessly as he raised the protective Ward.

Working as part of a team, with three others sharing the energy drain and Azim directing from their midst, Kelson soon discovered that merely maintaining the Ward, once established—even a Moving one—required far less power than he had first assumed. Actually to move required little concentration beyond making sure that the four of them remained in physical alignment. After an hour's practice, though they did not venture outside the room in which they worked, Kelson felt reasonably confident that he would be able to carry off his part in the first phase of the exercise for as long as it took—at least to the point when the actual transfer of power began.

For that, he would be handling far more and different types of power, helping channel Liam's energies as well as keeping his own in balance with those of the other three Wards; and Azim told him that there would be no opportunity to actually experience this part of the working until the day, for the power drain was considerable. Unspoken until their three assistants retired for the day was the certainty that this hemorrhaging of energy would have to be juggled according to how Liam's uncles focused any attack at the critical moment.

Against that likelihood, and before Azim allowed the King of Gwynedd to take a meal break, he showed Kelson how to bail out of the working and maybe save himself—though this would be a last-ditch option, if all hope of saving Liam was lost, and would entail abandoning Liam to his fate at his uncles' hands. A little later, before Kelson fell exhausted into bed, the two priests returned to go over all the external ceremony of the enthronement ritual, complete with diagrams. The exercise left Kelson's head spinning. Knowing that the morrow would see his first rehearsals with the Furstán brothers, rather than their stand-ins, he again allowed Azim to send him into deep, dreamless sleep.

Interestingly enough, finally working together with Teymuraz, Branyng, and Mátyás proved something of an anticlimax. Their initial encounter the next morning bristled with thinly veiled hostility at first; but with Liam in their midst, binding their energies into harmony, they soon progressed to marching along the corridors of the palace under an increasingly efficient Moving Ward, startling guards and sending small children scurrying.

After a midday collation, they progressed to the next phase: shifting the Moving Ward over a carriage-and-eight, similar in size to the great state carriage that, on the day of *killijálay*, would convey Liam-Lajos from the palace to the Quai du Saint-Basile and the caïque waiting to convey him upriver to Torenthály and Hagia Iób. The physical logistics required practice, with Branyng mounting the box beside the driver, Mátyás and Teymuraz perched on steps outside the two doors, left and right, and Kelson clinging to the rear of the carriage beside a footman; but actually maintaining the Ward required only minimal concentration, once they were ensconced.

Liam shot him a pleased grin as he alighted from Mátyás's side of the carriage, when they had returned to the king's palace after completion of the afternoon's rehearsal. Mátyás kept to the company of his brothers at the state banquet that evening, when the court entertained yet more new foreign arrivals who had come to witness the *killijálay*; but once, when both Mahael and Teymuraz were otherwise occupied, the youngest of Liam's uncles found occasion to glance sidelong at Kelson as he touched two fingers to his lips and then brushed them across the icon on his breast, at the same time meeting Kelson's gaze.

Kelson took the gesture to mean that Mátyás was trying to reassure him that he only played a part, that he honored the promise of fidelity he had made them in his private chapel, during that foray from the Nikolaseum. If only Kelson could be certain that Mátyás meant it.

Rehearsals continued the next day. That morning, the four of them set the Moving Ward around a carriage for a swift dash down the Avenue-du-Saint Constantine, then shifted to a caïque, where they held the Ward above Liam while the vessel rowed briskly upriver to Torenthály, combining two pieces of ritual action that would be played out as one continuum and at more sedate speeds on the day.

Landing at the quay at Torenthály, where Count Berrhones waited to cast his gimlet gaze over their efforts, they next tried their skill at maneuvering the Moving Ward over the white stallion that Liam would ride to his enthronement, up the Avenue des Rois to Hagia Iób. The animal was restive, only recently accustomed to Liam, and fought its handlers as the five of them approached; but it settled immediately as it came within the calming sphere of the Moving Ward, and allowed Liam to mount.

Horse and man became a fused unit of grace and channelled power, the great stallion tight-coiled and animated but utterly compliant as they set out along the avenue—for which Kelson was grateful, since his position required him to walk directly behind the great steed's steel-shod heels. Count Berrhones rode beside them on a smooth-gaited white mule, just outside the Moving Ward, and pronounced himself well satisfied with their competence as Liam dismounted before the golden doors to the church, where those involved in the inside ceremony waited to rehearse their parts. Inside, Morag, Ronal Rurik, and Mahael himself joined them for the first time.

There then ensued a full-scale walk-through of the ceremony itself—the latest of many, for most of those involved, but Kelson had seen only that very first run-through following Liam's return, watching casually from the sidelines, then blissfully unaware what his eventual role would be. Now designated as part of the all-important Moving Ward, he found himself observing from an entirely different perspective as they walked through the pattern of *killijálay* itself, taking Berrhones' exacting instruction, aware of Azim and Morgan and the others watching intently, proceeding right up to the moment when power would be transferred.

"We shall not rehearse any part of the actual transfer," Mahael said, there calling a halt. "To enact any part of the critical ritual without invoking its substance is to profane the legacy of Furstán. Laje knows what he must do."

"It can do no harm to mime the physical postures—" Berrhones began.

"It shall not be done," said Teymuraz, backing up Mahael. "Let us resume after the regirding, and proceed with the encrowning and acts of homage and the grand recessional."

"But, for the sake of King Kelson—" Berrhones began.

"He has only to hold steady, and to follow our lead," Mátyás said, with a sharp glance at Liam, who was looking rebellious. "For the sake of the *padishah*, let us not risk profaning the legacy of Furstán."

"Majesty?" Berrhones asked, finally appealing directly to Liam.

"Do as my uncles recommend," he agreed reluctantly. "We shall not rehearse any part of the rite of Furstán."

*M*uch later that night, after yet another semi-state banquet taken in the palace great hall, Bishop Denis Arilan sought the meeting place designated in a token he had received earlier in the evening. As he paused at a branching in the corridor, Azim stepped out of the shadow of a service stair, a little to his right, black-clad as usual.

"Come with me," he murmured, "and say nothing."

Silently Arilan followed down the spiral stair, half-feeling his way, for there were no torches. Azim seemed not to need the light. Down one level, they emerged before a bronze door entirely covered with a graceful, deeply incised script whose lines made a design of their own. The modest room beyond was lit by a single oil lamp suspended before an arched niche, with thick carpets underfoot. As Azim closed the door behind them, a woman stepped from the shadows and unveiled.

"Say nothing," Sofiana whispered. "Come. This Portal is in regular use by couriers. We must not be discovered here."

Even as she said it, Azim was urging him forward, hands set on his shoulders. Arilan felt Sofiana's shields enveloping the three of them, just before she took his hands, and he lowered his in response, for he had already felt the tingle of a readied Portal beneath his feet as he moved closer. Guessing their destination, he yielded to her control, as did Azim, finding reassurance in the brief swoop of giddiness that accompanied a Portal shift. As his vision stabilized and she released him, he recognized the expected Portal outside the meeting chamber of the Camberian Council.

Inside, only Barrett and Sion were seated at the great table beneath the purple dome. Sion rose as the three of them entered, looking concerned, one hand resting on Barrett's shoulder. Sofiana cast a glance at the empty places as she headed for her seat next to Sion.

"I see that Laran has not yet arrived," she said.

"And shall not, this night," Barrett said gravely. "Nor shall Vivienne, ever again. She is dying," he went on, lifting his blind, tear-filled eyes to the dark dome above them. "Laran is with her, and shall remain until the end, but he can do little."

Arilan caught himself from stumbling, en route to his seat beside Vivienne's empty chair, for he could not remember a time when the proud and sometimes difficult Vivienne had not been a part of the Council, bringing keen discernment and a shrewd intelligence to their deliberations, as well as her not inconsiderable power. Exasperating though she had been at times, and often maddeningly inflexible, she had always represented for him a link with the past and tradition. He could not imagine what the Council would be like without her. Nor had he realized she was ill; he had thought her only frail.

"What happened?" he asked as he sat, Azim taking his seat on the other side of Vivienne's chair, and Sofiana beyond Azim, beside Sion.

Barrett allowed himself a heavy sigh, himself suddenly looking more fragile than he had a few seconds earlier, before he had shared the news about Vivienne.

"She is old, Denis. We all grow old, if we are fortunate. It is her time. One day soon, it will be mine."

"But—"

"Denis," Sofiana said quietly, "she has not been well for some time. Even when last we met, she was more ill than she let it be known. She suffered a seizure some three days ago. Laran has been with her, and shall remain until—" She lifted both hands in an eloquent gesture of inevitability.

"Why did no one tell me?" Arilan whispered. "Three days—"

"Nothing could be allowed to possibly interfere with the king's preparations for the *killijálay*," Azim said quietly. "Even I did not know until an hour ago, lest my focus be distracted from teaching the king what he must know."

"In that, I am certain she would have wished that we proceed," Barrett declared, turning his blind face toward Arilan. "This is a critical time, and we must not let personal sorrows impede us in our work. Our brother Azim has kept us informed regarding his efforts to prepare Kelson for his part in the enthronement. He also informs us that you have something additional to report, which also touches on the concerns of the Council."

"I do," Arilan agreed, glancing at Azim—and wondering whether the other truly had not yet broached the subject of Kelson's intended marriage, if he had been in ongoing communication with the Council, outside their formal meetings. "I would have reported earlier, but when we first learned of it, we had no Portal access, and Azim advised that such news was best reported in person. In light of the news about Vivienne, his judgment was probably correct, since it would have been a personal disappointment to her on several counts—though I hope the Council will approve. The king has chosen his bride at last, and a private betrothal has been made."

Their startled looks, save for Azim, confirmed that the latter had not, indeed, shared the information with them.

"And the lady is—?" Sion asked.

"One whose removal from the marriage market may well make *your* task more difficult, in Llannedd," Arilan replied. "But we should have considered her before. I must say that I approve."

"Who is it?" Barrett demanded.

"He is marrying his cousin Araxie Haldane," Arilan replied, to varying expressions of surprise from the four who had not known. "Which means that she is *not* marrying Prince Cuan of Howicce, and that *he* is not marrying Noelie Ramsay."

Barrett's brow furrowed. "You're right that this would not please Vivienne—and it will not please the Mearans."

"The king has a better match in mind for Meara," Arilan countered. "He proposes that Noelie wed with his cousin Rory Haldane—an attachment that apparently developed last summer, when the two families met in Rhemuth to arrange the first Mearan marriage. This second Haldane match further offers the prospect of a permanent Haldane presence in Meara, for I am told that Rory is to be groomed as a future viceroy. These two Haldane alliances should ensure a peaceful resolution of the Mearan question in years to come."

"Well enough for *that*," Sion conceded, fingering his curling yellow beard in thoughtful reflection, "but the match that Kelson proposes for himself is the double-Haldane mating that Vivienne feared. What, indeed, might such a match produce?—the Haldane potential crossed with itself.

"Nor may I personally discount the difficulties that disclosure of this match will create for *me*, at home in Llannedd, though these are largely domestic." He sighed vexedly. "Sharp scrutiny will again fall on my mistress, the Princess Gwenlian, and her cousin Cuan, once it is learned that the supposed object of his matrimonial interest is to marry another. It will not be a pretty scene when this is brought to King Colman's attention."

Sofiana just controlled an impatient grimace. "With due respect, Sion, it is not the urgent priority of the Council to concern itself with the internal problems of Llannedd and Howicce at this time." She glanced at Azim. "This news is, indeed, most welcome, though it will require much further consideration. But just now, I agree that we must be far more concerned about the more immediate dangers of *killijálay*. Is it your conviction that Kelson is capable of working in the Moving Ward and thwarting any treachery of Mahael?"

"It would be foolish to contend that he is capable of thwarting *any* treachery of Mahael," Azim replied, inclining his head, "but I believe he is extremely capable. It remains to be seen whether belief and reality shall coincide, on the day. The morrow shall reveal all. By this time tomorrow, we shall know if we need worry any further regarding this marriage which seems to have several of you so concerned."

CHAPTER NINETEEN

Take away the wicked from before the king, and his
throne shall be established in righteousness.

Proverbs 25:5

*T*he day of *killijálay* dawned bright but mild, the heat of the past week tempered by cooling breezes conjured for the occasion by mages adept in weather-working. Kelson rose with the sun, standing at the open window of his chamber to watch the first long shadows retreat before the golden sunlight flooding across the tesselated floor. Very shortly, Dhugal came to inform him that his bath was drawn.

The water was tepid, warm enough to be comfortable, cool enough to refresh. Kelson let himself enjoy it until Payne and Brendan came to help him dress, Morgan bearing the richly embroidered ceremonial robe he was expected to wear as one of the four Pillars of the Moving Ward.

"Father Károly delivered this a little while ago," Morgan said, scowling as he laid out the garment beside a lighter-weight tunic of Haldane crimson that the king would wear beneath the ceremonial attire. "It's clear that *killijálay* usually occurs in the dead of winter."

Kelson eyed the heavy garment as he got out of the bath, dripping.

"It certainly wasn't designed with the summer heat in mind."

Dhugal snorted. "I think it was Father Irenaeus who mentioned that this one is actually from a lighter set, made for the ceremony to mark Alroy's coming of age. But they were never used," he added somewhat lamely, as he realized what he had said.

"We'll hope that isn't an omen," Kelson said quietly, for Alroy had died before the ceremony could be performed.

He declined further conversation as he quickly dried off and pulled on close-fitting black breeches, already feeling a knot in the pit of his stomach, all too conscious that Alroy almost certainly had met his fate at the hands of Mahael, who was very much a part of today's ceremony. While he let Brendan comb out his hair and braid it, he fingered the coral prayer beads his mother had given him—apt symbolism, he realized, for mediating the West, which ruled water. As Payne slipped short leather boots on his feet, he found his eyes drawn involuntarily to the robe never worn for Alroy's coming of age.

The robe of the West was the same celestial blue he now had come to associate with the holy color adorning church domes and other sacred buildings, stiff with silk embroidery and golden thread and semiprecious stones. The front of the garment fastened on the right shoulder to allow depiction on the breast of a symbol appropriate to the Quarter represented. This one bore a shimmering white crescent picked out in silver bullion and pearls, the symbol of the Western Quarter as used in Torenth and the East, the pearls alluding to the West's rule over elemental Water.

Embroidered scallop shells edged the cuffs of the wide sleeves and the deep slits on either side, amid waves of shaded silk threads, further evoking the imagery of water. Appliquéd along the full length of the back was a depiction of the Archangel Gabriel, with graceful hands upheld at shoulder-level in the posture known as *orans*, wings extended up and over the shoulders of the robe. The palms of the angel's hands were set with jewels, and Kelson glanced at the medal on the beads in his hand, showing it to Morgan when the other looked at him in question.

"Jehana gave me these, the night before we left," he said. "How could she have known? She thought it was meant to be her guardian angel, but I think it's Saint Gabriel."

"Holy Gabriél," Morgan said quietly, as Kelson touched the enamelled medal to his lips, then looped the beads around his neck. "Let us hope that the good archangel helps make your work light."

"My thought, precisely," Kelson replied.

He turned away to let Payne guide his arms into the sleeves of a thin cotton shirt, shaking his head when Brendan would have offered him the tunic of Haldane crimson lying beside the ritual robe. Though made of lightweight silk, it was still another layer he must wear all too soon; and a heavy Haldane state mantle would replace the Torenthi ritual garment, once Liam was empowered and enthroned and Kelson must shift role from angelic guardian to feudal overlord.

"Should you eat something?" Dhugal asked, as Kelson tucked the shirt into the waist of his breeches.

"I'm still of two minds on that," the king replied. "Magical ritual is usually best done on an empty stomach. On the other hand, it's going to be a long day. Alaric, what do you think?"

"Perhaps you should compromise and just receive Holy Communion," Morgan said. "Arilan will be here soon, to celebrate Mass for us."

"Maybe I'll have some additional bread and wine, after Mass," Kelson said. He sighed. "I am not looking forward to this, my friends. *Is* Mátyás true, or is this all an elaborate double- or even triple-cross, to bring me down? God, if only I could be certain!"

Arilan arrived soon after, with Azim, Saer, and Derry. After celebrating Mass for them, the Deryni bishop and Azim remained when Saer and Derry took the two pages to be about their business.

"Well," said Kelson, washing down a bite of chewy and substantial brown bread with a swallow of wine as Dhugal helped him into his Haldane tunic. "Have the two of you stayed to give me last-minute advice, or is Denis going to tell me how foolish I'm about to be?"

Azim only smiled faintly; Arilan bristled.

"Actually," said Morgan, forestalling comment by the bishop, "His Grace of Dhassa has stayed to give you a final blessing and then be on his way to Torenthály, since he insists upon being close-mouthed about who the players are and on whose side they might be playing. I begin to suspect the subtle hand of the Camberian Council in these recent goings-on."

"That is hardly fair!" Arilan retorted.

"Furthermore, since Prince Azim declines to clarify *his* somewhat enigmatic half-warnings about the brothers Furstán—and, indeed, has said he *may* not tell us more—I can only speculate that he comes under the authority of the same body that sometimes constrains Arilan's forthrightness—in short, that the Camberian Council is perhaps involved in machinations of their own, in the matter of the Torenthi succession. Have you any comment, Azim?"

The desert prince's expression did not change. "Pray, continue."

"Indeed, I shall. The Camberian Council do not allow themselves to interfere directly," Morgan went on, "so they're reduced to suggestion and innuendo, forcing would-be allies to react as adversaries. Except that all of us know that Liam-Lajos is the rightful king, and that Kelson is sworn to protect him, as his vassal. I therefore cannot imagine why either of you are playing these games with us. With Arilan, it's old habit—and we know that he is a member of the Camberian Council, because he once took me, Kelson, and Duncan to their secret meeting place. Azim was not then a member—but things change. Is he, Arilan?"

Arilan was occupied with a petulant study of the toes of his embroidered slippers. Azim gave him a long look, glanced appraisingly at Kelson and his companions, then back at the bishop.

"If you do not tell them, Denis, I shall," he said quietly. "If he was deemed worthy to be offered a seat on the Council, he deserves to know what he truly faces."

Kelson caught his breath, sensing a possible breakthrough. He could feel Morgan and Dhugal likewise tensed and attentive. Arilan looked up at Azim for a long moment—unreadable, implacable—then exhaled with a resigned sigh.

"Prince Azim is a member of the Council," he admitted. "Several other members will also be present to observe, for if Mahael does move successfully against his nephew, the ensuing dynastic wrangling will destabilize the entire East."

"Then, he *does* plan to attack Liam?" Kelson breathed.

"So we believe. But our source of information may not be true. Mahael has the support of Count Branyng, a very powerful and ambitious Deryni, and his two brothers; at least he thinks he does. There are—indications that Mátyás may be more loyal to Liam than to Mahael, and will try to defend the boy. Liam's mother has kept an outwardly civil working relationship with all three brothers, but may have her own priorities; she has done nothing to challenge Mahael regarding the death of her eldest son, but she cannot be unaware of the rumors. To *us*, it may seem unthinkable that a mother would connive at the deaths of her own children, but this is Torenth, and members of the House of Furstán have always been ambitious. Branyng has been seen to court her favors, but no one knows her true feelings about him."

"You might have told me all of this sooner," Kelson said sharply, when Arilan had finished.

"Such knowledge might have colored your interaction with the brothers during rehearsals," Azim interjected, before Arilan could reply. "Your shields will be stronger today, knowing that this is no rehearsal. And given what Denis has told you, I now may confirm that another person whose opinion I highly regard has assured me that Mátyás is to be trusted."

"And *you* might have told me *that!*" Kelson snapped back.

"And *that* might have betrayed you both to Mahael and to such others as are, indeed, fully committed to his treachery!" Azim returned. "Do not show *me* your indignation, Kelson of Gwynedd! You have few enough allies in what you must do."

Kelson forced himself to bite back further display of his frustration, drawing a long, slow breath. The implications of Azim's revelation were too complex to assimilate all at once, but at their core flared new hope that Mátyás could, indeed, be trusted—which Kelson had long felt, but now he was about to put that feeling to the ultimate test—and whatever his remaining misgivings regarding Mátyás, he did, indeed, trust Azim.

"Forgive me if I seem impatient," he said evenly, "but we have little time. If it is permitted, answer me this: It is my understanding that Liam will be at his most vulnerable just before Mahael renders up his share of the power of Furstán, when he will have dropped his shields in readiness for taking on Furstán's power. If Mahael takes that opportunity to attack Liam, and if Mátyás joins with me in attempting to defend Liam, will the Council support us?"

"It is not the policy of the Council to intervene directly," Arilan began.

"*No one* can intervene directly, from outside the Wards," Azim said pointedly, overriding him. "But if God is gracious, Mátyás will, indeed, prove both faithful and strong, and you and he shall be able to preserve Liam's life, and assist him to the full kingship that is his by right."

*H*alf an hour later, the turmoil of his doubts and fears schooled to discipline behind his shields, Kelson was poised on the back of the great state carriage as they had practiced before, weighted by his ceremonial robe and feeling the welcome breeze in his face as four matched pairs of white R'Kassan stallions bore Liam-Lajos toward the Quai du Saint-Basile and the state caïque waiting to convey them to *killijálay*. Perched on the steps to either side of the carriage, Mátyás and Teymuraz gazed straight ahead, each of them bearing the image of an archangel on his back: Mátyás, in the vibrant green of Saint Uriel—or Ouriél, as he was called in Torenth—and Teymuraz in the blazing reds and flame of Michaél. Branyng sat beside the driver, up on the box, in the gold of Raphael. The silvery sphere of their Moving Ward could not be seen in the bright sunlight, but Kelson could feel the drain of power it took to maintain it—though that was minimal while riding stationary as they now did.

Ahead, a lesser carriage drawn by three greys harnessed in troika carried Mahael, Morag, and Ronal Rurik, preceded by a troop of mounted Circassian guards in full array. Kelson's honor guard of Haldane cavalry followed directly behind Liam's state carriage, with Morgan and Dhugal at their head. The others of the Gwynedd delegation had gone ahead to Hagia Iób with an earlier procession of other official observers.

The Avenue du Saint Constantine was lined with hundreds of Liam's cheering subjects, kept in order by cordons of the city guard. Many waved kerchiefs or pennons of tawny silk, and some of the women cast flowers under the horses' hooves.

At the quay before the plaza fronting the Cathedral of Saint Constantine, state caïques were assembled to convey the investing party upriver. Liam's was white, with a gold-fringed canopy of purple damask stretched over a dais erected amidships, bordered with silver roundels bearing black Furstáni harts. As the state carriage drew up at quayside, fourteen pairs of oars rose in salute, in the hands of as many pairs of Truvorski oarsmen clad in pure white livery. Young girls in white gowns and with wreaths of flowers in their hair sang a song of welcome and cast rose petals and sweet herbs upon the fine Lorsöli carpet that liveried servants unrolled to the very door of the carriage.

Teymuraz jumped down from his step on the right and turned to open the carriage door as Kelson and Branyng also dismounted. In order to preserve their alignment for the Moving Ward, Mátyás was obliged to come through the carriage from the left, following Liam into the brilliant sunlight.

An even more joyous roar erupted from the waiting crowd as the *padishah* and his Moving Ward headed toward the gangway, treading on a perfumed carpet of flowers. Amid the splendor of the four Wards, the young king presented a contrast of utter simplicity and innocence as they boarded the caïque, his long, high-collared coat all of pure white wool save for the black Furstáni hart emblazoned on his breast and a fringed black silk sash bound several times around his narrow waist.

Bareheaded, the sun casting red glints in his dark hair, Liam made his way to the chair of state set beneath the canopy and took his place, looking neither left nor right. The Pillars of the Realm settled on stools below and around him. As the caïque pulled away from the quay, the swish of the oars provided lighter counter-point to the solemn beat of the master's drum, echoed by the shimmering bells that marked the pace for the lesser escort vessels.

All too soon for Kelson's tastes, they arrived at Torenthály. There, a smaller but no less vocal crowd waited to greet them: those privileged to keep vigil outside Hagia Iób during *killijálay*. As the young *padishah* disembarked, surrounded by his Moving Wards, white-clad maidens again cast flowers in his path as he made his stately way to the restive white steed awaiting him, its golden bridle held by two sons of dukes, snowy plumes adorning its headstall.

As before, the animal quieted at once, as it came within the calming sphere of the Moving Ward surrounding its master, lowering its head and standing motion-less while a third ducal son abased himself alongside to provide a mounting step. As the *padishah* settled into the golden saddle and gathered up the fringed golden reins, the crowd fell silent, dropping to their knees. Simultaneously, an emphatic shimmer of tiny golden bells accompanied the approach of eight proud Steppe lords moving smoothly into position around the perimeter of the Moving Ward, each bearing a gilded frame on which were mounted the source of the sound. Their purple robes had more bells sewn along the hems and trailing sleeves, and their tall black hats were likewise festooned with fine golden chains bearing bells.

They shook their hand-bells to set the cadence as the procession began moving slowly up the cobbled Avenue des Rois, in audible underlining of the shiver of power surrounding the investing party. Even as part of the source of that power, and having practiced the maneuver, Kelson felt a frisson of excitement as he walked in his appointed place behind Liam's steed. His Haldane lancers followed him on foot, led by Morgan and Dhugal. Ahead, men bearing the bright silk banners of all the provinces of Torenth led the procession toward its rendezvous with *killijálay*.

The Patriarch Alpheios was waiting before the door of Hagia Iób to receive them, attended by the twelve Metropolitans of the Holy Synod of Torenth, who stood six to either side, each man a blaze of golden vestments in the brilliant sunlight, each crowned with the rounded golden miter of Eastern usage, each with cross and *panagia* upon his breast and staff in hand.

As Liam alighted from his steed and relaxed the Moving Ward, allowing the animal to be led away—and giving those maintaining the Moving Ward a brief respite—Alpheios came to embrace him in the kiss of peace. In turn, the Metropolitans made him reverence, followed by the Grand Vizier, who welcomed Liam-Lajos in the name of the people of Torenth and bent to kiss the hem of his garment. Also on hand was Count Berrhones, staff of office in hand, who began deftly directing all but the immediate investing party and clergy to their places within, while servants changed the outdoor footwear of Liam and the Pillars of the Realm for soft slippers of embroidered felt.

Kelson kept his focus close as he watched Mahael make his way into the church with Morag and Ronal Rurik, followed by the rest of the state guests and Kelson's personal retainers. Morgan and Dhugal gave him glances that conveyed wariness and support as they passed. Arilan looked solemn, Azim serenely unperturbed. Kelson prayed for discernment and strength as Liam pulled the energies of his Pillars back into focus and again raised the milky dome of the Moving Ward.

At this signal, Count Berrhones rendered three measured raps with the heel of his great staff of office. Then, accompanied by three clear notes from Iób's Complaint, in a loft high above the great nave, the Metropolitans began to process into the church in two lines, led by four deacons swinging heavy, fuming censers and followed by Liam within the Moving Ward. Patriarch Alpheios brought up the rear, attended by two chaplains, his rich basso beginning the sonorous introit that signalled the start of *killijálay*.

"*Doxa en hypsistos Theo, kai epi gis irini, en anthropis evdokia. . . .*" Glory be to Thee, Who hast shown forth the light, glory be to God on high, and on earth peace, good will toward men. . . .

A choir of male voices took up the hymn, the rich harmony mingling with the rising clouds of sweet incense as the Moving Ward passed through the vestibule and into the church. Inside, the bearers of the banners of Torenth, who had entered by side doors, now lowered their banners before the *padishah*'s feet as a precious carpet over which he trod. Beneath the great dome, where lay the tomb of Furstán—today draped in a heavy pall of royal purple—those privileged to witness *killijálay* were ranged in ordered rows, well back from the tomb itself.

The Metropolitans passed beyond the tomb to stand before the iconostasis, flanking a golden chair of state set before the royal doors. From Kelson's perspective, the holy icons behind the Twelve seemed to gaze over their shoulders in mute and somber witness to what was about to transpire, almost animated by the flicker of lamplight on the gilt and jewels adorning them. Mahael and Morag had taken places before stools set to either side of the state chair, in token of their regent status, with Ronal Rurik standing behind his mother.

Watching carefully as he and his fellow Pillars approached the purple-draped tomb, Kelson slowed his pace to let the Moving Ward elongate and expand to compass it. Branyng skirted the tomb to the right, Liam passing to the left, Mátyás and Teymuraz moving slightly outward. Kelson stopped an arm-span from the head of the tomb, and Branyng came to a halt perhaps twice that distance from its foot. Kelson knew that Alpheios and his two chaplains stood directly behind him, just outside the Moving Ward.

As Liam and the other three Pillars made deep obeisance in the Eastern manner, in token of the Divine Presence acknowledged behind the iconostasis, Kelson bowed and crossed himself in a more familiar and restrained sign of respect. When the others had straightened, they turned as one to face the tomb, and Liam lowered the Ward to admit Alpheios, the dome of its power receding to a shimmering line of silver delineating their circle.

From behind, the patriarch passed Kelson on the left to pause halfway along the length of the tomb, bearing across his two hands a magnificent girdle studded with diamonds. This he raised in a gesture of oblation and respect, while the choir sang a short *alleluia*. Then he laid it across the foot of the purple pall and retreated to a position between Kelson and the tomb's head, where he again raised his hands.

"*Lajos ho Phourstanos*," he chanted, "thou hast been consecrated to thine office in thy youth, with the girding of the sword. Take now the girdle of thy rank and station, and prepare to take up thine inheritance, rendering due homage to great Phourstanos, in whose name thou shalt reign."

With Alpheios blocking his view, Kelson could see little of what was happening beyond the sweep of purple pall, but he knew that Liam was prostrating himself at the foot of the tomb. Thus far, the ceremony was largely symbolic, reiterating ritual performed at the time of Liam's girding nearly five years before. While the choir intoned another hymn—and while mostly disconnected from the others holding the Ward in temporary abeyance—Kelson reviewed the expected flow of action from this point forward, knowing that the real danger would come a little later, when even he did not know fully just how his own role would develop. As part of the Ward—and within its sphere, even though it was diminished—he was psychically blind to Morgan and Dhugal and other would-be allies outside the Ward. He could break it, if need be, but to break it was to halt Liam's full empowering—and that, he dared not do.

At least he was free to think about it all, so long as the Ward was lowered. He glanced at Mátyás surreptitiously, counting himself safe enough for now, while shielded behind Alpheios, but Liam's youngest uncle had closed his eyes, apparently deep in meditation, and Kelson dared not probe in his direction.

The hymn ended. Liam rose and took up the diamond-studded girdle from the foot of the tomb, lifting it in salute to his ancestor Furstán. A beam of sunlight lancing downward from the dome high above caught the stones and turned the girdle into a blaze of rainbow fire in Liam's hands. He bowed his head as he clasped it about his waist, after which Alpheios again raised his arms in exhortation.

"Bring now the Sword of Furstán, that his servant may take up his inheritance in the service of his people!"

His declaration evoked a single clear note from Iób's Complaint and a shimmer of bells from the Steppe lords. In response, the doors to the great church slammed back and six burly Albani guards slowly entered the nave, bearing upon a long purple cushion a great scimitar, more than half the height of a man. Its scabbard was inlaid with turquoise and lapis lazuli, and studded here and there with pearls and more precious stones: ruby and emerald and sapphire.

Lifting their burden above the tomb as they passed three to either side, the men laid its cushion upon the royal purple, the weapon's hilt toward Liam and its point toward the patriarch. Then they deftly eased the scabbard from the blade, being careful not to touch the latter, before laying the scabbard along the south side of the tomb and retreating from the church. Beyond Liam, his mother and Mahael had entered the precincts of the Ward while the deed was done, followed by Ronal Rurik, and now stood flanking Liam, with Morag in the north and Mahael in the south, the young prince behind. As the four deacons moved into position just beyond each of the four Pillars of the Realm, again swinging their censers, Holy Alpheios once more raised his arms.

"Now, in truth, begins the heart of *killijálay*. Now shall the servant of God, *Lajos ho Phourstanos*, take up his inheritance. Let us give honor to the Four Holy Ones as we invoke their protection!"

Liam crossed his arms upon his breast and bowed his head, as did his mother and uncle and brother. Kelson could feel the young king seizing the strands of power offered by the four Pillars, beginning to twine of them a far more powerful Ward than hitherto, and he yielded his share willingly, raising his arms to either side and bowing his head.

"I call upon the Holy Michaél," Alpheios intoned, from somewhere within a great silence that seemed to press inward from the edges of the Ward, focused on the sword upon the tomb. "May he stand with us in joy and gladness at this *killi-jálay*, to sanctify his servant, *Lajos ho Phourstanos.*"

Kelson heard Teymuraz gasp, but dared not lift his eyes to look.

"Also do I call upon the Holy Gabriél, to stand with his holy brethren, and upon the Holy Ouriél . . ."

Kelson hardly heard the rest of the patriarch's invocation, for a chill finger had brushed his spine, from beyond the confines of the Ward yet close at hand; an eerie whisper of benison and strength that enfolded him in an embrace that was both feather-light and definite. Finally daring to lift his gaze, he had an impression of mighty forms towering beyond each of his co-Pillars, almost-visible echoes of the Quarter Lords whose presence Alpheios was invoking, at once both familiar and alien. He, too, gasped with the wonder of it, hard-pressed to keep himself focused as a rainbow iridescence began to play over the arched dome of the Ward.

"Deathless Phourstanos, grant now to thy descendant that grace with which to grasp thy glory, that he may worthily wield thy power for his people."

Alpheios himself seemed suddenly to grow larger, though it was no physical largeness—and from Kelson's position behind the patriarch, and overshadowed by what he readily accepted as some manifestation of the archangel Gabriel, he could not be certain what was happening. Only dimly, from far outside the Ward, he thought he heard a collective gasp.

He knew what was meant to happen. He could feel Liam's defenses dropping away as the boy lifted both hands to reach out for the sword of Furstán and its power—sensed the flicker in Liam's concentration as Mahael and Morag laid their hands on his shoulders. For Morag, the gesture was but mime, for she had shared no part of Furstán's magic, but Mahael's focus was tight-coiled, in preparation either to give back his share of Furstán's might or to try seizing it all for himself.

Right up until that flicker of decision when it happened, Kelson kept hoping that Mahael would back down, would not attempt the treachery of which Mátyás had warned. But then power erupted from Mahael with staggering force, backed by Branyng and Teymuraz, but that bit off-focus because Mátyás was not supporting the attack.

Even so, it was enough to drive Morag to her knees and to strike young Ronal Rurik senseless. In that same instant, the boundaries of the Ward darkened, as if a curtain of starry night had been drawn over the proceedings, hiding from outside view what now unfolded.

That first attack buffeted Kelson almost past recovery, even though he had been expecting it; but immediately he found himself bolstered by Mátyás, who quickly bore Morag into his protection and began diverting their combined energy to Liam's defense. Alpheios, too, added his power to the protection of the young king, physically sheltering in the shadow of great Furstán's tomb.

Liam strained his hands toward the hilt of the sword of Furstán but could not quite touch it, shakily balanced between warding off Mahael's treacherous assault and keeping himself sufficiently open and focused to channel and receive the power his attackers were struggling to wrest away. The domed space within the Ward howled with a wind like a hurricane, though without physical manifestation, and ghostly flames roared above them in an unseen holocaust that threatened to consume not only bodies but souls.

From Mahael came a fresh onslaught of elemental force, part of the power of Furstán, with which he sought to rip the rest of it from his young nephew— demon lightning and a firestorm of shrieking power that scoured at every chink of potential weakness. From Branyng came the potent reinforcement of elemental Fire. Airy energies under the bidding of Teymuraz shifted and roiled, their focus uncertain.

But Mátyás stood firm upon the solid bedrock of elemental Earth, a steady bulwark from which to summon forth the molten energies deep in the earth's core and tap the wellsprings of supernal water in Kelson's wielding—augmented by Kelson's Haldane magic—a geysering outpouring of power to inundate the unseen conflagration and slowly quench it.

Branyng was the first to falter and then to crumple with a mortal cry, utterly spent, though Mahael himself backed deftly into his place in the East and surged even stronger, as if that had been his intention all along. Morag, as she drank in renewal from Mátyás's bolstering energy and began to regain her own equilibrium, soon sensed quite clearly what was happening and joined her focus to that of Mátyás and Kelson.

Fury flared from Mahael—rage at Mátyás's refusal to support him; it staggered Matyas to one knee, but he did not falter. Behind the raging storm of Mahael's anger and power, Teymuraz could not be seen. But as the energies surged and ebbed and balances shifted in the struggle, Liam at last found sufficient focus to seize the sword of Furstán.

The sudden surge of power channelled through the sword convulsed his body, wrenching a groan from his lips as he shuddered in both pain and ecstasy, hugging the hilt of the great scimitar to his breast as he fought to bind and tame the power that was his destiny.

In an eternal instant outside time, it was done. With a cry of triumph, Liam turned his face heavenward, lifting high the sword of Furstán, symbol of the Furstán power, thrusting it toward the dome above them.

In that instant, Teymuraz's support came slamming into the link held by Mátyás and Kelson, bending his strength to fuse with Morag's and then with theirs as, directed by Mátyás, they turned their combined strength on Mahael. The force of that onslaught bore him to the floor and smothered his power, pinning him helpless, even as Liam found his focus and sent visible confirmation of his empowering aloft in a beam of purplish light that pierced the top of the Ward sphere and splashed against the inside of Holy Iób's blue dome in a coruscating display of rainbow brilliance.

In that instant, the sphere of the Ward went from night-black to palest purple, still denying access but now allowing vision and hearing to those outside. A collective gasp swept through the great church, and Liam's Circassian guards immediately swarmed closer to surround the perimeter.

Slowly lowering the sword of Furstán, still overshadowed by its power, Liam turned his gaze to Mahael, still pinned but struggling in the East beneath the restraints directed by Mátyás, as augmented by his unlikely allies. Lifting his empty hand, Liam took from Mátyás the maintaining of those restraints.

Morag, kneeling between Mahael and the sprawled bodies of Branyng and her younger son, cradled the weakly stirring form of the latter in her arms and gazed up at her elder son with awe and bewilderment, apparently uncertain regarding Teymuraz as she glanced between him, Mátyás, and Kelson. Alpheios slowly rose from behind Furstán's tomb, but made no move to approach.

Kelson rose on shaky knees and came to hold out his hand to Mátyás. The Furstáni prince gave him a faint smile and then his hand, accepting his assistance to get to his feet.

"Is Branyng dead?" Liam asked, his gaze flicking among them, still taut with the aftermath of combat.

Mátyás nodded. "He is, my prince."

"Good."

Weaving a little, Liam walked unsteadily to stand over the sprawled Mahael, who lay with outflung arms, helpless to escape or offer further threat, but eyes ablaze with hatred and defiance. From beyond the starry purpled curtain of power that shrouded the Ward, Kelson caught the collective intake of breath as, very deliberately, Liam pointed the tip of the Furstán sword between his uncle's eyes.

"Mahael Termöd Furstán d'Arjenol, I take from thee that which was not thine to keep," he said—and with that, lightly touched the blade to Mahael's forehead.

Mahael's body stiffened and arched upward at the touch, throat opening on a silent scream as violet fire scoured down the blade to every extremity and into the deepest recesses of sanity. The bulging, wide-staring eyes were a mirror for his agony as Liam stripped away not only the power his uncle had purloined, but also Mahael's own power, ripping his mind in the process.

A faint whimper creaked from the feebly twitching lips, and his body went slowly slack as the fire then withdrew into the blade, leaving behind no reason or even awareness in the vacant, staring eyes as the sword of Furstán at last was lifted from his brow. *Liam-Lajos ho Phourstanos padishah* gave him not a second glance as he let the great scimitar sink to his side, then turned his gaze on Teymuraz, who had blanched but did not move from his crouched, wary position, still in the South.

"Laje, it was he and Branyng who betrayed you," Teymuraz whispered. "You know how strong Branyng was. And they used *me*! I only meant to play my part in the Wards, to be a part of your protection—but they tried to pull me into their treachery. Only barely was I able to break free!"

"The timing was, indeed, fortuitous, Uncle." Liam's cool tone left some ambiguity about how much irony he intended, as he turned his gaze to his mother and his remaining uncle. "Is this your perception?"

"Kill him," Mátyás said flatly. "He betrayed you, and will betray you again, if you allow him to live."

"Brother, do not abandon me, I pray you!" Teymuraz gasped. "You were aware how our brother did talk. Never did I think he would act upon his threats—you listened as well! But he had Branyng on his side—and I am not as strong as any of the rest of you. For a time, he pulled me into his link, forced me against my will. . . ."

"Mother?" Liam asked, coldly turning his face from Teymuraz. "If you ask for his death, I shall have him impaled, as is the prescribed manner of execution for traitors. As shall be done to Mahael."

Morag's jaw tightened, and Kelson glanced between her, Mátyás, and the young king in some surprise. That Mahael must be executed—and the sooner, the better—was only what Kelson himself would have done, under the circumstances; but the manner Liam had declared was nonetheless startling.

Yet even as a part of him recoiled, reminding him that Torenth's ways were not Gwynedd's ways, Kelson found himself recalling stark precedent that he himself had witnessed, at about the same age as Liam, when he and his army, on march toward their final confrontation with Wencit, another of Liam's uncles, had come upon the impaled bodies of several dozens of men left in warning by a retiring Torenthi force.

At the time, the stark brutality had seemed hardly mitigated by the discovery that the victims had been impaled *after* death. But the incident had shown quite clearly that impalement was known and practiced in Torenth, at least in time of war—and what was treason but the most insidious sort of warfare against one's sworn liege? Furthermore, it was no longer Kelson's place to interfere in the internal workings of Torenth—especially when its king had just proven himself worthy to stand in his own right, even as Kelson had been forced to do at a similar age.

"My son," Morag said, "I do not dispute that Mahael has greatly deserved his fate. But I—am not certain that Teymuraz truly betrayed you." Her face hardened as she glanced pointedly at Kelson. "Nor is it yet clear in my mind how you came to ally yourself with this—Haldane, who killed your father."

Liam hardly blinked, wisely declining to be drawn into public disagreement with his mother, only returning his gaze to Teymuraz. Kelson saw that he was starting to shake a little in reaction, the last of great Furstán's overshadowing leaving him, the great scimitar trembling in his hand. For a moment he feared the boy would falter; but Liam's voice was steady and dispassionate as he addressed his uncle.

"We have *killijálay* to complete," he said. "You will consider yourself under house arrest until I decide what to do with you. For the rest—"

He drew a deep breath and let it out slowly, in what Kelson knew was an exercise to stabilize his focus, then lifted a hand in arcane gesture. The Ward melted away like oil draining down the inside of a glass, leaving a silvery, glistening echo of a circle where the bounds of the Ward had been. Liam's Circassian guards were waiting to cross that line at a word from their master, and snapped to attention as he caught the eye of the guard captain.

"You will take the traitor Mahael before the gate to the Field of Kings, outside the precincts of Hagia Iób, and there execute him by impalement, that his ancestors may witness his shame." A rising frisson of revulsion and astonishment whispered among the massed observers, instantly cut short as Liam raised the hand not holding the sword, in a gesture both imperious and not to be ignored. "You will likewise impale the body of the traitor Branyng beside him. I shall expect to see evidence that my orders have been carried out, by the time I leave this place." He glanced at Teymuraz, who blanched visibly.

"Uncle, you will accompany the execution party as my official witness, that you may contemplate first-hand the justice done to traitors—even those of our family. I would suggest that you examine your own soul while thus engaged. You will remain in attendance upon the executed traitors until I give you leave to depart. Meanwhile, let the court physicians come and tend my brother and my mother."

He turned to the tomb of Furstán amid utter and shocked silence and carefully laid the sword of Furstán back on its velvet cushion, then bowed formally first to Alpheios, then to Kelson.

"Most Holy—and most honored friend and ally, Kelson of Gwynedd—let us now complete the *killijálay*."

CHAPTER TWENTY

*With that they cast away their weapons, and made
peace.*

I Maccabees 11:51

$\mathcal{T}$he Circassian guards took away the unresisting Mahael without further ado,
more of them removing Branyng's body. Several assisted Teymuraz to put
off his ceremonial robe before briskly conducting him from the premises as well.
Mahael seemed hardly to understand what was happening; Teymuraz understood
all too well. While physicians ministered briefly to Morag and the now conscious
Ronal Rurik, Count Berrhones began restoring order to the tatters of the investiture ceremony.

Moving to one side, Kelson shed his robe of the West and let Saer and Derry
help him into the stiff, cope-like mantle made of cloth-of-gold, that protocol
deemed requisite to his status as Liam's liege lord. He drew out from the neck of
his tunic his mother's prayer beads, letting the enamelled medal lie on his breast.
On his head Arilan placed the state crown of Gwynedd, with its leaves and crosses
intertwined. From Morgan, the king received the sheathed Haldane sword, which
he cradled in the crook of his left arm like a scepter, offering his right arm to
Liam.

Four Torenthi dukes had assisted Liam to don a long, coat-like mantle with
open sleeves that almost brushed the floor, so thickly encrusted with embroidery
of gold bullion and gems that the purple of the ground could scarce be seen; six
sons of counts bore the garment's long train. Mátyás was invited to take the place

of honor on Liam's right side, the robe of the North now set aside for a court coat of emerald-green damask, unadorned save for the richness of the fabric itself and an appliqued border of grapes and grape leaves. Morag and a shaky Ronal Rurik were conducted ahead by the four dukes, to take places of honor to either side and behind the chair of state.

Iób's Complaint resounded beneath the great dome in three long blasts as Alpheios led the twelve Metropolitans before the tomb of Furstán to render homage to the new *padishah*. Now confirmed in his powers, *Liam-Lajos ho Phourstanos padishah* received their reverence and allowed them to convey him forward, supported at either side by Kelson and Mátyás. In response and counterpoint to the invocation offered by the patriarch, the choir began to elaborate upon the theme:

"*Hagios ho Theos, Hagios Iskhuros, Hagios Athanatos, Eleison Hemas. . . .* " Holy God, Holy Mighty One, Holy Immortal One, have mercy on us. . . .

Processing to the steps before the iconostasis, preceded by Alpheios and his twelve fellow bishops, Liam was there girded with a smaller version of the sword of Furstán, its diamond-encrusted scabbard echoing the diamonds of the girdle he had received from the tomb of Furstán. He was then enthroned upon the chair of state by Kelson, whose privilege it was as his overlord.

Kelson moved, then, to one side, attended by Morgan and Dhugal, Arilan and Azim, his presence giving tacit assent as Alpheios placed upon Liam's head a golden diadem studded with rubies and emeralds and pearls, with great jewelled pendants hanging just short of his shoulders on either side. After what had gone before, Kelson was not surprised that the actual crowning seemed something of an anticlimax—yet the crown was, indeed, the outward symbol by which most men set apart their kings. Liam now possessed that symbol.

So adorned, Liam then received the homage of his subjects, beginning with his brother and heir, his mother, and Mátyás, followed in turn by the dukes, the counts, and then the lesser nobility of Torenth who were present.

When all had sworn, Liam himself rose and, accompanied only by Alpheios and a deacon bearing the gem-encrusted Book of the Gospel, came to present himself before Kelson, in accordance with his status as Kelson's vassal.

There, in accordance with Torenthi practice, he removed his crown and sank to both knees before his overlord, laid his crown at Kelson's feet, and bent to kiss a corner of Kelson's mantle. Then, by Gwyneddan custom, he offered his joined hands to Kelson, his eyes gladly meeting Kelson's as the other's hands clasped his and the deacon held the Gospel aloft as witness.

"I, Liam Lajos Lionel László Furstán, being of age, do hereby affirm that I am your man of life and limb and earthly worship, and remain in your fealty, and in my own right do render homage for all the lands of Torenth. Faith and truth will I bear unto you, as my suzerain, so help me God."

He bent dutifully to kiss both Kelson's hands, then the offered Gospel book. But when he looked up again, expecting to hear the oath returned, Kelson merely smiled faintly, still clasping Liam's hands.

"I gladly receive this expression of your faith, my friend and brother," he murmured, flicking a glance to Mátyás and summoning him with his eyes. "However, I am minded to somewhat alter our original intent."

Liam looked more bewildered than at any time in all the preceding trial as Kelson raised him up, and a murmur of question whispered among the assembled observers as Mátyás made his way with haste to join them. Morag looked startled, the assembled Metropolitans mystified.

Releasing Liam's hands, Kelson stooped briefly to take up Liam's crown from the carpet at his feet, turning it between his two hands as he glanced again at its owner.

"Liam-Lajos, King of Torenth," he said quietly, but so that his voice carried in the domed nave. "I have said from the beginning that it was never my intention that Torenth should remain indefinitely a vassal to Gwynedd. In keeping you at my side these last four years, I sought to expose you to the education and training you would need to govern Torenth in your own right, as a wise and benevolent sovereign, better acquainted with the ways of your more Western neighbors than your predecessors have been, so that relations between our two kingdoms should never again deteriorate to the level at which they have existed these two centuries past.

"Today you have proved amply, I think, that you are well prepared to reign, independent of the external control that I never wished to exercise. Saving a few notable exceptions, I have seen evidence that you are well loved by your people, and mostly surrounded by loyal men eager to serve you. In Count Mátyás, in particular, I believe you will find no wiser or loyal or more honest an advisor."

He flashed a grim smile at Mátyás. "Forgive me, my lord, but I fear I am sentencing you to spend far less time than you wish, tending your vines. But in what I hope will be a new era of peace between our two lands, I pray that you and your family may perhaps learn to find contentment nearer to Beldour, where your presence and wise counsel may provide assistance and support to your royal nephew in his duties."

Mátyás looked as if he could hardly believe what he was hearing, and Liam was still gazing at Kelson in wonder. Alpheios looked stunned.

"I therefore give you back your crown," Kelson said, extending it to Liam with a smile. "Before God and these witnesses, I release you from any *obligation* to render

228 ~ KATHERINE KURTZ

me service, and ask only that you and yours bear faith and truth to me and mine as *friends*—as I shall bear faith and truth unto you and yours. Thus, with God's help, may friendship prevail between us and between our eventual successors and between our two lands, in all the years to come."

Stunned, Liam took the crown, his eyes searching Kelson's. Then, with a little sob, he shifted it to one hand so that he and Kelson could embrace like brothers. The astonished murmurs of the assembled company turned to ragged cheers as the import sank in of what had just occurred.

The cheers became a roar as Liam drew back and set the crown firmly on his own head. And as he turned to face his people, seizing Kelson's hand and raising their joined hands in further symbol of their friendship, joyful pandemonium broke out. The approbation was not universal, but all present had seen how the King of Gwynedd came to the defense of a once mortal enemy, joining forces with men of Torenth against other men of Torenth and risking life and kingdom to protect their *padishah*. It was a beginning.

Only when the patriarch and his assisting clergy formed up to continue with the service did the cheering die away. The chair of state was shifted to one side, and Liam set his crown upon it before moving with his family to stand before the Royal Doors, as Alpheios entered the Holy of Holies to proceed with the service of the Divine Liturgy; the Torenthis did not call it Mass.

"*Stomen kalos, stomen meta phobou, proskomen ten again Anaphoran en eirene prosphein. . . .*" the choir sang. Let us stand upright, let us stand with awe, let us attend, that we may present the Holy Offering in peace. . . .

Watching from one side, with Arilan and Morgan and Dhugal and the others of his party, Kelson understood hardly a word of the rich liturgy that followed— and could see little, behind the royal doors that guarded the sanctuary—but occasional glimpses of common liturgical action provided enough familiar signposts that he at least was aware of the moment of consecration, which was the heart of Christian faith.

Following as best he could, he composed himself to make a spiritual communion rather than actually receiving, for he did not wish to offend Torenthi sensibilities, nor to detract from what now was Liam's celebration with his people. In addition, he found himself distracted by the knowledge that, even now, Mahael was being put to death in the most demeaning and excruciating manner, not far from the church door. He was not altogether certain he was in a fit state of mind to receive.

Accordingly, he offered up the focus of his prayers for the repose of Mahael's soul, and for that of the fallen Count Branyng, traitors that they were, his head bowed into the sheltering shadow of his right hand—and was faintly startled when Arilan lightly touched his forearm.

He looked up to see Mátyás before him. Beyond Mátyás, Liam was standing apart from the others before the icon of Saint Michael, far to the left of the iconostasis, head bowed over his clasped hands, presumably having received Communion. Others of the immediate royal party were in the process of receiving.

"My lord, Liam-Lajos requests that, if you desire it, you may come forward and partake of Holy Communion," Mátyás murmured. "Holy Alpheios gives his consent, and wishes you to know that you are most welcome. I myself have not yet received, and would be honored if we might partake together."

Kelson glanced at Arilan, who inclined his head in agreement. "It is not usual custom, as you know, Sire—but this has hardly been a usual day. Since both king and patriarch have extended the invitation, I cannot see any harm."

With a nod, Kelson removed his crown and handed it to Arilan, then went quietly with Mátyás. They fell in behind Count Berrhones. In response to Mátyás's glance, and following his gesture, Kelson crossed his arms on his breast, palms pressed to opposite shoulders, as was Torenthi custom. Letting Mátyás go ahead of him, he prayed pardon for any impropriety he might be committing in the cause of forging a closer bond with his new allies. When Mátyás stepped aside, Kelson listened with head bowed as Alpheios spoke the words customary in Torenth, dipping a morsel of wine-soaked bread from the chalice with a golden spoon.

"*To Kelsonous to anaxio Ierei, to timion kai panagion Soma kai Aima tou Kyrios kai Theou kai Soteros emon Iesou Christou. . . .*"

"The servant of God Kelson receives the Body and Blood of our Lord and God and Savior, Jesus Christ," Mátyás translated in a soft undertone, "unto the remission of sins and unto Eternal Life."

The form and words might be different, but Kelson had no doubt that the sacrament was the same—as was the sense of peace that descended upon him as Alpheios tipped the contents of the spoon into his mouth. As he swallowed, he thanked God for the peace conferred by the sacrament and also for the hope of a different kind of peace, between these two lands. The lingering comfort of that peace remained with him as Mátyás accompanied him back to his place with Arilan and the others.

But that peace did not prevail beyond the church doors. As the clergy and royal party emerged into the brilliant sunlight, to joyous cheers and shrill ululations from the waiting crowds lining the plaza before Hagia Iób, Kelson saw Liam's glance flick to their right, back along the extension of the Avenue des Rois that led to the Field of Kings, with its sea of pyramids and tombs.

There, behind a line of Circassian guards, lay the spectacle that Kelson had been at such pains to keep from mind during Communion, both far less and far more than he had expected. Still adorned in the finery they had worn to *killijálay*, as trusted members of the king's court, Mahael and Branyng seemed to stand erect and motionless beside the gates to the vast necropolis, heads lolling onto their breasts. Their long robes concealed the stakes upon which they had been impaled. Teymuraz stood within the gate between two guards, flanked by the dead men, head bowed like theirs. Kelson was glad he could not see any of the faces clearly.

"Bring my uncle," Liam said to a waiting guard, turning his back on the spectacle as he strode purposefully back toward his white stallion, accepting a leg up from a waiting attendant. "And you," he added, with a nod toward a guard captain mounted on a fine bay. "Give the loan of your mount to my friend, the King of Gwynedd. I would have him ride at my right hand, so to do him honor."

The first guard headed off immediately to do Liam's bidding, and the captain swung down from his bay, bringing it around smartly so that Kelson could mount. But just as he was settling into the saddle, letting attendants adjust his heavy mantle, a commotion exploded far behind them, within the gateway to the necropolis.

"Stop him!" someone screamed, on the tide of shouts of alarm.

As Kelson peered urgently in the direction of the growing uproar, he saw the Circassian guards beside the gate bowling back from a blaze of errant magic brighter than the sun, centered on Teymuraz, who bolted from between the bodies of his two dead co-conspirators and made for the heart of the necropolis.

"The Nikolaseum!" Liam cried, wrenching off his diadem and tossing it to a guard. "He's going for the Portal!"

Clapping heels to his mount, Liam took off in pursuit, scattering attendants and struggling to shed his heavy ceremonial robe as he went. Kelson was close behind, bending low over his horse's neck and juggling his crown until he could get it safely looped over one arm. Screaming people parted before them, and more mounted men fell in behind.

The cobbled avenue stretched the length of Hagia Iób before passing through the gate to the Field of Kings. The horses' steel-shod hooves slipped and skittered on the slick cobbles, threatening spills potentially deadly for man and beast, but they dared not slow lest their quarry make good his escape. At the gate ahead, the guards were picking themselves up, and a few had sufficiently recovered their wits to take up pursuit on foot, but there could be little doubt that Teymuraz's goal was, indeed, the Nikolaseum—and freedom, if he reached the Portal there.

"Teymuraz, stop!" Liam shouted. "Damn you, stop!"

They plunged past the bodies of Mahael and Branyng, through the gate of the necropolis—and gained better footing by shifting to the grass on either side of the cobbled avenue—but the Nikolaseum was still far ahead, and Teymuraz was pounding ever closer to its beckoning doorway. As they galloped past the pursuing guards, Kelson considered trying to stop Liam's wayward uncle with magic of his own, but it was futile even to contemplate proper focus of such magic from the back of a plunging horse.

Just that bit too far ahead of them, Teymuraz gained the steps to the Nikola-seum and lurched up them two at a time, plunging into the shadows of the door-way with a little cry of triumph. By the time Kelson and Liam got there, throwing themselves from their horses to scramble after, the memorial was as empty and as silent as the tomb it was.

"Damn and double damn!" Liam gasped, sobbing for breath as he bent to brace hands on knees, gulping in great lungsful of the cooler air inside.

Kelson could only stand panting beside him, bleakly scanning the empty chamber as he leaned both hands on one of the carved drums at the foot of Nikola's tomb. All at once, the future that so recently had looked so bright for Torenth had become shadowed by the dark prospect of future treachery that would not relent until either Teymuraz or Liam was dead.

Suddenly stifling under his heavy mantle, Kelson wrenched at its neck fas-tening and shed it in a stiff pool of gold and jewelled embroidery and appliqué. He set his crown upon it before sinking to a seat on one of the steps beside the tomb.

"How real a threat is Teymuraz, on his own?" he asked, slicking both hands back across his sweaty face and into his hair. "How much trouble could he be?"

Liam shook his head bleakly. "I do not know. A great deal, I suspect. We shall have to ask Mátyás."

Still breathing hard, he moved to the head of the tomb and went down on his knees to lay both hands flat on the Portal there, bowing his head. After a moment he looked up again, grimacing as he got to his feet.

"It's no use. I had hoped I might pick up some resonance of his intended des-tination, but—" Liam shrugged and cast his gaze unfocused toward the dome above, thinking aloud. "He could have gone to any of at least half a dozen places that I know of—and who knows what other private boltholes he and Mahael might have established in the past four years? Where, even, to start?"

"*I* would start by sending agents to check the places that you *do* know of," Kelson said, as the first of the foot pursuit appeared in the doorway of the Niko-laseum, winded and panting. "He might have been seen. At least that would give us some idea from where to expect his next move."

"I agree," Liam said, beckoning one of the guards closer. "We must begin somewhere—and hope that he will not have harmed any witnesses there may have been. Captain, you will coordinate with Count Mátyás to have all known Portals surveyed for passage by the traitor Teymuraz."

Mátyás himself came bursting through the doorway in time to hear the end of that order, and pulled up breathlessly as he saw only Liam, Kelson, and the hand-ful of guards.

"Out!" he said to the guards, as he staggered up the steps to Nikola's tomb, and the Portal square at its head. "Seek guidance on a plan of search from Holy Alpheios. I will join you shortly."

He sank beside the Portal square as the guards left to do his bidding, setting his hands upon the square as Liam had done, then let himself collapse upon it in a dejected sitting position. The labored breathing of the three of them echoed in the vaulted chamber.

"Gone with nary a trace," Mátyás said. "Why did I not insist that—" He shook his head, still catching his breath. "No matter. It is always better to err on the side of mercy, if one is not certain. To take another's life . . ."

As he shook his head again, Kelson cast him a faint, somewhat ironic smile. "Is it really true that you have never taken a human life yourself?"

Mátyás shrugged, himself smiling faintly. "Does Branyng count, or does that constitute a group effort?" he replied. "You would admit, I think, that the body count is generally low, among tenders of vines.

"But to answer your direct question, without possibility of ambiguous wording—no, I have never taken a human life." He grimaced. "Given the role into which you have thrust me, however, by declaring me Laje's protector and advisor, I fear that this shall not long be the case—nor should it, when dealing with traitors. And I fear that I did order the death of Count László—though he was a traitor, too. But there are some things worth killing for—and dying for, if need be. We shall hope it does not come to the latter."

"Amen to *that*," Kelson murmured.

He and Liam left the Nikolaseum very shortly, to be met by Morgan and Dhugal and several of the Torenthi lords Kelson had met in the past week, in addition to a contingent of Circassian guards. Liam kept his head high as they fell in with the guards to make their way back out of the Field of Kings. When they had passed between the bodies of Mahael and Branyng, Liam paused to beckon to one of the guard officers.

"I shall send orders regarding the eventual disposition of the bodies," he said. "Meanwhile, they are to remain where they stand, for the full three days and nights prescribed by law. You will post guards to ensure that this is done. Do you understand?"

The man drew himself to even more rigid attention. "I understand, Sire."

With a tight nod, Liam turned away to shrug back into his robe of state, to let Holy Alpheios set the crown back on his head. Then, with his hand on the shoulder of King Kelson of Gwynedd, he led a slow foot procession through a wildly cheering throng, back to the quay, where the fleet of state caïques was waiting to whisk them back downriver to the waiting celebrations.

CHAPTER TWENTY-ONE

And let just men eat and drink with thee. . . .

Ecclesiasticus 9:16

$\mathcal{N}$ ews of the betrayal at Hagia Iób, and from within the very bosom of the royal family, ought to have dampened the festivities that followed; but reports of King Kelson's astonishing response—how he had helped defend Liam-Lajos from treachery, then released the fully empowered *padishah* from his vassal status and given him back Torenth's independence—spread even faster than details of the thwarted attack by the royal uncles, or the escape of Teymuraz, or the hushed accounts of Mahael's justly deserved fate for his treason: impaled like a common criminal before the very gate of the Field of Kings, in the presence of the shades of all his ancestors.

The latter detail made but a grim footnote to the ecstatic reception the two kings received when the official party reached the Quai du Saint-Basile, before the great Cathedral of Saint Constantine. Mátyás was already there, via Portal, but only to report that the first agents to return had nothing to report of Teymuraz's likely whereabouts.

The procession back to the palace was a joyous affair, even more lavish than the one to the quai that morning, moving but slowly along a processional route now lined by cheering, shouting crowds waving ribbons in the colors of Torenth and casting flowers and palm fronds before the great state carriage. There Kelson now sat at Liam's side, not as suzerain but as equal. Mátyás rode slightly ahead of

Liam's right-hand carriage door, in demonstration of his loyalty to his royal nephew, and Morgan and Dhugal followed behind the carriage as escort to both kings.

So slow was their progress, because of the press of humanity, that it was mid-afternoon before the cavalcade reached the sprawling forecourt of Furstánaly Palace, where young girls in pastel gowns waited to strew rose petals before the royal party as they dismounted from the carriage. Mátyás briefly withdrew to a small staff room adjacent to a Portal used for official couriers, where his agents had been told to report as they returned with news, but soon returned with only a faint shake of his head as he rejoined the royal party.

The feast had been laid in the hanging gardens to catch the breezes, with long, damask-draped tables sheltering under the shade of silken canopies and groaning under the weight of gold and silver plate. Waiting were the highest ranks of Torenthi nobility, both men and women, who cheered Liam heartily as he passed among them to the dais prepared for him. After pausing to acknowledge their acclaim, he and Kelson retired briefly to shed their heavy ceremonial robes, emerging a short time later in lighter silks, more fitly attired to enjoy what remained of the day and evening. When they had taken their place at the high table, both kings put aside their crowns to recline on cushioned couches in the Eastern manner.

To the accompaniment of lute and drum, flute and lyre, and the intermittent lilt of women's voices drifting from behind a latticed screen, wave after wave of servants brought forth culinary offerings for the delectation of the noble guests. Kelson had Dhugal, Morgan, and Arilan close beside him; Mátyás and an appar-ently recovered Ronal Rurik ensconced themselves on Liam's other side, with a succession of other Torenthi dukes and counts and other courtiers rotating in by turns, to share the royal presence. Princess Morag held separate court from amid the highborn ladies permitted near the high dais, many of whom were veiled in the Eastern manner.

After the first hour, between courses, Liam began receiving petitioners infor-mally at table, vetted by Count Berrhones and attended by his brother, his mother, Rasoul, and Azim. Mátyás disappeared periodically.

Arilan stayed nearby, making himself available for counsel, as had originally been intended, but said little, being aware that his status was now uncertain, in light of Liam's change in status. In the dusky twilight, as weather mages set tiny spheres of handfire twinkling amid the branches of the trees, Kelson called Dhu-gal to his side and circulated among the guests. Hardly unexpectedly, much of the talk was of the betrayal of the *padishah* by his two elder uncles.

"I suppose it must be true, about them having contrived the death of Alroy Arion," Kelson heard one man say, as he and Dhugal passed by a knot of courtiers intent on a flask of Vezairi ale. "I never did trust Mahael—and Teymuraz may be the worst of the lot. . . ."

Others spoke of Mahael's fate. One such conversation, overheard en route to the privy, caused Kelson to draw Dhugal into the shadow of a pillar and feign avid interest in a pair of fire-jugglers as he strained to catch details.

"They say he danced very poorly," one elderly man was murmuring to another, as the pair stripped shreds of flesh from a roast peacock. "If you ask me, the executioners bungled the job." Both men wore the braided sidelocks and gilded leather wrist gauntlets of Steppes nobles. Their grey beards were braided as well, the moustaches twisted back behind their ears.

"Well, I doubt anyone was expecting an execution at a *killijálay*," the second man said, gesturing with a greasy bone. Both were also casting idle scrutiny toward the jugglers as they talked, their appetites apparently unaffected by the topic of conversation. "It takes finesse to impale a man properly, without piercing vital organs right away. Best if the victim's own struggles do *that*."

"True, it's the struggle that makes for a good dance," the first man agreed. "And cowards make the best dancers—straining upward on their toes to escape the inescapable. Of course, the length of the stake must be judged with precision. . . ."

Kelson could feel the gorge rising in his throat, and fought down queasiness as he seized Dhugal's elbow and the pair of them headed toward one of the balconies, gulping for breaths of fresh air.

"Do you suppose those men knew we were listening?" Dhugal asked, when they both had regained their equilibrium. "Surely no one could do what they described."

"It wouldn't surprise me," Kelson murmured.

He was trying not to imagine Mahael's "dance." Mind-ripped as Mahael had been, Kelson thought he would have been mostly oblivious to his fate, as his executioners set him in place; he hoped so. Still, it would not have been a quick death.

Not that Gwynedd's penalties for capital treason were necessarily much quicker. He had seen many a man slowly choke out his life at the end of a rope—and even beheading did not always guarantee a quick end, if the victim flinched or the headsman's concentration wavered. It had taken three blows to sever Conall's neck.

Memory of that particular execution, compounded by involuntary speculation surrounding Mahael's final moments, kept Kelson subdued for most of the next hour, though he declined comment when both Dhugal and Morgan remarked at his sobriety. For recollection of Conall had brought attendant memories of Rothana—and of Araxie, to whom he now was pledged in betrothal. He had been able to keep thoughts of both women mostly at bay in the face of the focus of the past few days, but his own fears and sorrows now began to intrude, as fatigue and relief made him start winding down. And interspersed with recollections of both women were increasing worries regarding the next likely moves of Teymuraz, as the twilight deepened and still no word came of the traitor's whereabouts.

The continuing lack of news put something of a damper on further celebrations, but when full darkness had fallen, Liam dutifully gathered his guests beside the terrace railing looking out to the east, where the domes of the cathedral and churches and even the minarets of the Moorish prayer halls of the city were lit to the rainbow hues of Deryni magic—like what they had seen at Saint-Sasile, but magnified tenfold. The display again brought a smile to Liam's lips, as he watched with Kelson and Mátyás at his sides, but the smile was no longer that of the innocence of youth. Much had changed in the fortnight since Saint-Sasile.

The celebrations were slated to continue long into the night, but soon after the lights had faded away over Beldour, Liam conferred briefly with Mátyás, then invited Kelson to bring Morgan, Dhugal, and Arilan to an impromptu meeting that Mátyás had arranged, of men he believed loyal to the newly enthroned king. Conspicuously absent were Morag and Liam's brother—both retired early, it was said, after their ordeals at Hagia Iób. But the Patriarch Alpheios and two of his senior Metropolitans were prominent among the Torenthis, which included Rasoul and several of the royal dukes. Azim was also in attendance. Liam made gracious apology for calling them from the festivities, declaring his intention to present each with a suitable token of his esteem at a later date, then shifted at once into the urgent business of the night.

"I shall not long keep you, my lords," he said, speaking to the dozen men whom Mátyás had convened at the long malachite table in the king's state apartments. "In light of the day's events, and lest you doubt my preparedness for the role I now assume, I thought to advise you regarding a few of the immediate concerns I shall ask you to address in the coming days and weeks and months. I regret that I have not been here to know you from my youth; that is the fault of no one here. In balance, however, I must tell you that I count it worth whatever inconvenience that may have caused, to have spent a time in squireship under the exacting standards of Duke Nigel Haldane, the uncle of my friend the King of Gwynedd."

He flicked a grateful glance in Kelson's direction as he made that statement, salute to a mentor become an elder peer in the course of the day's unfoldings. Kelson only inclined his head in satisfied acknowledgment, quietly reading the tenor of the room, hearing in Liam's gracious phrasing the moderation he had hoped and intended that the boy should learn at Nigel's side. Early into the afternoon, Liam had put aside his heavy state diadem for a simple circlet of gold; Kelson had eschewed even that symbol of rank, in token that he now was only a guest in this, Liam's restored kingdom.

"I have one item of personal business, however, before we proceed," Liam went on. "It reflects but one of the lessons that King Kelson has taught me." He glanced at Mátyás, then back at the men around the table. "One of the most important things I learned at the court of Gwynedd is the value of a loyal uncle—and I know that I shall rely heavily on mine, as I did today, to serve as one of my chief ministers. My friend King Kelson has suggested that ducal rank is appropriate for one in a position of such trust."

All Torenthi eyes turned toward Mátyás, who looked somewhat startled.

"I therefore give to my uncle, Count Mátyás Furstán-Komnéné, the titles and lands and revenues of Arjenol," Liam said, "for its late duke is attainted by his treason, and had no direct heirs with better claim. From what I have been told, Uncle, the vineyards are not so fine as those you already have," he added with a faint smile at Mátyás, "so you'd best keep Komnéné as well."

A ripple of guarded approval whispered through the room at this announcement, which had produced a faint flush of surprised pleasure on the face of Mátyás.

"I thank you, my prince."

"It is I who give thanks," Liam replied, before putting off his crown for more serious work.

In the half hour that followed, proceeding to an agenda Mátyás had prepared in anticipation of his brothers' probable betrayal, Liam outlined a general plan for the first year of his personal reign that left Kelson and his advisors with little doubt that Torenth was well started in the process of becoming a good neighbor to Gwynedd. Liam obviously had learned his lessons well at Kelson's court, and had put far more thought into the shape of his reign than any of them had dreamed. Though a few of the older dukes kept balking at old prejudices and old quarrels, Liam and Mátyás between them managed to defuse nearly all reservations—and with heartening support from the Patriarch Alpheios.

"Peace, Erdödy of Jandrich," he chided at one point. "It has done neither of our kingdoms any good to be at enmity these past two centuries. Our beloved land has seen too many of her best and brightest slain out of time—and all too many from pointless strife within our own borders. God now calls us to set this House of Furstán in order, led by the bold example of our bold young *padishah*." He inclined his head in Liam's direction.

"It was my sad duty to assist my predecessor in burying your brother, noble prince—an office I hope never to perform for you. For I pray that I may be long in my grave before you are called before God's holy throne of judgment, having died in my bed as a very old man, and having helped bring your sons into their manhood. I rejoice in your accession, bolstered by the might of Furstán. May you and they reign long and well, in wisdom and joy."

Such open and powerful support cheered Kelson; for, while he did not doubt that Liam would have his hands full, keeping his council focused on a new way of looking at relations between the two kingdoms, at least the boy would not have to contend with a clergy so recalcitrant as Gwynedd's had been, at the beginning of his own reign—closed to the very thought that powers such as had saved Liam today were other than seditious and evil. Deryni had long moved in the forefront of Torenthi politics, despite their small numbers—hardly surprising, given the heritage of Torenth's royal line. Acclaim like that just offered by the Holy Alpheios had not been given Kelson until far later in his reign, and boded well for the future of Liam's kingdom.

"I thank you, Holiness," Liam said quietly, apparently greatly moved by this unexpected expression of support. "Nor can I presently think of words to surpass the aspiration you have just expressed. Perhaps, therefore, you would be so good as to give us your blessing, before I allow these loyal men to return to the night's enjoyments—for I did promise that I would not keep you long, my lords," he concluded, as he rose to his feet and all hurriedly did the same.

When the patriarch had given his blessing, Mátyás dismissed the meeting in the *padishah's* name, signing for Kelson and his companions to remain as he drew Liam briefly aside to whisper in his ear and the others dispersed. At Azim's nod, Dhugal closed the door behind the last of the departing ministers, returning to where Liam had invited those remaining to gather closer at his end of the long malachite table.

"My uncle has pointed out another matter needing thought as a result of today's events," Liam said. "It concerns Bishop Arilan's continued presence at my court."

"Please allow me to clarify," Mátyás asked, before Arilan or Kelson could respond. "I would not have the good bishop feel that his presence is, in any way, resented or unwanted. On the contrary, I would request that his king permit him to remain among us for a time, to share his wise counsel, as had been originally intended. I am confident that your faith in Liam-Lajos is well-founded, Highness"—he nodded in Kelson's direction—"but I fear that *I* have not had the same benefit of exposure to the court of Gwynedd.

"Or perhaps Duke Alaric would consent to stay awhile," he added, turning a hopeful smile toward Morgan, "or at least return from time to time? I am told that he was one of Duke Nigel's most successful pupils. Perhaps he could teach this grower of grapes a little more of statecraft before casting him and his king adrift on their own."

Morgan only nodded, returning the smile as he recalled their conversation on the ride from Desse to Rhemuth; Arilan looked somewhat startled, but inclined his head in tentative assent as he glanced at Kelson, who grinned. Mátyás' request had been most gracefully put.

"I think none of us anticipated the day's developments," Kelson said. "And much has changed since it was agreed that Gwynedd should have an observer here. Torenth was then a vassal state, with an untried client king of tender years. But today has proven amply, I think, that Liam-Lajos is well able to take up the ruling of his kingdom. In restoring Torenth's sovereignty, I also yielded my right to impose my Haldane presence here.

"However," he went on, "if I can assist you by providing such ongoing advice as may be useful in shaping Torenth's future, I am happy to do so. Understand that I haven't had time to think this through yet—and I will need to consult with my own councillors of state regarding particulars—but I would certainly envision reciprocal embassies in both our capitals. And since it had already been agreed that Bishop Arilan should reside here for the immediate future, I see no reason to alter those arrangements at this time. I regret that I cannot spare Duke Alaric's services just now, but I am certain that he, too, will wish to continue the association."

"Perhaps," said Azim, "the *padishah* might wish to provide an additional Portal location here in Beldour—and King Kelson a suitable one in Rhemuth—to facilitate the future exchange of courtesies and assistance in your two kingdoms. For I believe that neither of you would wish to think that distance might dim the friendships that have been forged, these past days."

As Arilan glanced sharply at Kelson, apparently unaware that Liam had already given him the location of the Portal in the Nikolaseum, the king inclined his head. With everything else on his mind, there had been little time to spare for thinking about the full implications of knowing *any* Portal in Torenth, much less another right here in Beldour. The regular, if careful, use of Portals between the two courts would certainly enhance communications—and might well help facilitate a lasting peace, for the first time in centuries.

"As I said," Kelson replied, "I shall need to consult with others regarding specifics; but I, too, would be reluctant to lose what we have begun here."

"Certain specifics *should* be addressed immediately, regardless of our aspirations for the future," Arilan said, perhaps more sharply than he had intended.

"Indeed," Azim interjected smoothly. "We should by no means overestimate the progress made today, but I must point out that the escape of Count Teymuraz remains a cause for concern for all of you. For I think he will plot his revenge on all who were instrumental in his and Mahael's overthrow."

"True enough, my lord," Mátyás agreed, "but I think it unlikely he will soon seek his revenge here in Torenth. Though he and Mahael had a vast network of agents spread over a large area, those in Torenth will be wary of upholding previ ous alliances until they have taken the measure of the new *padishah*—especially as Mahael's fate becomes known."

"And what of those outside Torenth?" Morgan asked pointedly.

Mátyás inclined his head. "I would venture to guess that some will not feel so constrained. Undoubtedly, a few will still be available to Teymuraz, ready to work his mischief."

Kelson glanced at Mátyás, frowning. "Is there some danger of which I'm not aware? Given the friendship we both have pledged today, by deed as well as word, I must assume that we are not talking about any threat along our mutual border."

"Nay, I think you must look farther west, my lord," Mátyás offered, a trifle uncomfortably. "My brothers spoke often of preventing your closer alliance with Meara. At the time, I fear, thwarting their intention to kill Laje was far more important to me than protecting the western flank of a foreign king who had custody of *my* king, and whose true motives were yet unknown."

"You chose the right priority; you need not apologize," Kelson said, his mind quickly racing over the Mearan permutations—both those generally known and those as yet private. "But—what had they in mind, regarding Meara? I must assume that you refer to the coming marriage of Brecon Ramsay with my cousin Richelle."

"And to rumors that, as soon as those two are wed, you will announce a betrothal with Brecon's sister," Mátyás replied, raising a droll eyebrow.

"Ah," Kelson said, with a sidelong glance at his companions, who knew otherwise. "Well, it is, indeed, true that I hope soon to announce a betrothal for Brecon's sister," he said, to the obvious surprise of both Mátyás and Liam. "However, the match is not with me; it's with my cousin Rory, Duke Nigel's son and heir."

He watched as they exchanged startled glances. Liam looked pleased, for he knew Rory well, and might even have had some inkling of the relationship that had started to bloom the previous summer. Mátyás was smiling faintly, immediately grasping the political implications in far greater detail than were probably occurring to his nephew.

"You seem amused, Count Mátyás," Kelson observed.

Mátyás nodded good-naturedly. "And full of admiration, to see how well you continue to divert speculation regarding your own eventual nuptials. But the match is a good one for both Meara and Gwynedd—and of the heart, I would assume." He paused a beat. "But you still do not address the question of your own marriage."

Kelson shrugged, choosing his words carefully. "I think this is neither the time nor the place to elaborate on that subject, before official announcement is made to my own people," he said truthfully. "When that occurs, I can assure you that it will not be to the detriment of Torenth; but beyond that, I may not comment."

Liam grinned and shook his head, slapping an open palm on the table in ado-lescent glee. "It's no use, Mátyás. He won't talk about it. I spent three years at the court of Gwynedd, and believe me, he's a master at avoiding the question—though, God knows, it's long been a favorite topic of speculation, even among the squires and pages."

"Indeed?" Kelson said.

A knock at the door heralded a liveried Circassian guard, who came and whispered urgently to Mátyás as utter silence pervaded the room. Liam's uncle listened attentively, frowning, gave whispered instructions, then exchanged a glance with his nephew as the man left the room.

"Well. Teymuraz has made an appearance," he said. "He showed up at Saint-Sasile several hours ago, commandeered a war galley and crew, and put out to sea. In light of what we've just been discussing, of his previous intention to interfere with the Mearan alliance, it is just possible that he's headed for the Ile d'Orsal, perhaps to kidnap the prospective bride. I've asked that Létald be summoned."

As Mátyás bent his head to listen to Liam's urgent whisper, and the two con-ferred briefly in a staccato dialect that the Gwyneddans largely could not follow, Dhugal glanced at Kelson.

"What can Létald do?" he murmured. "We're nearly three days' sail from the Ile, even with a fair wind."

"There may well be a private Portal there," Azim volunteered, leaning in from Dhugal's other side. "The very genial Létald is a very private man, who does not make much of his Deryni roots, but it has long been believed that he has Portals, even if he little uses them."

"Are you suggesting that, if he does have Portals, we ask to use one to reach the Ile ahead of Teymuraz?" Kelson murmured, for he knew that Azim would be thinking of the other Haldane bride potentially in danger there.

"Precisely that," Azim agreed. "From there, the entire bridal party could be moved directly to Rhemuth, away from the reach of Teymuraz—if that is, in fact, his aim."

"Whether it is or not, getting them out of there is still the safest bet," Kelson muttered. "But I can't say I relish the notion of simply showing up back in Rhe-muth, several weeks early. I've spent my entire reign trying to avoid upsetting my subjects with blatant use of my magic."

"I suppose you could bring them through the Portal at Dhassa," Arilan said reluctantly, "and travel the rest of the way by horse. That isn't a difficult journey at this time of year. Teymuraz can't possibly have the Dhassa location—and I doubt very much that any of the Rhemuth locations are known here in Torenth."

He glanced at Mátyás, who had turned to follow their conversation—and who shook his head. Liam looked worried. Kelson watched all of them, racking his brain for other options, and found himself unaccountably anxious for Araxie, even though he knew that Richelle was likely to be Teymuraz's specific target, if he did contemplate an abduction from Horthánthy.

"All right, this isn't going to be easy for any of us," he said. "While we wait for Létald, let's consider the worst case. If Teymuraz is at sea, and heading for the Ile, he presumably does not have a closer Portal location than Saint-Sasile."

"Correction," Morgan said. "He does not have a closer Portal location that can also provide him with a ship and crew; but the question is moot. Neither do we."

"Perhaps we do," Azim said, as the door opened to admit Létald, looking more serious than Kelson had ever seen him. "My lord, have you been informed of the recent development?"

Létald was nodding as he headed for a chair that Mátyás indicated, one hand lifting in a gesture of forbearance. "Enough to share your concern—and to be anticipating what you are about to ask, though I am reluctant to breech so intimate a detail of my family's personal security. I'm told he left Saint-Sasile several hours ago?"

"So it would seem," Mátyás said.

"Well, that's a full day's sail," Létald replied, "so we have *some* time—*if* he's even headed for Horthánthy."

"Even if he isn't," Morgan said, "he's still sailing along your coast—or mine. You saw what happened today; you know what he's capable of. And the fact is, we *don't* know what his intentions are."

"Who *ever* knows, with Furstáns?" Létald muttered. "No offense intended," he added, to Liam and Mátyás.

Mátyás merely nodded mildly.

"Once we find out," Morgan went on, "dealing with him will present its own problems, as you will have gathered earlier today. Given the uncertainty, it might be best to withdraw your family to your winter palace on the mainland. I shall certainly have *Rhafallia* sail at first light, to fetch my wife and children away from Coroth and take them on to Rhemuth."

"We do need a Coroth Portal," Kelson murmured, glancing pointedly at Arilan. "But since we haven't yet got one, we're proposing to take the bridal party to Dhassa, and overland from there. Through your Portal," he added, to Létald.

"I should point out," said Mátyás, before Létald could answer, "that if my brother is intending to call at Horthánthy, it may not be only King Kelson's kin who are at risk."

Létald went very still.

"What are you saying?"

Mátyás looked faintly embarrassed. "Let us simply say that the name of your eldest daughter has been mentioned more than once by both my brothers as an object of . . . carnal interest. I won't repeat exactly what was said. In addition, I believe the fair Elisabet has from time to time been discussed among Gwynedd's ministers of state as a possible royal bride—has she not, Sire?" He briefly turned his glance on Kelson, who nodded. "One among many, to be sure, but perhaps it would be as well if she were not at home if Teymuraz comes calling for a Haldane princess and is thwarted in his intentions."

Létald's face had gone hard as Mátyás spoke, the last of his genial veneer melting away. After sweeping the others with his gaze, he returned his focus to Kelson, then to Liam.

"It seems we all must trust one another far more than we had planned or dreamed," he said quietly. "In granting access to my private Portal at Horthánthy, I shall require reciprocal access here and in Gwynedd. Dhassa will be acceptable for the latter, Bishop Arilan. Count Mátyás, what Portal will you offer here in Beldour?"

Mátyás looked immediately at Liam, but the boy merely inclined his head. "You must choose, Uncle," he said. "You know more of this than I."

*A*nd in the quarters of the Princess Morag, mother of the new king, a handsome, dark-haired young man in the braids and leather tunic of a sirdukar of royal horse waited for a servant to close the door behind him and withdraw. Morag was standing before the fireplace, one hand resting on the chimneypiece, and gestured with a be-ringed hand for him to approach. The events of earlier in the day had not at all altered the long-nurtured plan she now prepared to set in motion.

"I have a task for you, of a somewhat delicate nature," she said to the man, as he came and knelt to kiss the hem of her gown. "Stay, and I shall give you the whole of it," she added, setting a hand on his shoulder when he would have risen.

He bowed his head at the gesture, closing his eyes as her hand slipped round to cup the back of his neck. He remained thus for a handful of heartbeats, after which he raised his head, then got to his feet at her nod.

"It will not be easy, to draw Lord Derry aside without arousing his suspicions," he murmured.

"That is why I entrust this task to you," she replied. "I can trust no one else. He is very wary of us, but he is not Deryni—and he will not question a summons to attend Morgan and the other Deryni of King Kelson's party, whom he knows to be presently occupied in a closed meeting with my son. I need but a short time with him."

"You shall have it, my lady," the man said, inclining his head.

She watched him go, absently fondling an iron finger-ring found on the body of her brother, Wencit, following his death at the hands of Kelson of Gwynedd—who had also slain her husband. Not until many months later, while going through her brother's papers and magical diaries, had she discovered the significance and purpose of the ring—and learned that Sean Lord Derry, trusted aide of the detestable Morgan, once had worn its mate.

After that, it had taken nearly three years to find a mage capable of crafting a new match-mate. Meanwhile, she refined the functioning of the spell that once had made it such a powerful tool. The ritual for attuning the new ring to the old—and for augmenting the original spell—had required three days and three nights, during which she neither ate not slept. But now the new ring lay in a pocket of her gown, encased in purest gold to disguise its true nature. . . .

CHAPTER TWENTY-TWO

Therefore I purposed to take her to me to live with me,
knowing that she would be a counseller of good
things, and a comfort in cares and grief.

Wisdom of Solomon 8:9

ithin the hour, Kelson and his immediate party were gathered around the Portal in the staff room Mátyás had been using to direct the search for Teymuraz. It was also the Portal whence Arilan and Azim had made their visit to the Camberian Council with Sofiana the night before, though this was unknown to the rest of them. Létald and Azim had just disappeared from the Portal square; and as Mátyás invited inspection by the rest of them, Kelson noticed that Liam, too, was taking the opportunity to make the Portal's coordinates his own. Arilan looked uneasy about the entire operation.

"It isn't only Létald who will want the Dhassa coordinates," Kelson murmured aside to Arilan, as they stood back to watch Dhugal ease in to crouch beside Liam.

"I'm aware of that," Arilan muttered.

"I'm referring to Liam and Mátyás," Kelson said.

"That's what I'm aware of," Arilan replied, a little testily, but still very softly. "But the Portal is Trapped, if I set it that way—as is Létald's, I suspect. Or it will be, by the time all of this is finished."

Azim suddenly appeared again on the Portal square, causing Dhugal to rear back on his heels—though he had already finished what was necessary. As Azim's gaze flicked around the room, Kelson stepped forward where he could be seen easily.

246 ɣ KATHERINE KURTZ

"All's well at the Ile, I hope?" he said.

"For now. Come. Létald has started preparations there. I can take through two at a time."

Kelson found Mátyás at his elbow as he started forward. Smiling faintly, the Furstáni prince checked and gestured for Kelson to precede him. Kelson obliged, falling in at Azim's right and turning to face in the same direction, as Mátyás did the same on Azim's left.

"Play nicely, now, children," Azim said softly so that only they could hear, as he set a hand on the back of each man's neck. "Prepare yourselves."

Mildly bristling at Azim's indulgent tone, Kelson closed his eyes and drew a long breath to center, totally confident in the hands of the Deryni master—and confident in tandem with Mátyás, he realized as he settled into focus, though old suspicions died hard. As he let down his shields, he felt the firm and powerful embrace of Azim's mind enfolding his, carrying him deeper toward stillness. He yielded to it, vaguely aware of a surge of power—and caught his balance just slightly as the floor shifted beneath his feet.

He opened his eyes to a small, musty-smelling room lit by a standing rack of candles beside an open door. Beyond was a room paneled in light oak, with Létald standing behind a long council table, issuing orders to a handful of liveried servants. Kelson knew the room instantly, for he had often met there with Létald for discussions of business common to both of them; but he had never suspected the presence of a Portal this near.

"Wait with Létald," Azim murmured, propelling the pair of them off the Portal. He was gone again almost instantly, the feat betokening fine control. Still faintly disconnected from the jump, Kelson sank to a crouch to set his hands on the Portal square and imprint its location in his mind, faintly reassured to see Mátyás calmly doing the same. When they had finished, they rose together and went into the room beyond.

"I know the hour, and I know she detests having her sleep disturbed," Létald was saying to Vasilly Dimitriades. The lanky chamberlain was wrapped in a robe of sea-green silk, shoeless, his wide eyes and dishevelled hair making him look like a startled egret. "Ask her to summon my nieces as well. Say that I shall be there momentarily, with King Kelson."

Half an hour later, Kelson was standing uneasily in the solar chamber where he had come to speak to Araxie before, listening as Azim explained to Sivorn and her husband and daughters what had transpired at Beldour, and why the escape of Teymuraz might pose a threat to the two Haldane princesses. Morgan and Dhugal were with him, and Arilan, along with Liam and Mátyás.

"Accordingly, I would strongly recommend that you allow us to take you and the princesses to safety,"Azim concluded. "Your brother concurs in this proposal."

Sivorn cast a sour glance at Létald and made a moue. With her bright hair tumbled about her shoulders, she looked hardly older than her daughters, both of whom were sheltering somewhat bewilderedly in the embrace of their stepfather. Savile had dressed, but looked underslept; the women had merely thrown cloaks over their sleeping shifts. While Richelle's expression had been growing ever more indignant and even petulant, Araxie's suggested that she was already grasping the possible greater ramifications. It was unlikely that Teymuraz could have learned of her betrothal to Kelson, but he might well attempt to disrupt the marriage planned between Richelle and Brecon of Meara.

"It's out of the question," Sivorn said quite emphatically, a mutinous note in her voice. "Létald, please explain to Azim why we cannot possibly leave so soon. My seamstresses were counting on another full week before we left—and will probably still be stitching on the voyage. One simply cannot conjure royal weddings out of thin air!"

"The finery can be sent after," Létald replied. "The risk is very real. I won't have you endangering my nieces for the sake of fripperies."

"And why shouldn't they have fripperies?!" Sivorn retorted, with an emphatic stamp of her foot. "All brides are entitled to—to 'fripperies,' as you call them! Royal brides are *particularly* entitled to them. 'Tis little enough compensation for what *they* must often sacrifice, in the cause of duty!"

She was speaking of Araxie as well as Richelle, of course, though Mátyás and Liam were yet unaware of that. She let Savile draw her into the supporting circle of his arm with Richelle, but she looked on the stubborn edge of tears, head held high. As her husband and brother exchanged dismayed glances, it occurred to Kelson to wonder whether Sivorn realized that both her daughters were at risk, not just Richelle. But dared he raise the point in front of his new Torenthi allies, who were not yet aware of his secret betrothal? And ought he not ask Araxie herself before making such a revelation?

On impulse, uncertain whether she was capable of hearing him, he sent her the quick, tight-focused thought of his query. To his pleased surprise, Araxie's grey eyes flicked to his immediately, a faint smile touching her lips as the eyes briefly lowered in agreement. Thus emboldened, he came close enough to set a hand gently on Sivorn's shoulder.

"Aunt Sivorn," he said quietly, "it is precisely because of the nature of such sacrifice that I must insist that at least the three of you come away with us immediately. If necessary, the 'fripperies' can follow later—or we'll improvise. It's the marriages that are important—not the weddings."

He turned to take the hand Araxie offered, wearing the ring he had given her—sized to fit her in the days he had been away—and it occurred to him to wonder whether the potential relationship between the two of them also had become a better fit. Her hand felt reassuring in his, as if it belonged there.

"Gentlemen, I hope you will forgive my earlier evasions," he went on, lifting his gaze to Mátyás and Liam, "but I truly had intended that my council should be informed first. Under the circumstances, however, you should be aware that we now are speaking not of one royal bride but of two; for the Princess Araxie has consented to become my wife and my queen."

Liam's mouth fell open as Kelson lifted Araxie's hand to his lips, but Mátyás only nodded appraisingly.

"But—when did this happen?" Liam asked bewilderedly.

"When we stopped here before, en route to your enthronement," Kelson replied. He drew Araxie's hand into the crook of his arm and covered it with his.

"I have already indicated the importance of that second Mearan marriage, between my cousin Rory and Noelie Ramsay," he went on. "Since there had been speculation that I might marry the Lady Noelie, you will appreciate that, in the normal course of events, both marriages would have taken place before I announced my own intentions. However, the changed circumstances have put a certain urgency on our need to resolve all three matches."

Mátyás nodded sagely; Liam appeared a bit bemused. Sivorn was looking increasingly dismayed.

"Exactly how much urgency did you have in mind?" she asked a little peevishly. "I hope you don't expect me to conjure a state wedding overnight."

"No, not overnight," Kelson said with a smile. "And remember that the Mearan marriages aren't state occasions—just family celebrations, regardless of their diplomatic implications. I'm hopeful of arranging for both ceremonies on the same day, with a joint celebration to follow. After all, Noelie's family will already be in Rhemuth to see her brother wed. The third wedding can take place shortly thereafter."

"And just how shortly did you have in mind?" Sivorn heaved an exasperated sigh. "Kelson, it isn't just a matter of getting the bride and the groom in the same place at the same time."

"I know—'fripperies,' " Kelson said with a grin. "If it's any consolation, I'm certain Aunt Meraude and my mother will be prepared to lend a hand. Mother has been waiting a very long time for this."

"Then she deserves to see it done properly," Sivorn retorted. "Besides, it's my daughter we're talking about."

"*Maman*, we shall manage," Araxie said softly, with a pointed glance at Mátyás and Liam.

Sivorn glanced at them in turn, and reluctantly pulled herself back to the immediate situation. "I suppose we shall," she conceded. "Must we *really* leave so quickly, though?"

"I'm afraid you must," Kelson replied. "We simply don't know what danger there may be from Teymuraz. It will ease my mind considerably, to know that you and your family are safe in Rhemuth, under my protection. And as Létald has said, the 'fripperies' can be sent later. For that matter, I expect we can produce fripperies enough in Rhemuth," he added, with a cajoling wink. "My mother *is* a queen, you know."

The comment was enough to elicit a faint smile even from Sivorn, and her husband nodded his acceptance of the plan that was taking shape, finally speaking.

"How do you propose that we make this journey?" Savile said, as one hand stroked his wife's hair in reassurance. "If Teymuraz took ship from Saint-Sasile, he could be in these waters as early as midday—possibly sooner, with a fair wind. And if he is as powerful and unpredictable as you say—"

"I have a Portal at Dhassa," Arilan said quietly. "From there, it is only a few days' ride overland to Rhemuth."

"And there are several Portals at Rhemuth," Kelson said, before Arilan could elaborate. For he had decided that it was time to stop crippling himself by declining to use the strengths he had been given—and pointless to subject the women to the discomfort and risk of a land journey from Dhassa to Rhemuth. "I shall go ahead with Morgan and Dhugal to make arrangements, so that the arrival of the rest of you will cause as little comment as possible. The common folk have little cause to take much note of the comings and goings of those who live in a castle, unless it's a state occasion; and while my council may be unnerved initially, I have no doubt that any serious disgruntlement will be relieved quite quickly when I tell them I've finally chosen a queen."

The observation drew smiles from all present, and as Kelson glanced down at Araxie and squeezed her hand, she returned his gaze with a faint smile of her own.

"I do not envy you your task, my lord," she said. "I shall try not to disappoint them—or you." She pressed his hand before releasing it to turn and lay arms around her mother and sister, the bright braid of her hair like quicksilver down her back.

"Uncle Létald, we shall abide by your wishes in this matter, for I know you care only for our safety. *Maman*, would you please go and help Richelle begin packing? The maids will be hopeless if they are given no clear instructions. I would speak privately with the king before I join you."

Surprisingly, Araxie's calm declaration succeeded in clearing the room almost immediately. She gave Kelson a tentative smile as the door closed

250 ᚹ KATHERINE KURTZ

behind the last of them, then led the way to seats in the window embrasure, drawing her cloak around her before settling on one of the cushioned benches.

"You have obviously come to trust Mátyás and Liam," she said to him, as he sat down gingerly on the opposite seat. "I gather that the enthronement went well, other than for the betrayal by Mahael and Teymuraz." She wrinkled her nose in distaste. "Frankly, I never did like either of them. Until they both got so wrapped up with regencies, they used to be occasional visitors to Uncle Létald's court. I always thought Mahael was far too pompous for his own good, not to mention arrogant. And when Teymuraz wasn't molesting the female servants, he always gave me the impression he was trying to undress me with his eyes."

Kelson hastily lowered his own eyes, suddenly aware that his thoughts had been drifting in much the same direction, idly appreciative of the sweet line downward from her chin to neck to breasts, their curve just visible above the shadowed neckline of her long night shift—for the front edges of her cloak had parted as she tucked her feet up under her the way she had done when they were children.

Remembering those long ago summers of innocence, when both of them were very small, he reminded himself that he often must have seen, then, what now both stirred and unsettled him, for they would have splashed together in lake and stream and even bath with all the other young children of the royal household. But those children all were grown now, and some of them dead; and the comely young woman sitting across from him was no longer a childhood playmate but his future wife.

"Teymuraz—aye," he said, a little uneasily. "Mátyás did give me the impression that he is something of a womanizer—and hinted that he had spoken of your cousin Elisabet in rather salacious terms—Teymuraz, that is. Which is why Létald is moving his family to his winter palace until we know his intentions."

He drew breath and looked up at her again.

"Thank you for speaking up, by the way. I know it's awkward, leaving here a week ahead of schedule—and from your mother's perspective, I'm sure that the prospect of organizing not one but *two* weddings away from home is nothing short of daunting. But I wouldn't have asked if I didn't think it was important for everyone's safety. We really don't know what Teymuraz might try, even without his knowing about the two of us."

"I understand that," she replied. "And the two of us are the reason I spoke up." She studied him unabashedly in the dimness of the distant firelight. "I want to be a good queen to you, Kelson."

"I should have asked you more directly, before I told Mátyás and Liam about that," Kelson said hastily. "I—wasn't sure you would hear me."

"I was a little surprised myself," she admitted, "but certainly, no harm was done. I'm well aware that what happened at Liam's enthronement changed a lot of expectations on everyone's part—and I take it as a mark of your trust in our new allies, that you chose to tell them about us now."

He nodded. "It really is essential that I sort out the Mearan situation as quickly as possible. Now that you and Richelle will be safe in Rhemuth, I have no worries on that account—I can protect you there—but if Teymuraz were to try to get at me by sabotaging the Mearan alliance, it could set us back enormously."

Araxie gave him a tentative smile. "Would it help to know that I think you'll have an unexpected ally in the Mearan camp?" she asked.

"Oh?"

"Well, perhaps not totally unexpected—but unexpectedly useful. Richelle got to be rather good friends with Noelie Ramsay, while her own marriage negotiations were being worked out, and she thinks Noelie will be able to persuade her parents about Rory, once she knows you've given your blessing to the match. As you might expect, we talked about that development a lot while you were away. According to Brecon, Noelie is quite strong-willed, and generally gets what she wants."

Kelson nodded thoughtfully. "A good trait, so long as she's strong-willed on *our* side—and it's very useful to know." He smiled tentatively. "You do know, of course, that you're taking on royal consort functions already."

She shrugged and smiled wistfully. "I *am* a Haldane. And I confess to being relieved that I won't long have to maintain the charade that nothing has changed between us. Remember that when I agreed to marry you, I took on Gwynedd as well as Kelson Haldane; and I'm prepared to do whatever I can to help both of you, beginning right now, regardless of how many people do or do not know that we're planning to wed."

"I do appreciate that," Kelson said. He sighed. "I've put you in an awkward position. I'm sorry."

She pleated at a fold of her night shift, not looking directly at him. "The most awkward part, right now, is having only a very general notion of what went on today—but I will abide by your wishes, of course. Forgive me, I'm very new at this. But I hope you will remember that whatever talents and potentials I do have, I lay them at your feet—as my king, as my kinsman, and as my future husband."

Suddenly he sensed the direction of her halting declaration, again inviting him to share whatever limited rapport her present training might permit. And to his surprise, unlike the first time she had offered, he found that the notion no longer carried such a strong sense of betraying Rothana. Though he had sought to delay such intimacy, once he reluctantly accepted that he must marry Araxie, there had never been any question that it must come eventually. And perhaps now was, indeed, the time to begin building the more practical aspects of their future partnership, before the relationship became complicated by the emotional entanglements that would come with being husband and wife, both of them wed for reasons that had to do with duty rather than the heart.

And yet, as he turned to look at her—at the firelight gilding her cheek and the play of shadow on her lowered lashes—he found himself wondering at the grace of spirit that already had led her to commit her life to him, prompted not by love but by duty and familial affection—which, perhaps, was but another expression of love. She was very different from Rothana, but the two of them had held one another in affection since childhood. Love could grow from far less. And who, besides another Haldane, could truly come to love Gwynedd as he did?

"Araxie?" he said softly, reaching across to lightly brush the back of one of her hands.

She started at his touch, her fingers stopping their nervous pleating of her gown as her grey Haldane gaze lifted to his.

"Yes?"

Very gently he laid his hand next to hers, touching it but not clasping it, his fingertips barely brushing her little finger.

"I wonder that you're prepared to put up with me," he said, not looking at her directly.

She smiled tremulously. "I did agree to become your wife. Putting up with you comes with the arrangement."

He bowed his head, wondering how much he must have hurt her already. "I do want our marriage to be more than an arrangement," he said. "And more than just a dynastic coupling to beget the heirs I need. I hope you understand that it may take a little while to build such a relationship."

"Of course I understand."

"Yes. Well, I started things out rather badly when I was here before, by declining your very generous offer to attempt rapport. I want you to know that I'm not insensible to the courage it must have taken, to make me such an offer. At the time, it—seemed the best decision for both of us."

"And now?" she asked.

"That depends on whether you're still feeling brave," he replied, looking up at her. "God knows the circumstances have changed. And as my future queen, you certainly have the right to know about things that will affect how the two of us interact in the service of Gwynedd. Whatever else may or may not grow between us, I hope and pray that we may always rely upon one another as friends and helpmates."

"Well, of course," she retorted. "Duty be damned, if I didn't think we could manage at least *that*! Give it time, Kelson. We *have* time." She turned her hand to lightly clasp his. "As for me, you should understand that, as a Haldane, I have been brought up in the knowledge that, one day, I might have to marry solely for political reasons—maybe even with someone old enough to be my grandfather. To marry someone I've always liked and admired is a great blessing—even with the challenges that come with being your queen!"

He gazed at her in astonishment, only now beginning to appreciate the trust she was bringing to their commitment to marry.

"You really do mean that, don't you?" he said, though his powers left no doubt of her sincerity.

"Of course I do."

He felt a smile beginning to tug at the corners of his mouth, and he turned his hand in hers to lightly clasp it as well.

"Then, maybe we'd better make that attempt at rapport. I could *tell* you what happened today in Torenthály, but you'll grasp it far better if I *show* you. I'll go slowly. You needn't be afraid."

She turned her face full toward him, her fingers curling more boldly around his as she whispered, "I could never be afraid of you."

*B*ack in Beldour, Sean Lord Derry had time to be only briefly afraid. The message brought to him by the handsome young sirdukar in royal livery had mentioned only that his presence was requested by the new *padishah*. In fact, it was the new *padishah*'s mother who was waiting in the small audience chamber near the formal gardens—Morag of Torenth, whose brother's powerful magic once had forced Derry to obscene betrayals. By the time he saw her, she was too close to avoid, stepping from behind the door his escort was closing, her hand already lifting toward his forehead.

Nonetheless, instinct made him recoil—right into the sirdukar's arms, one of which clasped him tight against his captor's chest while a gloved hand smothered any hope of a cry for help. Her touch drained away any inclination to resist, stirring chilling and long-buried memories of an iron ring once placed on his finger by the detested Wencit, whose most profound compulsions yet slumbered in his mind, undisturbed or detected despite the deep probes and healings that Morgan had performed after Wencit's death.

Reawakened, those compulsions now drew him into docile oblivion, unable to fight them, his mind spread ready to receive and accept whatever instruction she cared to impose. . . .

CHAPTER TWENTY-THREE

*Exalt her, and she shall promote thee: she shall bring
thee to honour, when thou dost embrace her.*

Proverbs 4:8

No inkling of Derry's plight was even suspected by any of his would-be protectors, either in Beldour or back on the Ile d'Orsal. Even Derry's existence was far from Kelson's thoughts as he made his way back to Létald's conference chamber, having finally left Araxie to pack a few necessaries for her journey.

The king found himself surprisingly moved after their exchange. Though he had confined their rapport to a sharing of what had occurred earlier in the day, and his assessment thus far, of its aftermath, he had been astonished to discover how well both Azim and Rothana herself had prepared his bride-to-be—and he found that this, too, was less daunting a thought than it had been.

Given that Araxie herself had first broached the subject of psychic rapport, he supposed he should not have been surprised at her having achieved some level of competence in very basic skills usually associated with Deryni—or with Haldanes, which he was increasingly convinced were much the same. Augmenting these rudimentary skills, however, was a Haldane's keen appreciation for the political nuances with which he was wrestling, forged over a period of several centuries of Haldane history.

Which was not to say that he could wholly discount the profound differences between Araxie and Rothana. But he was discovering that Araxie compared more favorably than he had realized, and some areas of personality actually seemed far more complementary to his own—common points of family and heritage and expectation that would certainly help to make a partnership work, not only in their official duties and responsibilities but in their domestic interactions. It was not that Araxie's potentials were greater than Rothana's; they were simply different, and perhaps even better suited to the unique position in which Gwynedd's queen would need to function.

He could not yet bring himself to address the question of physical passion—bright-flaring kindling, where Rothana was concerned, in contrast to Araxie's clear, steady flame—so he had kept any hint of that aspect of his wants and needs carefully shuttered off during the interaction. But he could not deny that their shared rapport had moved him profoundly, or that some part of him had started to respond to her nearness. Most certainly, she would grace the consort's crown with intelligence as well as beauty, with gentleness and courtesy and even wit. Were it not for memories of Rothana. . . .

"Arilan has returned to Beldour with Liam," Morgan murmured, standing as Kelson joined him back in Létald's conference room. He had a map of the surrounding waters spread on the table before him, and laid aside a pair of callipers. "We thought it advisable that Torenth's new king not be too long absent from his capital, so soon after his enthronement, and that he ought to have a trustworthy advisor with him until the ripples settle from this afternoon."

"Did Mátyás go with him?" Kelson asked.

"No, he's with Létald, advising him on the defense of the island. Better him than me, since he knows what his brother might try. Dhugal is with them, standing in for you. Meanwhile, I've asked Arilan to assist Derry and Saer in organizing the departure arrangements at Beldour, first thing in the morning. How did it go with Araxie?"

Kelson nodded, more content than he had expected, as he sank into a chair across from Morgan. "Surprisingly well," he said. "Azim must be quite a teacher. Either that, or Haldane blood really does count for a good deal more than anyone ever dreamed."

"Probably a little of both," Morgan replied, "though that should hardly surprise you, knowing your own level of ability. May I take it, then, that you achieved a good level of rapport?"

"We did," Kelson said hesitantly. "She's far more accomplished than Rothana or even Azim had led me to believe. Part of that can probably be explained by the Deryni blood from her mother's side, but—she's a Haldane, too, Alaric. You don't suppose she might have the capacity to assume Haldane powers, do you?"

Morgan raised an eyebrow. "Now, that's an interesting thought. There's never been a Haldane queen regnant, so it's never occurred to me to wonder if the

power could be assumed by a woman. Nor am I aware of a Haldane ever marrying another Haldane, for that matter. But your grandfather and Araxie's father
were both sons of Malcolm Haldane—and where blood is concerned, nature
doesn't care which is the senior line. We already know that it isn't true that only
one Haldane can hold the power at a time.

"That means that, in theory, Duke Richard should have carried the same Haldane potential as his elder half-brother—your grandfather," Morgan went on,
warming to this new speculation. "And that should have passed to Araxie—and to
Richelle, for that matter. Of course, we don't know how the blood gets diluted,
down the generations. But if you're any example, it certainly hasn't lost its
potency in the senior line—and the trait seems to have bred true in Nigel's line."

Kelson had gone very still, his mind whirling with the diverse possibilities
suggested by the notion, not even recoiling as he usually did, at the oblique
reminder of betrayal by Nigel's eldest son. He had mentioned Araxie's possible
potential half-wistfully, still charmed by the rapport begun out of duty and then
embraced by unexpected stirrings of far greater compatibility than he dared to
hope for—and quite unprepared for the direction Morgan's speculations had
taken, once the question was raised.

"Then, you're saying that it might, indeed, be possible to awaken Haldane
potential in Araxie," he said slowly. "Good God, why did that never occur to me
before?—or to Rothana or Azim. If it had, they surely would have pointed it out."

"So one would think," Morgan agreed. "Unless, of course, some hidden purpose is at work." He paused a beat. "Does it signify, I wonder, that Azim is part of
the Camberian Council?"

A queasy knot stirred in Kelson's stomach.

"Why would the Council wish to hide such a thing?"

"I don't know. So far as I can tell, they have never been comfortable with the
notion of Deryni who do not fall within their definitions of what is proper. And
the fact is that there's a great deal that isn't known about Deryni or those who
somewhat resemble Deryni—like Haldanes.

"On that level," Morgan went on carefully, "it's a very good thing that Rothana
has set herself the task of bringing some of this into the open. Her vision of helping the Servants of Saint Camber establish a *schola* for Deryni is admirable, but the
dream is much too small. Someone besides scattered individuals and self-
appointed bodies operating in isolation must revive the ancient knowledge, and
gather it centrally, and encourage it to flourish in the open—and maintain standards of behavior, and chastise those who step beyond proper boundaries.

"What's more, it should be located in your capital," he said emphatically, stabbing a finger at the table for emphasis, "so that you can be its protector. And that
may also solve part of the Albin problem, because then he'd be there, and you and

Nigel could ensure that he gets the kind of education and training that will make him an asset to your House. And who better to be the patrons of such an undertaking than a Haldane king and queen, who share the powers and the consequences of those powers."

"You're speaking of me and Araxie," Kelson whispered, sensing where this was heading.

Morgan nodded. "Rothana got that part of the equation exactly right, when she chose Araxie for you—and I'll grant you that, in part, you and Rothana could have carried out some of this work, if things had been different. But she mustn't marry you, Kelson—and not alone because of Albin. She's Deryni, and she will need all her focus to gather the best Deryni minds to provide the foundation for such an enterprise. And you, with a functioning Haldane queen at your side, must provide the atmosphere in which such an enterprise may flourish—and Haldane heirs, properly educated in their heritage, to carry on your work."

Kelson slowly breathed out in a long, slow sigh, reluctantly accepting all that Morgan had said, already considering ways to implement this greater vision—and realizing, as he did so, that in letting go of part of his dream, by stepping back from marriage with Rothana, he was taking up an even greater dream, of which Araxie Haldane was an increasingly intriguing part.

"You've offered me a great deal to think about," he said slowly, glancing toward the door as footsteps approached in the corridor outside. "I'll want to explore this further, once we've returned to Rhemuth. Meanwhile, it's enough, for now, that I'll need to explain myself when we show up unexpectedly." He rose as Azim came into the room, another sheaf of maps tucked under one arm. "Is all well?" he asked.

Azim smiled faintly. "I was about to ask the same of you, but yes, all is well. Have you yet been to Rhemuth?"

Kelson shook his head. "I've only just returned from Araxie. We'll go now." He motioned Morgan toward the adjacent room. "Will you tell Létald where I've gone? It *is* his Portal, after all."

"True enough," Azim agreed. "Courtesy is prudent among magicians." He cocked his head. "You have not said whether I should be concerned for my most promising pupil."

"Araxie?" Kelson smiled sheepishly as Morgan slipped ahead of him into the Portal chamber. "I think that Haldane blood, coupled with your training, has yielded me a formidable consort—and I thank you. I don't think any of us have cause for worry on that count."

So saying, and before Azim could pursue the point, he went on into the room where the Portal lay. Morgan was already waiting on the Portal square, and set his hand on Kelson's shoulder as the king moved in to stand beside him.

"Which Portal?" he asked. "The library, I presume?"

Kelson nodded. "You take us through."

He closed his eyes and let his shields fall before Morgan's psychic embrace, surrendering control to the man who had become as much a father to him as his own had ever been. Thus enfolded, he was but faintly aware when Morgan reached out to bend the energies. The jump was smooth, but he was not expecting what awaited them at the other end.

CHAPTER TWENTY-FOUR

*Thy father and thy mother shall be glad, and she that
bare thee shall rejoice.*

Proverbs 23:25

*J*ehana of Rhemuth gave a little gasp as two dark-cloaked figures suddenly
materialized in the auxiliary library at Rhemuth. Seated in the window
embrasure but a few yards away, Father Nivard beside her and Barrett de Laney
opposite them, she had been listening spellbound as the two men, one very young
and one very old, engaged in passionate debate over shades of meaning in an
ancient poem's translation—a Deryni poem.

Such colloquia had been going on for the past week, nearly every night. She
could not rightly say how John Nivard had managed to make her understand,
where so many others had failed, that acknowledging and learning of her birthright
was not only permissible but laudable. Perhaps it came of her fascination with Barrett: more than old enough to be her father, but for whom she soon had found herself feeling strangely un-daughterly emotions. Indeed, when she learned that
Barrett came regularly to tutor Father Nivard, she had found herself contriving all
manner of excuses to be present.

She had told herself she was being foolish—had even confessed her foolish-
ness to Nivard—who had laughed gently and delightedly and assured her that
affection knew no difference of years.

"You are welcome to join us, if you wish," he said. "We meet here most
evenings. I know he would be glad of another pupil."

"He—does not work magic with you, does he?" she had asked—though she still would have come.

"No, mostly we read the old texts—and argue about them!" Nivard had said with a chuckle. "Since I work closely with the king, your son, Bishop Arilan has suggested that I not work mind to mind with—a Deryni from outside the king's counsels. He and Bishop Duncan have been my teachers of late, and occasionally Duke Alaric. There is no question regarding Barrett himself, of course," he added, "but as part of the king's household, I do have access to information that should not go outside it. You do appreciate that, I hope."

She did, indeed; and the reassurance had answered any lingering hesitation she might have had about further contact with the intriguing Barrett, who was blind yet not blind, and had given up his sight to save the lives of children. She had not yet summoned the courage to ask Barrett directly about the children—and Nivard did not know any of the details—but that snippet of information continued to intrigue her.

Thereafter, she had joined Nivard and Barrett almost nightly, often very nearly until dawn—which came early in full summer. And a few days before, when the sun had surprised them still in the midst of the night's disputation, Nivard had called a halt to offer up Matins with them, there in the slanting golden sunrise, and given them Holy Communion from a little pyx he had brought, laying out the elements upon her veil, spread upon the altar of the Portal square. Barrett had lit a single candle with handfire; and the golden glory of Nivard's Deryni aura had flared around him as he reverently gave each of them the sacred Body of Christ. She had wept with the beauty of it—and had shed yet another of her fears for the wonder of discovery.

Dawn was still far distant when Kelson suddenly appeared on the library Portal, Morgan at his side. Nivard rose immediately at the arrival of the newcomers, Jehana somewhat more slowly, both relieved and mortified. Her son's presence, and on the night following the Torenthi investiture, meant that he had survived—though his presence might bode something amiss regarding specifics; but the fact that he was accompanied by Morgan caused her a pang of acute embarrassment over the way she had behaved toward him for so many years. The pair looked equally surprised to see her there.

"Mother?" Kelson said, stiffening at the sight of Barrett, across from his mother and Nivard.

Barrett, too, had risen, hugging to his breast the scroll from which he and the young priest had been translating.

"Welcome home, Sire," he said easily. "I have been graced with another pupil during Your Majesty's absence. Your presence reassures me that you came to no ill in Torenthály, but I hope it does not portend unwanted complications."

So matter-of-fact a manner disarmed Jehana's tension, and she came down out of the window embrasure to throw her arms around Kelson, almost limp with relief as she hugged him to her, feeling against her cheek the smooth ripple of her prayer beads on his chest. He had remembered!

"There were complications," Morgan confirmed, as Kelson comforted his mother, "but for the most part, the outcome was favorable." He glanced past Kelson and Jehana at Nivard, who only smiled faintly and rolled his eyes, clearly in reference to Jehana. Kelson, meanwhile, was drawing back from his mother, wiping glad tears from her cheeks with a callused thumb. Only then did it register that she was not wearing her customary white robes, but a gown of forest green, with her auburn hair plaited in a long braid over one shoulder. She looked years younger than when he last had seen her, hardly a fortnight before. What—or who—had made her take up her life again, and put aside her widow's weeds? Surely not the young priest, who was hardly older than himself.

"My son—I worried so!" she whispered.

"And prayed, I'm sure," he said, with a touch to the beads around his neck, "which no doubt gave me strength. I'm fine—and Liam is fine. He did wonderfully. And Count Mátyás saved the day for all of us. His brothers had plotted to betray Liam during the transfer of power, but Mátyás managed to insert me into the investing party. It's a very long story, but Mahael is dead. Unfortunately, Teymuraz escaped. That's the only part of the day that didn't go exactly according to plan. Liam is now our ally, along with Mátyás, and there will be a lasting peace with Torenth."

Jehana was laughing through her tears as she listened; Nivard looked very pleased. Barrett's hairless head was bowed over his scroll, nodding slowly, a faint smile on his lips.

"Well done, indeed, Sire," he murmured. "This is news for much rejoicing. Shall I leave you now?"

Kelson drew his mother into the circle of his arm, glancing at Morgan and then at Nivard. Barrett's reaction suggested that he had not known of the day's outcome—which meant that the Camberian Council, at least as a body, probably did not know. Arilan and Azim did, of course, having been present, but Kelson had no idea how information was transmitted among the members of the Council—though Azim had told him others would be there. Much as the Council were a frequent source of annoyance to him, it was in everyone's best interests if they learned of this as soon as possible.

"You may leave if you wish, my lord," he said. "I apologize if I interrupted your tutorial. But perhaps there are others with whom you will wish to share this news from Torenth."

Barrett raised the emerald eyes, appearing to look right at Kelson.

"Thank you, Sire." He handed the scroll to Nivard with a nod, then took the young priest's arm to steady him as he moved forward and stepped down from the window embrasure, though he moved unerringly toward the Portal square as Morgan backed off and Kelson and Jehana moved aside.

"I bid you good night, Sire, my lady," he murmured as he stepped onto the square—and at once disappeared.

To Kelson's surprise, his mother hardly blinked. Quite illogically, he found himself wondering whether the elderly scholar could possibly be responsible for her transformation. Still amazed, he turned his gaze back to Nivard.

"Father, would you please go and fetch Nigel and Aunt Meraude—and Rory," he said. "I have some additional news that will concern all of them."

Nivard laid his scroll on one of the seats with a nod of agreement and departed immediately through the Veiled doorway. Morgan, with an appraising glance at Kelson, moved to follow.

"I'll wait in the next room," he said, just before he, too, ducked through the Veil and disappeared.

As soon as he had gone, Jehana turned to hug Kelson again, laying her head against his shoulder, now trembling a little.

"Darling, I've been so foolish, all these years. This past fortnight has been— quite indescribable. I don't even know where to begin!"

"Then, let's wait until we have more time," he said, hardly able to believe his ears. "I'm delighted, I can assure you, but you were the last person I expected to see here with Father Nivard and Barrett. I have other news for you, however, that I think—I hope—will please you even more than your news pleases me," he went on, as she drew away far enough to look up at him in question. "Mother, I've finally chosen a bride."

Joy mingled with disbelief and confusion on her upturned face.

"You've . . . chosen . . . Well, who *is* it?" she blurted, searching his eyes.

"Cousin Araxie."

She blinked at him, hardly able to take it in.

"But—wasn't she going to—"

"—marry Cuan of Howicce," he finished for her, grinning. "No, she isn't! Good Lord, if you knew how many times I've gotten that reaction!" He shook his head as he hugged her close again. "I like her very much, Mother. It was Rothana who suggested the match, just before I left for Torenth—practically *ordered* it, actually—but I find myself having to admit that we do have a great deal in common. Araxie and I discussed it when I stopped at the Ile, on the way to Torenth, and Bishop Arilan witnessed a private betrothal, with only her family and Dhugal and Morgan present. Rothana—apparently has been encouraging this for some time. The alleged relationship with Cuan has never been anything but a blind; he's in love with his cousin Gwenlian."

She was shaking her head in wonder as she gazed at him, her hands resting on his arms.

"Kelson . . . I hardly know what to say. Araxie is a darling girl, but I—know how much you cared for—for Rothana. . . ."

"And still care for her, deeply," he murmured, ducking his head. "But I've had to do some hard thinking in the past few weeks. Something that Richenda said, about Rothana always being meant for the religious life after all—and you know she's been with the Servants of Saint Camber for the past three years.

"Now she means to found a school, to see that our people are trained to the responsible use of their powers—and I'm going to give her a site here in Rhemuth for it, though she doesn't know that yet. It's ignorance that has caused so many of the problems between humans and Deryni—not the magic. Somehow I feel that I can say that to you now. Mother, what happened while I was away? To see you with Father Nivard and Barrett . . . with Deryni . . ."

Jehana ducked her head shyly, a flustered smile on her lips. "I—don't think there's time to tell you right now, son," she whispered.

"I think you might show me . . . ," he ventured, lifting her chin to gaze into the green eyes.

She had the grace to blush, shaking her head gently, but her gaze did not shrink from his. "Not yet. I'm learning, but I'm not ready for that."

"Then I won't press you," he said with a happy sigh, hugging her close again. "Meanwhile, you should know that I'll be bringing Araxie and Richelle and Aunt Sivorn here in the morning—and the rest of their family. There were—a few complications, because of the escape of Count Teymuraz. Which reminds me: With Sivorn to help, do you think that you and she and Aunt Meraude can manage to put together three weddings?"

"*Three?*" She drew back to look at him in blank astonishment.

"Well, yes." Smiling, he took her hand through the crook of his arm and led her up into the window embrasure to sit, briefly acquainting her with the developments regarding Rory and Noelie.

"The Carthmoor succession, and Albin's place in it, is the only remaining sticky point in *that* arrangement," he said in conclusion. "But I hope, in light of all the other developments, that Nigel will come around now."

"Ah." A grin came upon her face, the likes of which Kelson had not seen in years. "Well, I can tell you that Meraude and I managed to lay some groundwork for *that*, while you were gone."

"*Have* you?" he replied.

But the sound of voices in the next room precluded further exploration of that topic for the moment, since almost at once, Nivard poked his head through the Veil with a nod of apology.

"They're here, Sire," he said cheerfully. "Do you wish to come out, or shall I bring them in here?"

"We'll come out," Kelson said, rising to take Jehana's hand. "Perhaps you could keep watch here, by the Portal, in case someone comes through early."

"Of course."

The reunion with Nigel, Meraude, and Rory was ebullient; their reaction, when he linked with Nigel and Rory, a mixture of awed disbelief and relief.

"We'll be bringing the ladies through before first light," he said, reverting to speech for Meraude's benefit. Jehana had gone to her while Kelson briefed the two Haldanes, whispering excitedly, and Meraude looked astonished. "For now, I've told them they may bring only what they can carry. Morgan's *Rhafallia* will be sailing at dawn, and will bring what's ready now—they'll stop at Coroth to collect his family—and Létald's ship will follow with the rest in about three days, as soon as they arrive from Beldour.

"But I'd like to see the ladies settled in their quarters before the castle starts stirring. Though I'm feeling bold enough to bring them through the Portal—because I have little choice, under the circumstances—I'd rather not call attention to the way they arrived."

He grinned as he glanced back at Nigel, who still looked a little stunned.

"We'll discuss details when I come back," Kelson went on. "For now, once we get the ladies settled, I want you to convene a special meeting of the privy council at noon. Don't tell them why; don't even tell them I'll be there."

Nigel nodded.

"And Aunt Meraude, Nigel will explain what I've told him and Rory. I know it's a lot to take in, for all of you, but today's events have helped me understand how I've been needlessly crippling myself in several areas. If our new allies in Torenth have learned from us, we've learned equally from them. I think a lot of things are about to change—and for once, it's for the better."

He glanced at Morgan, who had been listening quietly against the door.

"Shall we?"

CHAPTER TWENTY-FIVE

*Then shall ye do unto him, as he had thought to do
unto his brother: so shalt thou put the evil away from
among you.*

Deuteronomy 19:19

*T*hey brought Araxie and her family through in the next hour, assisted by
Azim and Létald himself, passing them through the Veiled doorway and
lodging them in the state apartments already set aside for their expected arrival in
a week's time. In that predawn hour, their passage aroused only passing notice by
the occasional guard nearing the end of his watch and a few sleepy servants
already stirring to draw water and light fires for the day. Accompanied only by
Father Nivard, each of them cloaked and carrying a bundle—and with the four
wide-eyed half-siblings of Araxie and Richelle in the party, all of them under
ten—the new arrivals were assumed to be, at most, another contingent of
Mearan visitors arriving early for the wedding in a fortnight's time.

Kelson himself remained out of sight in the library, lest his own early arrival
invite comment before he had met with his council. He sent Rory to fetch Duncan. Morgan and Dhugal he sent after Létald, with instructions to continue on to
Beldour, report to Liam and Mátyás, and oversee the departure of the remaining
Gwynedd contingent to return home. They would return in time for the council
meeting at noon. When they had gone, only Azim remained with the king in the
little library annex.

"I shall return to Horthánthy and then to Beldour, in case my assistance is
needed in either location," Azim said to Kelson, watching him closely. "If I may, I

shall share the location of this Portal with Mátyás and Liam-Lajos; a direct link to you would be helpful."

Kelson nodded. "Agreed. Especially in these next days and weeks, communication will be vital. I shall make certain someone is always nearby. Perhaps Father Nivard will not mind sleeping in the library for the next few weeks."

"A prudent measure. There are many of Deryni blood at Létald's court, of varying degrees of competence, so it may be that Mahael and Teymuraz had agents there. If so, it is likely that our passage will have been remarked, even if they are not yet aware what happened today in Beldour. When I have consulted with Létald, I shall go on to Beldour to assist Morgan and the others in making certain that the Tralian ships depart immediately for home. Mátyás has promised to have his weather-workers conjure a fair wind to speed them to Horthánthy."

"How long will that take? The journey, not the conjuring."

"Perhaps three days, if they sail by night as well as by day. Meanwhile, we shall see if Teymuraz makes an appearance at the Ile."

"And if he does?"

Azim's black eyes narrowed. "Let us simply say that a very dim view will have been taken of his actions today, and he will be dealt with."

"By the Council?" Kelson asked.

Azim merely looked at him.

"What if he *doesn't* go to the Ile?" Kelson persisted.

Azim glanced away briefly, his gaze flicking over the outline of the Portal.

"Be assured that wherever he *does* surface, he shall find himself a pariah," he said softly. "Beyond that, I beg you not to ask."

Despite his absolute trust in Azim, Kelson found himself suppressing a shiver.

"Very well," he said. "I *shall* ask whether you have any further recommendations regarding *my* immediate actions, however."

"You have a marriage contract to negotiate between Rory and the Ramsay girl," Azim replied with a faint smile. "Between that and the practical considerations for accommodating *two* Mearan weddings, you will have your hands quite full. And while there will be no opposition to your own marriage, there are still formal documents to be drawn up, in addition to all the physical preparations for a royal wedding and the coronation of a consort—which must be done privily, until the others have been accomplished. Fortunately, you will find that many of the arrangements for the first celebration can be carried over for the second."

Kelson found himself smiling faintly. "You make the Mearan weddings sound like a dress rehearsal for my own."

Azim inclined his head in agreement. "In a sense, they are. And incidentally, the second Mearan match is a brilliant one, provided the Mearan parents raise no undue opposition. It is one that even the Council had not considered. They—also had not anticipated the match now in place between yourself and your cousin," he added, eyeing Kelson closely. "As her mentor, who cares greatly for her happiness, dare I hope that closer reacquaintance is proving more positive than you had expected?"

Thus phrased, the question demanded no commitment beyond what Kelson had already made—to give his earnest efforts to make the marriage work on a human level as well as a political one—but it underlined his growing recognition that he was, indeed, coming to care for Araxie.

"Let us simply say," he replied, "that I am increasingly confident that she will make a worthy queen. As for other aspects of our relationship—" He made himself draw a deep breath and let it out. "Azim, I can honestly say that only time will tell."

A little later, back at the summer palace of Létald Hort of Orsal, one whose first loyalties lay firmly elsewhere than with the master of that place watched unremarked from amid the guard detail outside Létald's council chamber—and drew smartly to attention in some surprise as the door opened, just at dawn, and Létald emerged with only his chamberlain, looking grim. In the glimpse the watcher managed just before the door closed, he could see no one else inside—and yet the Orsal's sister, along with her husband and children, had accompanied him there not an hour before, along with several servants carrying largish satchels. Despite the balmy summer night, all of the Lady Sivorn's family wore voluminous cloaks. The servants had not stayed long; but no one else had come out.

It was suspicious enough that Iddin de Vesca, a middle-ranking officer of the guard, contrived not to be among those who fell in to escort Létald back to his quarters, for he knew the chances of gaining any further information from Létald himself were extremely unlikely. The chamberlain, Vasilly Dimitriades, headed off in another direction, but he was no better prospect. Both men had Deryni blood, as did Iddin himself.

So he must be more resourceful. Certain risks were involved, but Iddin was well paid to take certain risks. As soon as the chamberlain had disappeared from sight and Létald and his guards had rounded the bend at the other end of the corridor, and the silence of the early morning had settled once again in that part of the palace, Iddin eased casually nearer the companion left behind: a stolid older man called Luric.

"A great deal of activity for so early in the morning," Iddin remarked.

"Aye," Luric agreed, hitching absently at his sword-belt. "I wonder what that was all about?"

Iddin did not give him time to speculate further, only seizing his wrist and exerting Deryni control, opening the door with his other hand as he pulled the compliant Luric into the room. He had primed the man to obey him, more than a year before, and to remember nothing of such encounters.

"Stay and guard the door," Iddin murmured, scanning the room.

It was, indeed, empty. And there appeared to be no other door out. He had never been in the council chamber before—indeed, Létald tried to avoid any serious work of government during the summer months, when he was in residence at Horthánthy—but Iddin knew what he had seen—and what might be one way of explaining it.

Drawing breath to trigger a centering and focus of his perceptions, he began circling the room to the left, casting out with his mind for another exit—and found evidence of a hidden door in the light wood panelling halfway along the left side of the room.

Running his hands over that section of the panelling, he searched for the outlines of the door, for what held it closed. The hidden lock yielded easily to his powers—merely a conventional latch behind an ornamental flap, worked by a key . . . or his mind.

He pushed gently at the door after shifting the wards in the lock. The small room beyond smelled of candle grease and damp. And beneath his feet, as he stepped farther in, he came up short against the distinctive tingle of a Portal—a recently active Portal.

Success at last! Mahael had told him that there must be a Portal here at Horthánthy, and this was the second summer Iddin had spent looking for it. He was well aware that Deryni blood ran deep in the von Horthy line, though they little used their powers save for shielding and Truth-Reading—and for this Portal, it now appeared.

He sank briefly to a crouch and laid his hands upon it long enough to capture its location, sought in vain for some trace of transit to other Portals, then rose and eased back out of the little chamber, closing the hidden door behind him and mentally resetting the lock. Luric was still listening at the door to the corridor, one ear pressed to the wood, and Iddin glided to him soundlessly to touch his wrist in command.

"Come with me," he said softly.

A few minutes later, after sending someone else to guard the council chamber, he had reached his quarters and had a plan for how best to proceed. He did not know where the Orsal had sent members of his family, or why, but the very fact that he had done so—and by what means—would be of great interest to his masters, as would the location of the Portal itself.

Drawing Luric inside, he closed the door and bade his unwitting accomplice sit beside him on the narrow cot. Keeping the man's wrist in his grasp, he closed his eyes and began centering, drawing Luric into trance with him, preparing to tap the other's energies to do what he must do.

Very shortly, he had achieved the desired level of focus. Reaching out with his mind, he set the Call. Though Mahael had never failed to respond within a few minutes, if only to advise of a delay, this time Iddin could detect nary a ripple. When, after a while longer, Iddin still had not made contact with Mahael, he shifted his Call to the next brother, Teymuraz.

The response was not immediate, but it came, strong and focused, somehow different from what Iddin had ever experienced with Teymuraz before.

I could not reach Mahael, Iddin sent. *I have news from Horthánthy. I have discovered a Portal at last—and Létald appears to have used it to send or take his sister and her family elsewhere.*

Indeed, came Teymuraz's reply. *Are you aware of what has happened?*

Iddin sent only a note of query.

You could not reach Mahael because he is dead—

What?

Defeated during killijálay, *with the connivance of my other dear brother and the King of Gwynedd,* came Teymuraz's thought, so potent that Iddin flinched from its power. *He then was executed by impalement, by order of our treacherous nephew—who now wields the full might of Furstán. I have only barely escaped.*

But—why would Létald—

That is what you must discover, came Teymuraz's sharp order. *He knows the circumstances of Mahael's death, and of my own flight from Torenthály. His very presence at the Ile, so quickly after, makes it likely that he has rightly guessed that I would act to disrupt the Mearan alliance planned by the Haldane. I had hoped to seize or kill the Haldane princesses.*

Then, do not come here! Iddin retorted. *That will be the reason he has sent them elsewhere. I know not what is planned, but I have never sensed such focus in Létald.*

Small wonder, Teymuraz replied, *for he will have allied with Mátyás and Liam-Lajos and the King of Gwynedd. Find out what you can—where the women have been taken. It may be that the Haldane has become brave enough to flex his powers, to take them to Rhemuth itself. We have long known that there are Portals there, though not their locations. Meanwhile, I shall adjust my own intentions.*

*L*ater that morning, after bringing Duncan up to date on all that had occurred, Kelson settled into a preliminary meeting with Nigel and Rory to discuss Mearan strategies, for they must present a united front when the full council met at noon.

"I don't really expect too much consternation at the manner of your arrival," Nigel said, "especially when they've heard your news. However, I must remind you that the Mearans are expected within a few days. They won't expect to find Richelle and her family already here. The wedding ship from Tralia wasn't originally expected to arrive for nearly a fortnight—and neither were you."

"The weather was fine, so they came early," Kelson said, without hesitation. "Richelle was eager to see her bridegroom."

Duncan nodded approvingly.

"Plausible—though it doesn't explain *your* presence."

"Hopefully, they won't think to ask," Kelson replied. "And we'll keep them too busy to think too much about it. Now, as to *your* part in all these matrimonial machinations—" He glanced at Rory, who looked vaguely anxious. "After I've told the council about Araxie, that's the perfect lead-in to announce *your* intentions—unless, of course, you're having second thoughts."

"Oh, no! I mean—well—"

"You *are* having second thoughts?" Kelson said lightly. "Rory, if you don't marry Noelie, I'm going to have to contend with her mother, when she learns I'm marrying someone else."

"I do want to marry her! It's just that—I'm not completely certain she'll have me, if I ask her." He twisted nervously at his signet ring. "What if I misread her interest? We never dared to speak of it, when she was here last summer—and since you asked me not to write to her . . ."

As his voice trailed off, Kelson rolled his eyes and sighed.

"*Now* you tell me. Well, at least I can reassure you on that count. Mind you, this is all second- and third-hand, but I have it from Araxie—who had it from her sister, who had it from Brecon—that *his* sister is . . . quite fond of you. . . ." He grinned as Rory closed his eyes and exhaled in a heavy sigh of relief.

"I also gather that her father dotes on his only daughter, and can deny her nothing. As we knew all along, her mother will be the sticking point. She had her heart set on a king for her daughter, and now she'll have to settle for *you*."

He gave Rory a playful dunt in the arm as he said it, and Nigel allowed himself a snort.

"The girl will do better than the mother did—not that Jolyon Ramsay isn't a decent man," the duke said. "Are the pair of you aware that she might have been either of your mothers?" he asked, to looks of surprise from both of them.

"Oh, yes. She was much at court before either Brion or I married—daughter of a Fallonese baron, but also, through her mother, a cousin of the then Hort of Orsal, Létald's father. Very ambitious—and quite a beauty she was, in those days.

She's still a handsome woman. The von Horthy blood would have made her a marginally suitable royal bride.

"But Brion married Jehana, and I married Meraude, so Oksana didn't get to be a queen *or* a royal duchess. Eventually she married Sir Jolyon Ramsay, the great-grandson of Magrette of Meara, who was the youngest sister of your great-grandmother Roisian, Malcolm Haldane's queen. If Magrette had been the eldest, it would have been she who married Malcolm—and a great deal would be different. For that matter, a great deal would have been different if Oksana had married Brion or me—but she didn't. Still, I'm sure she was hoping that, since she never got to be Queen of Gwynedd, her daughter might have done."

"You never told me any of this," Kelson said.

Nigel shrugged. "Gentlemen don't talk about the ladies in their past—and besides, once I set eyes on Meraude, there *were* no other contenders, so far as I was concerned."

"But if Oksana would have married the king's brother," Kelson said, "don't you think she might settle for having her daughter marry the king's first cousin?"

Nigel broke into a broad grin. "That's where a conspiracy between Noelie and her father may carry the day," he said. "By all reports, Oksana's marriage with Jolyon has been a contented one. If she can be persuaded that it would be a love match between Noelie and Rory *before* she discovers that you intend to marry Araxie, I think that might make all the difference. Oksana Ramsay is ambitious, but she's also quite a pragmatic woman—as you probably gathered during our earlier negotiations."

"That's true enough," Kelson agreed, well recalling the nitpicking over fine points of the marriage contract between Brecon and Richelle.

"Remember that the Ramsays have no wealth, and precious little land," Nigel continued. "The family fortunes will improve considerably with Brecon's marriage. However, balancing the distant possibility of marrying her daughter to a king, against the certainty of a match with a prince, I expect she'd rather see her daughter happily married to a prince than possibly end up with some pimply-faced local sprat for a son-in-law, with no prospects—and there aren't many princes available for the daughter of a simple knight. There is also the very real financial consideration that a double wedding here and now, with us bearing the bulk of the expense for all the royal trappings, will be very attractive."

Kelson only nodded, greatly heartened by Nigel's apparent confidence that the Mearan negotiations would be far less daunting than previously expected. He considered raising the question of Albin, now that Nigel seemed committed to Rory's match with Meara, but decided not to press his luck. First he must deal with his council, hoping that any uneasiness over his manner of return would be tempered by news of the success of his mission in Torenth and of his plans, at last, to marry.

*A*n hour later, behind closed doors, he had briefed his council on the circumstances of Liam's investiture the day before, advised them of possible eventual repercussions from Teymuraz—and announced his betrothal to his cousin Araxie Haldane.

"And no, she never intended to marry Prince Cuan of Howicce; he wants to marry his cousin Gwenlian," Kelson said, "so none of you need to make that comment. It appears that my future queen is well able to keep close counsel and carry out strategic negotiations with little help from anyone else."

Jaws dropped and smiles broke out among those who had not known. Nigel looked as pleased as if he had had some part in it; Jehana briefly closed her eyes in silent thanksgiving that it really was true. She was wearing a rose-colored gown this morning, her veil worked with a broad band of gold embroidery along the edges, and Kelson thought she had not looked so well since his father died. Morgan and Dhugal, returned from Beldour not an hour before, had reported that all was well with Liam and Mátyás, and flanked Kelson in silent support as he took in the reactions of his most trusted councillors. To his relief, both Duke Ewan and the two archbishops, sitting near Duncan, had adjusted quickly to the circumstances of his return via Portal.

"This is welcome news, indeed, Sire!" old Archbishop Bradene said. "All Gwynedd will rejoice to see a queen at your side at last!"

Duke Ewan was shaking his head in pleased disbelief, white teeth grinning in his grey-streaked beard. "Duke Richard's daughter. Who would have guessed? Congratulations, Sire. Claibourne wishes you every happiness!"

"You're aware, I'm sure, Sire, that a dispensation will be required," said Archbishop Cardiel, smiling, "but the degree of consanguinity is very slight. I suspect that a friendly bishop or two can be found to speed matters along—perhaps a few at this very table. And I assume that you will wish to delay any public announcement until after the Princess Richelle's wedding to Brecon Ramsay?"

Kelson glanced at Rory and contained a small smile. "Actually, we have hopes of yet another wedding—and I must ask that what I am about to tell you not go beyond these walls until negotiations can be completed, for reasons which will quickly become apparent. Many of you were urging me to make a match with Brecon's sister, Noelie. Obviously, that is not now an option."

"Good God, no!" old Ewan said, pursing his lips. "And her mother won't like *that*."

"I have no doubt that the Lady Oksana's initial reaction will be one of disappointment," Kelson replied, in droll understatement. "Happily—and Oksana will not have been aware of this, as I myself was unaware, until shortly before I left for Torenth—her daughter's heart was already inclined toward someone else, whose suit satisfies all the sound political reasons that would have made her a suitable consort for me, and will also answer both their hearts. It is my hope that Noelie's parents may be persuaded to give her hand in marriage to my cousin Rory."

This new announcement brought its own flurry of pleased commentary among Ewan and the two archbishops.

"To spare any possible embarrassment for the Ramsay family, due to higher aspirations," Kelson went on, "I intend to refrain from making public announcement of my own betrothal until both marriages have taken place, and in a manner that leaves no doubt that the marriage of Noelie with Rory is, indeed, a preference of the heart. It has been suggested that a double wedding would be appropriate—and would also appeal to the financial considerations of the Mearans, since both couples could be fêted at the wedding feast already planned for that night in honor of Brecon and Richelle. I would then plan to make my announcement at the end of the evening's festivities," he added, "which I'm certain will please all of Gwynedd."

"And, will it please the king?" Cardiel asked softly.

A silence fell on the room as the king stiffened slightly and then breathed out in a long sigh.

"I believe it will," he said, a little surprised that he was beginning to believe that. "I confess that, when I first approached my cousin on this matter, it was because that was what Rothana wanted, but now—" He allowed himself a faint smile.

"Fortunately, no great speculation will attach to the presence at court of the sister of the bride—especially since everyone seems convinced she's going to marry Prince Cuan," he added, with a wry grin. "We have known one another from childhood, and both have happy memories of those long-ago days. Meanwhile, I hope that the diversion of her sister's wedding—and that of Rory and Noelie—will give us opportunity to reacquaint ourselves as adults. I assure all of you that I am content enough; and I have no doubt whatever that the Princess Araxie will make an exceedingly worthy Queen of Gwynedd."

CHAPTER TWENTY-SIX

All these were honoured in their generations, and were
the glory of their times.

Ecclesiasticus 44:7

*A*t that same hour, the Camberian Council was meeting beneath the
faceted dome of their council chamber high in the mountains of Rhendall. It had taken more time than usual to assemble them, for the aftermath of the
Torenthi investiture the previous day was but one of the matters requiring the
Council's concern. The Lady Vivienne, whose service to the Council spanned
nearly half a century, had died peacefully in the arms of her eldest son during the
early morning hours, well into her seventy-sixth year, surrounded by dozens of
grandchildren and great-grandchildren and attended by the physician Laran ap
Pardyce, close friend of a lifetime.

Laran looked tired but also relieved, and had gently laid a single white rose
beside the white wand of office marking Vivienne's empty place at the great
octagonal table, before taking his own seat next to Barrett. Arilan and Azim, to
either side of Vivienne's empty chair, exchanged troubled glances after Laran had
finished telling of her final moments. Her passing had been gentle, but an era had
also passed.

"The funeral will be in two days' time," Laran said, in summation. "Count
Tibal, her eldest son, will lead the mourners. She's to be buried beside her hus-
band and a stillborn daughter in the family vault at Alta Jorda. Tibal will make his
Portal accessible to those who wish to attend."

"I shall be there," Sofiana declared. "I had made my farewells to Vivienne herself, of course, but I will wish to pay my respects to the family. Several of Tibal's children and grandchildren have trained at my court, over the years."

Azim also inclined his head. "I shall attend as well, on behalf of the Knights of the Anvil. She was ever a benefactress of our company."

"Perhaps they might provide pallbearers," Barrett said a little numbly. "I well remember the funeral of Michon de Courcy—dear God, has it really been more than thirty years ago? There could be no public display for the funeral itself, of course, else the de Courcys' Deryni blood would have been betrayed. But the interment that night, in the vaults at Valla de Courcy, was all that it should have been for a man whose family has sacrificed so much for our people.

"Six vowed Knights of the Anvil carried him to his rest, Azim, all of them arrayed in the full panoply of your Order—and none of them laid a hand on the coffin. He floated on a catafalque of golden fire. I could see it even without these poor, blinded eyes—as if the very angels had come to sing Michon home." Tears glistened in those eyes. "I shall never forget it—or Michon. Were it not for him . . ."

Arilan closed his eyes, well remembering his brother's grief the day word came of Michon's death, a full week after the burial. He himself had been too young to study with the great mage, but Jamyl Arilan had known Michon well, and had grieved for weeks, and had rarely spoken of him thereafter. Only after Jamyl's own death had his brother learned the significance of the bond the two had shared.

"We all owe much to Michon," Laran said softly, recalling all of them from their memories. "We and every other Deryni whose life he touched."

"We must not dwell on the past, when the future requires our attention," Azim said quietly. "Neither Michon nor Vivienne would wish it. I have already been in contact with my Order, and arrangements are being made for a suitable tribute.

"Meanwhile, however, the needs of this company must be considered," he went on. "Filling Vivienne's actual seat on the Council will require careful thought, especially in light of recent developments in Torenth, but a new co-adjutor must be selected more immediately, from among our present number. I submit that the Lady Sofiana is the only choice for that office—if she is willing."

Every face turned immediately in her direction, each with instinctive acknowledgment and agreement writ upon it, for Sofiana was among the most powerful and skilled Deryni to sit upon the Council in recent memory—the only successor really to be considered, once it became clear that Vivienne was in her final illness.

Sofiana herself bowed her head briefly, then lifted her eyes to them.

"*Volo*," she said quietly. I am willing.

Barrett dashed the tears from his eyes with the back of a graceful hand and gave her a formal nod. "I welcome my sister," he said. "Installation shall follow the funeral formalities at Alta Jorda." He lifted his sightless gaze on the rest of them, the emerald eyes still bright.

"That having been resolved, I think we must move on to other business," he went on. "Our sister's passing is not unexpected; merely accomplished.

"As has also been accomplished, and as Azim can confirm, King Kelson has returned to Rhemuth by Portal, bringing along his Haldane cousins from Horthánthy. There was concern lest Teymuraz attempt to interfere with the marriage arrangements presently moving forward. This marks a significant alteration in the king's stance regarding open use of his powers—for his council, at least, obviously will know that he has done this."

Sofiana glanced across at Arilan, already beginning to take up her function as a co-adjutor. "How will Kelson's council react to this news, Denis?"

Arilan shrugged. "I believe they will accept it, given the king's great success at Torenthály—and the news that he intends to wed at last. The humans who regularly advise him are comfortable enough with the few known to be Deryni—Morgan, Dhugal, Duncan McLain, and myself. It is also helpful that both archbishops have given their guarded support of us by making no official note that the changes in the Laws of Ramos already apply to two serving bishops sitting with them on the king's council. I would venture to guess that considerations of magic will be largely overshadowed by rejoicing at the king's marriage plans."

"Yes—to another Haldane," Laran said uneasily. "If Vivienne were already in her grave, she would turn over in it."

"Ah, yes, the double-Haldane match she feared," Azim said. "But let us not forget that Deryni blood also runs in Araxie Haldane's veins, friend Laran. Nor should you discount the fact that no one present, save myself, has ever worked with the lady—whose merits are considerable, I assure you. Indeed, only Denis has even met her—and that, only briefly."

"Indeed," Barrett agreed. "And remember that the king likewise carries Deryni blood. His mother is proving—quite an interesting pupil."

Laran merely rolled his eyes, being somewhat aware of Barrett's recent liaisons with Jehana of Gwynedd—if not altogether approving—but Arilan glanced sharply at Barrett. The others evidenced varying levels of somewhat surprised curiosity.

"You've been working with Queen Jehana?" Arilan asked Barrett.

"Oh, indeed—for most of a fortnight now," he murmured. "A most singular development. The queen discovered the connecting doorway into the library annex. Much to her surprise—and my own, I must confess—she also discovered that she could pass through the Veil that guards that doorway."

"Well, she *is* of the king's blood," Sion observed.

"She is, of course," Barrett agreed, "but no one thought she would ever make the attempt. As luck would have it, I was working in the annex at the time, sitting quietly in the window, so she did not notice me at first—though she did notice the Portal square in that chamber, and was greatly curious about it, thinking herself alone. She—ah—also displayed an unexpected ability to generate handfire before she realized I was there—much to her dismay. We were having rather a spirited conversation until Laran suddenly appeared on the Portal and frightened her away."

Barrett's fellow councillors were listening with varying degrees of amazement—apart from Laran, who folded his arms on his chest with a sour *humph!* Barrett appeared to be enjoying their discomfiture.

"Fortunately, she was brave enough to come back the next morning, and to make guarded inquiries of your Father Nivard," he added, with a nod toward Arilan, who had been Nivard's mentor. "He must certainly share in the credit for this apparent conversion on the road to Damascus. For the past week and more, thanks in no small part to the careful groundwork he had laid, the queen has returned to the library nightly for instruction regarding her Deryni heritage—and sometimes in the days as well. In this, young Nivard has been a particularly useful foil, by posing questions that I know will have occurred to the queen. Thus far, we have confined ourselves to cultural and theoretical topics, but I have reason to believe that there has been a . . . significant reappraisal on the queen's part."

Arilan looked utterly astonished, Laran somewhat grudgingly approving. Sofiana allowed herself a tiny smile. Sion merely raised a dubious eyebrow, knowing Jehana only by reputation.

"Can this be true?" Arilan murmured, though if it were not, making such a claim within the bosom of the Council would have been unthinkable.

Barrett inclined his head, his face unreadable. "It would not be appropriate for me to go into further detail at this time, but I have reason to be hopeful that we do have one less enemy—and perhaps even a new ally."

"I will believe *that* when I see it," Arilan muttered, shifting in his chair. "Unfortunately, that will not be soon, for I must return to Beldour, to keep watch on *those* allies. Létald's ships left for home early this morning, as you know. These next days and weeks will be a time of testing for Liam-Lajos, as he settles into his kingship and tries the mettle of his remaining advisors. I only hope that Count Mátyás is as loyal as he appears to be."

"Denis, Denis," Sofiana said with a musical chuckle, "what does it take to convince you of Mátyás's loyalty? Azim, tell him."

Azim smiled faintly as Arilan glanced at him.

"My lady Sofiana has been playing a dangerous game, this past year and more," he said, "but yesterday's outcome more than justified the risk. Mátyás came to our notice shortly after King Alroy's death, when his brothers called him to court to assist with the new regency for Liam-Lajos, for they knew that the young king liked and trusted his youngest uncle, and they hoped this might work to their advantage.

"What they had forgotten was that Mátyás was one of Sofiana's godsons, and had spent several years fostered at her father's court."

"It was a happy arrangement, for he is the same age as my second son," Sofiana said wistfully. "He was also a formidable pupil of the *ars magica*, even then— far more formidable than I felt his brothers should know. Had my father not died untimely, forcing me to take up my duties early, he might have stayed longer in Andelon. But my council recommended that the number of fosterlings at our court be reduced for the first few years of my reign, so Mátyás was sent to Lóránt of Truvorsk to complete his training.

"Fortunately, the good seeds had been sown on good ground," Sofiana went on. "When Mátyás learned that his brothers planned treason against their young nephew, he came to me for guidance. By then, I had become convinced that Kelson had no hidden agenda regarding Torenth; but overcoming two centuries of suspicion between the two kingdoms was more easily suggested than accepted. While, naturally, Mátyás would not agree to any measure that might further the interests of Gwynedd over those of Torenth, he was prepared to accept— depending upon circumstances—that it might be possible to trust King Kelson as an ally—which, as it happened, was well proven yesterday, to the joy of everyone save his traitorous brothers."

All Sofiana's listeners were nodding agreement by the time she finished, and she glanced aside at Azim before continuing.

"*I* had a hidden agenda, even if Kelson did not," she admitted, to varied reactions of surprise and consternation from the others on the Council, "and Azim has assisted me. I have come to know Mátyás very well in these past few years. The boy in whom I saw such potential has become exactly what I dared to dream: a young man of both power and conscience, in an unexpected position to make a difference.

"With that in mind, I have been grooming him for consideration as an eventual member of this body—not necessarily for Vivienne's seat, but it has been clear for some months that she must soon contemplate retirement. I did not expect that she would die in office."

"Are you proposing Mátyás as her replacement?" Laran muttered somewhat reproachfully. "The body is hardly cold."

"I apologize if this seems precipitous," Sofiana agreed. "Furthermore, I wish you to know that my assessment of the overall balance in these Eleven Kingdoms has somewhat altered, in light of yesterday's outcome. Not that I think any less of Mátyás; if anything, he has only risen in my estimation.

"But given the drastic reshuffling of alliances that will come with the death of Mahael, the outlawry of Teymuraz, and all the changes attendant upon the various Haldane marriages now being arranged, I now wonder whether we ought to look farther west for Vivienne's successor. I leave it to all of you to consider whether a seat again ought to be offered to Kelson—or whether some other might be better suited. But I wished you to know my thinking regarding Mátyás, and to be reassured on his behalf."

"This does, indeed, place matters in a somewhat different perspective," Arilan said thoughtfully. "How much does he know of the Council?"

"We have never spoken of it directly," Sofiana replied, "but, like most trained Deryni, he knows that we exist. Now that you have been reassured of his integrity, I hope you will take the opportunity to further your acquaintance with him. I believe he can become a most powerful ally in the cause of peace between your two kingdoms."

"I intend to do precisely that," Arilan agreed.

"I suggest, then," said Barrett, "that we adjourn now, so he may begin that task. Denis should not be long absent from Beldour, and it will take a few days to assess the situation there. In addition, there will be some significant domestic developments in the various kingdoms, because of the reshuffling of various nuptial arrangements—in Howicce and Llannedd as well as in Gwynedd and Meara," he added, with a nod toward Sion. "I suggest that we plan to meet again after Vivienne's burial."

Sion flashed a sly grin in his golden beard as all of them began to rise. "I was wondering whether anyone else had remembered my plight. Thank God we have not the political wrangling in Llannedd and Howicce that plagues the greater kingdoms—though King Colman is certain to be livid when he learns that his sister has been plotting all along to marry the heir of Howicce, who is *not* going to marry Araxie Haldane. *That* little illusion will vanish as soon as Kelson's marriage plans become public knowledge."

"And pray," said Barrett, "that news of Kelson's marriage plans does not precipitate a new crisis between Gwynedd and Meara as well. It is said that Oksana Ramsay has a formidable temper, when crossed—and she badly wanted a king for her daughter."

"If any king will do," Sion said lightly, "the girl *could* be matched with Colman of Llannedd instead of a prince of Gwynedd. . . ."

All eyes turned to Sion, who shrugged innocently and chuckled in his curly beard.

"I fear that more than one princess has declined his offers of marriage, after the way he jilted the Princess Janniver. Fortunately, I serve his sister, not Colman himself—and I am heartily in favor of dynastic marriages that also allow for genuine fondness. No, let my lady Gwenlian marry her cousin Cuan, whom she loves, and let Noelie Ramsay marry her handsome Haldane prince—and let Kelson of Gwynedd simply marry, so that everyone else can get on with their lives!"

*A*nd at Beldour, the Tralian galleys of Létald Hort of Orsal receded slowly downriver from the Torenthi capital, painted sails bellied by a fair wind conjured by Torenthi weather mages, bright banners aflutter in the rigging. Because Létald himself had returned by Portal to the Ile d'Orsal, where he remained to keep watch against the renegade Count Teymuraz, his son Prince Cyric now commanded the voyage home, with guidance available from Saer de Traherne and Sean Lord Derry, should he need it.

The newly affirmed *padishah* had seen them off personally at quayside, accompanied by King Kelson's new ambassador, the Deryni Bishop Arilan, and the uncle who was so much a topic of discussion by the Camberian Council later that morning, bidding a bittersweet farewell to Payne Haldane and Brendan Coris and Kelson's squire Ivo, who had been the boon companions of his squireship in Gwynedd. Kelson's contingent of Haldane lancers had lined the rails of Létald's flagship in salute to Torenth as they pulled away from the quay, with Saer and Derry performing the official leave-taking on behalf of their absent king.

Of that departing contingent, Derry alone was of interest to the veiled, dark-eyed woman who watched from a balcony of the tiered palace above the city, a cup of dark wine in her hand. A heavy finger-ring of iron adorned her other hand, match-mate to another worn by the departing man—though his had been plated with fine gold, to obscure appearance but not function, its outer surface incised with flowing Eastern motifs, and he believed it but a memento of his visit to the Torenthi capital. Calling on the link between those two rings, Morag of Torenth passed her own ring over the mouth of her cup, smiling as images took shape upon the dark surface of the wine.

"Yes, indeed," she whispered, seeing what Derry saw—and knowing she could hear what he heard, if she wished. "I thank you, my brother. Who would have thought they would fail to root out your magic? You have left me an exceedingly useful tool. I promise you that it—and he—shall serve Torenth well."

CHAPTER TWENTY-SEVEN

Come, and let us reason together.

Isaiah 1:18

$\mathcal{K}$elson was given two days' respite before he must deal with the arrival of the Mearans. By then, he and his Tralian kin had settled in quietly at the castle, with the story vaguely given out—and supported by his council—that the bridal party had simply elected to travel to Rhemuth somewhat sooner than originally planned, arriving late at night, with little fanfare.

Kelson himself kept a low profile, quietly conducting necessary business but staying mainly out of sight, lest he provoke too much curiosity. The work of the next few days saw the drafting of most of the documents necessary to support the second Mearan alliance he hoped to accomplish—and contracts for his own marriage with Araxie. Since only the council had been privy to his exact schedule regarding the Torenthi mission—or known of the full danger the jaunt had presented—few outside that privileged circle remarked that his return came somewhat earlier than anticipated, much less thought to wonder how the king had returned so quickly.

Meanwhile, the fugitive Teymuraz made no appearance at the Ile d'Orsal or any other place reporting back to Kelson or the young king recently enthroned at Torenthály. Bishop Denis Arilan, now greatly reassured regarding Mátyás as well as his young nephew, assumed the status of King Kelson's sole ambassador in the Torenthi capital, and made nightly excursions between Beldour and Rhemuth to report to the king—but only to report that there was nothing to report. Mátyás included him in such counsels as were appropriate to one not sworn to the service of Torenth, but Mátyás's energy and that of his royal nephew was turned increasingly toward setting up the workings of the new government: the first to operate outside the structure of a regency since the death of King Wencit, a full seven years before—for the regency of Wencit's successor, Alroy-Arion, had lasted nearly four years, and Liam's own regency for three. (One could hardly count the thirty days of Alroy's tragically brief majority.)

Despite initial and long-ingrained misgivings about anyone and anything Torenthi, Arilan found himself grudgingly impressed by nearly all the men Mátyás began calling to service on the Crown Council of the new *padishah*—but he did not pretend to understand the nuances of Torenthi politics. The ways of Torenth were not the ways of the West; and while he now had hopes that the two might settle into peaceful co-existence, he doubted seriously whether they would ever truly understand one another.

Azim, too, remained temporarily based at the court of Torenth, rendering such assistance to Mátyás as he could, in the ongoing search for some clue as to what had become of Teymuraz. It was he with whom Arilan spent much of his time, for neither was sworn to Torenth, and of necessity were excluded from much of the work of Liam's Crown Council. On the third day after *killijálay*, the second after the death of Vivienne, the pair duly attended Vivienne's final rites at Alta Jorda; but consultation with the rest of the Camberian Council, following the ceremony, produced no further developments regarding the whereabouts or intentions of the fled Teymuraz.

Kelson, meanwhile, was treading a narrow balance between political imperatives and personal priorities as the court at Rhemuth prepared for the arrival of the Mearan wedding party. Following two days of anxious fretting, word came late in the morning of the third day that the Mearans had spent the previous night a few hours' ride north of Rhemuth, and would arrive that afternoon: a modest cavalcade of perhaps two dozen riders and pack animals with, apparently, no pretense to the royal Mearan honors that many had feared Jolyon Ramsay might try to put forward, now that his son's match with Gwynedd was all but accomplished.

The king sent Rory with Lord Savile and an honor guard of eight Haldane lancers to escort the Mearans into the city, for he was well aware of the speculation that would attend the bridegroom's sister if he himself rode out to meet them. As further diversion, Richelle and Araxie elected to accompany their stepfather and their royal cousin, lightly veiled and gowned in the bright silks of their mother's homeland, Richelle to greet her bridegroom and both of them primed to help connive at Rory's romantic intentions.

It was late afternoon by the time the combined bridal party finally approached the city gates, where an anxious king was pacing one of the castle parapets, in only Dhugal's company. At midday, Morgan had ridden downriver to Desse, with young Sir Angus MacEwan and Kelson's squire Davoran for company, for Richenda and her two younger children were expected to arrive within the next twenty-four hours aboard *Rhafallia*. Likewise, Létald's ships from Beldour were expected to reach the Ile d'Orsal by nightfall. Duncan was waiting there to bring back Derry, Brendan, and Prince Payne; Saer and the rest of the royal entourage, including the Haldane lancers, would return on the Tralian wedding ship, now loaded with the "fripperies" left behind a few days before.

Straightening as the other wedding party came into sight, down on the road beside the river, Kelson watched with Dhugal as the cavalcade crawled along the final approach toward the city gate, using both hands to shade his eyes against the glare off the distant water.

"Well, that's reassuring," he murmured, noting the drift of blue silk banners gently astir on a light breeze. "About a dozen blue pennons mixed in with our lancers—livery silks, by the look of them, totally appropriate to a bridal party—and just the one armorial banner, up at the front, which definitely isn't the old Mearan royal arms."

"You didn't really think Jolyon would dare, did you?" Dhugal replied, also squinting against the sun.

"No, but you never know with Mearans," Kelson said, wondering whether any of them could see the red-clad dot of him, high on the walls of the great keep. "Hopefully, this branch of the family got its good sense from the Ramsay side. The Ramsays have always stayed carefully out of the wranglings of the more senior Mearan lines, tucked away up by Cloome—never a whiff of scandal or disloyalty. Still, the hope of a crown can do strange things to people."

Dhugal allowed himself a snort.

"Jolyon Ramsay is a very minor provincial knight whose son and heir is about to marry a Haldane princess and become an earl—and probably a duke, once their first son is born. He isn't likely to do anything to endanger that. Whatever else he may be, and however ambitious his wife may be, I gather that the good Sir Jolyon is a realist."

"We'll hope you're right," Kelson said, "and that the Lady Oksana can be similarly persuaded." He pushed himself back from the rampart, turning toward the cap-house that crowned the stairwell downward. "I'd better make my appearance. They'll be here soon. Dine with me later. Hopefully, they'll retire early. I'll need a dash of fresh perspective, after an afternoon contending with family."

Below in the castle yard, ranged on the great-hall steps, Sivorn had gathered her four younger children and the rest of her extended family to welcome her elder daughter's bridegroom and his family. The boys, aged nine and six, were standing to her right, eager for a glimpse of the expected new arrivals, for both had hopes that their new uncle-by-marriage might one day provide places for them as pages or squires. The youngest girl clung shyly to her mother's skirts; the eldest clutched a mixed posy of roses and delphiniums from the royal garden.

Behind them, Jehana waited with Nigel and Meraude and little Eirian. Kelson slipped into place among them, quite content to let Sivorn play hostess, as mother of the bride—and claim the focus of public attention. Jehana smiled him encouragement, apparently sympathetic to the delicacy of the next few hours.

He was pleased to note, as the first of the cavalcade clip-clopped into the castle yard, that his cousins had managed to arrange the principal players as they had hoped. Lord Savile properly led the procession, chatting amiably with the bridegroom's parents. The banner carried right behind them by a mounted herald bore the simple blue banner devised for Jolyon's Ramsay ancestor who had married a Mearan princess, with a chequy fess of silver and gold inserted between the three silver stars long borne by the Ramsays. A happy and animated Richelle rode directly behind the banner, at the side of her intended bridegroom.

To Rory had fallen the pleasant duty of escorting the sisters of both the bride and the bridegroom; nor did he look at all unhappy. The lancers properly followed behind, escorting the modest Mearan baggage train, and led that part of the cavalcade on toward the stable yard.

Kelson took the opportunity to survey the principals as they began dismounting, taking careful note of Jolyon and Oksana Ramsay, in particular— for they were the ones he must win over, in the next few days. They were a handsome pair, even if wilted and dust-begrimed from their journey: both of them on the tall side, both of them dark-eyed and graceful. Jolyon's soft-brimmed cap sported two eagle feathers; Oksana wore a large straw hat over the wimple mostly covering her dark hair—providing welcome shade, even if its appearance was less than regal. She pulled it off when she had shaken some of the dust from her skirts, handing it to the servant who came to take her horse away.

Behind them, Savile had also dismounted, and was directing the grooms come to take the horses. Richelle was being helped down by Brecon, a comely, well-proportioned young man of middling height, with sandy hair and dark, merry eyes, in whom a winter's separation from his affianced bride seemed only to have increased his affection. Brecon's sister, alighting with Rory and Araxie, had the same dark eyes, but her hair was almost Haldane-dark—and now that Kelson no longer felt obliged to consider her in his own matrimonial plans, he found himself far better able to appreciate her charms; she and Rory should produce very attractive children. He doubted there had been opportunity for the pair to have spoken privately, but it was clear that she was fond of both her Haldane companions.

Quickly servants disposed of the first few horses, making space for Savile to conduct the bridegroom's parents up the great-hall steps to be greeted by his wife. Sunlight glinted from wispy, fair hair going white at the temples as Jolyon swept off his cap in a courtly bow and his wife dipped in a formal curtsy.

"Sir Jolyon, you are most welcome to Rhemuth," Sivorn said before he could speak, offering him her hand. "And Lady Ramsay," she went on, as she exchanged a formal embrace with Oksana. "Or may I call you by your Christian name, since our children are to wed? Allow me to present my younger children, who were not with me last summer: the Lord Sivney, who perhaps aspires to service as a page or squire in Meara; young Sorley; little Siany, who is shy; and my darling Savilla."

The boys gave the newcomers gravely respectful bows, and Savilla presented her posy to Oksana with a smile and a graceful curtsy.

"The weather being fair, we came early from Horthánthy, as my daughters, no doubt, will have told you," Sivorn went on breezily, coming to receive her future son's salute. "Welcome, dear Brecon . . . and sweet Noelie. . . . We are delighted to see all of you again.

"I fear my brother is obliged to send his regrets," she continued, turning back to Jolyon and Oksana, "but his dear Nyya is soon to be brought to bed of twins— and in truth, no longer could he bear the prospect of both wedding bustling and a broody wife under the same roof." She smiled at their expressions of complete understanding.

"But please—come and be greeted by the king and the rest of our family, and then join us for refreshment," she went on. "I hope that your journey was not too wearying? The heat along the river can be most oppressive in high summer."

Thus disarmed of any further questions regarding the bride's early arrival at Rhemuth, Jolyon and Oksana allowed themselves to be ushered on for welcomes from other Haldane relatives, including Kelson himself, who bowed over Oksana's hand and exchanged a cordial handclasp with Jolyon, merely bowing to Brecon and Noelie as he joined in the general shepherding of the newcomers into the hall for refreshment.

The visitors soon were shown to the quarters prepared for them, where they all retired early, pleading fatigue of the journey. Kelson supped privately with Dhugal in his quarters, whence the pair later repaired to the library to wait until Duncan should come through the Portal from the Ile d'Orsal, with Derry, Brendan, and Payne.

Payne had found the experience exhilarating—his first direct contact with any aspect of Deryni magic save for having shields placed upon him, when Liam had first come to court three years before—and such work had always been done while he slept. Brendan simply had taken it in stride, like the good half-Deryni child he was, with scant experience of Transfer Portals, but not at all afraid to let Father Nivard bring him through, since Duncan had assured him it was all right.

As might have been expected, Derry showed signs that the experience had been less than one he would have chosen, given other options, but he had dutifully placed himself in Duncan's hands. He was pale as he and Duncan appeared on the Portal square, but looked palpably relieved as he set eyes on Kelson and Dhugal.

"He's fine," Duncan assured the king, before Kelson could even ask. "Relax, Derry, you did just fine—really. All you need now is a good night's sleep."

He gave Derry a reassuring buffet to the shoulders as he directed him toward Dhugal.

"Why don't you take him to Alaric's quarters and see him bedded down for the night?" he said to his son. Nivard had already taken Brendan and Payne through the Veil, and would see them to bed as well.

Kelson watched as Dhugal deftly received control from his father and took Derry through the Veil. When they were gone, Duncan turned back to the king. He looked tired—which was hardly surprising, for he had brought Payne through, taken Nivard back with him, then let Nivard bring Brendan while he had dealt with Derry. It was Derry about whom Kelson was concerned.

"*Did* he do just fine?" Kelson asked, motioning Duncan to a seat in the window embrasure.

"Well enough, I suppose. Nivard couldn't have brought him through without hurting him; he was skittish enough with me. But I offered him the chance to return with the wedding ship, if he preferred—and he chose the Portal. I gather he did well enough in Torenth. As I said, a good night's sleep should sort him out."

*W*hether, in fact, that night's sleep could be said to have "sorted Derry out" was open to debate. Certain it was that, an hour later, when he had been left deep in healing sleep in Morgan's quarters, that sleep had also left him even more open to the link again conjured between the handsome gold ring Derry wore and another like it, made of iron, on the finger of a woman gazing into an onyx scrying mirror in far-off Beldour.

After the fact, she could but retrieve visual impressions of what Derry had experienced since her last invocation of that link; but they were enough to tell her how Létald's ships had been met at the Ile d'Orsal by Bishop Duncan McLain, who was not often known to employ his Deryni powers; and how McLain had taken Derry, young Prince Payne, and Morgan's stepson to a Portal in Létald's summer palace—hitherto unknown to her, and still not accessible, since she had only its physical location, not the magical signature that marked its location on the inner planes.

While Derry watched in no little apprehension—for the scars of what her brother had done to him yet clouded his ability to willingly accept any aspect of Deryni magic where it concerned his own person—McLain had taken Payne onto the Portal and disappeared, reappearing momentarily with a Deryni priest introduced to young Brendan as Father Nivard, who then had taken Brendan away. McLain had then brought Derry onto the Portal square—at which time, had she been in the link and not just reading Derry's memory, she might have caught that Portal's signature—and also the one to which they had gone.

But equally likely was the possibility that McLain might have detected her presence, had the link then been in force. And Kelson had been waiting at their destination—another chance that she might have been detected. No, best she simply file away those physical locations against a time when she might investigate in person, or send Derry himself to the last one, at least. But that curious Veil through which Duke Dhugal had taken him was a great mystery. She wondered whether Derry could pass it again, unaccompanied.

Fortunately, young Dhugal's controls on Derry had not been nearly as firm as his father's—had not *needed* to be, for his purposes, simply to pass Derry through the Veil. She wondered whether it would surprise him to learn that the healing sleep in which he had left Derry had also made it that much easier to invoke her link. . . .

CHAPTER TWENTY-EIGHT

*T*he next morning brought Rory Haldane early to his royal cousin's apartments, very shortly after dawn. The duty squire admitted him to the royal bedchamber and then withdrew, as Kelson propped himself against a pile of pillows and settled in to hear Rory's news. It soon emerged that Rory somehow had managed to contrive a brief but private and very satisfying exchange with the Lady Noelie Ramsay.

"Then, she'll have you? Yes or no?" Kelson asked, grinning indulgently as Rory hemmed and hawed around much detail of their clandestine meeting.

"Well, we did kiss once or twice," Rory finally admitted, looking vaguely smug. "Well, maybe more than once or twice. I—ah—let her believe that you'd agreed to step back in my favor. But I did make it clear that I could make no formal offer for her hand until you'd approached her parents," he went on resolutely, recalling his duty. "And her mother is still keen for a crown for her. Kelson, what if—"

"Give me some time to work on that," Kelson told him, "and try to be patient. At least you know that the lady herself is willing."

Rory's grin suggested that if negotiations were very long protracted, neither patience nor restraint were likely to prevail before Noelie's willingness, but he drew a sobering breath and gave his royal cousin a formal bow of agreement before happily taking his leave.

Kelson resolved to begin the process of Mearan persuasion that very day—and a ready opportunity was already in place. To amuse the younger members of the court, Nigel had arranged a hawking expedition in the afternoon, as the day cooled down—for Jolyon had evinced a keen appreciation of the sport during their sojourn of the previous summer, and had inquired, soon after arrival, regarding some of the birds they had flown at that time.

To mingled relief and apprehension on Kelson's part, Oksana elected to spend the day in the ladies' solar, eager to gossip with Sivorn and Meraude and Jehana regarding her son's forthcoming wedding with Richelle. Kelson knew he could count on the three Haldane women to assist in the matter of Rory and Noelie, especially now that he himself was committed to Araxie; but Oksana was still a great unknown, so the situation made him somewhat apprehensive.

Having Noelie's interest confirmed, however, the hawking expedition did present an ideal opportunity to begin sounding the waters with her father, without the complication of Oksana's presence. Kelson found his opening late in the afternoon, when he at last contrived to draw Jolyon apart, away from courtiers or curious servants.

"My cousin Rory wishes me to speak to you regarding your daughter," he said to Jolyon, gentling the hooded peregrine perched on his fist and eyeing the Mearan sidelong. "Unbeknownst to you or to me, it seems that the two of them became quite fond of one another last summer, while you and I were hammering out the details of the other marriage with my House."

Jolyon had tensed as Kelson spoke, arrested in the act of stroking the breast feathers of his own hawk, and looked somewhat bewildered. "Sire, I—confess myself somewhat taken aback. I—had not expected a request on behalf of Rory."

"Their mutual attraction came as something of a surprise to *me*, I must confess," Kelson said, "but I hope I may speak frankly in this matter. I am not unaware that your lady wife had hoped that I might offer for your daughter's hand.

"As it happens, however, *they* have chosen otherwise," Kelson went on, sparing Jolyon any embarrassment of having to confirm or deny. "Nor can I say that I disapprove, because it seems to me a match of hearts, and one which also fulfills the political alliances that would have been served by a match between myself and Noelie. I see that you had never considered such an arrangement," he added, when Jolyon did not immediately speak.

Jolyon seemed to be searching for words, though Kelson did not have the impression that the other man was precisely distressed by the notion.

"There is much to be said," Kelson went on carefully, "for a state marriage that also embodies honest affection. All my life, I have observed the fondness in the marriage of Rory's parents, who also married for love, and I very much believe that Rory himself is the same kind of man as his father, for whom a match of hearts is very important—and he believes he has found it in your Noelie."

Jolyon gazed off across the meadow before them, returning to the absent stroking of his bird. "It is the happiness I have always wished, for my little girl," he finally said. "It is her mother who aspires to titles."

"She shall have happiness as well as title, if you allow her and Rory to wed," Kelson replied. "I am prepared to revive one of the ancient Mearan dukedoms for them, on the day the marriage takes place—and *that*, I would suggest, could be done in conjunction with the nuptials already scheduled between Brecon and Richelle. Not to put too fine a point on it, but such an arrangement would also save you the expense of a separate wedding for Noelie. She could return to Meara with both a husband and a title."

"Surely Nigel would not allow his heir to live in Meara," Jolyon ventured, in tactful allusion to the *reason* Rory was Nigel's heir, known by all.

"The details of that arrangement have yet to be worked out," Kelson admitted, "but such would be my wish, if it is theirs—much though I would miss his counsel here at court."

Jolyon slowly nodded. "A very tempting prospect. I expect that I would see a great deal more of my eventual grandchildren." He summoned up a tentative grin. "You've anticipated most of the arguments that my dear wife is sure to raise. She throws things when she's angry, you know—and it's no secret that she'd set her cap for *you* as a match for our daughter."

Kelson snorted. "She and the kin of every other well-bred young woman in the Eleven Kingdoms, of marriageable age and situation. But I can't marry them all."

"No, just one will suffice," Jolyon agreed. "And all Gwynedd will rejoice on that day. But you're certainly narrowing the choices available. Dare I ask whether you are any nearer a decision?"

"You may—and I am," Kelson admitted, "though you will appreciate that I may not say more at this time. But be assured that, by stepping aside for Rory, I mean no slight to your daughter. On the contrary, it's my respect for her and my affection for my cousin that move me to this decision—which will allow *them* to satisfy both duty *and* genuine affection. I should be honored and delighted to have Noelie as my cousin by marriage."

"I understand what you're saying," Jolyon said impatiently, "but you and I are men. Getting her mother to see it that way may be somewhat more difficult."

"I don't doubt that," Kelson replied, "but if you care as much about your daughter's happiness as you say you do, you'll find a way to convince her."

"I'll certainly do my best." Jolyon cocked his head, pretending profound interest in his fidgeting bird. "You said you were nearer a decision, in your own case—may I ask how near?"

Kelson had to smile faintly at Jolyon's persistence.

"Near enough—though I know you will appreciate that I may not say more until a public announcement has been made—and I shan't allow that until both your children are wed."

"To spare my daughter's feelings?"

"As much to spare her mother's feelings," Kelson said with a strained smile. "Rory assures me that your daughter has no sense of settling for less than she desired."

Jolyon grinned broadly. "She's a passionate lass—as is her mother. It has always been difficult to deny either of them what they wanted—and if anything, the daughter is more determined than the dam. I hope young Rory knows what he's taking on!"

"That, fortunately, is not my concern," Kelson said. "May I take it that he has your permission, then?"

"I shall still have to placate my wife—but, yes, he has my permission," Jolyon replied. "May I ask, however, that you say nothing to anyone else until I give you leave? I would prefer to handle this in my own way."

"I wouldn't dream of interfering."

"And don't be surprised at any shouts or screams or sounds of breaking crockery coming from our quarters tonight," Jolyon went on. "For everyone's peace of mind, I think it best if my wife and I take our evening meal there in privacy; the youngsters may join in whatever public arrangements have been made. I should also point out that the details of the second marriage contract have still to be worked out, but I promise you I'll not be unreasonable. I only want my girl to be happy."

His gaze flicked out across the meadow, where Rory, Noelie, and Araxie were racing their horses flat out after a gyring hawk. Somewhat nearer, in the shade of a sprawling oak, Richelle was sitting with her back against its trunk and Brecon's head in her lap, laughing as she dropped grapes into his open mouth.

"They seem happy enough with *their* arrangement," Jolyon observed.

"Yes, they do," Kelson agreed. "I think all of us will do well by both these matches."

"We shall see," Jolyon said, gathering up his reins. "Remember, not a word . . ."

Later in the afternoon, Rory rode over to where Kelson and Dhugal were watching from afar as Nigel flew a great gerfalcon, eagerly observed by Jolyon and Brecon and several squires. Noelie and Araxie had joined Richelle under the giant oak, the three of them chattering happily as they sipped at ale cooled in a nearby stream, attended by several adoring pages.

"Did you ask him?" Rory breathed, his eyes alight with anticipation. "You two were alone for a very long time."

"I asked him," Kelson admitted, "but he's asked that I not discuss it yet."

"He hardly looked at me, when I passed him a while ago," Rory whispered. "Is he angry? Did he think me presumptuous?"

"I told you, I mayn't speak of it," Kelson repeated, though he smiled as he said it, and Dhugal was doing his best not to grin—for Kelson had told him, mind to mind, in strictest confidence.

Rory closed his eyes, letting out a tiny, relieved sigh as he realized Kelson was teasing. "He's agreed. I understand why it can't yet be discussed. Dear God, I'll burst, having to keep it all bottled up. I want to tell the world!"

"You can't even tell Noelie yet," Kelson said calmly. "I am given to understand that we might expect shouting and the sounds of breakage later tonight, when Jolyon confronts his lady wife. If you doubt your ability to appear oblivious to such a scene, I suggest you pretend an indisposition for the evening. The marriage contract has yet to be negotiated." He cocked his head at Rory. "If you wish, I *can* block your memory of this until tomorrow."

Rory favored him with a darting grin. "And miss the delicious feeling of happy conspiracy that I'm enjoying at this moment? Not a chance! You shall see a prize-winning performance of 'innocence' for the rest of the day! I promise I won't let you down, Kel."

As he rode off, shading his eyes to watch another hawk strike, Dhugal glanced at the king.

"You've made him a very happy man."

"*Jolyon* has made him a very happy man," Kelson replied. "I'm just glad I was able to be the bearer of *good* news for a change."

Rory was as good as his word. All through the remainder of the afternoon, he maintained a convincing façade of decorous nonchalance, equally courteous and attentive to all in the royal party, never betraying any hint that he had knowledge of what had been discussed between Kelson and Jolyon, or even that a discussion had taken place.

On the way back to Rhemuth, Jolyon himself contrived to ride at Rory's side, the two of them soon dropping back from the others to talk privily. After a while, Rory sent a page forward to request that Nigel drop back to ride with them. The three seemed to have achieved an easy camaraderie by the time the hawking party dismounted in the castle yard.

Morgan had returned from Desse with his family while they hunted, and came to the door of the hall with Richenda to watch as hawks and horses were taken away and their riders began to disperse. Kelson bounded up the great-hall steps when he saw them, saluting Richenda with a kiss and then bending to greet Kelric and accept a kiss from Briony, who was holding the hand of "Uncle Séandry." The latter looked a trifle weary, but apparently well enough recovered from his experience of the night before.

"All's well?" Morgan murmured aside to the king, as Nigel shouldered past them with only perfunctory greeting, trailed uncertainly by Rory.

"I hope so." Kelson hailed Rory and drew him aside with Morgan, jutting his chin toward Nigel. "He didn't dig in his heels, did he?"

Rory shook his head, somber. "No, he's in favor of the marriage. I think he's realizing, though, the pressure this will bring to bear on the question of the Carthmoor succession. I haven't dared to mention it."

"And Jolyon?"

"He seems well enough content—but he still has to contend with Oksana. It isn't over, by any means. However, I was left with the firm impression that there will be either a marriage or a murder."

"Good God, let it not be murder!" Kelson said in mock alarm. "All we need is another war with Meara."

Very shortly, Jolyon announced his intention to retire early, being wearied from the day's outing. He tendered Rory a broad wink before disappearing up the turnpike stair. Kelson dined that evening with Morgan and Richenda, Duncan and Dhugal also joining them. The short summer night was only just descending by the time they finished eating, but Morgan's sidelong glances at his wife made it clear that he would appreciate an early departure on the part of all three of their supper guests.

Accordingly, Kelson soon took his leave, declaring his intention to attend to some correspondence before retiring. Duncan and Dhugal followed his lead—and were, in fact, debating whether to adjourn to Kelson's quarters to continue drinking—when Davoran, one of Kelson's senior squires, came to him with a message that he was wanted in the withdrawing room behind the great-hall dais.

"Shall I come along?" Dhugal asked, as his father lifted a hand in resigned leave-taking and headed off for the night.

Kelson started to say yes, but the squire was quietly shaking his head.

"Apparently not," Kelson said. "Why not, Davoran?"

"A lady, Sire. Actually, two of them. But they said I was to bring only you."

With a shrug, Kelson followed Davoran down the stair, through the great hall to the withdrawing room. There he found Araxie and Richelle, fresh from conversation with their mother regarding the afternoon's gossip in the ladies' solar. When Richelle had given Kelson a quick hug, she slipped outside to keep watch before the door with Davoran, leaving Kelson alone with Araxie. A single torch burned in a cresset by the door, but otherwise the room was dark.

"Come away from the door," she said, drawing him into the shadow of the fireplace. "I couldn't think where else was safe to meet you, at this hour. *Maman* has just told us the most extraordinary thing—and I think I now know what might answer nearly all Oksana's desires."

"If you know *that*, then tell me, by all means. Jolyon is breaking the news about Noelie and Rory, even as we speak."

"Then, consider a title for her and Jolyon. That's what she wants and has never gotten, Kelson. She wanted to be Brion's queen—but he married Jehana. Then she wanted to be Nigel's duchess—and *he* married Meraude. That's one of the reasons she so desperately wants Noelie to be *your* queen."

"I'd gathered that much, from things Nigel's told me," he said, though he had not, indeed, considered a title for Jolyon.

"Then, suppose you were to create a ducal title for her and Jolyon?" she went on eagerly, almost as if she were picking up his thoughts. "Perhaps give them the one you were going to give to Brecon, when he and Richelle have their first son. Brecon would still receive that title, once his father passes on. He's quite devoted to his sister, so I suspect it wouldn't make a great deal of difference to *him*, so long as he and Richelle have sufficient income—which they will, of course, as Earl and Countess of Kilarden. Meanwhile, Oksana would enjoy the ducal title she missed when Nigel didn't marry her. For *her*, that's even better than having her daughter be queen."

Kelson had listened in growing astonishment as Araxie unfolded her proposal, at once aware that it was the absolutely perfect solution to at least that part of the Mearan tangle—and wondering why *he* had not thought of it. In a sudden impulse of sheer delight and gratitude, he seized her face between his two hands and kissed her—and started back, in even greater astonishment, as he realized what he had done.

For the life of him, though, he could not bring himself to take his hands from those downy cheeks, like silk beneath his fingers. Her own hands had lifted of their own accord to lightly clasp his elbows, and she looked no less surprised than he, the soft, rosy lips slightly parted in wonder, those wide eyes of Haldane grey glinting in the torchlight, shyly inviting but not presuming.

He could feel his heart hammering in his breast as he bent to kiss her again, more mindfully this time, stirring to her response as her hands slid up his arms to rest upon his shoulders. As he tasted and then drank more deeply of a gentle, poignant yearning, the sweeter for being quite unexpected, he let his hands quest into the pale, silken hair, feeling her mouth melt under his, the taut length of his body gradually pressing her against the wall behind as a delicious tension began to stir in his groin.

But it was not the fiery rush of near-unbridled passion that had threatened to overwhelm him that one time he had actually held Rothana in his arms. Rather, a slower welling up of longing from someplace deeper than mere physical response, though promising similar resolution, once unleashed. As he let himself at last acknowledge that longing, instinct bade him tenderly enfold her in his shields—and her own shields answered, briefly merging and mingling with his in exquisite rapport.

It lasted but an instant, for neither had planned it, nor was ready for more; but that glimpse of shared vision and mutual discovery was a tantalizing taste of the deeper communion hinted at in their one previous venture into rapport—and was sufficient for now, ratifying guarded hopes and easing fears on both their parts—acknowledgment that there *was* a bond both of need and of tenderness growing between them, which might very well be love. Kelson could feel her trembling in his arms—and his own trembling—as, at last, he reluctantly ended their kiss to rest his lips against her cheek and simply hold her softly to him, like some precious, fragile bird.

After a moment, as his pulse rate settled, he finally drew back enough to look at her, still suffused by wonder. She was smiling, tears brimming in her eyes, and he bent to gently kiss away their wet saltiness.

"Am I to take it," she whispered huskily, "that you approve of a title for Oksana?"

In a burst of sheer exhilaration, he laughed aloud and set his hands on her waist to lift her off her feet and whirl her once around him, smartly kissing her again as he set her back on her feet.

"Not only do I approve," he declared happily, "but I think that with you at my side, darling coz, we may become the most fortunate king and queen ever to grace the throne of Gwynedd! We *can* make this work, Araxie! I know that now. There are still a few loose ends to tidy, but we can do that!"

He drew a deep breath and took both her hands in his, lifting first one and then the other to press it to his lips, feeling her contentment, sharing it—and knowing that, at last, he had let himself loose the final chains binding him to dreams with Rothana that were never meant to be.

"There *is* one thing I must ask you, though," he warned, gazing down at her with an expression of mock gravity.

Her serene expression assured him that she did not, for a moment, think herself in serious jeopardy.

"And just what is that?"

"Whatever made you carry on that charade with Cuan of Howicce, especially once Rothana had approached you about a match with me?"

"Why, Cuan is a pleasant young man, and he dearly loves his cousin Gwenlian," she replied, her hands still in his. "Since, at the time, I had no other prospects I seriously favored, I was glad to help their cause. After all, I hadn't seen you since I was six.

"Fortunately, you'd already turned up alive by the time I heard that they thought you dead. I wept when I heard of Conall's execution, but I knew why you had to do it."

Kelson dropped his gaze, regretting it anew.

"Don't look away," she said, jiggling his hands. "You are king. You will have to do many things you would rather not do—though I . . . think . . . that perhaps you have changed your mind about at least one of those things. I know I have."

He dared to look up at her, still finding it hard to believe that he *had* changed his mind.

"In any case, Cuan provided an agreeable ruse to keep me from being shunted into some far less salubrious marriage," she said. "And since I knew he and I were never going to marry, I was able to enjoy the titillation of appearing to be wooed, fooling everyone. I shall miss that; Cuan was great fun." She heaved a wistful sigh.

"Meanwhile, Rothana had come along. And there's something you should understand, that there wasn't time to explain, when you came to me at Horthánthy and we first agreed to marry. I met her twice during that first year after Albin was born—en route to and from Nur Hallaj, to show him to her parents. Sometime between those two visits, she had already begun to conceive the part of the dream she hoped to salvage out of Conall's tragedy: to restore Deryni to the full partnership with humans that it can and should be. She means to start by building a school."

"Ah, I *do* know about *that*," he interjected. "Richenda told me—though apparently she didn't know about your part in all of this. I've already started looking for a site, right here in Rhemuth. Actually, Duncan's looking. It's rather an exciting proposition: the first Deryni *schola* under royal patronage in nearly two centuries."

"And you're the first *Haldane* to achieve the full potential of our blood in nearly two centuries," she said. "With your support of this enterprise, just imagine the difference we can make!"

"You're a Haldane, too," Kelson reminded her. "I've done quite a lot of thinking about that, in the past week or so. It's occurred to me that if it was possible to awaken Haldane powers in Nigel—and we know that Conall was brought to astonishing levels of power—why not other Haldanes? Why not you, as well?"

She merely cocked her head, considering, neither daunted nor repelled by the notion.

"There's never been a Haldane queen, so I'm sure it's never been tried," she said. "But that might explain why Azim and Rothana were able to bring me along so well—that or my Deryni blood," she conceded. "And maybe regular exposure to other Deryni also helps. But whatever the answer, I'm certainly willing to do whatever you think best, to help you do what *you* need to do."

"What an incredibly brave queen you shall be!" he whispered, lifting one of her hands to kiss it. "We'll certainly speak more of this later. Just now, however, it's occurred to me that I probably ought to go, before both of us are missed at the same time. People will talk."

"About what?" she said with an air of wide-eyed innocence. "After all, it's still believed that I'm all but engaged to marry Cuan—and you *are* my cousin."

"Sweet cousin," he said with a faint, lazy smile, bending to kiss her lips again.

She sighed softly, contentedly, as they parted, then glanced toward the door.

"You may be right about people talking. Besides, I'm dying to know what success Jolyon is having with Oksana." She wrinkled her nose at him, the way she had done when they were children. "I haven't heard any screams or shattering crockery. . . ."

"Neither have I," Kelson replied with a chuckle. "And I think I'd like to approach Nigel about your suggestion regarding titles. That touches on *his* title, and Albin's—one of those loose ends I mentioned earlier."

He bent down and kissed her lightly on the lips again, smiling, and gave her hand a squeeze before he released it.

"I'll go out first. I suggest you wait a few minutes before following."

He found himself smiling as he left the room—and caught Richelle in a quick, brotherly hug before heading up to his quarters, sending Davoran to summon Nigel and Rory to join him.

Nigel was *not* smiling, by the time Kelson had laid out his proposal.

"I hope this isn't a threat to stop Rory's marriage from going forward, if I don't capitulate."

"Of course not. But I think it's time you accepted the fact that, whatever Conall did, it has nothing to do with his son—Rothana's son, your grandson."

Rory was staring at his father, white-lipped with the tension.

"I beg you not to destroy what should be a time of joy for all of us," he said. "I don't *want* the title that should be Albin's. He's done nothing to warrant being disinherited. And I don't *need* his title. Kelson very generously has offered me one of my own. I'd be founding a new branch of the family."

"Then I'll give Carthmoor to Payne," Nigel said stubbornly. "Besides, Rothana doesn't want Albin in the succession, either. Kelson, he *could* endanger your own succession. Why can't you accept that?"

"I must accept that at *any* time, anyone farther along the succession *might* try to supplant those above him—just as Conall did," Kelson said. "A king who cannot answer such challenges does not deserve to keep his crown.

"But I'll make you this counteroffer. Restore the ducal succession to Albin. His mother still intends him for the church—and that's *my* problem, to convince her to let him make his own choice. But if, for whatever reason, he doesn't marry and continue his line, the succession *then* passes to Payne, rather than Rory—because Rory will already be a duke. And I'll provide a title for Payne as well, whatever else happens, when he comes of age. That's your ultimate intention, after all, isn't it? To see all your descendants provided for?"

Nigel was tracing patterns on the tabletop with one callused finger. He did not look up as he slowly began to speak.

"When I lay under Conall's spell," he said, "I was aware of what was going on around me. I could make no movement, could give no sign that I was aware—but I was. And I—think—I want to believe—that Conall truly did not mean to do what he did. He was a willful boy, growing up—proud, sometimes arrogant—but he was truly concerned for the honor of our House. I think that the—power he used against me was—a flexing of desperation, trying to salvage something from the chain of events he'd unwittingly set in motion, which had led, he thought, to your death. If you *had* been dead, he was, indeed, correct that, as *my* heir, it was important to secure the succession into the next generation—a necessity with which you are intimately acquainted," he added, with a wry glance at Kelson, who slowly nodded in agreement.

"In that, at least," the king said, "he knew his duty."

Nigel briefly bowed his head, then went on.

"My son was also ambitious—and jealous—for which both of us have suffered. But I wonder if his fall perhaps came as much from his frustration at being denied access—or so he perceived—to what he believed to be his Haldane birthright." Nigel sighed. "Had we known then what we know now, regarding the Haldane potential, it might have been possible to admit him legitimately to some part of that heritage, as you have done for me—and he could have become a valuable and reliable member of your court.

"But his association with Tiercel de Claron, at that point in time, was particularly unfortunate," Nigel went on dully, "for the allure of forbidden power proved all too provocative, and the circumstances of its getting precluded his receiving adequate training in the responsible use of that power. Once he had caused Tiercel's death, and declined to own up to the consequences of his actions, he set himself upon a path of ever more convoluted deception from which there was no turning back.

"The rest, I fear, was largely the result of trying to hold together the illusions he himself had wrought; and when you returned, the time of reckoning had arrived. Unfortunately, some things could not be undone."

"No, they couldn't," Kelson said. "But having seen his son—your grandson—can you honestly wish that *he* could be undone?"

Nigel shook his head. "Of course not. When I look at Albin, I see Conall as he was at that age—so full of life and intelligence and curiosity about the world. But then I remember Conall's betrayal."

"And when *I* look at him," Kelson replied, "I see Rothana's son as well, who might have been *my* son. And it was of *her* love and loyalty that he was conceived, Nigel, to carry on the Haldane name and heritage—which he still can do. No, hear me out," he added, when Nigel would have interrupted.

"I've had to accept that she will never bear my sons, but I hope and believe that, in time, Albin Haldane will carry on some part of the dream she and I shared. Meanwhile, the bride I have chosen—at Rothana's urging—is a Haldane like ourselves, who will give my own sons an equally precious legacy. She's already showing me the kind of queen she'll be. In fact, it was she who suggested the title for Oksana.

"As for Rothana, I have come to realize that what she now is offering to Gwynedd—and to me—may be more precious to future generations than any scores of further children of her flesh. Both Araxie and Richenda have acquainted me with some of what Rothana has envisioned for the Servants of Saint Camber and the school she means to establish. Perhaps, in fact, that is a more important function, weighed against the future of this realm.

"To that end, I intend to offer her land here in Rhemuth for her new *schola*, with the Crown to be its patron. I've already asked Duncan to find me a suitable site. Given that we cannot change the past, my fondest wish for the future would be that Albin may embrace the fullness of his Deryni heritage, both at his mother's knee and here at court, and come into his manhood instilled with the responsibilities as well as the privileges that are his birthright.

"If he still chooses a religious life after all of that"—Kelson threw up both his hands—"that's in God's hands. But in the fullness of time, it's Albin whom I would wish to have at my side as Duke of Carthmoor after you, to help me rule Gwynedd alongside my own sons, and Morgan's sons, and Dhugal's sons—and with Rory's sons and Richelle's sons ruling in Meara, as my deputies, binding the peace throughout our realm. But for all of that to happen, I need you to restore Albin to the Carthmoor succession, and acknowledge him as your heir."

Nigel said nothing for a long moment, only staring at his hands folded on the table. When he finally spoke, he did not look up.

"I will agree to this," he said quietly, "if Rothana will agree."

N igel's capitulation considerably reinforced Kelson's intentions regarding the Mearans. By the time Jolyon came to him the next morning, to report on progress or lack thereof, the king had decided on precisely the terms o the offer he would make to Sir Jolyon Ramsay and his wife.

"The silence was far more frightening than if she had screamed or thrown things," Jolyon concluded, slumping on the bench opposite Kelson, in the win dow seat of his private reception chamber. When he said nothing more, Kelson raised an eyebrow.

"I take it that, eventually, she did speak?"

"Not really. She went white at first, then bright red. Then she burst into tears and took to her bed. I slept in another room. She was sitting at the window when I rose this morning, gazing out over the gardens. She still hasn't spoken more than two words. I've asked that food be sent up to her."

"I see." Kelson considered, then sat forward slightly.

"Very well, I have a proposition for you, that hopefully will sweeten her dis position," he said. "How, if we were to make a slight alteration to the marriage contract between Brecon and Richelle, whereby *you* would receive the ducal title that I had proposed to bestow on Brecon upon the birth of his first son by Richelle?"

Jolyon's jaw dropped.

"It would still pass to him upon your eventual death, of course," Kelson went on enjoying Jolyon's astonishment, "and he'd still be Earl of Kilarden for the interim but you and your lady wife would enjoy ducal rank and revenues for your lifetimes."

He sat back in his chair in no little satisfaction.

"As for your daughter, I've already told you that I would create a separate ducal title for Rory—and I am happy to inform you that Nigel has agreed to le him step back from the Carthmoor succession, and to reinstate his grandson Prince Albin, to his proper place as heir. There are still some details to be worked out with Albin's mother, but that needn't concern you."

Jolyon had gone very still as Kelson unfolded his proposal, and shook his head in wonder as the king looked at him expectantly.

"Sire, you truly wield powerful magic of an entirely different sort than I had dreamed. Nigel approves of this?"

"He accepts it, which is much the same thing," Kelson countered. "What say you? Would it please your lady wife that both she and your daughter should be duchesses?"

Jolyon grinned. "You are far more shrewd a judge of women than I had realized, Sire. I do agree—for the sake of both our Houses."

"Excellent." Kelson smiled faintly. "I cannot change the past, Jolyon, but, God willing, I can build strength upon it. May I inform the ladies of my household that they may look forward to that double wedding we discussed?"

"You may, indeed." Jolyon sighed. "I must confess myself greatly relieved that I shall accomplish the marriages of both my children in one fell swoop, and to the honor of all concerned."

"Then I shall have the necessary documents prepared," Kelson said, rising. "Please convey my kindest respects to your new duchess."

CHAPTER TWENTY-NINE

So foolish was I, and ignorant.

Psalm 73:22

$\mathcal{N}$ ot until the new marriage contract was agreed could the betrothal be announced of the Lady Noelie Ramsay to Prince Rory Haldane; but during the next several days, the two were seen increasingly in one another's company, along with her brother and the king's cousins and the growing numbers of noble wedding guests arriving from near and far to witness the historic union of Brecon Ramsay, the Mearan heir, with his Haldane princess.

The bridegroom's mother basked in the attention showered on the bridal couple and their kin, gracefully sharing in the diversions devised to entertain the guests of Gwynedd. While the fact that Gwynedd's king had not chosen Noelie of Meara for his bride still rankled with the Lady Oksana, the prospect of her own ducal coronet as well as one for her daughter considerably eased the disappointment.

A few days following agreement of the basic arrangement, a morning when Kelson was still closeted with Jolyon and their respective advisors to hammer out details of the legal provisions—for Jolyon's impending promotion to ducal status somewhat altered previous expectations—the Duchess Meraude invited Jolyon's wife and daughter to join them in the breeze-cooled solar where she, Jehana, and Sivorn and her daughters—all the royal ladies of Gwynedd—were contentedly stitching on wedding finery, sharing the latest gossip of the court. Included at last in this world of grace and privilege, Oksana soon settled into the status to which she had always believed herself both destined and entitled, happily confirming their speculations—as yet unverified by official announcement—of a second Mearan marriage with Haldane royalty. More, no mother could ask.

Jehana was much relieved at this final evidence of Oksana's capitulation, for she had been well aware of her son's uneasiness over the Mearan situation. She sat with them for a while, working fine embroidery on the collar of a shirt for Kelson, but after a while she excused herself and went down to the library. As expected, the door was locked, for Father Nivard would be with Kelson, performing his usual secretarial duties; but the young Deryni priest had given her a key of her own, with the droll comment that it would not do to have her reputation compromised, were someone to see her crouching before the door to work its lock with her powers.

She smiled at the memory as she opened the door and entered, closing and locking it behind her. Inside, the drapes had been drawn to keep the sun from fading the manuscripts stored there, but there was enough light to make her way to the passageway to the adjoining chamber. She no longer paid much mind as she passed through the Veil that divided the two rooms. Nor was she at all discomfited to see Barrett sitting in the window embrasure, as he had that first night she met him, again with a scroll unfurled on his lap. He laid the scroll aside and turned his face toward her as she came into the room.

"My lord Barrett, I had expected you might be here," she said, coming to take the hand he extended to her, keeping it in hers as she settled opposite him. She dipped her head to press his hand to her forehead in fond and respectful salute, pupil to teacher. "I have happy news. My nephew Rory is to be permitted a marriage of love—to the Lady Noelie Ramsay. There were fears that his mother would not allow the match, for she hoped that Kelson might wed her daughter, but she seems well enough content. The promise of a ducal coronet has sweetened her disposition."

"I am pleased for the lady, and for young Rory," Barrett said, smiling gently, "and I am pleased that *you* are pleased." He patted their joined hands with his free one, then drew back, looking faintly wistful. "It is a great blessing, to marry for love."

"Yes, it is," Jehana replied. His expression made her wonder whether Barrett had ever married, and whether it had been for love. She had loved Brion dearly, in the beginning; she tried not to dwell on how she herself had blighted that love by refusing to acknowledge that part of him that was magical, how she had wasted so much time denying what he was, what *she* was. Barrett had assured her that it was not too late to take up her destiny, to learn to be all that she *could* be, in the fullness of her Deryni heritage; but it was too late to share any of that with Brion.

"I never expected that I would have any say in who I married," she said after a moment. "Princes and especially princesses learn from birth that their marriages must satisfy dynastic needs before needs of the heart. I grieve for Kelson, that his own heart has been obliged to endure such disappointments in his young life, but I hope and pray that he and Araxie may find contentment together. In some respects, she reminds me of the woman I might have become, had things been different."

"Does she?" Barrett murmured, though the words were not really a question.

"Aye, she has spirit and grace, and I think she cares for him more than he knows. They greatly enjoyed one another's company when they were children. And she has willingly embraced what she is, determined to put her gifts to the service of this land." She glanced down at her hands. "I could not always admit that we bear gifts, in our powers. For far too long, I thought mine were a curse."

"You have come a very long way, Jehana," he said.

"Yes, but is it far enough?" she asked with a tiny sigh.

He smiled and reached across to pat her hand again, then leaned back in the cushions of their window seat, closing his eyes to the warm summer sun.

"I remember days like this, when I was young," he said. "My father's castle had the most extraordinary gardens. I remember a particularly enticing arbor, thick with fragrant vines. As a very young man, I was fond of slipping away from my tutors to hide away there. I would stretch out in the dappled shade of a summer's afternoon, lulled by the buzz of honey-heavy bees, and practice herding clouds while I gorged on grapes that I had hidden to cool in a nearby spring that morning."

"You can herd clouds?" Jehana said in amazement.

"In those days, I could," Barrett said with a shrug. "It is not as frivolous as, perhaps, it sounds. The skill is useful in weather-working, as is the ability to change the shapes of clouds. But both require physical sight. That was before I learned the cost of power that could be turned to such benevolent purposes."

"Has that something to do with how you lost your sight?" she dared to ask.

He smiled faintly and shook his head. "Not cloud-herding, or any form of weather magic. But I was young and impetuous then, and probably thought myself invincible, as the young often do, especially if blessed with abilities above the ordinary."

"That night we first met," she said softly, "you said something about saving children, and your sight having been the cost?"

"Some other time, perhaps," he said almost brusquely.

"I'm sorry, I didn't mean to pry—"

"It isn't that. One day, I shall tell you, if you really wish to know."

"Then—"

"You reminded me of yet another thing I miss: the chance to see the wonders of God's creation, the colors and textures of a beautiful garden. I have a garden where I now dwell, and the scents convey something of the colors I used to know—but it isn't the same."

A silence fell between them for a score of heartbeats, underscored by the poignancy of Barrett's loss, until suddenly Jehana found herself conceiving a notion that, before, would never have occurred to her.

"The gardens here at Rhemuth are very beautiful," she said tentatively. "I could—show you my memories of them. Or perhaps I could even take you through the Veil to walk through them in person!" she suddenly blurted. "Oh, Barrett, do you really suppose that I could? I can't imagine that Kelson would mind."

"I can't imagine that he *wouldn't*!" Barrett retorted. "But on the other hand," he said, after a beat, "it should be possible, at least in theory—to pass through the Veil in conjunction with someone like yourself, who *is* permitted to pass. It's frankly never occurred to me to wonder, because I simply respected your son's wishes that no outside Deryni should have access to the rest of the castle."

"You never thought to ask or wonder about that?" Jehana said, amazed.

"I honestly did not. But I cannot ask you to compromise your son's intentions."

"You didn't ask; I offered," she replied. "He obviously has great regard for you, or he wouldn't allow you to be *here*. Oh, Barrett, I *would* like to try, to see if it's something that I can actually do! You've taught me so much. Let me try; allow me to return some of the gift you've given me, by sharing my garden."

As she reached across to take his hand again, she felt him shudder faintly. But then his hand closed on hers and he bowed his head.

"Very well, let us try," he whispered hoarsely.

"Yes, come!" She rose and urged him to his feet. "Who knows? Perhaps we can simply walk through, hand in hand—I have no idea. But on such a wonderful summer's day, would it not be a shame not even to try?"

He said nothing as he let her lead him to the Veil. She could feel his hand cold and trembling in hers, and she turned to watch him as she eased backward into it and tried to draw him through as well. But as his hand in hers drew near the Veil, he drew it back with a hiss of discomfort.

"I cannot!" he gasped.

"Did it hurt you?" she asked, wide-eyed.

Lips pressed tightly together, he shook his head and reached out blindly to test the limits of the Veil, grimacing as he finally drew back a pace.

"I did not expect it to be easy," he murmured. "Take my hand and try again to draw me through—but slowly. *If* this can be done, it will require considerable adjustment on my part."

She did as he asked, but with no better success. As he bowed his head, nursing a hand obviously still in some discomfort, she came back through the Veil to lightly touch his arm.

"I'm sorry," she whispered. "I had hoped—"

"And *I* had hoped," he replied. "But there might be another way." He threw back his head, the emerald eyes flicking upward almost as if they could see, then turned his face to her again, a faint smile lifting the corners of his mouth. In that moment, he looked half his age.

"Tell me, are you feeling exceptionally brave today?"

She looked at him with no little apprehension.

"Why do you ask?"

"I propose to show you *my* garden, since you cannot show me yours. But to do that, you must trust me enough to let me to take you through the Portal."

Her stomach did a queasy flip-flop, and her eyes darted at once to the Portal square. They had avoided discussing Portals thus far, but she had known this moment would come, or one like it. Oddly, the prospect of actually using a Portal did not fill her with nearly as much dread as she had expected.

"I would very much like to see your garden," she found herself saying, far more calmly than she felt. "Will you forgive me for being just a little frightened?"

He smiled faintly. "If you are only a little frightened, we have come far, indeed."

"I suppose I have." She drew a steadying breath and squared her shoulders. "What must I do?"

Unerringly he moved onto the Portal square and extended a hand in invitation. "Join me here, and stand in the circle of my arm."

She obeyed, laying her hand in his and letting him turn her away from him, his hands resting on her shoulders from behind. She stifled a little gasp as he drew her gently against his chest, his right hand slipping lightly around to bracket her throat in the angle of thumb and fingers. She could feel her pulse fluttering within the compass of that embrace, but she closed her eyes and made a conscious effort to relax, for she trusted him utterly.

"Perfect," he whispered, lips close beside her ear. "Now, still your mind and think of nothing at all. . . . See those white clouds I mentioned earlier, drifting lazily in the dappled sunlight . . . and let your thoughts drift with them. Draw a deep breath and let it all the way out, very slowly. And now another."

Gladly she let herself be guided by his voice.

"Good. Drift amid the shifting clouds . . . and very soon, you shall feel my mind enfolding yours, soft as those clouds . . . but don't resist. Just relax and let me do all the work . . . relax. . . ."

Despite her apprehension, she could feel herself stilling inside, akin to that serenity that, only a fortnight ago, had been approachable only in prayer. It had come to her, in a moment of awed wonder, that the two states were not at odds.

The touch of his mind, when it came, was gentle but sure, coaxing her into greater stillness. She hardly felt the brief shifting of energies, only staggering a little as the floor seemed, momentarily, to drop from under her feet.

But *he* was there to steady her, his arms close around her shoulders, and she never felt a trace of fear. Breathing in a whiff of mellow leather and damp and a hint of sweetness that reminded her of church incense, she opened her eyes to a dimness quickly dispelled by the flare of handfire immediately before them—conjured for her benefit, she knew at once, for the chamber in whose corner they stood was uniquely suited to one without physical sight.

It seemed to have no windows, but its walls were hung with textured tapestries and carved wood panels: artistic embellishments to please the hand as well as the eye. Across the room, two thickly upholstered chairs were set within the embrace of a huge inglenook, a thick sheepskin rug at the foot of each, a round table nestled between the pair. On this table were stacked half a dozen heavy, leather-bound volumes bristling with bits of parchment marking places in the text: clear indication that Barrett's scholarly pursuits were not confined to the library at Rhemuth.

"The décor, perhaps, is not to your taste," he said beside her, quite aware of her perusal of the room around them.

"On the contrary," she said, "the room reflects its owner." She reached out a tentative hand to stroke the silken satin stitches delineating the curve of a courser's sleek flank, then fingered the gold laid-work on the rider's raiment. "Even if you couldn't see these things with your mind, you could see them with your fingers, couldn't you? Barrett, it's beautiful."

He smiled and took her hand, threading it through the crook of his elbow as he began leading her slowly toward the door.

"I am told that it is," he said quietly. "It serves this old bachelor well enough. I can speak with greater authority regarding my gardens."

The door opened before them as they approached, admitting them to an arched cloister walk opening onto an expanse of garden in a riot of colors and textures and scents. The air was cooler than in Rhemuth, touched with a clean salt tang as she filled her lungs with it.

"We're near the sea," she murmured, eyes half-closed. "There's a freshness to the air that reminds me of summer days in Bremagne. Barrett, where are we?" she asked, turning to face him.

He smiled with faint irony. "Not so very far from Bremagne, as it happens—but perhaps it is best if I do not tell you precisely where."

"Is it home, then?" she asked.

"As much of home as I have now," he replied. "I was born in the Purple March, but I have not lived there for a very long time."

"Not since—you lost your sight?" she dared to ask.

His lips tightened, pain flickering briefly in the emerald eyes as he turned his face toward the path ahead and started them along a walkway laid with crushed clam shells of a startling whiteness. The garden's sweet perfumes accompanied them as their garments brushed against close-growing lavender and sage and comfrey.

"There is nothing more precious than the young of a people," he said quietly, when they had walked along for several dozen strides in a silence broken only by the crunch of their footsteps against the distant cry of sea birds. "Twenty-three young ones would have burned that day, had I not intervened."

Horrified, she stared at him open-mouthed.

"Someone would have burned children?"

"Several of my people had been teaching them in secret, against the Laws of Ramos. The penalty was death. The teacher with them that day paid with his life at the time they were discovered. They cut his throat and left him to drown in his own blood—and in the presence of those little ones. The local lord meant to burn the rest—and none of them more than ten years of age."

"And you stopped it?"

He halted unerringly before a cut-stone bench and sank down on it wearily, loosing her hand as he did so.

"Aye, but at greater cost than even I could have imagined at the time. In what I imagined was noble self-sacrifice, I offered to trade my life for theirs: a mature Deryni, trained and dangerous, for the lives of two dozen little ones, who *might* survive to replace me." He closed his eyes briefly.

"A few did. And I—expected to be burned, in place of the children. But they started with my eyes instead. Then one of the other hedge-teachers from the forbidden *schola* came charging in to rescue me—and paid with *his* life." He dropped his head into his hands with a weariness come of having relived the horror all too many times.

"He was bolder than I; he used his magic to free me. But the archers cut him down as we fled, and he later died of his wounds. His wife had been present, and soon miscarried of what would have been their first child—*another* life lost."

Jehana's eyes had filled with tears as she listened, her thoughts flashing back to those halcyon months when she had carried Kelson beneath her heart—and the daughter who had survived only hours.

"You did a brave thing," she whispered.

"Brave, or foolish?" he replied. "I was young and arrogant, and lost not only my sight—and, therefore, a great deal of my own effectiveness—but the life of another trained Deryni, and a child who might, one day, have followed in his work."

"But you saved all those other children," Jehana ventured. "Surely that counts for something."

"Perhaps. But many of them died anyway, later on. For them, my folly only prolonged the inevitable—and lessened my usefulness to future generations of our people."

A silence fell between them, broken only by birdsong and the drone of bees and the distant boom of the surf.

"I think," Jehana finally said, "that you still have spent your life more fruitfully than I have done. By denying what I am, I threw away my heritage, the love of a good man—and have tried the patience of my only son almost beyond enduring, when what he needed most was my support."

"Ah, but when he needed that support the very most—at his coronation, when he still was vulnerable—you gave it to him," Barrett said gently. "And would have given up your life for him, in that moment."

"That's true," she said wistfully. "My own moment of divine folly, I suppose— and I would not change one heartbeat of that hour, when I gambled my life for the life of my son. But there are other things I would change, if I could. How could I have been so bli—"

She stopped as she realized what she very nearly had said, her cheeks flaming crimson, but thankfully he could not see them—though he reached across in that moment to gently take her hand.

"Dearest lady, you are very brave, indeed—and believe me, it is far better to finally see clearly than to continue cursing the darkness. I have mostly made peace with my darkness—and I think, perhaps, that you are also making peace with yours. Believe me, the worst blindness does not come from a lack of physical sight."

With that, he rose and gently drew her to her feet, tucking her hand through the angle of his arm.

"But come now, and let me show you more of my garden. Let me see it through *your* eyes. And I shall show you how it seems to me. . . ."

CHAPTER THIRTY

*Building an house unto the Lord, great and new, of
hewn and costly stones, and the timber already laid
upon the walls.*

I Esdras 6:9

*F*inalizing the marriage contract between Rory and Noelie took the better
part of a week, interspersed with the normal business of the court and the
growing press of wedding guests, arriving almost daily, though the attachment of
the pair was soon an open secret. It therefore came as no surprise when, at a formal court convened for that purpose, the official announcement was made that
Prince Rory Haldane, first cousin to the king, would marry the Lady Noelie Ramsay of Meara a week hence, on the same day her brother married the Princess
Richelle Haldane.

"I think there can be no doubt that this will be a true union of hearts, in addition to the obvious dynastic benefits that will accrue to all," Kelson said, smiling,
when Archbishop Bradene had witnessed the exchange of their betrothal vows.
"To seal the dynastic aspect of this union, I have decided to revive and bestow
upon my noble cousin the ancient title and style of Duke of Ratharkin, on their
wedding day . . . and I have it in mind that, during the next year, your new duke
shall take up residence in this royal duchy as my viceroy Meara."

A ripple of pleased surprise ran through the hall, especially among the Mearans, for even Jolyon had not known of Kelson's plan to name Rory viceroy. The
granting of viceregal status to Meara all but restored her ancient status as a principality, with the future Dukes of Ratharkin to spring from Mearan blood as well

as Haldane. Oksana stood with mouth agape, for her daughter would be vicereine as well as duchess—all but a queen.

"I gather that Meara is content," Kelson said mildly, with a smiling glance across the still-murmuring Mearans—which elicited a cheer.

"I have more to offer Meara," he said, as they settled again. "In further token of the importance I attach to this double sealing of our joint fortunes, by virtue of the forthcoming marriage already arranged between Lady Noelie's brother Brecon and my cousin Richelle, I have decided to somewhat amend what I announced at the time of their betrothal." He glanced benignly at the couple, then at Brecon's parents—still stunned at their daughter's good fortune.

"It is still my intention to create Brecon Ramsay and my cousin Earl and Countess of Kilarden on *their* wedding day," he went on. "However, it has occurred to me that a son ought not to outrank his father, and that this would be an appropriate time to acknowledge the Ramsay family's long-standing loyalty to our Crown and Realm. Accordingly, that creation will be subsidiary to a second ducal title that I intend to revive for Brecon's father—this title eventually to pass to the Earl and Countess of Kilarden and their issue."

Jolyon had closed his eyes, his face gone very still, as another frisson of excitement whispered among the other Mearans present. Oksana was holding onto her husband's arm in what appeared to be a death grip, joyful tears streaming down her face: confirmation, indeed, that Kelson had succeeded in defusing any lingering resentment over a perceived rejection of her daughter, and had bound Ramsay loyalty inextricably to Gwynedd.

Glad enough that he could create at least a little happiness amid the cold realities of arranged marriages and dynastic alliances sparked by politics and wealth rather than affection, Kelson allowed himself a faint smile as he went on.

"Therefore, on the eve of their children's marriages with my House, I shall create and establish Sir Jolyon Ramsay as Duke of Laas—and the Lady Oksana shall be Duchess of Laas. By these divers creations, and by promulgating these marriages, it is my fervent hope that the hostilities that have long marred relations between our two lands will cease, and peace will prevail at last."

Amid Mearan elation over the restoration of so many of their ancient titles, any niggle regarding the muddled succession status of one of their new dukes went largely unremarked. Afterward, as the court dispersed, Nigel quietly absented himself from the hall, as well-wishers flocked equally around the happy couple and the bride's parents. Only Kelson knew that, as agreed, Nigel had dutifully signed the appropriate documents that morning, restoring Albin to the Carthmoor succession—as would meet with general approval, once it became known, for the original decision had never been a popular one. But it would take more than a piece of parchment to admit the boy to his grandfather's heart.

Fortunately, with both the Torenthi situation and Meara largely resolved—and, apparently, the issue of his own marriage—Kelson could now turn some of his energies to a more satisfactory resolution of such domestic loose ends. And in that, he had engaged the willing assistance of his future queen, his mother, and several of the other ladies in his life.

"That will have been difficult for Nigel," Morgan remarked aside to Kelson, as they and Dhugal headed toward the council chamber, where Duncan was waiting to brief them on his site proposals for the Deryni *schola* to be established.

"At least he signed the Carthmoor documents," Kelson replied, as Derry and Father Nivard fell in behind. "And fortunately, the women of my family have far better sense than the men about dealing with such things. Araxie and Richenda have charge of resolving the next phase of *that* problem, with some invaluable conniving on the part of my mother and Aunt Meraude."

"Indeed?" Morgan said, with a raised eyebrow.

"Don't ask," Kelson muttered. "Or better yet, come along with me to the basilica later this afternoon, for the final inspection of the new chapel. *That's* progressing as well."

They spent the next hour studying Duncan's site recommendation, which, to Kelson's surprise and delight, now centered on the basilica itself, with its adjacent monastic complex and a cluster of ancillary buildings nearby that could be incorporated later.

"It will already have a Saint Camber focus, from the chapel," Duncan pointed out, letting Kelson and the others inspect the rough ground plan he had brought. "That will definitely make it attractive to the Servants. And best of all, it's within the walls of the outer keep—and therefore, under your direct control, for security purposes. Most of the buildings are usable as they are, and there's plenty of room for expansion. The advantages of having a Portal there already, and the secret passageway connecting that part of the outer yard to the castle, are things I don't think we want to mention to the Servants yet, as selling points, but all in all, I don't think you could ask for a better location."

Kelson nodded, casting his gaze over the ground plan of the area, and the accommodations encompassed.

"I like it. And it brings to mind something else I've been considering." He looked up thoughtfully at Duncan, sitting opposite him in the plain black cassock of a working priest, though his bishop's amethyst marked his actual rank.

"The new *schola* will need an ecclesiastical visitor—one who's sympathetic to the unique needs of such a foundation. In short, a Deryni bishop—and not one who's already attached to a diocese of his own, like Arilan," he added, anticipating the objection Duncan was about to raise. "It might take you out of the running for further episcopal advancement, at least for a few years, but maybe that's no bad thing. I told Bradene, before I approved your election as an auxiliary bishop, that I wouldn't allow you to accept any titular bishopric besides Rhemuth or possibly Valoret. I need you too badly here, with *me*."

Duncan was smiling resignedly, well aware of Kelson's affection, and his own key role in Kelson's governing strategy, and knew it was fruitless to gainsay him, even had he wished to do so.

"How, if you were to have Cardiel make you rector of the new *schola?*" the king went on. "That wouldn't have to interfere with your other present duties as his assistant. I could give you the living of the basilica; I've never liked having you all the way down at the cathedral anyway. Alaric, what do you think? Would Rothana go for it?"

Morgan was nodding, obviously intrigued by the possibilities.

"I confess, I hadn't thought that far ahead," he admitted. "But the arrangement *would* seem to be tailor-made—provided Duncan is willing to take on yet more administrative duties."

"There wouldn't be that many, in the beginning," Duncan said, already warming to the idea. "It would be a gradual shift in emphasis. Besides, I'd have first access to all the teachers we'd bring. There's still so much to learn. . . ."

"That's settled, then, as far as I'm concerned," Kelson said, satisfied. "You can stop looking for additional sites—at least until we're ready to open our *second schola*. Rothana may fight me at first—she'll see it as one more ploy to get Albin here at court—but apart from that, I don't see how she can possibly fault the logic. We'll have a good look at the facilities later this afternoon, when we go down to see the Camber chapel—and that's a good reason to insist that Nigel come along." He sighed. "Now we'll just hope that the next piece falls into place—and *that*," he said, "is in the hands of the ladies."

*K*elson duly assembled his handpicked inspection party shortly after noon—Dhugal, Morgan, and Nigel—and set out as soon as the latter met them at the appointed rendezvous in the cooler shade of the royal gardens, immediately beneath the gaze of the great hall. Duncan had preceded them down to the basilica, in readiness to receive the two archbishops coming up from the cathedral.

As they headed on through the gardens toward the wicket gate and long stair down to the basilica level, between the inner and outer wards, Kelson briefly reviewed what he had proposed to the others regarding the location for the *schola*.

Nigel listened with keen interest, apparently past his sulk of earlier in the day, as they passed from the public precincts of the royal gardens on through the area set aside for the exclusive use of the royal family, to skirt bustling evidence of domestic tranquillity.

On this fine afternoon, Meraude and Jehana had invited the Mearan brides and their mothers to bring their needlework into that garden, where some of the young children of the royal and noble ladies gathering for the coming wedding festivities were playing happily with the four-year-old Princess Eirian, under the watchful eyes of the assembled ladies. Rory and Brecon had taken the older children and some of the royal pages down to the river to swim their ponies in the shallows north of the city. Brecon's father and Baron Savile accompanied them, for it now was likely that several of the latter's children would be fostered to one or the other of the new noble households soon to be established in Meara.

The smaller boys, Morgan's Kelric and Sorley, Sivorn's six-year-old, were happily engaged in floating toy boats in a nearby pond, looked after by a maidservant, while their sisters ran and played with Eirian and Conalline—the child Nigel knew, if he recalled her name at all, as Amelia: a merry three-year-old with rosy coloring and a shock of chestnut curls, who had often caught his eye when he made his daily visits to play with his daughter. But he thought her merely one of many among the young children of one or another of his wife's ladies-in-waiting, who were permitted to live at court and have their offspring educated with the royal children.

Morgan's daughter Briony and Sivorn's youngest girl, Siany, rounded out the bevy of little girls presently running and playing in the garden. Richenda gave Kelson a slight nod as he and his party approached, herself discreetly keeping a low profile since her arrival back at court, lest she disturb the still fragile and tentative overtures of peace newly being displayed toward her by Jehana, who previously had shied away from any contact with the Deryni duchess.

Meanwhile, Araxie and "Uncle Séandry" had been drafted to supervise the girls, who were whooping with delight as their adult playmates took the part of very menacing wild beasts, creeping along behind hedges and along garden paths and suddenly looming to roar and snarl most ferociously, hands upraised like claws—and sometimes bolting into pursuit, to delicious squeals of terror and flight.

"Papa!" Briony squealed, as she spotted Morgan, in her exuberance nearly bowling over Eirian as she flung herself into her father's arms and Eirian raced toward Nigel.

Little Conalline fell down, tripped up by the enthusiasm of her elder playmates, but Eirian stopped immediately to comfort her, before the younger child could burst into tears, and made the pouting lower lip disappear before she continued on to greet her sire.

"Papa, have you come to play with me?" Eirian asked, reaching up for his embrace, and wrapping legs around his waist and arms around his neck as he lifted his daughter to kiss her and be kissed in turn. "I've missed you so!"

"What, since breakfast?" he returned, wide-eyed with indulgent amazement.

The ladies rose in the king's presence as he and his three dukes halted amid the milling, laughing children, the royal and noble ladies among half a dozen ladies-in-waiting helping with the needlework, all of them bobbing in casual curtsies. Noelie had been seated between her mother and her soon-to-be mother-in-law, with Richelle beside *her* mother, all of them chattering and stitching happily. Araxie, flushed and breathless from chasing children, stopped to scoop up Conalline and brace her on her hip before coming with Derry to greet Kelson.

"Good morrow, cousin. You find us awash in children and contentedly stitching up another wedding. Do you go now to inspect the new chapel?"

"We do," he replied, though the exchange was for Nigel's benefit, and all planned in advance. "But, how is it that you are free to frolic with these fair damsels, rather than being relegated to stitchery?" he asked, taking Conalline's little hand and bowing over it to bestow a courtly kiss.

"We picked Araxie!" Briony announced, from Morgan's arms. "Mummy said we could pick a grown-up to help Uncle Séandry play with us. Araxie is fun! She was pretending to be a ferocious lion! 'Melia was scared, but she's only little."

"*Not* scared!" Conalline blurted, lower lip outthrust in petulant denial.

"Well, she doesn't look scared to me," Kelson agreed, leaning over to kiss Eirian's hand as well, where she perched contentedly in her father's arms. "In fact all of these fair demoiselles look quite brave to me."

"Indeed, they are," Araxie said. "In fact, they've been so very brave, I was wondering whether they should be rewarded with a special outing this afternoon." She leaned closer to the men, as if in conspiracy, particularly careful not to exclude Nigel. "Actually, Lord Derry and I were wondering whether *we* might have a bit of an outing this afternoon—an escape, actually. I've been telling the girls about Saint Camber. Maybe we could come along to see the chapel, so that Maman and the other ladies madly stitching bridal finery can have an hour's peace."

"I don't know," Nigel said doubtfully, eliciting a pouting frown from his daughter. "A building site is hardly the place for small children."

"True enough," Dhugal said cheerfully, stooping to receive the embrace of Araxie's youngest sister, the seven-year-old Siany, who had come to offer him a flower. "But the building work is all but finished, I hear. The scaffolding has all been taken away, and they're just doing the final cleanup. Besides, the archbishops will be charmed. Who could resist such little angels?"

He grinned as he gave Siany a hug, for he was a favorite among the children. Simultaneously, Eirian planted another kiss on her father's cheek.

"Please, Papa, can we come?" she pleaded. "We'll be good, I promise! We'll hold Cousin Araxie's hand and be ever so quiet in church. Oh, please, Papa!"

Morgan, with an armful of daughter, arched an eyebrow at Araxie, whose youngest sister was now watching eagerly from her side, tugging on her sleeve. Richenda, too, had drifted over to join them.

"Oh, please!" Siany begged, turning her earnest gaze from her sister to Kelson. "Please, Sire, let us come."

"All four of you?" Kelson said, somewhat skeptically.

Four little chins nodded solemnly, each surmounted by a pair of wide, sober eyes.

"Kelson, I really don't think—" Nigel began.

"No, this is a chance for them to learn something important," the king replied. "It's been a long time since our children could learn about Saint Camber. And it isn't as if we have anything to do except take a look around. Eirian, are you sure you and the others can be good, if we let you come? If you misbehave, I shan't let you come along next time."

Eirian nodded, smiling happily around the two fingers she crammed into her mouth.

"Did you hear that?" Araxie asked Conalline, jogging her gently to get her attention. "Will you stay right with me and always hold someone's hand, if you're asked?"

As Conalline nodded solemnly, Richenda laughed and came to take Briony from her father's arms.

"I'll come along as well, Nigel," she said. "If the girls start getting restless, Araxie and Derry and I will bring them back. What could be more charming, than an impromptu outing on such a beautiful day?"

Nigel rolled his eyes, well aware that he had been bested, though with no idea how much. With resigned good humor, he set his daughter back on her feet and took her hand, falling in with the others as the little band bade farewell to the women settling back to stitch and made their way on toward the postern gate, and the long stair leading down to the basilica. Before they left the garden, following Siany's example, all three of the younger girls paused along the way to pick more flowers, for Araxie had explained that it showed good manners to bring a present when visiting a special friend.

"We're going to visit God!" Conalline declared, tilting back her curly locks to regard Nigel with sea-grey eyes, beaming as she held up a fluffy pink chrysanthe-mum in one little hand. "Do you think he'll like this one?"

"Why, I should think He would, indeed," Nigel assured her, charmed and utterly disarmed.

It was a fine summer day, not too hot, and the girls were models of eager decorum, chattering happily with the surrounding adults as they made their way out the postern gate and down the long steps to the basilica yard. Their presence made the little procession festive, something of a celebration, and brought a smile to those who saw the king, his uncle, and two dukes in their midst. Duncan was waiting in the church porch with the two archbishops and Father Nivard, beloved of all the children, and crouched down genially to greet them as the four little girls mounted the basilica steps ahead of the king, each of them with several flow-ers in hand.

"Why, what is this?" he asked, surveying all the children at eye level and accepting a hug from Briony. "Thank you. I see we have very important visitors, in addition to the king."

"We brought flowers for God," Briony announced, holding up a by now somewhat bedraggled stalk of hollyhock.

"Why, so you did," Duncan replied. "That was a very fine thing to do. And I see that all of you have brought flowers. Shall we give some of them to Our Lady? Or maybe one of you would like to be the very first person to give a flower to Saint Camber."

"I do, I do!" Eirian declared, tugging at her father's hand, as the other three joined in.

"Suppose Araxie and I organize this, while you go and inspect the new chapel," Richenda said to Kelson, laughing as a minor uproar broke out among the children and Araxie made shushing sounds behind an upraised finger. "We'll go visit Our Lady first, and leave her some flowers, and then we'll give some to Saint Hilary. This is his church, you know."

The prospect obviously appealed to her young charges, so she and Araxie headed off amid a happy chatter of childish voices, with Derry bringing up the rear, leaving Kelson and his three dukes with Duncan, the archbishops, and Nivard.

"They begged to come along," Kelson remarked with a shrug. "One should never discourage children who ask to go to a church. I hope they won't be too disruptive."

Cardiel smiled. "Children are always welcome in God's house, Sire. How else should they learn about Him? Come. I think you'll be pleased with what's been done."

The basilica was dim and cool and welcoming after the heat of the summer day. Their footsteps echoed on the marble floor as they passed down the north aisle, under the gaze of serried saints looking down from the stained-glass windows along the bays and statues of saints set into niches in the wall. Just before the transept, one bay had been opened to create a doorway arch, presently screened by a hanging of canvas to reduce dust and noise from the building site. As they approached it, Father Nivard moved ahead to pull the canvas aside.

The little chapel beyond was a shimmering jewel of simplicity, its walls clad with pale grey marble, the ceiling ribbed and vaulted to support a soaring dome. A graceful labyrinth design had been laid in the tessellated floor, in opalescent white and pale shades of grey, its convoluted path meandering from the arched entryway ever toward the center, where tiny golden tiles marked out a copy of the seal of Saint Camber, like the one set in the floor of the cathedral down in the city—the same that had triggered Kelson's Haldane powers at his coronation nearly seven years before. Though comparable in size to other side chapels that had been grafted onto the basilica over the years, the scale of the chamber gave the impression of a larger, airier space, flooded with light that streamed from high windows on two sides, mostly filled with clear or very pale amber glass. Kelson thought it might accommodate twenty to thirty people, depending upon how closely they stood—and probably but one celebrant at the small altar set against the east wall.

Stepping through the arch into the center of the space, Kelson cast his delighted gaze around the place as the others silently followed at his back. The workmen polishing the floor left off their work and retreated to the cloister garden beyond a small, arched door, for a much appreciated break from their labors.

No statue graced any part of the chapel. Nor had any attempt been made to invoke the imagery more traditionally associated with Saint Camber, in his own time; no emphasis on Camber's magic, but rather on what he had accomplished. Instead, set into the wall above the still-bare altar, a finely detailed mosaic depicted the crowning of King Cinhil Haldane by Camber of Culdi, on the morning of the Haldane Restoration.

The saint wore an earl's coronet and mail and a bright surcoat of red and blue, a sword girt at his side, and held the crown of Gwynedd aloft in offering—as Camber had, indeed, crowned Cinhil Haldane, ending the Interregnum of the Festils. The kneeling king was arrayed in mail and steel and Haldane crimson, hands clasped before him in thanks either to God or to the man who had helped him win back that crown. Though crown, king, and saint were surrounded by a golden glory, softly shimmering in the long, slanting sunlight filtering through the windows high in the western wall behind them, the manner of its depiction made it unclear whether the light was meant to be metaphorical or literal, enabling observers to form their own conclusions about whether Camber's assistance had come solely from his Deryni powers, from mere political astuteness, or the actual will of God.

Arched above the mosaic, worked as a decorative border to contain it in the angle of the ribs springing into the dome, polished golden letters had been set amid the little tiles, spelling out the legend: SANCTUS CAMBERUS, SALVATOR DOMUS HALDANI, DEFENSOR HOMINUM, ORA PRO NOBIS. Saint Camber, Saviour of the House of Haldane, Defender of Humankind, pray for us. . . .

"I think it came out rather well," Duncan said, when Kelson had drunk his fill of the visual delights of the place and turned to him in approval. "Very subtle— nothing to frighten anyone. And those sympathetic to his cause will understand." He glanced around them. "They're nearly finished with the floor. Then it only needs a final cleaning, to wipe down the last of the dust and such. Everything will be ready on the day. I hope you're pleased."

"Pleased? I'm delighted," Kelson said, looking to Morgan and Nigel and then the archbishops for their opinions. Everyone looked well-satisfied. "It's everything I imagined, that I hoped for. Has there been much local comment? How widely is it known what's being done here?"

Archbishop Bradene smiled. "I'm glad that you approve, Sire. There's been a great deal of careful groundwork laid while you were away—which has only been helped by your success in Torenth. And putting the first chapel here, rather than in the cathedral, was exactly the right choice, since it will allow gradual access and awareness to develop among the people—hopefully without generating any resentment or hostility. Word of mouth being what it is, there's certainly some awareness, but we don't foresee any opposition. And the consecration will be private, of course. I understand that Duncan has some interesting things planned."

Kelson grinned as Duncan assumed an expression of innocence, blue eyes cast briefly toward heaven, then shrugged.

"It will be a bit different," he allowed with a smile. "Lady Rothana has given me some guidance from the Servants in planning the ceremony."

"That should be interesting," Kelson said. "And I expect they'll continue to have input here—because I intend this for the site of the first Deryni *schola* in two centuries," he added, only grinning at the startled but not at all disapproving looks on the faces of his two archbishops. "That's the second part of my mission here this afternoon. I thought I'd have a look around while I'm here. Duncan can brief you in more detail after I've gone. This is marvellous. I'm very, very pleased."

They spent another few minutes inspecting finer points of the chapel's decor, after which Duncan began drawing them back toward the main body of the basilica. He ushered the archbishops past the canvas curtain, then followed, as Richenda and Araxie came into the chapel from the cloister garden with the children, each of them now clutching half a dozen flowers. Kelson paused, as did Morgan and Dhugal, leaving Nigel scant choice but to pause as well.

"We've been out to the cloister garden," Richenda announced, rolling her eyes as the four little girls trotted off to put their flowers on the altar, Siany in the lead, all of them chattering away, pointing at the mosaic of Saint Camber and King Cinhil. "I tried to keep them from trampling brother gardener's tidy flower beds. After they'd visited Our Lady and Saint Hilary and several other venerables and given them all flowers, they decided they hadn't enough left for Saint Camber—and I thought you'd appreciate the extra peace and quiet."

"Papa, I can't reach!" Eirian cried, glancing back in appeal as Briony stretched up to place her flowers beside Siany's.

Nigel came at once to lift his daughter up, Morgan and Araxie helping Briony and Conalline.

"Who can tell me who that is?" Araxie asked the children, as she lifted Conalline to show her the mosaic.

"Saint Camber!" they cried in chorus.

"An' King Cinhil!" Eirian chimed in. "My papa's great-great-great-grandpapa! Saint Camber helped him be crowned. See? Uncle Kelson, is that your crown?"

"Well, it might be," Kelson said, moving closer to look up at it. "Certainly, if Saint Camber hadn't helped my many-times great-grandfather, I wouldn't have any crown at all!"

As Kelson spoke, little Conalline turned in Araxie's arms and held out a flower to Nigel.

"You give this flower to Saint Camber?" she asked.

"Well, of course," Nigel replied, taking it with courtly grace. "I would be honored. Thank you very much, Amelia."

As he placed the flower, she wiggled to be put down beside Eirian, who crowed, "More flowers!" and went racing toward the door to the cloister yard.

"That's enough flowers for Saint Camber!" Richenda called out, as Derry started after her and Briony. "But why don't we take some flowers back to your mummies? That would also be a very nice thing to do . . . !"

Her voice trailed off as she and Dhugal followed all four children out of the chapel, leaving Araxie with Kelson, Nigel, and Morgan. As the four of them drifted toward the doorway, Nigel still charmed and smiling absently after them, Araxie glanced at Kelson, then laid a hand on Nigel's sleeve.

"That's your granddaughter, you know," she said quietly.

Nigel blinked blankly and turned to her in astonishment.

"What?"

"That's your granddaughter," Araxie repeated, her cool grey eyes engaging his, not in challenge but in simple assertion of fact. "And I should think that, by now, it's clear that that little girl is someone you ought to have in your life. She adores you, Nigel. Please don't let Conall's poor judgment deprive you of such sweetness."

Gaping at her, Nigel slowly closed his mouth, swallowing with difficulty, then turned to look accusingly at Kelson.

"You set me up," he said reproachfully.

Kelson only shook his head, smiling faintly. "I didn't set you up—though I wish I could take credit for it."

"But, how—?"

"You'll have to ask your wife and my mother about that—and your son," Kelson said. "While I was away, they found the child's mother and brought the pair of them to court. Eirian has been lonely, with her brothers so much older, so Aunt Meraude thought it would be lovely to have your granddaughter as a companion."

"The mother is a sweet girl, Nigel," Araxie said. "No one else at court knows who she is—besides Rory, of course. She's learning fine embroidery, and Meraude likes her very much—as does everyone else who's met her. And Amelia is Conalline's second name. If calling her by that name will make it easier for you to accept her, that's a concession that all of us can live with." She paused a beat. "But can you really live with knowing that you're denying yourself the joy of that little girl? Hasn't everyone suffered enough by now, for Conall's errors? You can end it. All you have to do is say the word."

Nigel turned away from all of them, saying nothing, head bowed. Kelson hardly dared breathe, and Morgan and Araxie likewise were silent. After a moment, Nigel reached out with a trembling hand to pick up the flower that Conalline had asked him to place on the altar. As he lifted it to inhale its fragrance, tears were brimming in his eyes.

"Dear God, what have I done?" he whispered. He swallowed audibly. "A part of me is furious that you've tricked me into letting her into my heart, but another part is rejoicing that she's not just a charming child who plays with my own little girl; she's my granddaughter!"

Kelson dared not speak as Nigel turned to face him, not allowing himself to flinch from his uncle's gaze. But Nigel hardly seemed to see him. Laying the flower back on the altar, he turned away like a man in a trance and moved slowly to the door leading to the cloister garden.

Through the archway, they could see Richenda, Dhugal, and Derry moving amid the flower beds with Conalline and the other children, ensuring that the girls did not totally denude the garden. As Nigel passed on into the garden, halted, and then began walking slowly toward his granddaughter, Morgan cast a pleased glance at Kelson, then left him with Araxie, who slipped an arm through Kelson's with affectionate contentment as the two of them gazed after.

"You did it," Kelson murmured, glancing at her sidelong in frank admiration. "And if he accepts Conalline, he'll accept Albin. It's only a matter of time."

She smiled contentedly and briefly leaned her cheek to touch his shoulder. "The credit really goes to Aunt Meraude and your mother," she said, "but I must confess that it's been fun helping extend the conspiracy—even more fun than my Cuan charade. You're accumulating a rather formidable array of ladies to help you behind the scenes, cousin. I think I shall enjoy being your queen."

"*Do* you?" Kelson said lightly, though with rather more satisfaction at that reassurance than he had dreamed possible. "I think I shall enjoy that as well."

Beyond them, in the garden, Nigel was crouched down on his hunkers to talk to Conalline, who was offering him another flower. Nigel's expression was almost beatific.

*B*y the time the king and his party had finished walking the grounds and surveying the buildings at the basilica, and he and Araxie had returned to the castle with Morgan and Dhugal, Nigel was not in evidence. He had accompanied Richenda and Derry back to the castle with the children, Eirian's hand in one of his and Conalline's in the other; but the private gardens now were empty. The ladies had retired to their respective quarters, the children were down for naps, and Meraude herself was nowhere to be seen—though Jehana came at once, when her son made inquiries at the ladies' solar.

"Nigel did look inordinately pleased when they came back," Jehana told Kelson with a droll smile, when he inquired as to the whereabouts of his aunt and uncle. "He drew Meraude aside, and after a few minutes, she laughed aloud and threw her arms around his neck. Then the two of them disappeared into her private chambers. They looked like a pair of newlyweds. I take it that he's pleased with his new granddaughter."

"Besotted!" Araxie declared happily. "And it's thanks to the plotting that you and Aunt Meraude did. Thank you, Aunt Jehana!"

Jehana inclined her head, herself smiling. "And thank *you*," she said, and looked at Kelson. "Will this make it easier now, to deal with Albin's situation?"

"I hope so," he replied. "But even if Nigel has come around, we still have to convince Rothana. She'll be here in the next few days."

"Then, we'd best see that we're ready for her," Jehana replied. She cocked her head. "Is it to be Conalline or Amelia?" she asked.

Kelson shook his head. "I don't know; that's for him to decide. I wasn't going to question the details of the miracle. I don't care what he calls her, as long as he accepts her—and Albin."

"I think that he'll accept them both," Araxie said. "And I think I now know how to approach Rothana." She slipped her hand into Kelson's and smiled. "Trust me, both of you," she murmured. "It will be all right."

CHAPTER THIRTY-ONE

And they lay wait for their own blood; and they lurk
privily for their own lives.

Proverbs 1:18

*A*t least an inkling of the afternoon's events had been gained by an erstwhile enemy of Gwynedd, observing from far Torenthály. The Princess
Morag Furstána, mother of Torenth's new king, drew a deep breath and closed
down the psychic link whose physical focus was the ring of iron on her left hand,
sitting back from her mirror of onyx to reflect on what she had seen, turning the
ring on her finger.

She was beginning to like the hapless Sean Lord Derry, who wore its mate.
Furthermore, what she was seeing, through his eyes, of the court of Gwynedd
and its king suggested that her own preconceptions, and many of the beliefs about
the Haldanes, long held in Torenth, perhaps were not entirely accurate.

Kelson of Gwynedd, despite his youth, was a temperate and fair-minded
monarch, both clever and sensitive, greatly respected and admired by all—at
least by everyone in Derry's circle of acquaintance. Duke Nigel Haldane, the
king's uncle, seemed every bit the noble and courteous knight whose praises her
son continued to sing.

Young Dhugal McLain, apparently the king's closest boon companion, lacked
the polished manner or guile of Torenthi courtiers; but he was unswervingly honest and loyal to his friend, and apparently uncontaminated by any taint of
unseemly ambition. Even the long-detested Morgan, whom she held responsible

for the deaths of her husband and her brother, was coming to seem a moral and even honorable man.

Then there was the very interesting Araxie Haldane, niece of the Hort of Orsal and cousin of Kelson, who seemed to be spending increasing periods of time with the king. It was Derry's belief—though no official announcement had yet been made—that she was the woman Kelson intended to marry.

Meanwhile, Araxie's sister was set to marry the heir to the Mearan throne— if Meara had still had a throne—and her bridegroom's sister now was going to marry Duke Nigel's son Rory. Derry had witnessed the announcement, this very morning, and was somewhat involved in logistic arrangements for the upcoming wedding festivities.

Weddings and weddings and—perhaps—weddings, if the speculation about Kelson was true. Morag was mulling these very interesting develop- ments, wondering how best to turn any of this information against Gwynedd— wondering, indeed, whether it was *needful* to continue thinking in terms of turning anything against Gwynedd—when power flared behind her, from her private Portal.

She came to her feet at once, for Teymuraz was standing there, hands clasped easily behind his back, merely looking at her.

"What are you doing here?" she whispered, cursing herself for nine kinds of fool for having neglected to ward the Portal against his use. But she had never dreamed that he would dare to return to Torenthály.

Her brother-in-law merely inclined his head.

"I've come to plead my case. I couldn't go to Laje or Mátyás. Laje is too well guarded, and Mátyás would never listen to what I have to say."

"Why *should* he, after your performance at *killijálay*? And why should *I* listen? You helped Mahael try to kill my son!"

"Dear, dear brother's wife, I did not think he meant to go for Laje. The plan was to kill Kelson of Gwynedd—or so I thought. So did Mátyás. That was the purpose of luring Kelson into the Moving Ward."

"But when Mahael and Branyng turned on Laje as well—and on you and Ronal Rurik—I saw their treachery for what it was, and joined my powers with yours to help defeat them."

It was a preposterous tale, if plausible in parts—and at least some of it was a lie—but she now was curious how far he would go.

"If that is true, husband's brother—that you are loyal to my son—why did you run?"

Teymuraz gave a snort, stepping from the Portal square to come and take a stemmed cup from the tray on the table between them, glancing sidelong at the scrying mirror toward her end of the table as he filled the cup from a fragile green glass flagon.

"By then, it was clear that Mátyás had allied himself with Kelson of Gwynedd. I feared that they would persuade Laje that I was a traitor."

"Do you so doubt the fidelity of your *padishah?*" she retorted. "The word of an honest man cannot be impugned by the lies of false witnesses."

"Our beloved *padishah*, your son, has been tainted by exposure to the West," Teymuraz said coldly, setting down his cup untasted. "He is too far corrupted now to ever be a proper Furstán! Best to cut our losses. Bypass Liam-Lajos, and put Ronal Rurik on the throne."

"Or you?" Morag countered. "With Mahael dead, you are now heir presumptive after Ronal Rurik, until he should produce an heir. Mahael killed my first son—and who knows whether you had a hand in that? You're now proposing that I countenance the killing of my second son. What is to prevent the killing of the third as well?"

"Then, take the crown yourself," Teymuraz whispered, resting both hands on the table to lean closer to her, "and breed more sons. You could be a formidable queen—and empress, if you chose. No woman may rule Torenth, but by Festillic House law, a woman *could* rule Gwynedd—and then she could conquer Torenth. Even now, you are titular Queen of Gwynedd, if only you will reach out and take it! In fact, you and I could rule an empire uniting all the Eleven Kingdoms of old!"

"You're mad!" she stated flatly. "Why am I even listening to you? Do you really think that I could harm my sons, or allow you to do so? And for what? To rule beside you?" She drew herself up proudly. "My son rules, Teymuraz, and his sons will follow him. And if not this son, I have another—and *he* shall have sons!"

"And meanwhile," Teymuraz purred, "the Haldane and my treasonous little brother will overcome them both, by kind words and insidious alien ideas and treacherous half-truths, and Torenth will be changed forever! Do you not see that they must be stopped?"

"You *are* mad," she whispered, real fear stirring in her breast, fatally aware, between one heartbeat and the next, that she had greatly underestimated him; that, very likely, she would not be granted time enough to throw magic between them before he killed her.

She bolted anyway, in a sudden shimmer of tiny golden bells at throat and ears— for the door, for the Portal—for anywhere that would take her from this viperous presence. But he was moving even as she moved, overturning the table in a deluge of shattering glass to catch her by one wrist and wrench her around like a drover cracking a whip, seizing her head between his hands and giving it a sharp twist.

The sound of her own neck snapping was the last thing she heard. But the last thing she felt was the brutal thrust of his mind into hers, ripping it asunder—a searing conflagration that scoured into the depths of sanity in a long-drawn agony that went on . . . and on . . . and on. . . .

He revelled in his moment of triumph. With her head lolling bonelessly on her broken neck like a broken doll, light and life fading from the startled, staring eyes, he held her limp body tenderly to his own, as a lover holds his beloved, one hand clasped behind her back and the other thrust into her hair as focus for his rending while he ruthlessly tore from her every vestige of what had made her what she was, regretting that she had driven him to do what he had done—for she had been a handsome and spirited woman.

But the power was sweet, and the knowledge sweeter still—secrets he had not dreamed she possessed, keys to greatly further his ambitions.

"You should have joined with me, brother's wife," he whispered, when it was done, finally letting her down beside the stain of wine spreading upon the priceless Bhuttari carpet. "I fear you shall not live to regret that decision."

Crouching there beside her lifeless body, he gently shifted her head to an angle of mere repose, then covered her face with her veil of royal purple. Only then did he take from her hand the heavy iron ring—Wencit's ring; he remembered it well. He had long wondered what became of it.

He closed it briefly in his hand, smiling, then rose and went to a locked cupboard secreted behind a tapestry of rich Vezairi work, broken glass crunching beneath his boots. Both the lock and less ordinary safeguards yielded at once to his touch, and he breathed a silent whistle under his breath as he ran a hand down the stack of bound volumes.

"So, brother's wife, *this* is what became of Wencit's notes. And all these years, you kept them from me. . . ."

Pulling the books from their safe place, he cradled them possessively to his chest and carried them to the Portal square, casting a final look at the sprawled, purple-clad form lying beside the overturned table.

"Greet my brothers for me in hell, dearest Morag," he said aloud. "And say that I shall send the other one to join them, as soon as I may."

*T*he body was not discovered until the morning, when Morag's servants came to draw her bath and bring a light repast. Their screams brought guards, who summoned other guards and sealed off the room. Mátyás was there within a quarter-hour, summoned from Beldour; Liam-Lajos soon after, closely accompanied by four bodyguards with drawn scimitars, sent by his uncle to fetch him.

"Who has done this thing?" Liam whispered, from the open doorway of his mother's apartment. The vizier and two of his officers were crouched beside the sprawled body of his mother while a fourth man, robed all in white, probed for evidence of the violence done to her mind, his slender hands set lightly along her temples. From farther across the room, Mátyás looked up from examining the Portal square, rising to come to Liam and draw him into the room, bidding the guards stay outside as he drew the door shut.

"It was Teymuraz, without a doubt, my prince," he said softly. "I have taken steps to ensure that he cannot return the same way, but he does have access to a Portal now, I know not where. I have already sent Janos Sokrat and Amaury Makróry to ward such others as are most strategic, beginning with your own in the royal apartments."

"I passed them on the way here," Liam said, nodding numbly, grief like a grey veil upon his face as he turned to look back at his mother. "Did she suffer?"

"Not physically," Mátyás replied. "Her neck was snapped. The end would have come very quickly."

"But he mind-ripped her, didn't he?" Liam said through tight jaws.

"I fear he did," Mátyás admitted. "I cannot lie to you."

"Nor would I wish it." Liam drew a deep breath and let it out. "You must tell Bishop Arilan what has happened—and Lord Azim—and they must inform King Kelson. If Teymuraz would kill his own kin, God knows what else he might do. I now do not doubt that he played some part in my brother's death; I feared it before, but I did not really think he could have done it—though that was before Mahael's treachery."

He glanced around the room, trying to think what Kelson would do—or Duke Nigel—trying *not* to think about who lay there amid the shards of a shattered life. "Was anything else disturbed? Can you tell yet whether anything is missing?"

"Among a woman's trinkets, who can say?" Mátyás replied. "These were her very private quarters. A wall-safe stands open, there behind the tapestry, but we do not know yet what it contained. All the servants will be questioned. I have sought already for traces in the Portal, as to where he might have gone, but without success. Beyond that, I confess I know not what else to do."

Nodding numbly, Liam walked over to the trellised window and gazed out through the brass grillwork, resting his hands at head level on the wooden frame that held the screen in place. After a moment, with a glance at the white-robed mage still working on Morag's body, Mátyás came quietly to join him, slipping an arm close around his shoulders but saying nothing.

"Tell me, Uncle," the young king whispered after a moment, "is a land worth saving, when it can spawn such as killed my mother this way?—and from the bosom of our own family. Perhaps I was too long in Gwynedd, but we of Torenth seem a murderous lot. The pages of our history are filled with regicides and fratricides and patricides and other kin killing kin. And I am expected to rule such men, when I cannot restrain my own House!"

A stifled sob rose in his throat, his loss welling up, and his hands slid down from the window frame to cover his averted face, shoulders shuddering in silent grieving—all at once, not the puissant sovereign of a powerful and ancient kingdom, but a fourteen-year-old boy mourning the loss of his mother. Containing his own sorrow, offering what comfort he could, Mátyás let his shields enfold the pair of them and drew his nephew gently away from the glaring light of the window, his body shielding the boy from the covert glances of the vizier's men as they moved into the sheltering privacy of the next room.

CHAPTER THIRTY-TWO

But her end is bitter as wormwood, sharp as a two-edged sword.

Proverbs 5:5

$\mathcal{K}$elson received the news of Morag's murder toward midday, as he prepared to ride down to the cathedral with Dhugal and Morgan and Derry. The latter was particularly pleased to be included in the king's company, and well content to be back in Rhemuth, for he had not much liked the idea of going into Torenth with Morgan—or the manner of returning from there!—and facing up to the fears residual from his long-ago experience at the hands of a Torenthi king.

Happily, nothing had happened to frighten him unduly. And he had gone as Morgan's aide—a duty he greatly enjoyed under normal circumstances, and for which he had first entered Morgan's service as a green young knight, on the very day of his dubbing by Kelson's father—for it was not often that he was free to resume that early role as aide and boon companion. He had enjoyed the part of the Torenthi venture that involved serving Morgan, as he was enjoying these past days spent in Rhemuth, often at Morgan's side.

As he helped the groom hold Morgan's horse for him to mount, it came to him that he would have preferred a less pastoral existence than the one his life gradually had become. For some years, duties of a more responsible nature than an aide's—and far less fun!—had kept him based at Coroth, Morgan's capital, there to assist in the smooth running of his lord's household during his frequent and often prolonged absences from Corwyn in the service of King Kelson. In the early months of Morgan's marriage to the Lady Richenda, Derry and a few trusted officers of Morgan's staff had provided sympathetic companionship and support for their lord's new duchess—Deryni, and the widow of a traitor, and mother of a possible rival for her affections among later children she hopefully would bear for Morgan—and very, very much alone. Derry soon had taken on a role of a surrogate younger brother for the lonely Richenda, and had quickly become "Uncle Séandry" to her young son, and to her children by Morgan, as these began to come along. By no word or action had Morgan or anyone else attached any blame to Derry for what he had been forced to do seven years before, under the compulsions of Wencit of Torenth. Nor had anyone around him any inkling that those compulsions had been renewed, and again sunk into abeyance, at the death of Morag of Torenth.

Derry was swinging up on his own horse, the king and his two dukes already mounted, preparing to move out, when Father Nivard came dashing down the great hall steps with the first stark details.

"There's been murder done in Torenthály!" he said, puffing to a halt as he caught himself on Kelson's stirrup.

"Not—"

"No, not Liam or Mátyás," Nivard assured him, as the others kneed their horses closer. "Morag."

"Morag?!" Kelson repeated, stunned.

"I have no details," Nivard said, gulping for breath. "Thank God I caught you. Bishop Arilan and Prince Azim are waiting in the library."

They bailed off their horses and went at once, Kelson sending Derry to summon Nigel as well. In the library's annex, close by the Portal by which he and Arilan had come, Azim quickly began a stark recital of the facts as then were known. He had hardly begun when Nigel arrived, though Derry remained with Father Nivard in the outer library, being reluctant to pass through the Veil again.

"Certain it is that Teymuraz performed the deed, but his motive is uncertain," Azim finally said, by way of summary. "It may have been vengeance, it may have been an instant's decision. There is evidence of a sudden and violent struggle. He must have shaken her as a terrier shakes a rat, for her neck was snapped like a twig. But that manner of death is also one of the surer ways to facilitate a mind-rip."

Kelson exhaled forcefully, feeling a little queasy, trying not to imagine Morag's final moments. Mind-ripping itself was a thing difficult to do and more difficult to justify. Most often, it occurred as an accidental side effect of too much power wielded with too little control and too little knowledge. Occasionally, it happened in the course of other necessity, as when Liam had ripped the mind of

Mahael while taking back his purloined power, but deliberate mind-ripping was an obscenity abhorred by all Deryni of any scruples.

"In practical terms," Kelson asked Azim, with a sidelong glance at his companions, "what are the implications, if Teymuraz succeeded in taking on the full accumulation of Morag's knowledge? I know it's possible to extract specific information, even from an unwilling source, if one knows what one is looking for. It's my understanding that Wencit himself trained his sister—and while I know it isn't customary for women to receive the same training as men, I can tell you, from firsthand experience, that she was very, very strong. Does this mean that Teymuraz now has access to whatever Wencit taught her?"

"I cannot answer that," Azim said. "With intent and preparation, it is possible, in theory, to distill and integrate the flow of memory and knowledge as it is drawn. On a very small scale, this can be done without harm to the subject or to the one who seeks such knowledge; we do it every time we probe another mind. I have even heard it said that the ancients had the ability to tap the memories and knowledge of a dying mage and draw from him the essence of what should be preserved and passed on to succeeding generations."

All of them were gazing at the desert prince in wonder.

"Mind-ripping, whether planned or incidental to some other intent, does not allow the leisure for such sifting and distilling," Azim went on. "By its very nature, it is a very sudden and violent act. Hence, Teymuraz will also have obtained a great deal that is worthless, along with what he sought. An individual's everyday thoughts and memories are of little interest to anyone else besides that person, even one such as Morag.

"Accordingly, he now will need to spend the time to sift and refine away the dross, before he can make much use of what he has stolen. Not to do so is to court madness, if he too long delays. I do not think he will be so brash as simply to run amok, without some plan. He has gone too far, risked too much. He could bide his time for a decade, even two, and still be in his prime. He will not throw that all away."

"You're saying we *have* time, then?" Arilan asked.

Azim inclined his head. "With luck, I think it likely—though there are no guarantees. A great deal depends upon the strength of the assistance he can rally. Mátyás is aware of some of those who might aid him—both the political supporters and those who might assist him in the magical work he must do—but we dare assume nothing.

"Meanwhile—and this much is certain—he will have gained access to a Portal; my Order has already begun to make inquiries regarding the many sites known to us—some of them perhaps known to Teymuraz. It is now more than a week since he sailed from Saint-Sasile, so he could have made landfall almost anywhere; but there are few Portals in Gwynedd or the far West, and few likely to be known to him. This means it is probable he has sailed south and west, perhaps around the horn of Bremagne, until he reached a friendly port he knew and could make his way to a Portal."

Kelson's heart sank, thinking of the many miles of coastline stretching southward along the Southern Sea. Finding Teymuraz now seemed even more impossible than he had first believed.

"What next, then?" he asked. "How much at risk is Liam? And how is he holding up? He's just lost his mother."

"He is a Furstán, and has faced far worse, in his young life," Azim replied, though not without compassion. "But Mátyás is at his side, as are other good men, and as I shall be. He is no longer your concern. You are no longer his lord."

"I shall always be his *friend*, Azim," Kelson answered. "I care very much what happens to him, and to Mátyás, and to their people."

Azim inclined his head in an eloquently Eastern gesture of assent. "I have never doubted that, my prince. But you must allow him to stand or fall on his own merits, assisted by his own people—the cause for which every true king will lay down his life, if need be. If he cannot do that, Torenth shall never truly be his land."

Kelson briefly averted his gaze, knowing Azim was right.

"Please convey my sympathy on the death of his mother," he said quietly, "and say that if ever there is any way I may render assistance, of whatever kind, he has only to ask."

"I believe he knows that, Sire."

"Just tell him."

"I shall do so," Azim agreed.

*A*fter Azim and Arilan had gone, Kelson and his companions likewise quit the library annex, though by means of the Veiled doorway rather than the Portal. After sharing with Derry and Father Nivard an abridged account of the implications of Morag's murder, focused on his concern for the now motherless Liam and the impact, on Torenth, of her death, Kelson asked Nivard to offer Masses for Morag's soul for the next three days. Out of deference for Derry's uneasiness regarding things Deryni and their magic, he did not go into the details he knew Nivard would want to know; but he had already asked Dhugal to brief the priest later on—and to share the news with his father, for Duncan should be told as well.

The news of Morag's murder, coupled with the arrival of the Tralian wedding ship at Desse later that day, forced him to abandon his earlier plans to ride down to the cathedral—for that had been their intended destination. After closeting himself for the afternoon with his council, he was obliged to carry out hosting duties in the great hall that night, for the day of the great Mearan wedding fete was fast approaching, and guests were arriving daily.

Nor was he able to get away the following day, for he must make his appearance at the first of Morag's Masses in the morning, followed by attending to a host of dreary duties related to the upcoming festivities, for Saer de Traherne brought the baggage train up from Desse, with the Tralian bridal finery. He also brought back the detachment of Haldane lancers who had accompanied the king to Torenth—and Ivo Hepburn, Kelson's other senior squire. Kelson did deputize Morgan to ride down with Richenda and Araxie, to advise Archbishop Bradene that he wished the Servants of Saint Camber to be housed at the basilica when they arrived, not the cathedral; and having done that, he bade them return by way of that basilica, to make direct arrangements there.

It was yet too soon to consider how he might help Liam and Mátyás in any concrete way, far away in Torenth; but the news of Morag's brutal murder only underlined the importance of proceeding with the establishment of a Deryni *schola* under Crown patronage. The events of the past month had amply shown how the might of Deryni magic could feed the power of ambitious men; and only knowledge and responsible training in the use of that magic—especially its benign uses—could combat the kind of turmoil presently seething in Torenth.

CHAPTER THIRTY-THREE

Gather my saints together unto me; those that have made a covenant with me by sacrifice.

Psalm 30:5

The Servants of Saint Camber numbered twelve plus one, as they rode through the gates of Rhemuth the evening before the scheduled consecration of his new chapel. Rothana was in their company, with her young son—as, indeed, were several others of the band accompanied by children. Mother and son lodged that night in the accommodations provided for the Servants in the monastic establishment adjacent to the basilica, though usually Rothana stayed at least a few days with her son's grandmother up at the castle, having no wish to deprive Meraude of access to her only grandson, no matter the cloud of guilt that continued to vex both Nigel and Rothana because of the deeds of the boy's father.

Word of their arrival came as a relief to Kelson, up at the castle, though he made no attempt to see Rothana that night, having already laid a different strategy from the one she might be expecting, at least regarding her son. She would be happy enough to hear that he did, indeed, intend to marry Araxie; but her intentions regarding Albin remained the final point of contention between them. Rather than tackling that in private, he had decided to present his latest proposition in the context of the offer he now planned to lay directly at the feet of the Servants, before the expected ceremony at midday. And he would frame that in a way that he hoped the Servants would be unable to ignore—or refuse.

Accordingly, the king marshalled his accomplices and reinforcements for an early arrival at the basilica the next morning, with Morgan, Dhugal, Araxie, and Richenda to attend him at the meeting. Meraude and Jehana came as well, along with Richelle, to dote on little Albin in the cloister garden while his mother attended to the Servants' business.

Bishop Duncan McLain, now provost of the basilica chapter—and incipient rector of the *schola* to be established there, though only he and the king's companions yet knew it—was on hand to greet the Servants at midmorning, as they began to congregate in the cobbled cloister yard for the ceremony yet an hour and more away, inviting them to bide their time in the dim coolness of the chapter house, adjacent to the south transept. When most of them had obligingly filed into the chamber, largely unaware exactly who Duncan was, besides a bishop—evident by ring and cross and purple cassock—Duncan glanced farther along the eastern cloister range toward the arched doorway that led into the nave, and nodded broadly.

At once, Kelson and his chosen four came walking briskly along the colonnade—two dukes, a duchess, and a royal Haldane princess—all of them richly but quietly attired, as became the solemnity of the coming event, all of them wearing coronets of their rank. He fell back to let the others precede him before himself entering the chapter house.

The Servants were milling quietly inside, murmuring among themselves, and only gradually became aware that their ranks were being infiltrated. As Kelson casually followed his four toward the apsidal niche enlarging the east end of the little chapter room, where was set the simple chair of stone from which the house's abbot normally presided, Duncan quietly closed the door behind them. As the king's companions took the first four places before the stone bench set against the north wall, Kelson himself claimed the abbot's chair. Thirteen pairs of eyes were fixed on him uncertainly, Rothana's among them, as he and his companions sat, without ceremony.

Kelson let the silence deepen for a few taut heartbeats, then briefly allowed his shields to flare visibly about his head, his four co-conspirators doing likewise, in unmistakable affirmation of what, if not who, they were. A murmur passed among the Servants, though none showed any fear, and a few flared shields of their own to show that there were Deryni among them as well, though most were human. Most of them had recognized both Kelson and Dhugal by now, having made their acquaintance when the pair first discovered their long-hidden enclave in the remote mountains of Carcashale.

But when Duncan abruptly vacated his place before the door and came to join the king, flaring his Deryni aura as the others had done and maintaining it as he quietly took a place at Kelson's left, the Servants' murmuring died away and they moved at once to the stone benches set along the south and west sides of the little chapter room, sitting obediently at the king's gesture of leave. The Servants might

be little impressed by the presence of a king whom most had seen in his naked-
ness, as he prepared to face the ritual they called the *cruaidh-dheuchainn*, the *per-
iculum*, the ordeal by which true vision of Saint Camber was tested—and which
test Kelson of Gwynedd had passed to their satisfaction; but the open presence of
an undoubtedly Deryni bishop at that king's side engaged their complete attention. Rothana looked puzzled and vaguely suspicious, seated among the Servants
along the south wall.

"I bid you welcome," Kelson said to them, as Duncan let the glow of his
shields die away, merely standing beside him. "I apologize for the somewhat dramatic nature of my coming among you, but you will understand my reason in a
moment. I trust that, by now, all of you have had a chance to inspect your patron's
new chapel. I hope you are as pleased as I am, to see this milestone in our labors
of the past several years."

Utter silence greeted this declaration—not hostile, but certainly wary.

"Various of my Deryni advisors have guided me in the design of the chapel we
shall consecrate a little later today," Kelson went on, glancing toward the four
seated along the wall to his right. "It is my most earnest prayer that this holy place
will serve as a fitting focus to encourage the rediscovery and open veneration of
your august patron once more. Indeed, the two ladies seated here at my right have
named themselves particular patrons of the work you have striven to advance for
the past century and more: my cousin, the Princess Araxie Haldane, and the Lady
Richenda de Morgan, wife of my trusted friend and advisor, the Duke of Corwyn."

He indicated Morgan and Dhugal, sitting beyond the women. "Many of you
will remember the MacArdry of Transha from our brief sojourn among you, a few
years ago. He is now Duke of Cassan and Earl of Kierney as well as Earl of Transha.
Bishop McLain you have already met." He glanced up at Duncan with a nod. "As is,
by now, apparent, all of us are Deryni or of Haldane blood—which may well be
the same thing. Perhaps some of you will help us to learn more of that."

Before him and to the left, ranged on the stone benches set along the sides
and back of the room, the Servants of Saint Camber turned coolly appraising
glances on those he had named. All of them, men and women, were garbed for
their patron's celebration in simple grey robes girt at the waist with a cincture of
knotted red and blue cord. Though a few of the men were close-shorn, some even
tonsured, most wore the *g'dula*, their version of the Border braid that Kelson and
Dhugal favored. A few of the men wore belted swords as well.

The women conveyed more of the impression of a religious order. Though
the Servants were a lay order, most of the older women wore coifs and wimples
covering their hair, reminiscent of religious habit. The younger ones, including
Rothana, seemed to favor veils of fine, gauzy white linen over hair neatly dressed

in a knot at the nape of the neck, bound across the brow with a braided torse of red and blue cord. Kelson recognized several faces among them, including—he thought—a young woman called Rhidian, who had spoken for the Quorial, the Servants' eight-person governing body: one of the few he was definitely certain was Deryni. Then, she had been a girl-woman, disturbingly wise-seeming and direct for one so young.

It was she whom Kelson had expected to speak, if not Rothana herself; but instead, an elderly woman whom Kelson also recognized, the *ban-aba* Jilyan, slowly rose, according him a dignified inclination of her head.

"We thank the king's friends for their patronage, my lord king," she murmured, "and we also thank Your Grace. Please know that we are grateful for the work that all of you have done on behalf of our patron, the Holy Camber. If God wills it, this will be but the first of many shrines to his memory, where those of our race may draw inspiration to take up their heritage, for the good of all our people."

"That is my most fervent wish as well, Ban-Aba," Kelson replied, giving her the title she was accorded among the Servants, roughly equivalent to an abbess. "In support of that aspiration, I wish to offer a proposal to the Servants of Saint Camber, as further evidence of my support of your work. Please be easy," he added, gesturing for her to sit—and deliberately avoiding Rothana's eyes. "You need not give me your answer until after we have properly reinstated the Blessed Camber in our noontime observances, for I wish to give all of you the opportunity to meditate upon my proposal, while we offer our prayers together."

The ban-aba glanced at Rothana as she sat, in a look of question, but Rothana only shrugged, for she knew nothing of the king's plans.

"I shall not mince words, then," Kelson went on briskly. "In the nearly seven years since coming to my crown, as I have sought to redress the errors of the past—especially as they concern our Deryni heritage—it has become increasingly obvious that only knowledge can eradicate the misconceptions upon which two centuries of persecution were founded. Changing the law is a start—and I have begun that process, as is evidenced by the presence of several Deryni priests among my immediate entourage, including the good Bishop McLain." He gestured toward Duncan. "But only the education of our people into the fullness of their heritage will enable them to properly take their rightful place in this kingdom.

"Accordingly, I make you this proposal. I am prepared, under certain conditions, to grant substantial lands and revenues here in Rhemuth for the foundation and support of a royal *schola* or collegium, under the direct protection of the Crown, whose purpose will be the identification and proper education of Deryni. I am informed that such collegia once existed, to train Deryni in the responsible use of their powers, and I am determined that they shall exist again."

"You mentioned certain conditions," said a thickset man seated next to Jilyan—Brother Michael, the hard-nosed spokesman of the Quorial, another Deryni.

Kelson inclined his head. "They are few, Brother Michael—only three, in fact. They are not negotiable, but I think you will find them acceptable. First of all, the quarters I propose to give this first royal collegium lie here within the walls of Rhemuth Castle's outer ward—the abbey precincts of this very basilica, with whose accommodation you are already familiar—with ample room for expansion. Foundation of your *schola* here will enable me to give you the protection of the Crown, should there be initial opposition to your work until the people learn that they have nothing to fear from Deryni. And of course, I would expect that a substantial number of the Servants of Saint Camber would relocate to Rhemuth, to support this endeavor."

"That is acceptable," Jilyan said flatly, before any of the others could comment, though Rothana looked startled at the last part. "What else?"

"The new collegium will require a rector, who should be a cleric, even though you are a lay order, for it will still be attached to the basilica—which will continue to function as such, under royal warrant. In the past, this would have given cause for grave concern, since the Church and Deryni were at odds with one another in law, but the law has now been amended.

"Accordingly, I have asked a Deryni cleric to accept this position, should you agree to be a part of this endeavor. Bishop McLain, who presently is auxiliary here in Rhemuth, as well as having charge of this basilica, is willing to serve in this capacity, and to work with the archbishop and the synod of bishops to integrate the training of Deryni clergy with the work of the collegium. Through Duchess Richenda, Princess Araxie, and your own Lady Rothana and their contacts in the East, he will be able to assist in the recruitment of suitable teachers, so that our task of education may go forward."

The look on Rothana's face declared her taken totally by surprise, clearly intrigued by the prospect of the college itself—for it was a logical extension of the dream she and Kelson had shared for Gwynedd—but well aware that her participation in the exercise would bring her into far closer ongoing contact with Kelson and the court than she had planned . . . and as yet uncertain what might be inferred from Araxie's presence.

"This is both generous and farsighted, Sire, and I am certainly willing to serve in an advisory capacity," she began, "but I should prefer to remain based in—"

"For this to succeed," Kelson interjected, cutting across her objection, "I shall need your presence here, Rothana. This is my third and final condition." His gaze locked on hers, reaching out to her for some vestige of what they once had shared. "I wish you—no, I *ask* you, as Deryni—for the sake of this land for which you have already offered up so much, to accept appointment as lay assistant to the rector, to be the interface between the Servants and my council—and be resident here in Rhemuth."

"Sire—"

"Perhaps it would be best if we now suspend this discussion until after the ceremony," Kelson said firmly, flicking his gaze over the rest of them. "I ask that, as we witness the reinstatement of your saintly patron, all of you meditate upon what I have proposed. I shall certainly do so. Afterward, I shall speak privily with the Lady Rothana," he added pointedly, "for I think much will depend upon her decision. Meanwhile, I thank you for your time and ask you to excuse me, for I must go now to prepare for the ceremony that has brought us here."

With that he rose, summoning Dhugal and Morgan with a glance as he strode briskly out of the chapter room, Duncan following, hoping that this abrupt and uncharacteristic ending of discussion had gotten Rothana's attention. The Servants streamed after them amid a murmur of amazed and excited speculation, as soon as the four had disappeared through the doorway—except for Rothana, who was left with Richenda and Araxie, looking somewhat stunned.

"Whatever can he be thinking?" she said, turning dark eyes on the pair of them bewilderedly. "The offer for the *schola* is generous, but I cannot—"

Richenda went to close the door to the chamber, staying then to lean her back against it, as Araxie came to sit beside Rothana.

"A great deal has happened, most of it very good, indeed," she said, touching a sympathetic hand to Rothana's shoulder.

"Then—he *did* ask you to marry him, did he not?"

"He did, of course, though it's not yet been announced. Rory and Noelie are to wed first, as you hoped—and that has changed a few things you may not have reckoned on."

Briefly she told Rothana of the Mearan titles, and Nigel's concession regarding the Carthmoor succession, with the subsequent reinstatement of Albin as Nigel's heir, and of Nigel's acceptance of little Conalline.

"Though she's to be called by her second name, Amelia," Araxie concluded. "Meraude suggested that. The mite's poor mother never would have named the child for her father, had she dreamed that the girl would be acknowledged as Conall's natural daughter. But I think that none of us need the constant reminder of *him*."

"Araxie, that was wicked of you, to manipulate poor Nigel!" Rothana murmured. "And Meraude, and Jehana—"

"And me," said Richenda, coming from her post by the door to join them, sitting on Rothana's other side. "And even Oksana Ramsay, for that matter."

"No one can change the past," Araxie said. "But Conall's children should have the chance to know their grandparents—and Meraude and Nigel should know the joy of their grandchildren. Little Amelia is a darling child . . . and Eirian already adores her."

Rothana closed her eyes, blinking back tears.

"Albin shouldn't be at court, Araxie," she whispered. "He could become a danger to your sons some day."

"Frankly, I think he's more likely to become a danger to my sons if he *isn't* at court," Araxie said bluntly. "You've focused so closely on proper training for Deryni—how about proper training for a man? Albin is a Haldane, a prince of Gwynedd. His grandfather is the most *parfait* knight in all the realm, and his cousin is the King of Gwynedd—himself already well respected throughout these Eleven Kingdoms as a noble and virtuous liege of exceptional honor. And his mother is Deryni, about to found the first Deryni *schola* in this land in nearly two centuries. What better examples could a boy have?"

"But I've—promised him to the Church. . . ."

"A promise that was made when you thought there were no better options, for him *or* for Gwynedd," Araxie answered. "How many bishops would you like me to have dispense you from that promise? I can have Kelson get as many as you like. Rothana, it simply isn't right that Albin should have to suffer for what his father did—and he doesn't *need* to suffer, unless you insist upon it!"

"Would it be such suffering, to be brought up for the Church?" Rothana asked.

"Unless that's what *he* wants, the answer is yes," Araxie replied. "If you accept Kelson's offer, you and he and Albin and all of us can have very good options, indeed. You would be here, close at hand, to help and advise Kelson—and me! And Albin can learn the fullness of his Deryni heritage, and his heritage as a Haldane, and then decide what kind of a life *he* wants.

"In the fullness of time, that could be as Duke of Carthmoor, as is his birthright—or he could pass that title on to Payne and *his* sons, if he *should* decide he wants to pursue a religious vocation. But there can't be anything much sadder than—than being forced into a religious life when you don't want to be . . . or being denied one, if that's what you're really called to do."

Rothana looked up at Araxie, clearly taken back by that last observation.

"Marriage, even to Kelson, would have been a compromise, wouldn't it?" Araxie ventured, after a beat.

"Life is full of compromises. . . ."

"True enough," Araxie agreed. "But sometimes, if we're very fortunate, we are given a second chance, to assemble a better set of compromises.

"You'd already made several, by the time Kelson turned up alive—maybe because you were still searching for your greater purpose. I don't think it was to be a nun . . . or a wife . . . or even a queen—but I do think you were meant to be a mother, and in a far broader sense than simply bearing children of your body—though Albin is a treasure who compensates for a great deal of the sadness that's come along with this journey of discovery.

"I think that what you've just been offered by the man you once thought to wed may well present a choice that is little compromise at all: to be the mother of a new renaissance of Deryni learning—right here, centered on the *schola* that you and the Servants of Saint Camber can build at this basilica, working with all of us. I think *this* is your true vocation, Rothana. It's the work you're called to do—for yourself, and for Kelson, and for God."

Rothana was actually smiling faintly by the time Araxie wound down, her former resistance all but dissipated.

"Sweet, fierce, passionate Araxie," she said gently. "You know me better than I know myself. What an advocate he has in you. And you've come to love him, haven't you? I hoped you would."

Araxie ventured the beginning of a smile, suddenly gone shy.

"He was the beloved playmate of my childhood. We are building on the affection we shared then—and yes, I think I do love him . . . and am coming to love him more, as the days pass." She looked up boldly.

"But I do not begrudge you the love that you and he shared. That would be as foolish as denying the past, which cannot be changed. All three of us—he and you and I—understand the duty to which we were born; we cannot abdicate that duty and still be true to who we were meant to be, not only for ourselves but for God and those around us.

"The wonder of what is now unfolding—thanks, in no small part, to your generosity of spirit—is that the three of us can still do nearly all the things that you and he dreamed of. It will just be divided up a little differently than any of us anticipated—and maybe what we need to do for our Deryni race was always more than just two people could ever hope to accomplish."

Rothana was gazing up at her bemusedly, tears trembling on her lashes, slowly shaking her head.

"You are wiser than I dared to hope, and gracious beyond reckoning. Having feared that I had lost all, I find that I yet have been granted the chance to share some precious part of the dreams that he and I dreamed. I count myself among the most fortunate of women."

She rose, her head held high, like the queen she very nearly had been, and Araxie and Richenda rose as well.

"In love, I wish you a profound joy of our beloved Kelson, my dear friend. How ever did I choose so well? Be his wise and gentle queen, and bear him as many sons and daughters of your love as you both desire." She lifted a hand to gently brush Araxie's cheek. "I pray that, in the final reckoning, you may count me as a loving sister, and that you will permit me to share some small part of your life with Kelson, and to know his children, and to be the friend of both of you, and of them. For I have come to love both this land and its king, and I would serve them and their queen, as well as our people."

She drew herself up and dashed away the last of her tears with the back of her hand.

"I shall accept the king's appointment for the *schola* we shall found here together, and help teach those sons and daughters their heritage beside my own son. Would you tell him that for me?"

"Of course."

"Thank you. I beg you to excuse me now. The hour will soon be upon us to see Saint Camber restored, as our advocate. And first, I must see that my son has not been a burden to his grandmother."

*T*he chapter house lay adjacent to the end of the basilica's south transept, opening into the cobbled yard that lay in the angle of that transept with the long nave. Under the arched colonnade that ran along that side of the nave, the Servants of Saint Camber were assembling before the door at the southwest corner of the yard, preparing for the entrance procession that would enter the basilica through that door, pass down the long nave, and enter the new chapel through the arched doorway just before the north transept. The women had sheaves of flowers cradled in their arms, and several small children were proudly clutching single blooms.

A man at the head of the procession was leaning on the staff of a bright banner divided red and blue behind the length of a silver-robed depiction of their saint, whose upraised hands were holding aloft a golden crown. Toward the back of the procession, Meraude and Jehana were talking to one of the woman Servants with apparent interest, little Albin between them. The boy was dressed in a miniature version of the adults' grey robes, his Haldane-black hair caught back in a stubby *g'dula*, head tipped back to follow the conversation of the two grown-ups with apparent interest.

A few of the others invited to attend the coming ceremony had also been making their way across the cloister yard since Kelson emerged from the chapter house, slowly disappearing inside to find places in what would be a crowded chapel. He had been observing their comings and goings from the shadows of a doorway giving access to the south transept, with Morgan, the duke's two young children, and Derry, who had been charged with looking after the pair while their parents were occupied in the chapter house—and Richenda was still occupied. Derry was crouched down beside Morgan's son and heir, who was showing "Uncle Séandry" a pair of banded river stones he had picked up from a gravel path on the way there. Morgan had one hand resting lightly on his daughter's shoulder, where it played gently with one of her curls as he peered idly back toward the chapter house for some sign of her mother. Kelson's glances in that direction had a more impatient quality.

Following the exodus of the king and his Deryni dukes and bishop from the chapter house, the Servants had spilled after them in twos and threes, all of them whispering excitedly among themselves as they withdrew to the far side of the yard; but neither Rothana nor Araxie nor Richenda had yet emerged. The yard was slowly emptying of everyone except the Servants waiting to process in. Dhugal had withdrawn with Duncan to help him vest, and would be serving Mass for his father, Deryni acolyte for a Deryni priest.

Kelson sighed and leaned heavily against the doorjamb, folding his arms across his chest.

"What do you think is happening in there?" he murmured.

"I think," said Morgan, "that between my wife and your future wife, Rothana probably doesn't stand much of a chance."

"Then why is it taking them so long?"

"I couldn't say. But women's magic is often more subtle than ours, and sometimes does take longer. You'll see; just wait."

"I hardly have a choice," Kelson muttered.

Even as he said it, the door of the chapter house opened far enough for Rothana to emerge. Kelson stiffened, slowly unfolding his arms from across his chest and straightening, but she took herself purposefully across the yard toward the Servants at a brisk pace, head down and looking neither right nor left, briefly greeting Meraude and Jehana as she took Albin in charge. The four of them then moved farther up along the line of Servants, where Rothana and her son ducked into their place and the two Haldane ladies continued on through the door ahead and disappeared.

"So, what happened?" Kelson asked under his breath.

"We'll see, soon enough—though perhaps not until afterward," Morgan said, still fondling his daughter's hair as she leaned against him. "We should be going in, though."

Ignoring him, Kelson craned his neck toward the Servants' procession in hopes of getting a better look at Rothana and Albin, but they were shielded behind other grey robes. In the belfry chamber atop one of the west towers of the basilica, a bell began to ring out the Angelus, the salutation prayed to the Queen of Heaven at morning, noon, and night: three sets of three strokes, followed by nine solemn rings.

Angelus Domini nuntiavit Mariae . . . The Angel of the Lord declared unto Mary . . . and she conceived of the Holy Spirit. . . .

"Where *are* they?" Kelson whispered, wishing desperately for Araxie and Richenda to reappear.

He bowed his head and tried to pray, seeking reassurance in the grace-filled phrases of the beautiful devotion; reflecting that, in a sense, just as that angelic messenger had sought Mary's assent, whereby the world might be redeemed through her willing participation in the Incarnation of the Christ, even so were his own messengers seeking the assent of Rothana—not to take on the redemption of the entire world; only to stay on and be a willing participant and helpmate in the bettering of this small part of it that was *his* world, this land of Gwynedd. That she might insist upon withdrawing fully from his world, he was not prepared to accept.

The bell in the tower paused, then began ringing again, in a regular but more spritely tempo, now summoning worshippers to the service soon to begin. A quiet bustle behind Kelson marked the approach of the now white-vested Duncan, a cassocked and lace-surpliced Dhugal, and the two archbishops—and Denis Arilan, quietly lurking behind them, though the latter was not vested for celebration; indeed, he wore but the plain black cassock of an ordinary priest.

Instantly sobered—for Arilan could only have come here by means of the Portal elsewhere in the basilica—Kelson stood his ground against the purple bustle of bishops pressing past him to join the Servants and drew back with the Deryni bishop into the shadows of one of the side altars in the south transept, hoping there was no new crisis in the Torenthi capital. Derry drew Morgan's children inside, to head for the Saint Camber chapel, and Morgan ducked outside.

"I hope your presence doesn't mean there's more trouble in Beldour," Kelson said distractedly, keeping one eye on the doorway to the sun-drenched cloister yard. "How is Liam bearing up?"

"As well as can be expected," Arilan said. "Once he's gotten through his mother's funeral, he should be fine. As you know, they do things differently in Torenth. Even if it weren't for the circumstances of her death, it won't be just a simple Requiem Mass he'll have to face."

Dark silhouettes briefly eclipsed the glare of the open doorway: Araxie first, heading immediately in the direction of the service about to begin—away from Kelson; then Morgan, a hand on his wife's waist and head bent to hear her whispered comments. But there was no time for the king to make inquiry of the three as they passed briskly on along the transept to disappear westward down the nave.

"I don't suppose there's any progress finding Teymuraz?" Kelson asked mechanically.

"No, Mátyás is still working on it; and Azim has his Order putting out feelers, but there's still no sign. He may be lying low, as Azim said he might.

"But I didn't come about that. This is an important day for Deryni, and I wanted to be here to witness it. Hopefully, no one will think twice about how I got here; no need to be *too* blatant. But we'd better go in. They won't start without you, and we shouldn't keep them waiting."

Still tight-wound, Kelson let Arilan escort him back down the nave toward the knot of people clustered before the Saint Camber chapel. The arch opening into the chapel had been swagged with a thick garland of flowers, their scent clean and citrusy amid the sweeter note of incense, and the space beyond was closely packed with the Servants and the dozen or so members of the king's family and immediate household, numbering about a score.

The chapel itself was bedecked with more flowers, adorning the sills of the high windows and festooning the doorway leading out to the gardens. At noon, no window caught the sun at an angle that could illuminate the chapel directly, but sunlight spilling from the garden door cast a wash of gold on those standing nearest. At the front of the chapel, two standing candelabra flanking the altar served to bring to life the gold of the mosaic behind—the crown in the hands of Saint Camber, and the nimbus of power surrounding him and King Cinhil.

Kelson eased himself into a place just inside the archway from the nave, beside Morgan and his son. Richenda stood beyond, with Briony, Jehana, and Father Nivard. Besides the Servants and their children—and Rothana and Albin—most of the rest packed into the little chapel were his kin: Nigel and his family, Sivorn and her family, and the Ramsays of Meara, who were about to be family, whose second son, Brother Christophle, had arrived the day before, to see his brother and sister wed. Arilan remained quietly at the rear of the half dozen folk standing in the archway, for he would slip away as soon as the proceedings were concluded, to return to Beldour.

As Duncan and the archbishops entered without fanfare, Dhugal setting aside a processional cross, little Kelric crept his small hand into the king's and settled in contentment between Kelson and his father. Touched by that innocent affirmation of trust and honest affection, Kelson schooled his thoughts toward prayer.

The ceremony of dedication and consecration that followed was exceedingly simple—and profoundly moving. After offering up a collect for their intentions, answered in antiphon by the Servants, Duncan proceeded to asperse and then to cense the inside perimeter of the chapel, passing sun-wise from the east, across the great arch leading to the nave, then behind the Servants and back along the northern wall, establishing—though such was never said—protective Wards of a very special nature: not to physically prevent any normal ingress and egress to the chapel, but to contain and enhance the meditations that might be offered there in times to come. These Wards would remain in place indefinitely, and be maintained by the prayers and particular intent of all Deryni working prayerfully within them.

Assisted, then, by Bradene and Cardiel, Duncan purified the virgin altar with water and incense and anointed it with holy chrism on the five consecration crosses carved at its corners and in the center. And it was with the pointed presence of an archbishop at either side that he laid his hands flat upon the marble and allowed a gleam of silvery handfire to briefly wash out across the surface. As he bent, then, to reverently kiss the altar, both archbishops did likewise before the three of them drew back to let Dhugal dress the altar for celebration of the Eucharist.

The ensuing Mass followed the same general pattern of those being celebrated upon countless altars elsewhere in Christendom. But the Lesson was taken from an early account of the life of Saint Camber, the *Acta Sancti Camberi*, read with fervor by the ban-aba Jilyan. And the Gospel text that Father John Nivard delivered from the midst of the Servants, selected from the tenth chapter of Saint John, took on new meaning for those giving witness to this historic occasion.

"I am the good shepherd, and know my sheep, and am known of mine. As the Father knoweth me, even so know I the Father: and I lay down my life for the sheep. And other sheep I have, which are not of this fold: them also I must bring, and they shall hear my voice; and there shall be one fold, and one shepherd. . . ."

In more pointed illustration that a new perspective was being offered this day with the reinstatement of this chapel dedicated to a Deryni saint, the Offertory was the opening canon of the *Adsum Domine*, anciently the office hymn of the Deryni Healers, who once had given freely of their precious gifts for the good of all—sung by Duncan in the common tongue, so that there might be no mistaking the aspiration that all Deryni of good faith might use their gifts only in benevolent and upright service.

Here am I, Lord:
Thou has granted me the grace to heal men's bodies.

Here am I, Lord:
Thou hast blessed me with the Sight to See men's souls.
Here am I, Lord:
Thou hast given me the might to bend the will of others.
O Lord, grant strength and wisdom to wield all these gifts
only as Thy will wouldst have me serve. . . .

Duncan then kindled celestial fire to light a pure white taper, which he took
to a sand-filled metal tray on legs, set just inside the door to the cloister garden.
There he set the light as a symbol of the beacon all prayed would shine forth from
what was begun today.

And at the consecration of the sacred Elements, as Duncan lifted up first
the Host and then the Chalice, he briefly let the glory of his shield-light
enfold What he offered up, in visible affirmation of the Celestial benison
attendant upon the sacramental act—this physical focus of Word made Flesh,
which at last might be celebrated by Deryni without stifling this joyful manifestation of the unique gifts they brought to this outward expression of their
faith.

Not even among the Deryni present were there many who, hitherto, had
been witness to such magic. Deryni and humans alike bowed humbly before the
wonder, which showed forth yet another glimpse of how man's yearning might
reach toward Divinity. Not a few were moved to tears, some still moist-eyed as
they came forward to receive the Sacrament. Most of the children were yet too
young to have made their first Communion, but each came eagerly to receive a
blessing.

As Duncan touched the head of one such child—Nigel's little granddaughter, come forward hand-in-hand with Princess Eirian, with Nigel shepherding
both girls—Kelson reflected that the Deryni priest was as much a father to these
little ones as he was to Dhugal, who lifted the paten under Nigel's chin as he
then received the Sacrament, a hand on the shoulder of each child, the polished
gold reflecting God-glory upon that reverent face. Surely, it was always meant to
be this way—this community of humans and Deryni joined before God in common intent, the two races sharing all of life in harmony, even as they shared this
Sacrament.

Afterward, when Dhugal had declared the final dismissal and the little congregation had begun to disperse to the cloister garden, lighting candles as they
went out the garden door, Kelson remained in a back corner of the chapel and
buried his face in one hand, elbow propped on the other, and turned his thoughts
to a final prayer for the success of what they had begun today. He had somewhat

lost track of what was going on around him when a touch at his elbow made him look up.

It was Richenda, faintly smiling, who slid her arm through his and jutted her chin toward the door to the cloister garden. There, where many slender, honey-colored tapers now bristled around the white one Duncan had set there in the tray of sand, Rothana was lifting Albin up to light one of his own from one of those already set in place, her lips making a rosy *O* as she helped him stick it in the sand.

She smiled at his expression of pleased satisfaction as she set him down; then she took another candle from the basket of new ones underneath the rack as she crouched down beside him to whisper briefly in his ear. He nodded gravely, intent on her instructions as she put the candle in his hand, then nodded and, propelled gently forward by her hand, trotted off through the garden door, she trailing a few yards behind.

Kelson glanced at Richenda in question, but she only shook her head and urged him toward the doorway, where Araxie had just come back in.

"Don't say anything, and don't go out there," the latter whispered, holding a finger to her lips. "Just watch from here."

At her direction and Richena's guiding, Kelson allowed himself to be eased far enough into the doorway to peer out into the garden, where Albin could be seen running along one of the paths amid the flower beds, his candle clutched in his little fist, toward a knot of brightly dressed adults. Nigel was among them, his back toward the doorway, and looked down in surprise at the small person who tugged at the tails of his long robe of royal blue and wordlessly offered him a candle.

For just an instant Nigel froze, his gaze flicking past Albin's backward-tilted head to the boy's mother, who was slowly approaching with hands clasped behind her. Then he sank to a crouch before his small petitioner, slow joy suffusing his face as he took the candle the boy offered and began to speak to him. His companions melted back as Rothana drew near—Rory and Brecon and Noelie—and when Rothana reached the pair, she, too, exchanged words with Nigel.

Both of them were smiling as Nigel rose and, with his grandson's hand in his, began slowly walking back toward the chapel door with him, gazing down at the boy's upturned face in wonder, listening to an outpouring of earnest chatter. Following after, Rothana noted the king and his two companions watching from the doorway, and gave Kelson a deliberate nod.

"She's agreed?" he asked Araxie, as she and Richenda drew him back into the nave to give mother and son and grandfather their privacy.

"Yes, to *all* of it," Araxie said happily. "She'll accept the appointment to found her *schola* here, and live here, and help us in our work—and the rest, you can see."

Over by the tray of burning candles, Nigel had lifted Albin so that, together, they could light the candle the boy had given him. As Rothana joined them, the three of them set its base into the sand amid the others.

CHAPTER THIRTY-FOUR

When a man's ways please the Lord, he maketh even his enemies to be at peace with him.

Proverbs 16:7

$\mathcal{K}$elson spent the rest of that day in contentment, meeting again with the Servants and, later, with Rothana and Araxie. Together, they began to address some of the plans unfolding for the future. The morrow would see the celebration of the Mearan weddings—and given the day's developments, Kelson knew that he could announce his own nuptial intentions with a glad heart.

But that night, shortly after he had retired, well satisfied with the outcome of the day, his squire Davoran came to wake him, with word that Lord Derry was asking to speak with him, sent by Father Nivard.

"Sorry if I woke you, Sire," Derry said. "I'm to tell you that Duke Mátyás wishes to see you."

"Mátyás? Here?"

"He said you weren't to be anxious, sir. The duke is alone. He says nothing is wrong. But he asks to speak with you."

Pulling on a loose robe, Kelson knotted a cincture around his waist and thrust his feet into felt slippers. The midnight summons, coming from a Torenthi prince, would have made him wary in previous times; but apprehension touched him only regarding the news Mátyás might bring, for he trusted Mátyás himself. Gesturing for Derry to lead the way, he padded softly after him, his squire Davoran quietly following behind.

Nivard was waiting in the library, and preceded him through the Veil. Derry and Davoran remained in the outer room. In the chamber beyond, Mátyás turned at the king's arrival, dressed all in black, eerily illuminated by a sphere of handfire floating a little beside his head so that he could peruse an open book in his hands. He laid the book aside as Kelson straightened from the arch of the Veiled doorway. His only adornment was the holy icon hanging from his neck, glowing like a lighted jewel upon his breast.

"Thank you for seeing me, my prince."

"It's Kelson—please," the king said, gesturing toward the seats in the window embrasure. "Is Liam well?"

"Well enough—Kelson," Mátyás replied, inclining his head in thanks for the courtesy. "He grieves for his mother, and fears for our lives, and dreads the public obsequies over which he must preside in a few days' time. The latter is what brings me here tonight."

"Does he wish me to come?" Kelson asked. "If it will bring him comfort, I shall do so. But I would not wish to intrude. Azim has reminded me that I must allow him to make his own way as a king. But as a friend, I wish to do anything I can, to ease his task."

Mátyás nodded. "Azim told me of your conversation. No, what my nephew would ask is far less than that, and little likely to compromise either of your crowns. The time is weighing heavily upon him, as he waits to see his mother entombed in the Field of Kings. Meanwhile, the friends of his childhood are here in Rhemuth. It is Brendan and Payne whom he misses most; but he also grew fond of Prince Rory, who is to wed tomorrow.

"It occurred to me that it might lift his spirits if he could escape from Torenthály for even a few hours, to witness Rory's marriage. I would keep him in my charge, to protect him, so that you need not take special precautions for our safety. We would come disguised, and place ourselves wholly in your desire as to where we may and may not go—whatever you require. It—would mean a great deal to him."

Kelson slowly nodded, for he could sense no guile in any word Mátyás uttered. And it was a courtesy easy enough to grant—though, to do it, he would have to give Mátyás the location of the cathedral Portal, for there was no other way to safely bring the pair in and out of the cathedral tomorrow, even disguised.

"Wait here," he said, rising. "I'm going to ask Morgan to join us. There's a Portal in the cathedral, but if I take you there unescorted, Morgan will kill me when he finds out, if you haven't already done so."

The statement brought a smile to Mátyás' lips, as intended. A quarter-hour later, Morgan was ducking through the Veil to join them, Mátyás having spent the intervening time reviewing progress on the search for Teymuraz.

"A galley matching the description of the one he took from Saint-Sasile was spotted off the Horn of Bremagne four days later, heading south," Mátyás was saying. "We have learned of no further sightings, but Azim has turned the direction of his search toward the southron lands. Duke Alaric," he acknowledged, rising as Morgan came toward them.

"Mátyás." Morgan glanced toward Kelson, who had also risen and stepped down to meet him, staying the Torenthi lord with a gesture.

"A moment, Mátyás, while I acquaint Alaric with our intentions."

Taking Morgan's wrist, the king gave him the gist of what had passed between him and the uncle of the King of Torenth, relieved when Morgan only nodded, faintly smiling.

"Please join us, my lord," he said, motioning toward Mátyás as he headed toward the Portal square. "Kelson somewhat overstates, but I would, indeed, have been angry, had he taken you to the cathedral unescorted. I'll go ahead, to make sure it's clear," he said to Kelson. "You'd best tell Nivard and Derry we'll be unavailable for the next little while."

As Kelson ducked his head back through the Veil to alert Nivard, Morgan positioned himself on the Portal square, bowed his head as he composed himself, and vanished. When he did not reappear, after a count of ten, Kelson moved onto the same square with Mátyás, took the other's wrist, and extended his shields around them both as the Torenthi mage smoothly retracted his and yielded control. A moment to stabilize their position—to reach toward their destination— and then Kelson wrenched the energies. In the space between two heartbeats, they were standing in the sacristy of Rhemuth Cathedral, before the vesting altar. Beside the door that led out to the nave, Morgan was peering through the little squint that looked into the sanctuary, with its high altar.

"Everything dressed for tomorrow," he said, "and no one about. Take your time."

Softly Kelson stepped back from Mátyás, so the other could crouch alone on the Portal square to learn its location. The dark head of the Torenthi prince briefly bowed as he laid his hands on the fine mosaic that delineated the square. Kelson watched in silence. After a few seconds, Mátyás rose.

"I have it," he said. "At what time tomorrow may we come? I think this sacristy shall be a busy place."

"The procession is to arrive here at noon," Kelson said, "so all the clergy should be out by then. Morgan will be here to see you to a place where you can watch. I'll tell Rory that you and Liam will be here."

Mátyás nodded. "Thank you. This will mean much to him." He came to peer out the little grille in the sacristy door, orienting himself to the transept beyond, then returned to the Portal.

"I shall not keep you longer," he said. "I shall return directly to Torenthály. Again, my thanks."

When he had vanished, Kelson turned to Morgan.

"Did I just do a foolish thing?" he asked softly.

"Are you asking if I trust him, my prince?" Morgan countered.

"I suppose I am."

"Then, I must answer that I do," Morgan replied. "I think he is an honorable and compassionate man, and Liam is fortunate to have him. And we are fortunate to have him for a friend. But for now, I think we should go back whence we came. Come, I'll take you through. Tomorrow will be a very long day—and I left a very warm and loving woman in my bed."

Chuckling, Kelson moved back onto the Portal and let Morgan take them both back to the library Portal, where Derry and Davoran were waiting to conduct them back to their respective beds.

*T*he movements of Derry, at least, did not go unremarked that night—and not by any of those who saw him at his work in Rhemuth Castle. In a room atop a tower in the foothills of distant Alver, close by the Bremagni border, Teymuraz closed down the link that had given him access to what Sean Lord Derry saw and pushed aside the bowl of ink in which he had scried it, turning the iron finger-ring under his thumb.

Only a few days ago had he finished sifting through the knowledge wrenched from the dying Morag, and kindled the link through the ring that gave him access to the court of Gwynedd through the eyes of Sean Lord Derry, aide to the powerful Duke Alaric Morgan—who was Deryni, but ill-trained, and did not know of the cuckoo in his nest. Teymuraz was still feeling out the limits of the link through the rings, but the results were extremely promising, thus far.

All must be intuited through the eyes of Derry himself, of course; Teymuraz had not yet managed to get much past mere observation, though with concentration, he was starting to have an effect on Derry's movements and even on his will. For the last several days, Teymuraz had been in the link during nearly all Derry's waking hours, and sometimes in his sleep, ever stretching the limits of his control.

Tonight, quite unexpectedly, his diligence had begun to pay off. It was difficult to know precisely what was going on, on this night before the great wedding celebration in Rhemuth, but Derry very definitely had brought word to his king that his own two-faced and deceiving brother Mátyás was in the castle—and apparently in the library to which Derry conducted the king, though no one but the Deryni priest Nivard was there when they arrived. But then priest and king apparently had walked right through a wall, Nivard emerging almost at once, apparently quite nonchalant about the entire matter.

From their quiet converse of the next little while, Teymuraz had gathered that another chamber lay beyond that wall, the connecting passage guarded and disguised to humans by some spell—but try as he might, he had not been able to get Derry to go closer. Derry feared it, as he feared most magic, though it had not always been so—and small wonder that he feared, given what Wencit had done to him—though his devotion to the Deryni Duke Alaric Morgan was such that he made himself go beyond his fears, most of the time. Piecing together what snippets he could actually pull from Derry's memories, rather than what he saw through Derry's eyes, Teymuraz concluded that a Portal lay on the other side of that wall, to which the King of Gwynedd had given Mátyás access.

That impression was reinforced when the king soon emerged briefly to have Derry fetch Morgan, who also walked through the wall. And after another interval, Kelson had again emerged to say to Nivard that they would be unavailable for the next little while, suggesting that the three of them—Kelson, Morgan, and Mátyás—intended transfer to yet another Portal: vilest betrayal of Torenth, on the part of Mátyás, to ally himself with Kelson of Gwynedd, even in the intimacy of shared magic.

But the payoff had come when Morgan returned, Derry accompanying him back to his quarters. There Morgan had told his aide how Mátyás and Laje planned to come through a Portal in Rhemuth Cathedral on the morrow, there to witness the nuptials of the Mearan heiress with Prince Rory Haldane, beloved of Laje. He even told Derry the approximate location of the Portal. Teymuraz had known that he would be able to observe the wedding through Derry's eyes, but this promised more tempting opportunity.

Smiling, thoughtfully turning the iron ring on his finger, he laid himself down on a couch draped with silks and composed himself for darker work than he had done since he killed Morag.

CHAPTER THIRTY-FIVE

We have heard of thee, that thou art a man of great power, and meet to be our friend.

I Maccabees 10:19

*K*elson woke the next morning to the distant bustling sounds of the castle awakening, aware that the long anticipated day finally had arrived. He knew that the servants would be about their preparations for the wedding feast to come, that the invasion of wedding guests would be already assembling, preparatory to the planned exodus to the cathedral in a few hours' time; that the bridal parties would be making their final nervous preparations.

Not being a formal part of the bridal procession, for he himself was only a wedding guest today, Kelson had good excuse to keep apart from most of the bustle. After a leisurely bath, he picked at a plate of cheese and bread and fruit while Ivo plaited his hair in a neat Border braid and clubbed it up, then let him and Davoran dress him in a long Haldane tunic of crimson silk, girt at the waist with a belt of silver plaques, from which hung a long Border dirk set with a ruby in its pommel. This was not a day for swords.

When they had pronounced him fit for public viewing, he hooked his coronet over one arm, finishing off the last of a particularly fine pear, and went down to join Morgan, Derry, and Dhugal, who were waiting to ride with him to the cathedral. In the hall, the participants in the official procession were starting to assemble. He detoured briefly to inform Rory that Liam and Mátyás would be present, much to Rory's delight. He saw Araxie heading up the stairs with fresh flower garlands for the brides' hair, but she was gone before he could greet her.

The morning was fine, not as warm as many previous days, and Kelson found himself able to relax as he and his companions rode casually down the long, winding thoroughfare toward the cathedral, to witness this culmination of many months of planning and negotiation and domestic interaction. At a brief court convened the previous evening, he had confirmed the creation of Jolyon Ramsay as Duke of Laas, so that Oksana could wear her coveted ducal coronet for the wedding festivities. He was quite content to let her share in some of the attention, on this day when both her children would be wed to royalty.

Happily, as they rode out the castle gates, no one was much interested in him today; he still was carrying his coronet hooked over his arm, much to Dhugal's amusement. But Morgan made him put it on before they reached the final approach to the cathedral square. The crowds gathering along the route of the procession gawked at all the noble riders descending from the castle, and occasionally gave a ragged cheer, but most of their adulation was being saved for the brides. Remembering the last time he had been part of such a procession, en route to his ill-fated marriage to Sidana of Meara, Kelson was well glad that the day was not his, and that he had this opportunity to lay to rest the ghosts of that other wedding with a more joyful one, before he came along this route with Araxie.

At the cathedral, all was in readiness. A stir passed among the wedding guests as Kelson was led to his place in the choir by Bishop Duncan, escorted by Dhugal, Morgan, and Derry. He was the king, after all. After Duncan had departed, the four of them settled back to watch the arrival of other guests—Mearan kin of the Ramsays, most of the court of Gwynedd, and finally the mothers of the brides and bridegrooms, a Haldane princess and—now—two duchesses.

Kelson nodded to Oksana as she took her place across the choir from him, amid Mearan kin and nobles, glad to note her contented smile. His own mother was a few places down from him, gowned and crowned as a queen of Gwynedd, not far from Meraude and Sivorn. Beyond, he could just see Araxie and Rothana—and Azim, taking a place between them.

The roar of the crowds outside announced the coming of the bridal party. As the cathedral bells began to ring the noonday Angelus, Morgan and Derry slipped out of the choir and briefly disappeared, returning momentarily with two black-clad and closely hooded figures who slipped quietly into shadowed places just within the choir screen, not far from Kelson. Very soon, the choir began to sing an introit from the rear of the great nave—a selection from the Song of Songs—and the bridal procession began.

First came the two bridegrooms walking side by side: Rory, all in the royal blue of his father's House, no circlet yet adorning that glossy head of Haldane-sable hair, clouted back in a neat Border braid; Brecon in the lighter blue of his

Ramsay ancestors, his robe embroidered across the chest with a broad band of gold and silver chequy, echoing the Ramsay arms, his sandy hair merely tied back with a twist of gold and silver cord. Both wore the white belts and golden spurs of their knighthood, for both were yet simple knights, though Rory had been born a prince. Behind them came their supporters: Rory's uncle, Saer de Traherne, and Brecon's younger brother, Christophle, a pleasant-looking young man in monastic robes, whose arrival in time for the wedding had been a near-run thing. Kelson had met him briefly the day before.

Then the ecclesiastical procession: cross and torches, thurifers and choir; the two archbishops, all in snowy vestments, coped and mitered; and a bevy of little girls—at least a dozen of them—shepherded by Richelle's little sisters, each carrying a ribbon-bedecked basket from which they strewed flower petals before the brides.

Noelie came first, on the arm of Jolyon Ramsay—his pale head now ducally adorned, as from yesterday's court—then Richelle on her stepfather's arm, each with hair unbound and crowned with roses, each being given in marriage to a man she adored.

Kelson turned his eyes away as the couples knelt each before an archbishop and exchanged their vows, remembering how he had spoken those same words before this very altar—had it really been more than four years ago?—sealing the same marriage promises before God, in hope of a great peace to be born of their union.

But only blood had come of that brief marriage: Sidana's blood, draining away upon those holy altar steps, and with it, a tiny portion of his soul. He would never know what might have been, had Sidana lived; just as he would never know what might have been, had Rothana married him instead of Conall; but he knew he would never forget Sidana of Meara, his silken princess.

Abruptly he wished that his marriage to Araxie need not take place here, where Sidana had died—though no other place was fitting to crown the queen so long awaited by his people. Though Sidana was long gone, at rest in her tomb in the crypt below, the offering of her blood would always lie before this altar, ultimate sacrifice for the cause of peace.

He bowed his head briefly in one hand to whisper a prayer for her. But as he dared to glance at her distant Mearan kin—at Brecon Ramsay with his Richelle, at Noelie Ramsay and Rory—it occurred to him that perhaps these Mearans could forge the peace she had failed to secure, not by spilling their blood but by merging it with Haldane blood—in marriage, not in murder.

By the time the vows had been exchanged, the rings given, the blessings bestowed, he could rest content enough with that notion, offering up that intention during the nuptial Mass that followed, receiving the Sacrament as a tangible symbol of his determination to carry forward with the work he knew he must achieve, as he built upon the new beginnings taking form for himself as well as the Mearan venture.

When the final dismissal had been given, each of the bridegrooms came to present his bride before the king, Rory and then Brecon, before retreating up the aisle for the procession back to the castle, and the wedding feast to come. The parents of the couples followed after, the wedding guests falling in informally behind, as the great cathedral bells began to peal and the cathedral began to empty.

Kelson lingered with Dhugal as Morgan brought Liam and Mátyás over to him. Derry had been sent to the sacristy, to alert them when the clergy had finished unvesting. Liam looked tired—and older—but he managed a smile as he pushed back his hood and he and Kelson exchanged nods.

"I'm very sorry for your loss," Kelson said to him. "I wish there were something I could do."

"Allowing us to come today is a great boon," Liam replied, smiling faintly. "It was good to see Rory wed. I wish him every happiness."

"Would you like to give him that wish in person?" Kelson asked. "I've thought of a way it can be done discreetly." He glanced at Mátyás. "I cannot grant you free passage from the room with the Portal that you know, but I can take you to another, in the precincts of the basilica within the outer walls. It will become somewhat known, soon enough, since Saint Hilary's is to become the home of our first Deryni *schola* in Gwynedd in many years."

"Indeed?" Mátyás said. "That is very good news. Laje, would it please you to speak briefly with Rory before we return?"

Liam's broad grin required no further confirmation. Attended by Morgan and Dhugal, Kelson and his Torenthi guests began making their way slowly toward the sacristy, detouring to show Mátyás and Liam the great seal of Saint Camber set in the transept crossing. As Kelson briefly explained how the seal had figured in his coming to full power, drawing parallels with Liam's inauguration at Torenthály, he caught a flicker of movement beyond the choir screen, up before the high altar: Rothana, pointing out some feature of the vaulting above to Araxie and Azim. Only then did it occur to him that, in all the turmoil of the past few weeks, he had neglected to inform Mátyás and Liam of the official announcement that would be made at the wedding feast shortly to commence, of the forthcoming marriage that had occupied so much of his own focus during those other ceremonies just concluded.

Sending Dhugal to ask Araxie's attendance, he drew the Torenthi pair back through the arch of the choir screen, away from the curious eyes of the last wedding guests straggling out the cathedral's great doors.

"I thought you had already gone," he said, as Dhugal brought her—wearing a look of innocence, but he knew that she had recognized his companions, and must at least guess what he intended. "Liam-Lajos, King of Torenth, and Duke Mátyás Furstán d'Arjenol—you will, of course, remember my fair cousin, the Princess Araxie Haldane." As he took her hand, he swept a glance behind him in exaggerated gesture of assuring himself that none could overhear, then lowered his voice conspiratorially. "It is also my honor to officially present my future queen—as all Gwynedd will shortly learn, now that today's weddings are accomplished."

Liam had begun to grin at this pronouncement, and Mátyás nodded sagely, pleasure in his eyes.

"My official congratulations, Sire," he said, "and my felicitations to you, Princess. May your marriage be as sweet and as fruitful as my own has been."

With a murmured word of thanks, she gave him her hand to kiss. Liam shook his head in admiring disbelief and glanced at Kelson.

"Then it really is true," he blurted. "When you told us at the Ile, so much else was going on, I later wondered whether I might have dreamed it all. And no one guessed—*no* one! All the squires were wrong. Princess, you were meant to marry Cuan of Howicce!"

"No, I think I was meant to marry Kelson of Gwynedd," she said happily, slipping her arm through his and casting him a contented smile as Kelson glanced down at her.

Following a moment's further light converse regarding the plans for the evening, Derry appeared in the arch of the choir screen and indicated that the sacristy was clear of clergy.

"I'd best go back with Azim and Rothana, then," Araxie said. "At least a few of us should arrive back at the castle by conventional means—not that anyone is likely to notice, in all the milling about. You should see all the horses still waiting outside."

Kelson nodded his agreement, raising a hand in summons to Derry.

"I'll send Derry with you," he said. "He's none too happy about Portals, from all reports. Morgan and Dhugal and I will take Liam and Mátyás through to the Portal at the basilica. There's a tunnel from there that I'll have to show you, one day soon. It gives access to several different locations in the castle. Derry, please go with Araxie, would you? We'll join you shortly."

So saying, he gave Araxie into Derry's hands and turned to begin shepherding the others toward the sacristy. Morgan was already moving in that direction, Dhugal right behind him. He did not see the flicker of consternation that passed over Derry's face as he hesitated and started to turn, glassy-eyed, one hand pulling a short dagger from its sheath.

But he caught the flash of the blade out of the corner of his eye as it arched upward, in the same instant that Derry thrust Araxie from him and seized Mátyás's arm, whirling him to drive the steel up and under the ribs—unprotected by armor or even mail, for Mátyás and Liam had come for a wedding.

It was Araxie who kept it from being an immediately fatal blow, scrambling for balance and then throwing herself against Derry's knees with enough force to slightly deflect his aim and loose his hold on the weapon, even as Kelson and Dhugal wrestled him to the ground, struggling like one possessed—as indeed he was, in that instant. At the same time, Morgan launched himself toward the silk-robed form of Teymuraz, who suddenly reared out from behind a pillar, an iron ring glinting on his clenched fist and triumph blazing in his dark eyes.

"Go reign in hell, brother!" he screamed—then bolted for the sacristy and escape, for Liam had whirled in focused outrage and was raising a hand toward him, the power of Furstán already stirring.

Mátyás was sinking to his knees, clutching at his side, Araxie scrambling to catch his weight as he crumpled, intent on keeping him from falling on his wound. Behind them, from up in the choir, Azim had bolted toward them with hard-eyed intent, Rothana not far behind him, drawn by the cry of Teymuraz and the scuffle centered on the king and the power roiling amid it.

Derry's struggles ceased as Teymuraz fled, going limp under the sprawled weight of Kelson and Dhugal, pinning him to the floor. By the time Morgan could reach the sacristy, Teymuraz was well away. Azim arrived hard on Morgan's heels, assessed the situation in an instant, and briskly shouldered him aside, with an admonition to get back to the others while he secured the Portal against any further intrusion by the fled Teymuraz.

Morgan was breathing hard when he got back to the scene of the devastation wrought by Teymuraz. Dhugal had scrambled to the aid of the stricken Mátyás, who lay gasping and faintly writhing with his knees drawn to his chest. Though Morgan could see no blood, Mátyás's hand was clutched to his left side where, close between his body and the angle of his elbow, the hilt of Derry's dagger protruded at a downward angle, black against the black silk of his robe.

Mátyás bit back a moan as Dhugal drew his left arm out and away from his body to get a look at the wound, giving his wrist into the keeping of the wide-eyed Araxie. Liam was easing his uncle's head onto his knees, already working to ease the pain, softly whispering something that sounded like *su-su-su* . . . Beyond, Kelson was sitting astride Derry's chest, apparently in control of *that* situation.

Sick at heart—for *he* felt responsible for Derry's defection—Morgan crouched down opposite Dhugal. He could see that Derry's blade, rather than piercing the robe, had driven a sheathing of the fine silk into the wound—and fortunately, had not become dislodged in the scuffle; for that plug of silk, stayed by the blade, was all that was keeping him from bleeding out his life.

As Dhugal used his own blade to hurriedly rip an opening and gain access to the wound, Mátyás sensed Morgan's added presence, and turned his face toward him, away from the wound.

"I have heard," he whispered, around a cough that brought up blood, "that you have healing powers. Now would be a very good time for a demonstration."

"Just lie easy," Morgan said softly, with an urgent glance at Dhugal, whose eyes had gone a little glazed with trancing as his agile fingers pressed and probed around the wound.

"It's deep," Dhugal murmured, "but a rib deflected the angle just enough to miss the heart—though only by a hairsbreadth. It's in the lung, though—and apt to do more damage when it's pulled—but it can't stay."

Kelson heard the chilling words from his perch astride Derry's chest, where he was binding Derry's wrists with Araxie's veil—strong enough for now, and what was presently at hand. Derry was starting to stir, the blue eyes heavy-lidded, vacant. Rothana had joined them, and was running her hands above his forehead, a finger's breadth away, frowning. Araxie gave Mátyás's hand into Liam's keeping and moved to join her as Azim came to crouch on Derry's other side. Briskly sliding one hand from Derry's shoulder to his hands, Azim hissed as he found the heavy gold ring on Derry's finger.

"*That* explains!" he said emphatically, twisting off the ring and flinging it from them in a rare show of pique, to bounce a few times with a dull *thunk!* until it rolled to rest a few yards away.

"Leave it!" he said to Kelson—and to Morgan, who was hesitating between Derry and Mátyás. "Go, go! He needs you more. I will deal with this."

As if both of them had simply ceased to exist, Azim then laid one hand on Derry's forehead and the other on the bound wrists, his eyes summoning first Rothana and then Araxie into the link. As they settled closer to Derry and Azim, the two women laying their hands on Azim's, Kelson shifted from his sitting position astride Derry's chest and eased onto his knees between him and Mátyás. He held both men in his affection, in different ways; and both were now poised on the edge of mortal peril.

Morgan had already pivoted on his knees to lean across Mátyás's chest and observe Dhugal's investigations. A ragged frill of black silk now bloomed from around the place where the blade disappeared into Mátyás's side, where Dhugal had cut away Mátyás's robe to get at the wound. Mátyás winced as Dhugal probed around the entry point, and tried to stifle a cough; his breathing was labored, his eyes were closed. Liam looked like a man whose heart was being slowly ripped from his chest, one hand locked in his uncle's hand and the other laid across his brow.

"It's a narrow blade," Dhugal was saying, "so it isn't going to leave much of an exit channel. Just wide enough to let his life out, if we don't move fast, once we pull it. I don't know that I can get even a little finger in—and I think the wound is deeper than that. But I've got to have contact, in order to visualize that kind of healing."

"Then, we'll have to widen the channel as the blade is pulled," Morgan murmured. "Pull the silk first, else you'll have no edge. Dangerous, but at least Derry always keeps his weapons sharp."

Both fascinated and faintly sickened by this clinical discussion of what must be done, Kelson scooted closer on his knees, torn between the battle being waged for Mátyás's life and the silent but no less deadly battle being waged behind him, for Derry's soul—for he knew that Azim's focus was on yet another resurgence of the magic Wencit of Torenth had laid upon Derry many years go.

"You've more experience at this," Dhugal said to Morgan. "Maybe you'd better do it."

"No, your hands are smaller. I'll handle the power flow—and we'd better do it *now*. Mátyás, my friend," Morgan said, laying his hand on the other's forehead and signing with his eyes for Liam to take his hand away, "it's time to do or die, and I mean that quite literally." He quirked a faint smile as Mátyás opened his eyes. "I'd hoped not to have to put our friendship to the test like this, but I need absolute and unconditional trust from you. Dhugal will need to tap a lot of energy, for this to work. So will I—and you've got to serve as a backup reservoir. I can't predict how deep I'll need to go—or whether we can even do this."

Mátyás stifled another cough, turning his head briefly aside to spit out blood. Liam, white-faced, gently wiped his uncle's mouth with a fold of his sleeve.

"Only tell me what I must do . . . my friend," Mátyás whispered, his dark eyes searching Morgan's. "I give myself willingly into your hands."

"Close your eyes," Morgan murmured, shifting thumb and little finger to rest on the eyelids, as Mátyás obeyed and he, too, closed his eyes briefly. After a moment, he clasped his other hand around the wrist of Mátyás's outflung hand and glanced at Dhugal, nodding for him to proceed.

Kelson could not bear to watch too closely as Dhugal bent to his work— Liam looked like he might faint, his uncle's head still cradled on his knees—but it went quickly, as he knew it must—either to save Mátyás's life or to speed its end. One second, Dhugal's hand was on the hilt of Derry's dagger, his other hand poised to follow where the blade had been; the next instant, the dagger was out, Dhugal's forefinger thrust deep in the wound, his other hand pressed close around it, he and Morgan both with heads bowed, deep in healing trance.

Kelson sensed the battle being waged, but Mátyás did not move beneath Dhugal's hands, only breathing softly, shallowly, in the same rhythm as Dhugal and

Morgan, until Dhugal slowly drew his bloody finger from the closing wound—of which only a faint discoloring remained, surrounded by a smear of blood.

Breathing a heavy sigh, Dhugal laid his hand flat over the former site of the wound and gave Liam a reassuring nod. Morgan, too, sighed and pulled back as Mátyás opened his eyes in wonder, lifting his head and questing a hand to his side.

"You may be a little sore," Dhugal said. "And you might cough a bit of blood for a day or two. But this shouldn't slow you down much."

Behind them, Azim was now untying Derry's hands. Derry himself lay pale and unmoving, eyes closed. The desert prince cast an approving glance at Mátyás, who lay his head back gratefully on Liam's knees.

"*That*," said Azim, with a nod toward Mátyás, "is one of the things my niece must have taught in her *schola*. And *this*," he continued, as he freed Derry's hands, "should never have been allowed to continue for long."

Kelson blinked at him in astonishment, and Morgan turned to face him, as Azim made a *tsk*-ing sound with his tongue.

"Most appalling," he said to Kelson, as he handed Araxie's veil back to her with an apologetic shrug for its condition. "There have been three very powerful and highly skilled Furstáns poking about in his mind, in the past seven-year. Yon Alaric made a fair job of cleaning up after the first, considering his lack of formal training, but more must be done. The most recent intruder has left him badly used."

Morgan went a little grey, scooting closer on his knees, and Azim settled back on his haunches, briefly contemplative, bracing graceful hands on his thighs.

"I can resolve this now, if you will," he said. "The process is relatively straightforward, if tedious."

"But—when did this happen?" Kelson asked.

"In Beldour, while all of us were occupied with the aftermath of *killijálay*. Oh, Morag was very subtle."

"We didn't know," Kelson said, appalled.

"Of course you did not. How could you, without the training to recognize the signs? It is magic of a darker sort, which I would not expect to fall within the purview of a Haldane's knowledge."

He cast a sour glance at the unconscious Derry, then back at Kelson.

"A Haldane may, perhaps, aid in its resolution, however—and in doing so, learn how to safeguard against it in the future. As I said, the work will be tedious rather than difficult, and taxing only in the energy required; but I shall be here all night, if I have not assistance. I would prefer to spend the time refocusing the search for Teymuraz himself. For with that ring—unless he has sense enough to discard it, which I think he will not do, in his arrogance—we have now a means to trace its link back to him. Fetch it for me, please, Rothana—and only grasp it in a fold of your skirt. I would not have you touch it."

As she rose obediently to do his bidding, Azim returned his gaze to Kelson, cocking his head in question.

"I shall ask of you the same thing Alaric asked Mátyás: unconditional trust—for I shall need to draw deeply from your energy reserves, lest I deplete my own and have none left for Teymuraz. Do you consent?"

"*I* consent," Morgan said, before Kelson could speak. "Derry is my responsibility—*my* vassal, as well as my friend."

"And you have already given much of yourself in the saving of Mátyás," Azim replied. "Best let another serve this need."

Without comment, Kelson scooted closer to the Deryni master, settling close beside him and the hapless Derry. Not to assist was unthinkable, given all that Derry must have suffered, over the years, from what had been done to him by Wencit—and in the service of Morgan and himself.

To his surprise, Azim then turned to Araxie, who seemed not at all dismayed by the way he had briskly taken charge—or perhaps, as his sometime pupil, she was used to his forthright manner.

"And you, child—will you stretch your wings with us?" he said. "What I will ask is well within your ability. You may consider it your rite of passage, from neophyte into the ranks of working Deryni—for such you must be, now to share in the work of our friend, the King of Gwynedd."

He smiled as he said it, and held out his hand, and her eyes laughed as she put her hand in his, slipping easily into trance as her head bowed and her eyes closed with the ease of utter trust, pupil to master. Himself already poised to do the same, Kelson could sense their rapport like a sweet note of harmony faintly vibrating just beyond the range of hearing. After a moment, Azim held out his other hand to Kelson.

"And now you, young Haldane."

Drawing a deep breath, Kelson set his hand in the master's and slowly exhaled, closing his eyes, letting his shields fall away, yielding up control. The embrace of Azim's shields bore him gently downward into a tranquil resting place, away from any physical sensation, where he found himself content to float in quiet limbo, waiting. . . .

Azim briefly drew back. Kelson waited, vaguely aware of power stirring still deeper within him. When Azim returned, it was to draw him into harmony with the sweetly pulsing skein of presence that was Araxie—like the shimmer of music on moonlight—as yet, a skein of less substantial strands than his, but strong, like the silk that had bound Derry's wrists.

Delicately Azim began to tease out precisely the threads he needed for his task, from both his charges. Kelson sensed it as a gentle but insistent drawing forth, from some depth he had not known existed, and he gave willingly and gladly. For Azim wove of the threads a fine, shimmering net with which he quickly sifted out the last vestiges of Wencit's taint from Derry's mind, healing as he went, in a magic altogether different from the healing done for Mátyás.

When, at last, Azim's need slowly abated, Kelson was allowed to settle back into that tranquil resting place. He sensed a beginning of withdrawal, and prepared himself to slowly start to surface; but curiously, he found himself impeded.

Stay yet a while longer, came Azim's thought, gossamer soft. *One need yet remains. You shall come to no harm.*

Kelson sensed a further gentle probing, different from before. Then, in a faintly giddying upward spiral, he was being drawn toward the surface—bobbing back into full consciousness with control and shields restored.

He opened his eyes, sight quickly stabilizing any lingering disorientation. Azim had drawn their hands down upon Derry's chest while they worked, and pressed Kelson's before releasing it, bending then to kiss Araxie's hand before releasing her as well. Derry appeared to be sleeping peacefully now, his color better, apparently restored.

"Well done, children. An excellent piece of work. I thank you. On that note, I think it time we were all of us about our various obligations. Rothana, that ring, if you please."

"But—what, exactly, happened?" Morgan asked, as Azim got to his feet, himself scrambling to rise as Kelson also stood up. Mátyás was sitting up now, apparently none the worse for his ordeal save for a tattered robe. Dhugal sat cross-legged beside him and Liam, looking altogether pleased.

"Ah. *That* I can now explain with somewhat greater certainty, having seen the extent of interference in his mind," Azim said. "Walk with me to the Portal, all of you, for I must be soon away. Rothana, stay you with Derry."

The others scrambled to their feet and fell in with him as they began moving slowly toward the sacristy.

"What, exactly, happened is that the magic Wencit set some years ago in young Derry was never fully rooted out—which is not your fault, my lord Alaric; you did not know. Kelson can show you later what we did. Save that this failing had left snippets of memory troubling to Derry, the matter might have ended there—except that the match-mate to *this* ring"—he held up the ring he had taken from Derry—"was the same that had belonged to Wencit, and which had bound him to the one you took from him and, most rightly, destroyed after Wencit's death.

"I can only surmise the general unfolding of events since that time," he went on, turning the ring in his fingers. "Morag, who was Wencit's sister, came into possession of his ring after his death. Presumably, she also obtained knowledge of what it was and what it could do. Whether Wencit himself told her, I do not know. But she learned its history and had another made, binding it to her brother's ring, and his to her, and laying plans against the day when she might use it—preferably against the two of you," he said, with a nod toward Morgan and Kelson, "for you had caused the deaths of both brother and husband.

"She knew of Derry's connection with the original link," he went on. "She had him brought to her while he was in Rhemuth, overcame him, and ascertained that enough remained of what Wencit had sown to re-establish the old link with this— which she cleverly disguised by encasing it in gold, leaving Derry with the belief that it was a trinket he had acquired while in Rhemuth." He displayed it again between thumb and forefinger. "Through its link, she would have been able to see everything that he saw, and to hear what he heard, so long as the link was open."

"Then, did Teymuraz take it, when he killed my mother?" Liam asked.

"So it would appear—and learned to reach far deeper into the link than your mother had done, to bend Derry's will to his—as Wencit had done, when he first set the link. Perhaps, in time, she would have done so as well; but Teymuraz took it from her before she progressed that far, so we shall never know. I did make a thorough sifting of Derry's memories since acquiring the ring in Beldour. Only in the last few days had there begun to be interference with his will, so we may conclude that all Morag did was to observe.

"Not so, Teymuraz, of course—though he shall never use *this* link again." He closed the ring in his fist, his gaze hardening briefly before his usual benign expression returned. They had reached the sacristy, and Azim paused before the open doorway.

"You may rest assured that Derry is now free of whatever hold Wencit—and his kin—had on him. He may regret missing the wedding festivities, but I would have him sleep a full night and a day. Do you see to it," he ordered Dhugal, who dipped his head in unquestioning agreement. "He will remember nothing of this when he wakes. And if no one of you tells him"—he swept an admonitory glance over all of them—"he need never know of this final obscene assault on his will. Nor will he ever be haunted by what is now past."

Morgan glanced back across the nave at Derry, peacefully asleep under Rothana's watch, greatly regretting that their ignorance had caused the faithful Derry so much pain.

"Thank you, Master Azim," he said quietly. "We all have much to learn from you."

"We have much to learn from one another," Azim said, nodding toward the clean flesh visible through the hole in Mátyás's robe. "And my niece's *schola* here in Rhemuth will be only the beginning. But for now, Kelson of Gwynedd," he continued, tucking the false ring into his robe, "I must take this to my brethren, for I hope it may lead us back to Teymuraz. Liam, I would recommend that you and Mátyás return at once to Beldour, much though I know how you will have anticipated the wedding festivities here in Rhemuth. I shall keep you informed regarding Teymuraz.

"Meanwhile, my king," he said, returning his gaze to Kelson, "I believe you have wedding guests awaiting you back at the castle—and I think," he added, with a glance at Araxie, "that you have a very important announcement concerning this young woman, whose true mettle only now begins to emerge. You would be well advised to marry her as soon as you may, and crown her your queen."

CHAPTER THIRTY-SIX

Come unto her with thy whole heart.

Ecclesiasticus 6:26

*K*elson took Azim's wise counsel and did exactly that. He and Araxie were wed a week later, to the joy of all Gwynedd. He would have done it then and there, but even Deryni kings and queens cannot conjure such magics on the spot.

Abandoning all royal precedent, he rode with his own wedding procession only as far as the cathedral square, there dismounting to give the state crown of Gwynedd into the keeping of his uncle, the Duke of Carthmoor, while he waited to receive his bride, who approached beneath a canopy of gold-fringed golden silk, attended by her sister, a bride of the week before.

Lord Savile, their stepfather, had led her along the flower-strewn processional route from the castle, his hand set proudly on the headstall of her mount, and clasped an affectionate hand to the king's shoulder as he gave over its velvet lead-rein. As Kelson gazed up at his bride, he could put aside the memories of that other bride he had led to this place, for he had no doubt that the patterns of the past had been broken.

The cheers of the crowd swelled in happy rejoicing as the king led his bride from under the canopy, traversing that last expanse of the cathedral square amid a bevy of brightly clad children, among them those of the ill-fortuned Conall, strewing flowers in their way—he in a sweeping robe of tissue gold powdered with tiny scarlet Haldane lions, she on her honey-colored palfrey, gowned in the pale golden silks of her mother's homeland and crowned with golden roses still moist with the morning dew, both of them aglow in the golden sunlight—or was it the shimmer of their magic, mute testament to the love that had grown between them?

There before the great cathedral doors, kneeling upon a prie-dieu all but smothered under flowers, they made their vows before Duncan McLain like any other bridal couple in the land, there before the sight of all who could crowd into the square behind them.

I, Kelson, take thee, Araxie, to be my wedded wife. . . .

When he had given her a ring, and at last they kissed, the square erupted in rapturous cheering as the cathedral bells rang out the Angelus and then continued pealing as he led her inside to be crowned, preceded by a hastily organized procession of the families of them both, who had ranged the steps informally to either side to witness the exchange of vows. Liam of Torenth and Mátyás were quietly among them, along with Azim—and Barrett de Laney, his arm clasped by Kelson's mother in more than mere affection between master and pupil.

Rothana, too, was close by Azim's side, her son beside her, clad in the royal blue of his Haldane father, her presence no longer a stabbing reminder of what might have been, but a quiet promise of new roads opening before all of them— and with the steady and joyful support and love of the woman at Kelson's side: his queen, his wife, his soul's true mate.

As was customary, Kelson and his bride went first to the side chapel of the Virgin to offer up the roses of her bridal crown, while family and the nobles of his court arranged themselves to witness her sacring as queen. In this, too, Kelson had decreed that precedent should be broken.

As the pealing of the bells died away, in preparation for her crowning, Kelson conducted his bride to a modest kneeling bench set upon the seal of Saint Camber, where he had achieved his own epiphany as a true Haldane king, there presenting her before the archbishops and the holy Presence of the altar beyond. He then stepped back amid his family and closest friends, retrieving his own crown from Nigel, as Araxie knelt to receive anointing from the hands of Archbishop Bradene, was adorned with a royal mantle of tissue gold embossed with their Haldane lions, and Archbishop Cardiel then brought forward the glittering, pearl-bestudded crown of Gwynedd's consort.

Cardiel, most assuredly, was not Deryni; but as he raised the crown above her head and intoned the holy words of royal consecration, it seemed to Kelson that another presence moved to overshadow the good archbishop, laying hands upon Cardiel's hands as he set the crown on Araxie's head. The glory that blazed briefly around her was not visible to human eyes, but even Cardiel seemed to sense it.

Morgan, standing at Kelson's right, saw it, as did Dhugal and Duncan, standing on his other side. The thought crossed Kelson's mind that the vision could be mere illusion; with the number of powerful Deryni focused on this moment, who knew what they might summon forth?

But the vision was of but an instant, and apparently unnoticed by those of merely mortal vision. As Kelson went to raise her up, his own crown upon his head, the bells began to peal again, their varied voices cascading down the scale in joyous affirmation that Gwynedd, indeed, had a queen at last. The kiss the two exchanged was honey-sweet, and he hardly remembered taking her back up the aisle and into the sunlight, to accept the adulation of the cheering multitudes outside.

Their wedding feast was the one they had mostly missed the week before, with none of the stiffness of protocol that nearly always had marred Kelson's enjoyment of state occasions in the past. Certain it was that all of Gwynedd had given their hearts to the king's fair Haldane bride. Content to let the night unfold in due time, he let himself enjoy the long-drawn festivities of the afternoon and evening, sampling but sparingly of the culinary offerings tendered by a never-ending succession of eager pages and squires, though many a morsel he took from Araxie's own hands, minds caressing every time their eyes met.

When, at last, as the summer twilight began to fall, and the ladies of the court came to sing her to her bridal chamber, he rose with the men to drink her health in courtly salute, lingering in a flurry of final good wishes from his closest friends before himself retiring from the hall.

The song they sang to light him to his bride was the same they had sung when Jatham wed the Princess Janniver, what seemed a lifetime ago; but the words of the old Transhan folk tune now sang to him of joy and gentleness, not loss and sorrow. Conducted to the outer chamber of the queen's apartments, now Araxie's domain, it was Morgan and Dhugal who helped him to undress, adorning him in a robe of scarlet silk, while the ladies sweetly sang from beyond Araxie's door and the men answered, in ardent counterpoint, Rory's rich tenor leading the refrains.

When the song had died away, the ladies emerged and Kelson went in to his bride. Duncan had already blessed the bridal bed. And given the other blessings already dispensed in the course of the day, no others seemed necessary, though the women sang a final bridal blessing as they departed, their voices slowly receding behind the door Kelson closed softly behind him.

Araxie was propped amid the pillows of the queen's great bed, which was hung with airy silks and softly lit by a sphere of golden handfire hovering just above her head. In that light, she, too, seemed to be kissed with finest gold, her pale hair spread upon the pillows, one lock trailing across the shoulder of a nightdress of gossamer silk. Her grey Haldane gaze met his with utter trust as she held out her hand to him.

Smiling, he came to take it, mounting the step up to the great bed and sitting beside her in a rustle of scarlet silk.

"You know, of course," she said, as he bent to kiss her hand, "that we're expected to make a son tonight."

She was smiling playfully as his eyes darted to hers, briefly startled; but then he, too, smiled and bent again to turn her hand in his, letting his tongue caress her palm—thrilling to her delicious shiver as she laughed delightedly, in an echo of long-ago childhood happiness, and reached her other hand to clasp a handful of his scarlet silk, drawing him into her embrace.

"I do believe that's what's required," he said huskily, happy contentment swelling in his breast as he brushed fingertips along the line of her cheek. "Gwynedd expects—"

"—every man to do his duty!" she finished for him, laughing, just before he hushed all further commentary, at least with words, with the sweet questing of his lips to hers, tasting and then drinking deeply of her yielding in a heady union of duty with growing desire, as Kelson of Gwynedd at last came into his full kingship with his true queen.

Appendix I
INDEX OF CHARACTERS

ALARIC Anthony Morgan, Lord—Deryni Duke of Corwyn and King's Champion, age thirty-six; husband of Lady Richenda, father of Briony and Kelric; cousin of Bishop Duncan McLain.

ALBIN Haldane, Prince—posthumous son and heir of the late Prince Conall and Princess Rothana, age two-and-a-half.

ALPHEIOS, Archbishop—Patriarch of All Torenth and head of the Orthodox Church of Torenth.

ALROY, King—late ruler of Torenth (1121–1123), Deryni; eldest son of Lionel Duke d'Arjenol and Wencit's sister, the Princess Morag; succeeded by his brother, King Liam-Lajos II. Many in Torenth believe Alroy's "accidental" death was contrived by Kelson to eliminate a rival who had come of age.

AMAURY Makróry, Lord—son and heir of Róry Makróry, reigning Count Kulnán in Torenth, age twenty-nine; Deryni.

AMBROS, Father—chaplain to Queen Jehana.

ANGUS MacEwan, Sir—newly knighted son and heir of Graham Earl of Kheldour, age eighteen.

ARAXIE Léan Haldane, Princess—younger daughter of the late Prince Richard, Duke of Carthmoor and Princess Sivorn; sister of Richelle and niece of the Hort of Orsal; age eighteen.

ARKADY II, King—Deryni ruler of Torenth (1025–1080), grandfather of King Wencit and Princess Morag, brother of Prince Nikola.

AYNBETH—a daughter of Létald Hort of Orsal, age six.

AZIM, Prince—a younger brother of the Emir of Nur Hallaj, uncle of Princess Rothana, and an accomplished Deryni master; member of the Camberian Council.

BAHADUR KHAN, King—ruler of the desert kingdom of R'Kassi.

BARRETT de Laney, Lord—elderly blind Deryni; coadjutor of the Camberian Council.

BERRHONES, Count—Torenthi courtier and master of ceremonies of the *killijálay*; Deryni.

BRADENE, Archbishop—scholarly Archbishop of Valoret and Primate of All Gwynedd, age sixty.

BRAN Coris, Lord—traitor Earl of Marley and first husband of Richenda; father of Brendan; killed by Kelson in 1121.

BRANYNG, Count—a Deryni master and Count of Sostra in Torenth, age thirty.

BRECON Ramsay-Quinnell, Sir—son of Sir Jolyon Ramsay and Lady Oksana, and titular heir to the Throne of Meara; brother of Noelie and Christophle; age twenty-four.

BRENDAN Coris, Lord—Earl of Marley, son of Richenda and the late Bran Coris; age eleven; a page to his stepfather, Alaric Morgan.

BRION Donal Cinhil Urien Haldane, King—ruler of Gwynedd (1095–1120) and late father of Kelson.

BRIONY Bronwyn de Morgan, Lady—daughter of Alaric Morgan Duke of Corwyn and Lady Richenda, age five.

CAMBER Kyriell MacRorie, Saint—Deryni former Earl of Culdi and restorer of the Haldane monarchy in 904; patron of magic, whose status as a saint was revoked by the Statutes of Ramos, and then restored by King Kelson and the Church of Gwynedd in the year 1125.

CARDIEL—see THOMAS Cardiel.

CECILE, Sister—companion to Queen Jehana.

CENTULE, Prince—younger son of Centule V Grand Duc du Vézaire, and a representative of his father to the Court of Torenth.

CHARISSA, Princess—late Festillic Pretender to the Throne of Gwynedd, killed by King Kelson in a duel arcane in 1120, when her pretensions passed to King Wencit.

CHRISTOPHLE, Brother—younger son of Sir Jolyon Ramsay of Meara and Lady Oksana, age eighteen.

CINHIL I Donal Ifor Haldane, King—first ruler of Gwynedd of the restored Haldane Dynasty (904–917), and ancestor of all the later kings of Gwynedd.

COLMAN, King—ruler of the United Kingdoms of Howicce and Llannedd, age thirty-five; formerly betrothed to Janniver Princess of Pardiac; his heirs are his half-sister, Princess Gwenlian (in Llannedd) and his cousin, Prince Cuan (in Howicce).

CONALL Haldane, Prince—late eldest son of Duke Nigel and Lady Meraude, husband of Princess Rothana, father of Prince Albin and Conalline; executed by Kelson for treason in 1125.

(CONALLINE) AMELIA—natural daughter of Prince Conall by his mistress, Vanissa; age three.

CUAN, Prince—a cousin of Colman II King of Howicce and Llannedd, and his Heir Presumptive to the Throne of Howicce, age eighteen; presumed suitor for the hand of Princess Araxie Haldane.

CYRIC von Horthy, Prince—eldest son and heir of Létald Hort of Orsal and Prince of Tralia; age twenty-two.

DAVORAN—a squire to King Kelson, age sixteen.

DENIS Michael Arilan, Bishop—Deryni Bishop of Dhassa, and a member of the Camberian Council; age forty-four.

DERRY—see SÉAN Seamus O'Flynn.

DHUGAL Ardry MacArdry McLain, Lord—foster brother to King Kelson and member of the Privy Council of Gwynedd, age twenty; Duke of Cassan, Earl of Kierney and Transha, Chief of Clan MacArdry; son of Duncan McLain by Maryse MacArdry; Deryni.

DOLFIN—Kelson's senior squire, age eighteen; only survivor of accident at High Greldour Pass that nearly claimed the lives of Kelson and Dhugal in 1125.

DONAL BLAINE II Aidan Cinhil Haldane, King—former ruler of Gwynedd (1074–1095) and father of King Brion and Duke Nigel.

DUNCAN Howard McLain, Bishop—Deryni Auxiliary Bishop of Rhemuth, age thirty-six; former Duke of Cassan and Earl of Kierney, which titles he resigned to his son, Dhugal MacArdry McLain.

EDWARD Ramsay, Lord—a younger son of the Earl of Cloome in Meara and ancestor of the current representatives of the House of Quinnell through his marriage with Princess Magrette of Meara; died 1078.

EIRIAN Elspeth Sidana Haldane, Princess—daughter of Nigel Duke of Carthmoor and Lady Meraude, age four.

EKATERINA, Princess—daughter of Rotrou, Hereditary Prince of Jáca, age seventeen.

ERDŐDY, Duke—Deryni Duke of Jándrich in Torenth, age thirty-three.

EWAN III MacEwan, Duke—Duke of Claibourne and Hereditary Earl Marshal of Gwynedd; father of Earl Graham, grandfather of Sir Angus; age sixty-one.

FURSTÁN I von Furstán, King of Torenth—Deryni founder of the House of Furstán, and first King of Torenth (537–566).

GAETAN—a servant at Horthánthy.

GRAHAM MacEwan, Lord—son and heir of Duke Ewan (and Earl of Kheldour by courtesy), father of Sir Angus, age thirty-nine.

GRON, Duke—Grand Duke of Calam in the Connait, and representative to the Court of Torenth from the Connaiti Council of Sovereign Princes.

GWENLIAN, Princess—half-sister of Colman II King of Howicce and Llannedd and his heir presumptive for Llannedd; age nineteen.

HALDANE—surname of the ruling House of Gwynedd.

HUSNIYYA (Niyya), Princess—wife of Létald Hort of Orsal and Prince of Tralia, mother of Prince Cyric, Rezza Elisabet, Rogan, Marcel and Marcelline, Aynbeth, and Oswin.

IDDIN de Vesca—an officer of the guard in the service of the Hort of Orsal.

IMRE I, King—last King of Gwynedd of the House of Furstán-Festil (900–904), who sired an incestuous son on his sister, Princess Ariella; killed in 904 by King Cinhil I.

IRENAEUS, Father—Orthodox Torenthi chaplain to young King Liam-Lajos.

ISARN, Prince—sovereign ruler of Logréine, one of the Forcinn States.

ITHEL Quinnell, Prince—late Hereditary Prince of Meara, son of Caitrin Pretender of Meara and Lord Sicard MacArdry, brother of Queen Sidana and Prince Llewell, executed by King Kelson in 1124.

IVO Hepburn—a squire to King Kelson, age fifteen.

JAMYL Arilan, Sir—late brother of Denis Arilan; Deryni; died 1107 from injuries incurred in service to King Brion.

JANNIVER, Princess—daughter of Pons Prince of Pardiac in the Connait; formerly betrothed to Colman II King of Llannedd and Howicce; age twenty-three.

JÁNOS Sokrat—blind Deryni advisor to the Court of Torenth; a master of the Moving Ward.

JATHAM Kilshane, Sir—former squire to King Kelson, enamored of the Princess Janniver; age twenty.

JEHANA, Queen—Dowager Queen of Gwynedd, mother of Kelson and widow of King Brion; Deryni, age thirty-nine.

JILYAN, Mother—ban-aba (i.e., abbess) of the hill folk of Saint Kyriell's.

JOHN Nivard, Father—Deryni priest ordained by Bishop Denis Arilan, age twenty-five.

JOKAL of Tyndour—early Deryni Healer, scholar, and poet.

JOLYON Ramsay-Quinnell, Sir—titular Prince of Meara, husband of Oksana, father of Brecon, Noelie, and Christophle, age fifty.

JOWAN—late squire to Prince Conall.

JUDHAEL Quinnell, Bishop—late Prince of Meara, illegal Bishop of Ratharkin, nephew of Caitrin Pretender of Meara, executed by King Kelson in 1124.

KAMIL, Prince—eldest son and heir of Princess Sofiana of Andelon and Lord Reyhan, age thirty-one.

KÁROLY, Father—Torenthi Orthodox priest.

KÁSPÁR, Duke—Deryni Duke of Truvorsk in Torenth.

KELRIC Alain Morgan—son and heir of Alaric Morgan, Duke of Corwyn and Lady Richenda, Deryni, age three.

KELSON Cinhil Rhys Anthony Haldane, King—ruler of Gwynedd (1120–) and Overlord of Torenth, son of King Brion and Queen Jehana, formerly married to Sidana (died 1124); Deryni; age twenty-one.

KITRON—early Deryni scholar, author of *Principia Magica*.

KYRI, Lady—a former member of the Camberian Council.

LARAN ap Pardyce, Lord—Deryni physician and member of the Camberian Council, age sixty-three.

LÁSZLÓ, Count—Deryni Count of Czalsky in Torenth, age twenty-seven.

LÉTALD, Hort of Orsal and Prince of Tralia—sovereign ruler of Orsal and Tralia (1101–), Overlord of the Forcinn States, husband of Princess Husniyya, father of Cyric, Rezza Elisabet, Rogan, Marcel and Marcelline, Aynbeth, and Oswin; brother of Sivorn and uncle of Princesses Araxie and Richelle; age fifty.

LIAM-LAJOS II Lionel László Furstán d'Arjenol, King (called "Laje")—Deryni ruler of Torenth (1123–), middle son of Lionel Duke d'Arjenol and Princess Morag, brother of King Alroy Arion II, whom he succeeded; hostage of King Kelson; age fourteen.

LIONEL, Duke—late Deryni Duke d'Arjenol in Torenth (1100–1121); husband of Princess Morag and father of the late King Alroy Arion II, King Liam-Lajos II, Prince Ronal Rurik, and Princess Stanisha; half-brother of Mahael II Duke d'Arjenol (his successor), Count Teymuraz, and Count Mátyás; killed by King Kelson in 1121.

LLEWELL Quinnell, Prince—late second son of Caitrin Pretender of Meara and Sicard MacArdry; brother of Prince Ithel and Queen Sidana; executed by King Kelson in 1124 for the murder of his sister.

LÓRÁNT, Duke—late Duke of Truvorsk in Torenth (1105–1122), a Deryni master who trained Count Mátyás; father of Duke Káspár.

LURIC—a soldier of the guard in the service of the Hort of Orsal.

McLAIN—see DHUGAL, Duncan.

MAGRETTE, Princess—third daughter of Prince Jolyon II, last sovereign Prince of Meara; wife of Lord Edward Ramsay, a younger son of the Earl of Cloome; her descendants include the last representatives of the princely House of Quinnell.

MAHAEL Furstán d'Arjenol, Duke—Deryni co-regent of Torenth with his sister-in-law, Princess Morag; half-brother of Lionel late Duke d'Arjenol (whom he succeeded), full brother of Count Teymuraz and Count Mátyás, uncle of the late King Alroy Arion II, King Liam Lajos II, Prince Ronal Rurik, and Princess Stanisha; second in the line to the Torenthi throne, age thirty-seven.

MARCEL—son of Létald Hort of Orsal and Princess Husniyya, twin to Lady Marcelline, age fourteen.

MARCELLINE—daughter of Létald Hort of Orsal and Princess Husniyya, twin to Lord Marcel; age fourteen.

MÁTYÁS Furstán-Komnéné, Count—half-brother of Lionel late Duke d'Arjenol and full brother of Duke Mahael and Count Teymuraz, uncle of the late King Alroy Arion II, King Liam-Lajos II, Prince Ronal Rurik, and Princess Stanisha; Count of Komnéné in Torenth, and fourth in line to the Torenthi throne; Deryni, age twenty-seven.

MERAUDE de Traherne, Lady—Duchess of Carthmoor, wife of Duke Nigel, mother of the late Prince Conall, Prince Rory, Prince Payne, and Princess Eirian; sister of Lord Saer de Traherne; age thirty-seven.

MICHAEL, Brother—*coisrigte* or member of the priestly caste of the hill folk of Saint Kyriell's.

MICHON de Courcy, Lord—a former member of the Camberian Council, died 1098; Deryni.

MORAG Furstána, Princess—Deryni sister of Wencit late King of Torenth and widow of Duke Lionel; titular Festillic Queen of Gwynedd; co-regent of Torenth with her brother-in-law, Duke Mahael; mother of Alroy Arion II late King of Torenth, Liam-Lajos II King of Torenth, Prince Ronal Rurik (the Heir Presumptive), and Princess Stanisha; age forty-eight.

MORGAN—see ALARIC, BRIONY, KELRIC, RICHENDA.

NIALL—a page to King Kelson, age eleven.

NIGEL Cluim Gwydion Rhys Haldane, Prince—Duke of Carthmoor, uncle of King Kelson and Heir Presumptive to the throne of Gwynedd; husband of Lady Meraude and father of the late Prince Conall, Prince Rory, Prince Payne, and Princess Eirian, grandfather of Prince Albin; age forty-one.

NIKOLA, Prince—late younger brother of Arkady II King of Torenth, whose life he saved at Killingford (1025), at the cost of his own; Deryni.

NOELIE, Lady—daughter of Sir Jolyon Ramsay and Lady Oksana, sister of Brecon and Christophle, age twenty.

OKSANA, Lady—wife of Sir Jolyon Ramsay and mother of Brecon, Noelie, and Christophle, age forty-eight.

ORIN—early Deryni scholar, author of the Codex Orini, who died 675.

OSWIN—youngest son of Létald Hort of Orsal and Princess Husniyya, age three.

PAYNE Haldane, Prince—youngest son of Duke Nigel and Lady Meraude, brother to Rory and Eirian; squire to King Kelson, age twelve.

QUERON Kinevan, Dom—early Deryni Healer and scholar, author of the *Annales Queroni*, who died after 928.

RADUSLAV, Lord—Torenthi courtier, grandson of Count Berrhones, Deryni.

RALF Tolliver, Bishop—Bishop of Coroth in the Duchy of Corwyn.

al-RASOUL ibn Tarik, Lord—Moorish Deryni emissary of Torent to the Court of Gwynedd, a master architect and builder; age forty-seven.

RATHER de Corbie, Lord—Tralian baron and ambassador to the Duchy of Corwyn in Gwynedd, age sixty-two.

REYHAN, Lord—consort of Sofiana Sovereign Princess of Andelon, and father of Prince Kamil and Prince Taher.

(REZZA) ELISABET, Lady—eldest daughter of the Hort of Orsal and Princess Husniyya; age twenty-two.

RHIDIAN—young Deryni woman, member of the Quorial of Saint Kyriell's.

RICHARD Haldane, Prince—late half-brother of King Donal Blaine Haldane, hence uncle to Brion and Nigel; husband of Lady Sivorn; father of Princesses Richelle and Araxie; died 1114.

RICHELDIS, Queen—consort of King Donal Blaine II, mother of King Brion and Duke Nigel; died 1118.

RICHELLE Haldane, Princess—elder daughter of Prince Richard Duke of Carthmoor and Princess Sivorn, sister of Araxie, niece of the Hort of Orsal; age twenty.

RICHENDA, Duchess—widow of Bran Coris Earl of Marley and mother of the current earl, their son Brendan; now wife of Alaric Morgan Duke of Corwyn, mother of Briony and Kelric; Deryni, age twenty-nine.

ROGAN, Prince—second son of Létald Hort of Orsal and Princess Husniyya; age seventeen.

RONAL Rurik, Prince—youngest son of the late Lionel Duke d'Arjenol and Princess Morag, brother of Liam-Lajos II King of Torent and the late Alroy Arion II King of Torent; Duke of Lorsöl and Heir Presumptive to the Throne of Torent; Deryni, age ten.

RORY Haldane, Prince, Sir—second son and designated heir of Nigel Duke of Carthmoor and Lady Meraude, brother of Payne and Eirian; age eighteen.

ROSANE Haldane, Princess—infant daughter of King Brion and Queen Jehana, who died a few hours after birth in 1108.

ROTHANA, Princess—widow of Conall Haldane, mother of Prince Albin; Nabila (or Princess) of Nur Hallaj, niece of Prince Azim; cousin by marriage of Lady Richenda; Deryni, age twenty.

ROTROU, Prince—Hereditary Prince of Jáca, father of Princess Ekaterina.

SAER de Traherne, Lord—Earl of Rhendall and brother of Meraude Duchess of Carthmoor, age thirty-five.

SAVILE, Baron—husband of Lady Sivorn, father of Sivney, Sorley, Siany, and Savilla; age forty-seven.

SAVILLA—daughter of Lord Savile and Lady Sivorn, age eleven.

SÉAN Seamus O'Flynn, Lord—Earl Derry, former aide to Alaric Duke of Corwyn and now his lieutenant, Deputy Regent of Marley, occasional member of the Privy Council of Gwynedd, age thirty-one.

SÉANDRY, Uncle—Briany de Morgan's pet-name for Séan, Lord Derry.

SIANY—daughter of Lord Savile and Lady Sivorn, age seven.

SIDANA Quinnell, Lady—Princess of Meara and first wife of King Kelson, murdered by her brother on her wedding day in 1124.

SION Benét, Sir—Under-Chancellor to the Royal House of Llannedd and newest member of the Camberian Council; a descendant of Sir Sion Benét, who was a cousin of Earl Jebediah and a friend and supporter of Saint Camber; age forty-two.

SIVNEY—son and heir of Lord Savile and Lady Sivorn, age nine.

SIVORN, Princess—sister of Létald Hort of Orsal; widow of Prince Richard Haldane Duke of Carthmoor and wife of Savile Baron Kishknock; mother of Princesses Richelle and Araxie by her first marriage, and Savilla, Sivney, Siany, and Sorley by her second; age thirty-nine.

SOFIANA, Princess—Sovereign Princess of Andelon, wife of Lord Reyhan; mother of Princes Kamil and Taher; aunt of Lady Richenda; member of the Camberian Council; age forty-eight.

SOPHIE—maid to Queen Jehana.

SORLEY—son of Lord Savile and Lady Sivorn, age six.

STANISHA, Princess—posthumous daughter of Lionel II late Duke d'Arjenol and Princess Morag, sister of Liam-Lajos and Ronal Rurik; age six.

SULIEN of R'Kassi—early Deryni scholar, author of the *Annales Sulieni*.

TAHER, Prince—second son of Sofiana Sovereign Princess of Andelon and Lord Reyhan, Deryni; age twenty-eight.

TEYMURAZ, Count—half-brother of Lionel late Duke d'Arjenol, full brother of Duke Mahael and Count Mátyás; uncle of the late King Alroy Arion II, King Liam-Lajos II, Prince Ronal Rurik, and Princess Stanisha; Count of Brustarkia and third in line to the Torenthi throne, Deryni; age thirty-three.

THOMAS Cardiel, Archbishop—Bremagni former Bishop of Dhassa, now Archbishop of Rhemuth; age forty-eight.

TIBAL, Count—son of Lady Vivienne de Jordanet, now Count de Jordanet in Joux, Deryni; age fifty-four.

TIERCEL de Claron—late member of the Camberian Council, who trained Prince Conall in the use of his Haldane potential.

UNGNAD, Count—Deryni Count of Fajardô in Torenth.

URSULA, Lady—granddaughter of Braon, late Prince of Howicce; age nineteen.

VANISSA—former mistress of Prince Conall, and mother of his natural daughter, Conalline Amelia; age twenty.

VASILLY Dimitriades—Chief Chamberlain to the Hort of Orsal; age forty-one.

VIVIENNE de Jordanet, Lady—coadjutor of the Camberian Council; mother of Tibal Count de Jordanet in Joux; age seventy-five.

WENCIT, King—late Deryni ruler of Torenth (1110–1121), brother of Princess Morag, uncle of King Liam Lajos II; killed by King Kelson in a duel arcane in 1121.

Appendix II
INDEX OF PLACES

ALTA JORDA—seat of the Jordanet family in Joux.

ANDELON—a sovereign principality immediately bordering the Forcinn States to the south, currently ruled by Princess Sofiana.

ANVIL OF THE LORD—a large desert region lying to the east of Jáca, Bremagne, and Alver, and south of R'Kassi, consisting of a number of small independent Moorish states.

ARJENOL—a large duchy in eastern Torenth, closely associated with the royal House of Furstán; recent dukes include Lionel II (1100–1121) and his half-brother, Mahael II (1121–).

BELDOUR—capital of Torenth, sited near the confluence of the Beldour and Arjent Rivers.

BREMAGNE—a large kingdom situated across the Southern Sea to the southeast of Gwynedd, currently ruled by King Ryol II, brother of Jehana Dowager Queen of Gwynedd.

BRUSTARKIA—a county of western Arjenol, currently ruled by Count Teymuraz.

CALAM—a sovereign grand duchy of the Connait, currently ruled by Grand Duke Gron III.

CARTHMOOR—a royal duchy in southeastern Gwynedd, just southwest of Corwyn, currently ruled by Duke Nigel, uncle to King Kelson.

CASSAN—a duchy in western Gwynedd which includes the Earldom of Kierney; recent dukes include Duncan (1121–1125) and Dhugal (1125–).

CIRCASSIA—an emirate in Libania.

CLAIBOURNE—a duchy far north in Gwynedd, encompassing much of the ancient principality of Kheldour; currently ruled by Duke Ewan III.

CLOOME—a small earldom in the southwestern region of Meara.

THE CONNAIT—a confederation of sovereign states located west of Gwynedd and south of Meara, loosely governed by the Connaiti Council of Sovereign Princes.

COROTH—capital city of the Duchy of Corwyn in Gwynedd.

CORWYN—a duchy located in the southeastern corner of Gwynedd, ruled since 1091 by Duke Alaric Morgan.

CZALSKY—a county of northeastern Torenth, currently ruled by Count László.

DERRY—a small earldom located north of Corwyn, currently held by Earl Séan O'Flynn.

DESSE—the principal inland port town of Gwynedd, located south of Rhemuth on the confluence of the Rivers Eirian and Molling, and representing the farthest navigable point on the Eirian into Gwynedd.

DHASSA—a free holy city of eastern Gwynedd, once an independent Prince-Bishopric, situated between Gwynedd and Mooryn; currently the seat of Bishop Denis Arilan.

EASTMARCH—an earldom in eastern Gwynedd, currently held by Earl Burchard de Varian.

ELEVEN KINGDOMS—ancient name for the entire area including and surrounding Gwynedd.

FALLON—a small kingdom lying south of the Forcinn States and north of Bremagne.

FIANNA—a small sovereign county lying between Fallon and Logréine, south of the Forcinn States, known primarily for its wines.

FORCINN STATES—a group of five sovereign states located south of Torenth and Tralia, under the overlordship of the Hort of Orsal (who is also Prince of Tralia).

FURSTÁNÁLY—principal palace of the Kings of Torenth in Beldour, famous for its Hanging Garden, one of the seven architectural wonders of the world.

FURSTÁNAN—a Torenthi town located near the mouth of the Beldour River.

GREAT ESTUARY OR TWIN RIVERS STRAIT—the waterway between Corwyn and Orsal leading to the mouths of the Western and Beldour Rivers in Torenth.

GWYNEDD—the central and largest of the Eleven Kingdoms, held by the Haldane family since 645; recent kings include Malcolm (1025–1074), Donal Blaine II (1074–1095), Brion (1095–1120), and Kelson (1120–).

HAGIA IÓB'S—the oldest Christian church in Torenth, located in Torenthály; burial place of Furstán I, first King of Torenth.

HORTHÁNTHY—the summer palace of the Hort of Orsal on the Ile d'Orsal.

HOWICCE AND LLANNEDD—two kingdoms located in the southwestern portion of the Eleven Kingdoms, united under the personal rule of King Colman II.

ILE D'ORSAL—an island off the coast of Tralia in the Southern Sea, constituting the original settlement of the Orsal family; it includes the town of Orsalis.

JÁCA—a sovereign principality lying to the east of Fallon and west of the Anvil of the Lord.

JÁNDRICH—a duchy of northern Torenth.

JOUX—a sovereign duchy of the Forcinn States.

KHELDOUR—an ancient sovereign principality located in the far north of the Eleven Kingdoms, now a part of Gwynedd.

KIERNEY—an earldom in western Gwynedd, now a secondary holding of the Dukes of Cassan.

KILARDEN—an earldom in northern Meara.

KILLINGFORD—site of the bloodiest battle fought in the history of the Eleven Kingdoms, between Gwynedd and Torenth, at a ford on the Falling Water River north of Valoret in the year 1025.

KILSHANE—an ancient extinct barony in Kierney.

KOMNÉNË—a small county in southwestern Arjenol.

KULNÁN—a county of western Torenth.

LAAS—the ancient royal capital of Meara, located on the west coast of that country.

LENDOUR—an earldom in south central Gwynedd, now a subsidiary title to the Duchy of Corwyn.

LOGRÉINE—a sovereign principality of the Forcinn States.

LORSÖL—a duchy of southeastern Torenth.

MARLUK—a Torenthi duchy lying on the south side of the Beldour River, currently merged with the Crown.

MEARA—a former sovereign principality in the far western region of the Eleven Kingdoms, now part of Gwynedd.

NIKOLASEUM—the seven-tiered monument erected at Torenthály by Arkady II King of Torenth to the memory of his brother, Prince Nikola; it is considered one of the seven architectural wonders of the world.

NUR HALLAJ—one of the Forcinn States, bordered on the east by the Kingdom of R'Kassi.

NYFORD—a port town in southern Gwynedd situated at the confluence of the Eirian and Lendour Rivers.

ORSAL AND TRALIA—a principality lying east of Corwyn across the Southern Sea, and south of Torenth, ruled by the von Horthy family, whose current prince, Létald, bears the title Hort of Orsal and Prince of Tralia; the Principality of Tralia is the mainland portion of the country.

ORSALIS—the town and harbor of the Ile d'Orsal.

ÖSTMARCKE—a duchy of eastern Torenth, situated to the west of Arjenol.

RATHARKIN—the new capital of Meara after the union of Meara and Gwynedd in 1025, displacing Laas; seat of the Bishop of Meara.

RHEMUTH—the capital city of Gwynedd, called "the beautiful," seat of the Archbishop of Rhemuth.

RHENDALL—an earldom of western Kheldour, in northern Gwynedd.

R'KASSI—a great desert kingdom lying south of Torenth and Tralia and east of the Forcinn States.

SAINT CONSTANTINE'S CATHEDRAL—the chief seat of the Archbishop of Beldour and Patriarch of All Torenth, currently Patriarch Alpheios I.

SAINT GEORGE'S CATHEDRAL—seat of the Archbishop of Rhemuth, currently Archbishop Thomas II Cardiel.

SAINT HILARY'S BASILICA—the ancient royal basilica located within the walls of Rhemuth Castle, of which Bishop Duncan McLain is rector.

SAINT KYRIELL'S—a village located in the hills northeast of Caerrorie, where some of the Servants of Saint Camber went into exile after the imposition of the Statutes of Ramos in the tenth century; rediscovered by King Kelson in 1125.

SAINT-SASILE—a monastery in the southern Torenth town of Furstánan on the Beldour River.

SOSTRA—a county of western Torenth, centered on the town of the same name.

SOUTHERN SEA—that part of the Atalantic Ocean lying between Gwynedd and the Forcinn States, Fallon, and Bremagne.

TORENTH—major kingdom bordering Gwynedd on the east, whose recent kings include Wencit, or Wenzel II (1110–1121), Alroy Arion II (1121–1123), and Liam-Lajos II (1123–).

TORENTHÁLY—the country seat of Torenth's kings, located north of Beldour, which includes the Church of Hagia Iób, the Nikolaseum, and the Furstáni royal tombs.

TRALIA—see Orsal.

TRANSHA—an earldom in Gwynedd bordering Kierney and the Purple March, now owned by the Dukes of Cassan.

TRUVORSK—a duchy of central Torenth.

VALLA DE COURCY—the estate of the de Courcy family in Gwynedd.

VALORET—the old capital of Gwynedd during the Festillic Interregnum (822–904), and the seat of the Archbishop Primate of Valoret and All Gwynedd.

VÉZAIRE—a sovereign grand duchy of the Forcinn.